JAMES BALDWIN AND TONI MORRISON

JAMES BALDWIN AND TONI MORRISON: COMPARATIVE CRITICAL AND THEORETICAL ESSAYS

Edited by
Lovalerie King and Lynn Orilla Scott

palgrave
macmillan

JAMES BALDWIN AND TONI MORRISON: COMPARATIVE CRITICAL AND
THEORETICAL ESSAYS

Copyright © Lovalerie King, Lynn Orilla Scott, 2006.

First published in 2006 by
PALGRAVE MACMILLAN™
175 Fifth Avenue, New York, N.Y. 10010 and
Houndmills, Basingstoke, Hampshire, England RG21 6XS.
Companies and representatives throughout the world.

PALGRAVE MACMILLAN is the global academic imprint of the Palgrave Macmillan division of St. Martin's Press, LLC and of Palgrave Macmillan Ltd. Macmillan® is a registered trademark in the United States, United Kingdom and other countries. Palgrave is a registered trademark in the European Union and other countries.

ISBN-13: 978-1-4039-7073-2
ISBN-10: 1-4039-7073-4

Library of Congress Cataloging-in-Publication Data

James Baldwin and Toni Morrison: comparative critical and theoretical essays/
    co-editors, Lovalerie King, Lynn Orilla Scott.
        p. cm.
    Includes bibliographical references and index.
    ISBN 1-4039-7073-4 (alk. paper)
    1. Baldwin, James, 1924—Criticism and interpretation. 2. Morrison, Toni.—Criticism and interpretation. 3. African Americans in literature. I. King, Lovalerie. II. Scott, Lynn Orilla, 1950-

PS3552.A45Z724 2006
810.9'89607309045—dc22   2006041603

A catalogue record for this book is available from the British Library.

Design by Macmillan India Ltd.

First edition: October 2006

10 9 8 7 6 5 4 3 2 1

Printed in the United States of America.

Transferred to digital printing in 2007.

For our Children
Eric and Erin King
Sara, Ziba, and Margaret Scott

CONTENTS

ACKNOWLEDGMENTS

"We wish to express very special thanks to Randall Scott for taking on the monumental task of indexing this volume."

We would like to ackowledge the following colleagues, associates, friends, and relatives for their professional and moral support: Trudier Harris, Iyun Osagie, Marilyn Atlas, our generous, dedicated, and talented contributors, and the editors and reviewers at Palgrave. We thank you one and all.

INTRODUCTION: BALDWIN AND
MORRISON IN DIALOGUE

LOVALERIE KING

In the second half of the twentieth century, no two authors did more to shape an African American literary tradition and gain a broad national and international audience for that tradition than James Baldwin and Toni Morrison. Born only seven years before Morrison, Baldwin began his professional writing career a full generation ahead of her. His work in fiction and nonfiction opened up new discursive terrain in African American literature and influenced a number of younger writers, including Morrison. The two authors first met in the 1970s, when Morrison was an editor for Random House; they became friends who read and respected each other's work. In a 1987 interview, shortly before Baldwin's death, Quincy Troupe asked Baldwin what he thought of Toni Morrison. He replied,

Toni's my ally and it's really probably too complex to get into. She's a black woman writer, which in the public domain makes it more difficult to talk about . . . Her gift is allegory. *Tar Baby* is an allegory. In fact all her novels are. But they're hard to talk about in public. That's where you get in trouble because her books and allegory are not always what they seem to be about. I was too occupied with my recent illness to deal with *Beloved*. But in general, she's taken a myth, or she takes what seems to be a myth, and turns it into something else. I don't know how to put this, *Beloved* could be the story of truth. She's taken a whole lot of things and turned them upside down. Some of them you recognize the truth in it. I think that Toni's very painful to read . . . Because it's always, or most times, a horrifying allegory; but you recognize that it works. But you don't really want to march through it. Sometimes people have a lot against Toni, but she's got the most believing story of everybody, this rather elegant matron, whose intentions really are serious, and according to some people, lethal. (rpt. in Standley 284)

Morrison spoke likewise of Baldwin's believability, truth telling, and elegance while relating her indebtedness to him during a three-hour discussion of her work on cable television (C-Span 2001). Responding to this viewer's question about Baldwin's influence on her intellectual life and literary production, Morrison said she admired his courage, intellect, ferocity, and mostly his clarity:

> He was able to talk about very serious situations of race, and violence, and love in language that was both scathing and at the same time, loving. Extraordinary feats he accomplished in a kind of truth-telling manner that I hadn't heard before. He wasn't calling names, he wasn't posing, he wasn't even vengeful. There was an elegance to his language that was about race but was not racist. And I just never had experienced that kind of language before in the fifties and sixties, so I owe him for teaching me that there was such a thing as that kind of language. I owe James Baldwin that. (C-Span 2001)

Morrison had expressed similar sentiments earlier in her 1987 eulogy of Baldwin: "You gave me a language to dwell in, a gift so perfect it seems my own invention. I have been thinking your spoken and written thoughts for so long I believed they were mine. I have been seeing the world through your eyes for so long, I believed that clear, clear view was my own" (Troupe 76). Significantly, it was during a 1984 interview published in *The Paris Review* that Baldwin characterized his early essay "Everybody's Protest Novel" as the beginning of his *"finding a new vocabulary and another point of view"* (rpt. in Standley 237; my emphasis).

In the 1987 interview with Quincy Troupe mentioned above, Baldwin noted the problems he was having with the editor of *Giovanni's Room* (1956):

> You see, whites want black writers to mostly deliver something as if it were an official version of the black experience. But the vocabulary won't hold it, simply. No true account really of black life can be held, can be contained, in the American vocabulary. As it is, the only way that you can deal with it is by doing great violence to the assumptions on which the vocabulary is based. (rpt. in Standley 285)

Certainly, Baldwin's particular approach to the burden of racial representation in American literature, his resistance to dominant constructions of race and gender, and his reinvention of a racially inflected language are of specific importance to the development of Morrison's art as well as her criticism.

For example, in a 1984 interview with Julius Lester, Baldwin noted that "the effort on the part of the Republic to avoid the presence of black people reflects itself in American literature fatally, to the detriment of that literature" (rpt. in Standley 228). Morrison explores this same idea in two of her most popular works of nonfiction: "Unspeakable Things Unspoken: The

Afro-American Presence in American Literature" (1989) and *Playing in the Dark* (1992). Clearly, Baldwin and Morrison realized that politics is no stranger to American literature and literary criticism. Their insistence on literary approaches to sociological issues mirrors that of other writers and critics, from W. E. B. DuBois to artists and critics associated with the Black Arts Movement of the 1960s and early 1970s, who understood that there is no necessary contradiction between art and politics. Indeed, Morrison stated that position clearly and explicitly in a 1974 conversation with Alice Childress (rpt. in Taylor-Guthrie 3).

While Morrison found inspiration in the nuance, beauty and strength of Baldwin's language, the literary influence was certainly not a one-way street. For example, in *If Beale Street Could Talk* (1974) and *Just Above My Head* (1979), Baldwin explores intraracial dynamics, including the problem of racial self-hatred and the possibilities of the family as a place of resistance to white hegemony, through plot structures and devices that suggest an engagement with Morrison's family stories in *The Bluest Eye* (1970), *Song of Solomon* (1977), and other novels. Asked during a 1980 interview with Wolfgang Binder which of the new authors he found promising, Baldwin answered, "They are not all young. One is Sterling Brown, and then there are Gwendolyn Brooks and Toni Morrison" (rpt. in Taylor-Guthrie 207). During a 1971 conversation taped for television and later published as *A Dialogue* (1973), Nikki Giovanni asked Baldwin, "What do you think about the younger writers? . . . Are we in your opinion moving ahead?" Baldwin's response was, "I can never express to you, to what extent I depend on you. I mean you, Nikki Giovanni, and I also mean your generation" (*Dialogue* 16).

Both Baldwin and Morrison supported and promoted the work of younger writers. Baldwin wrote the foreword to Louise Meriwether's *Daddy Was a Number Runner* (1970), for example; in a cover blurb, he had high praise for Gayl Jones's *Corregidora* (1975)—which Morrison edited—and he wrote a preface titled "Stagolee" for Bobby Seale's *A Lonely Rage: The Autobiography of Bobby Seale* (1978). A number of younger and older black writers benefited from Morrison's position as an editor for Random House, beginning in the 1960s; for almost two decades, she nurtured the careers of such writers as Toni Cade Bambara, Lucille Clifton, Henry Dumas, and Gayl Jones. Moreover, Morrison recently reintroduced Baldwin's work in *James Baldwin: Collected Essays* (1998) and *James Baldwin: Early Novels and Stories* (1998), making it readily available for a new generation of scholars now studying his writing.

While Baldwin has most often been read in the cultural context of the 1950s and 1960s, in the context of "protest," or more recently as a progenitor of black, gay writing, Morrison is most often read and studied in the context of other women writers, especially black women writers, and in projects involving postmodernist and poststructuralist modes of inquiry. Our engagement with these two authors suggested a number of areas in which comparison and contrast would be valuable and contribute to a richer understanding of African American literature and culture. The contributors to this volume obviously saw similar potential in a comparative exploration of their work.

Several essays illuminate how music becomes both theme and an innovative method of literary construction and style for each author. In "Baldwin's Bop 'n' Morrison's Mood: Bebop and Race in James Baldwin's *Another Country* and Toni Morrison's *Jazz*," Keren Omry examines each author's engagement with the "idea of ethnicity as a dynamic and infinite process of creation and re-creation" (12). She argues that "through their emphases on performativity and creative impulses," both authors "explore the implications of perceiving blackness as a process that relies on consent," a process that carries "many potentially destructive as well as productive possibilities" (31). Omry concludes that we can see *Another Country* (1962) and *Jazz* (1992) as part of a larger project that assists in destabilizing and undermining "the divisive borders of social, racialized construals, offering instead a much more complex and diverse cultural model" (32).

Similarly, Anna Kérchy's "Narrating the Beat of the Heart, Jazzing the Text of Desire: A Comparative Interface of James Baldwin's *Another Country* and Toni Morrison's *Jazz*" examines the transgressive characteristics and potential of Baldwin's and Morrison's narrative styles. Like Omry, Kérchy notes the significance of the creative process in each author's work; their texts "transgress conventional discourse, show ways of flight from the prisonhouse of language, and provide heterogeneous, alternative identifications (with the desiring subject-in-process or the polyphonic, choral narrative voice[s]) beyond the ideologically prescribed subject position" (58). In language that itself mirrors jazz, Kérchy tells us that Baldwin and Morrison challenge "their readers to participate actively in the composition of the jazz story and text, filling in gaps, musing over mysteries, tracking disseminated meanings, tracing floating signifiers, playing with open possibilities at the numerous entrances and exits of the self-deconstructive texts, vibrating sensitive chords, and voicing written melodies" (58).

Trudier Harris takes a different approach to subject position and narrative construction in "Watchers Watching Watchers: Positioning Characters and Readers in Baldwin's 'Sonny's Blues' and Morrison's 'Recitatif.'" Harris illustrates how Baldwin's and Morrison's positioning of characters in these two short stories "mirrors how readers are positioned in reading them" (104). Each author creates an investigative narrator who is "intent upon solving puzzles surrounding other characters" (117). The reader, according to Harris, becomes a shadow detective, following the narrator's path, or deviating from it on the basis of our own desires (117). Noting the manner in which both authors make use of music—and specifically a blues ethos—in giving form and shape to their characters, Harris points out that "as we watch both sets of characters reach significant points in their journeys, we are astute enough as readers to know that we are caught in another of our received traditions about African American literature: most of it does not end 'happily ever after' . . . The struggles continue" (118).

In "Playing a Mean Guitar: The Legend of Staggerlee in Baldwin and Morrison," Quentin Miller examines each author's use of the folk figure Staggerlee, a character often associated with black militancy and the blues. Miller points out that insofar as Staggerlee is associated with black militancy in Baldwin's and Morrison's fictions, he is "a powerful figure who can inspire and awaken the type of anger needed for social change" (146). He notes importantly that neither author ignores Staggerlee's more disturbing implications; rather, they allow characters such as Leo Proudhammer of *Tell Me How Long the Train's Been Gone* (1968) and Milkman Dead of *Song of Solomon* to "play their own version, modifying what they have heard and making it their own" (118).

Baldwin and Morrison also devote substantial literary space to healing, spiritual evolution, and love relationships within the black community. Michelle H. Phillips' essay "Revising Revision: Methodologies of Love, Desire, and Resistance in *Beloved* and *If Beale Street Could Talk*" explores the deployment of "love" in each author's work as "a foundation for change because of its capacity to open the mind and the heart" (79). She argues that Baldwin and Morrison use love (and desire) as a means for resisting the limitations of established frameworks for revision. In both novels, asserts Phillips, "love . . . has the invaluable capacity of 'bearing witness' to circumstances removed from sight . . . Love produces the intersubjective recognition and commitment necessary for a promising future" (79).

In "Revising the Incest Story: Toni Morrison's *The Bluest Eye* and James Baldwin's *Just Above My Head*," Lynn Scott argues that both novels "expose the ideological uses of incest stories to normalize cultural scripts about race and sex and render other subjects and stories 'unspeakable.'" The unspeakable, unnameable thing in *The Bluest Eye*, for example, is racial self-loathing brought on by the "total force of cultural assumption that links beauty to being white, an assumption that maintains white power and is enforced by the attitudes and actions of the white and black communities" (98). In *Just Above My Head*, the unspeakable, unnameable thing is homophobia "hidden through a psychoanalytic discourse of incest as desire and taboo." In both cases, the unspeakable is "given form in the story of an incested African American daughter" (98).

In "Refiguring the Flesh: The Word, the Body, and the Rituals of Being in *Beloved* and *Go Tell It on the Mountain*," Carol Henderson argues that "both writers use place—Morrison, "the Clearing" and Baldwin, the "Threshing Floor"—as avenues for 'clearing space' in order to refigure the flesh (151). Henderson concludes that both *Go Tell It* (1953) and *Beloved* (1987) "imagine a reclaimed spiritual past that stands on the edge of time, healing the disfigurements of a tortured soul shaped by the vestiges of history" (162). Keith Byerman's exploration of preachers in these and other works resonates with Henderson's essay on several points. In "Secular Word, Sacred Flesh: Preachers in the Fiction of Baldwin and Morrison," Byerman argues that preachers fail when they "insist on a moral dichotomy between the Word and the body" (202). He notes the ways that Baldwin and Morrison strive to show that "words alone cannot meet the needs of living beings. Instead, their meaning must be performed so as to connect the body to the Word" (202). Byerman illustrates how both authors come to the same conclusion from different vantage points and through different means.

In "Resistance against Racial, Sexual, and Social Oppression in *Go Tell It on the Mountain* and *Beloved*," Babacar M'Baye examines the crucial importance of communal memory of the past in Baldwin's and Morrison's works, asserting that these two texts "explore the impact of slavery and racism on African Americans and European Americans since the time before the Emancipation Proclamation." M'Baye writes that through their engagement with the anxieties related to the violence of slavery and racism, the authors show that "the invention of whiteness as a hegemonic identity that is antithetical to blackness is the major obstacle to successful cross-racial relationships in the United States" (184).

Jon Mirin and Richard Schur focus exclusively on Baldwin's and Morrison's nonfiction in "The Art of Whiteness in the Nonfiction of James Baldwin and Toni Morrison" and "Unseen or Unspeakable? Racial Evidence in Baldwin and Morrison's Nonfiction," respectively. Mirin examines the roots of Morrison's *Playing in the Dark* in several of Baldwin's earlier essays, noting that "Baldwin['s] and Morrison's primary aim in regard to whiteness has been to unravel the ways white America has shaped itself in opposition to blackness" (237). They "map distinct but analogous chains of ill-effects resulting from the same historical cause: the birth of America's art of whiteness" (237). Mirin asserts that scholars engaged in projects of "explicating the ways race functions in art now and tomorrow must look to Baldwin for a fuller understanding of Morrison" (238).

Richard Schur's essay departs from legal scholar Jon-Christian Suggs's (*Whispered Consolations* 2000) exploration of interfaces between the American legal system and African American literature leading up to the

Brown v. Board of Education decision in 1954. Schur engages with Suggs's analysis of the uses of literature to expose the flaws in the legal system by linking Baldwin and Morrison to hip hop culture; he argues that we must extend Suggs's thesis in order to account for the ways that contemporary narratives "continue to write over dominant American discourse" (219). Schur asserts that if "previous generations relied on producing images of black respectability, texts of searing social realism, and arguments against the irrationality of legalized racism, [then] critical race theory . . . and hip hop culture deploy irony . . . to deconstruct stereotyped images of African American life in literary and legal discourse" (219).

The last two essays in the volume, E. Frances White's "The Evidence of Things Not Seen: The Alchemy of Race and Sexuality" and Keith Mitchell's "Femininity, Abjection and (Black) Masculinity in James Baldwin's *Giovanni's Room* and Toni Morrison's *Beloved*," examine the reification of heteronormativity as a problem in each author's work. In an ironic parody of one of Morrison's central questions in "Unspeakable Things Unspoken: The Afro-American Presence in American Literature," White asks "what intellectual and political feats she [Morrison] has had to perform to erase black queers from her consciousness" (258). In regard to Baldwin, White asserts that his less-than-powerful response to attacks on his homosexuality during 1960s, specifically Eldridge Cleaver's charge that Baldwin's homosexuality was a sign of racial self-hatred, was in part due to Baldwin's own narrow vision of masculinity, which left him vulnerable to such attacks. Though he suggested in "Here Be Dragons" (1985) that "he believed that all males contain elements of the female," Baldwin actually "devalued womanhood." Baldwin, she continues, "could not defend himself against the assertion that he was like a woman" (254). On this point, Keith Mitchell is in agreement.

Mitchell notes that Baldwin and Morrison "seek to expose systems of oppression that threaten (black) masculinity and, by extension, (black) heteronormative relationships," but in doing so they reify heteronormativity. Each author "erases important aspects of the African American experience that would . . . flesh out the rich history and contributions of all African Americans, not just of those who conform to the very same patterns of behavior prescribed by white society's notion of normalcy that Baldwin and Morrison are supposedly fighting against" (280).

The thirteen essays in this volume help to illuminate the literary relationship between James Baldwin and Toni Morrison; they provide evidence that reading Baldwin and Morrison next to each other opens up new avenues of discovery and interpretation related to their representations of African American and American literature and cultural experience. Their contributions to the American cultural landscape as artists and cultural critics reverberate throughout the world. The relationship between the two authors was clearly reciprocal, and both African American and American literature are richer traditions for that fact.

WORKS CITED

Baldwin, James. *A Dialogue: James Baldwin and Nikki Giovanni.* Philadelphia: Lippincott, 1973.

————. *Another Country.* 1962. London: Michael Joseph, 1979.

————. "Everybody's Protest Novel." 1949. Rpt. in *Baldwin: Collected Essays.* Ed. Toni Morrison. New York: Library of America, 1998. 11–18.

————. *Giovanni's Room.* 1956. New York: Delta Publishing, 2000.

————. *Go Tell It on the Mountain.* New York: Bantam Doubleday Books, 1953.

————. "Here Be Dragons." (Orig. "Freaks and the American Ideal of Manhood." Playboy, January 1985). In *The Price of the Ticket.* New York: St. Martin's/ Marek, 1985, 677–690.

————. *If Beale Street Could Talk.* 1974. New York: Dell, 1988.

————. *Just Above My Head.* 1978. New York: Dell, 1990.

————. "Sonny's Blues." 1957. In *Going to Meet the Man.* New York: Dell, 1964. 86–122.

————. *Tell Me How Long the Train's Been Gone.* 1968. New York: Random House (Vintage), 1998.

C-Span 2. " In Depth: Toni Morrison." 2001.

Jones, Gayl. *Corregidora.* 1975. Boston: Beacon Press, 1986.

Meriwether, Louise. *Daddy Was a Number Runner.* 1970. New York: Feminist Press, 2002.

Morrison, Toni. *Beloved.* New York: Knopf, 1987.

————. *The Bluest Eye.* New York: Holt, Rinehart, and Winston, 1970.

————. *James Baldwin: Early Novels and Stories.* New York: Library of America, 1998.

————. *Jazz.* New York: Knopf, 1992.

————. *Playing in the Dark: Whiteness and the Literary Imagination.* Cambridge, MA: Harvard University Press, 1992.

————. "Recitatif." In *Confirmation: An Anthology of African American Women.* Ed. Amiri Baraka (LeRoi Jones) and Amina Baraka. New York: Quill, 1983. 243–261.

————. *Song of Solomon.* 1977. New York: Plume, 1987.

————. "Unspeakable Things Unspoken: The Afro-American Presence in American Literature," *Michigan Quarterly Review* 28 (Winter 1989): 9–34.

————, ed. *James Baldwin: Collected Essays.* New York: Library of America, 1998.

Seale, Bobby. *A Lonely Rage: The Autobiography of Bobby Seale.* New York: Times Books, 1978.

Standley, Fred L., and Louis H. Pratt, eds. *Conversations with James Baldwin*. Jackson: University Press of Mississippi, 1989.

Suggs, Jon-Christian. *Whispered Consolations*. Ann Arbor: University of Michigan Press, 2000.

Taylor-Guthrie, Danille, ed. *Conversations with Toni Morrison*. Jackson: University Press of Mississippi, 1994.

Troupe, Quincy, ed. *James Baldwin: The Legacy*. New York: Simon and Schuster, 1989.

BALDWIN'S BOP 'N' MORRISON'S MOOD: BEBOP AND RACE IN JAMES BALDWIN'S *ANOTHER COUNTRY* AND TONI MORRISON'S *JAZZ*

KEREN OMRY

James Baldwin and Toni Morrison, two pivotal figures in the African American literary canon and cultural history, use their fiction and nonfiction to grapple with vital social and aesthetic challenges by exploring diverse aspects of African American experience. Toni Morrison's work engages in an ongoing dialogue with Baldwin's ideas, a dialogue made explicit in her second-person tribute to his legacy, "Life in His Language": "I never heard a single command from you, yet the demands you made on me, the challenges you issued to me, were nevertheless unmistakable, even if unenforced . . . I have been seeing the world through your eyes for so long, I believed that clear, clear view was my own" (75–76). The implications of Baldwin's influence are made clear as she goes on to comment that "[i]t was you who gave us the courage to appropriate an alien, hostile, all-white geography because you had discovered that 'this world [meaning history] is white no longer and it will never be white again'" (77).

For both Baldwin and Morrison, the concepts of race and ethnicity, the distinctions between them, and the definitions and the boundaries of each are central issues. Although not always defined in these terms, both authors make a distinction between two conceptions of blackness—that real or perceived difference that underlies African Americanness in all its expressions. The first, for which I shall be using the term *race*, is a static, narrow, and biologically determined category that serves as the primary ideological context for racism in America.[1] The second, which I refer to as *ethnicity*, is a much more dynamic and fluctuating category that is centrally based on cultural affiliation.[2] In my attempts to differentiate coherently between these terms, I will hereafter use the term *blackness* to refer to the very basis of this categorization. Although this term is inevitably inflected with racial as well as ethnic connotations, I choose it carefully with the hope that it is simultaneously representative of some implicitly incontrovertible impulse for historical and social categorization and sufficiently neutral to deflect the burden of implications suggested in the other terms already defined.

Paul Gilroy describes blackness as a metaphysical condition that creates, as much as it is created by, the social surroundings of modern existence, rather than as any fixed and static identity (160). Thus Gilroy's "blackness" is reflected in my definition of ethnic identity, which emphasizes the intangibility and fluidity of the concept. Furthermore, by assigning agency to his conception of blackness—"creates, as much as it is created by"—and focusing on the process of identification itself, Gilroy adds new dimensions to *ethnic identity* (a term virtually inextricable and only subtly different from *ethnicity*). The act of affiliation suggested in *ethnic identity* manifests the central distinction between *race* and *ethnicity*.

This idea of ethnic identity as a dynamic and infinite process of creation and re-creation is relevant for both Baldwin's and Morrison's writing. The attempt to create something new, to move beyond the inherited, confining terms of race, was reflected in music being developed, mainly by African American musicians, from the 1940s—namely, bebop. Bebop becomes a conceptual model by which these two authors seek productive ways to consider ethnic identity and rewrite the historical processes that laid so much stress on the biological conceptions of race.

In his writing, Baldwin examines the relevance of the social, political, and physical landscape of America to the experiences of African Americans. Similarly, Morrison's work explores the shifting notions of self in direct relation to the social and physical environment. By looking at how Baldwin and Morrison explore the tensions between a culturally imposed collective and a socially constructed individualized identity in *Another Country* (1962) and *Jazz* (1992), I hope to examine how they introduce jazz as a primary means of reconciling these opposing and potentially destructive forces.[3] As will be demonstrated below, what emerges from these literary projects is the beginnings of a new formulation of blackness that incorporates communal consent as one of its defining features. Morrison returns to this reconfiguration in a later novel, *Paradise* (1998), but its various implications—the dangers and the benefits—are already hinted at in these earlier texts.

In his landmark *The Birth of Bebop* (1997), Scott DeVeaux positions bebop as "the point at which the yardstick [his metaphor for the history of jazz] comes into balance," for it is "the point at which our contemporary ideas of jazz come into focus" (1). Citing Bernard Gendron, he goes on to describe bebop as "both the source of the present—'that great revolution in jazz which made all subsequent jazz modernisms possible'—and the prism through which we absorb the past. To understand jazz, one must understand bebop" (3). The pivotal role played by bebop as a musical moment where the past and the present meet is a central trope in *Another Country* and *Jazz*. Bebop has an ambivalent relation to its musical ancestry. As will be described presently, beboppers attempted to resolve this ambivalence in what can be described as mechanisms of performativity, mechanisms also adopted by the two authors in their literary endeavors to achieve a parallel reconciliation.

The ambivalence toward the musical past was, according to DeVeaux, the direct result of the prolonged encounter with dominating white aesthetic standards. An expression of this interdependence can be seen in the comment made by Dizzy Gillespie regarding the beboppers' general attitudes to the blues: "The bebop musicians didn't like to play the blues. They were ashamed. The media had made it shameful" (343). By the 1940s, the blues had been problematized in the popular imagination, being directly—and often exclusively—linked with a vernacular culture, which denied both its aesthetic richness and the sociocultural history that informed its development. By rejecting the heritage of the blues form, opting instead for a dialogic relationship with the blues rhetoric, the beboppers participated in a double-pronged racializing process: not only are the blues deprived of their musical and ethnohistorical complexity, but the boppers themselves become actors in a black-and-white masquerade that presupposes an inherent, racially (pre)determined relationship to jazz (269). This image of the masquerade is particularly useful for understanding the relation of bebop to its past, since the association with masks, minstrelsy, parody, and mimicry recalls the role played by performance in conceptualizing race in American history.[4]

In his study of racial thinking in African American literature, *Authentic Blackness: The Folk in the New Negro Renaissance* (1999), J. Martin Favor introduces a performative context to his discussion of blackness, with particular reference to the writers of the Harlem Renaissance. The notion of performativity begins to complicate the history of race in America, adding new dimensions to the understanding of blackness, for it suggests that conscious choice and artificial constructs are central features of configurations of blackness. Thus, the model of performativity casts new light on the history of performance, from minstrelsy in its many forms through to bebop. It complicates the processes of mimicry and parody and exposes their biting social critique, but also focuses on the complex racial thinking underlying them and highlights the serious implications and possibilities of imitation. Bebop, which was often associated with a fine-tuned performative sensibility (the staple horn-rimmed glasses, beret, and goatee sported by many of the boppers), is firmly located within this self-conscious tradition. Beboppers often used standard jazz pieces, not infrequently written by white composers, and by exploring the harmonic possibilities of the underlying chords, they reached new frontiers in musical experience.[5] The characteristic whirlwind of notes frustrated popular demands for facile entertainment, commenting on both the nature of market demands and its relation to the possibilities of jazz. These elements of role playing and performativity point to how some African American artists use their creative impulses to explore ways of making something new, redefining their space and rewriting their narratives, processes that function centrally in these novels.

Dissonance: Racialized Divisiveness and Performed Identities

In *Another Country*, Baldwin recognizes the complexity of racial identity and implies that there is a distinction between an inherited and a chosen identity or—as Werner Sollors proposed in *Beyond Ethnicity* (1986)—between descent and consent. Music is one of the principal mediums through which Baldwin explores blackness. By examining the relation of the various protagonists to music, Baldwin examines the idea of an intrinsic, racialized musicality. In a novel so involved with creativity in general and music in particular, it is significant to note that in all the references and musical quotations, as well as among all the characters of the novel, there is no white musician.

The question of a biological or inherent association to music—specifically jazz—has always been present in jazz discourse but becomes particularly germane with bebop. Bebop was, in many ways, a direct response to the popular success of what was perceived as a watered-down appropriation of African American musical forms. With the mass appeal of swing bands, a market largely dominated by white musicians, some African American jazz players sought to recapture the creative authority denied to them in swing. It has been generally acknowledged that one motivation for pursuing the breakneck speed so prevalent in bebop was to exclude the supposedly less talented white musicians. Furthermore, as bebop gained prominence, virtually exploding onto the scene once the recording ban of 1942–1944 was lifted, it was often associated with a racially subversive movement, as a revolutionary model for change. On the other hand, partly because of the constraints of World War II, but also partly because of a concentrated focus on the integrity of the music as the primary goal of bebop, this musical moment also saw an unprecedented presence of mixed-race bands and genuine interracial creative cooperation.[6] As DeVeaux's argument regarding the importance of bebop in jazz history suggests, bebop stands at the cusp of a conceptual, as well as a musical, transformation. Bebop both completes the trajectory of a racialized past, manifesting a racial divisiveness, and—as will be demonstrated at length below—formalizes a new ethnic cohesiveness.

Resonant of the racial politics surrounding bebop's production and aesthetic motivations, Baldwin's novel struggles to understand the relation of biological conceptions of race to music, a relation explored through the association of each character with the music. Baldwin does not preclude the white characters from creative possibilities. In fact, all the protagonists of the novel are preoccupied with a creative impulse—with the arguable exception of Cass, a detail significant in terms of the various gender issues raised in the novel and in terms of her relationship with her husband, Richard. Nevertheless, music is reserved primarily for the black world within the text. The characters seem to be placed on a hierarchy, qualified according to their relation to music. Steve Ellis, the producer, is reduced to a bumbling buffoon through his inability to relate to or communicate through music. The doubtless intentional irony of this inability, in light of his career as a music and television producer, serves to enhance the farce. Although both Vivaldo and Eric are white characters, they are given a heightened integrity through their intimacy with music.[7]

What seems to be an intrinsic difference between the musical creativity of the white characters and that of the black characters is also apparent in their ability (or inability) to grasp music. Vivaldo remembers an incident from his past in Harlem, where he had been swindled by a prostitute and her pimp. As the man confronted him, Vivaldo hears the woman humming a tune: "He couldn't quite make out the tune she was humming and this, for some insane reason, drove him wild" (69). A parallel reaction is later repeated on a larger and much more personal scale. Vivaldo remembers a song that Ida often sings: "Just above my head, / I hear music in the air. / And I really do believe / There's a God somewhere" (307). This unidentified song suggests to Vivaldo a world from which he is excluded. He comments that "[p]erhaps the answer was in the songs," but what the answer is and to which questions, he does not know; he cannot actually hear the music in the air.

> What in the world did these songs mean to her? For he knew that she often sang them in order to flaunt before "him" privacies which he could never hope to penetrate and to convey accusations which he could never hope to decipher, much less deny. And yet, if he could enter this secret place, he would, by that act, be released forever from the power of her accusations. His presence in this strangest and grimmest of sanctuaries would prove his right to be there; in the same way that the prince, having outwitted all the dangers and slaughtered the lion, is ushered into the presence of his bride, the princess. (308)

But Vivaldo cannot enter this sanctuary; he is blocked from this realm by the barrier of his culture, and no matter how closely he approaches its gates he is barred from this language full of symbols and mythology. He must resort to the familiar European fairy-tale metaphors to fill the incomprehensive gaps in the musical language in which Ida is fluent. Implicit in the cultural exclusion are the same stereotypes that abound in racial thinking—that is, that the difference in Vivaldo's and Ida's musicality stems from the fact that he is white and she is black. Baldwin is conscious of these associations and exploits them in his illustrations of the very different kinds of musical conversations that Ida and Vivaldo each have in another scene with the jazz musicians in the bar where Ida is about to perform for the first time.

Listening to the musicians, Ida fully understands the language of the music and the meaning being communicated. Vivaldo, on the other hand, is aurally and emotionally confronted by the music and defies it:

> Ida watched with a bright, sardonic knowingness, as though the men on the stand were beating out a message she had commanded them to convey; but Vivaldo's head was slightly lowered and he looked up at the bandstand with a wry, uncertain bravado; as though there were an incipient war going on between himself and the musicians, having to do with rank and colour and authority. He and Ida sat very still, very straight, not touching—it was as though, before this altar, touch was forbidden them. (249)

Thus, the only way that Ida and Vivaldo can hope to communicate with each other is within the realm of music; physicality as a communicative substitute is insufficient here. The relationship among sexuality, music, and communication is very complex in the novel—the role of each is often dependent on the existence of the other. I will discuss this relationship at length, but it is significant to note that at this point physical contact cannot be resorted to as a medium to bridge the gap in communication created by the music. Ida is an active participant in the creative musical process; the language of the music is her own. Vivaldo, on the other hand, remains an outsider and interacts with the musicians on an external and political level, straining to match their strength in a virtual contest of communication in order to withstand his inability to interconnect with the music. The irreconcilable difference between Ida and Vivaldo would seem to support the racial exclusivity of bebop, asserted by some of its proponents. However, Baldwin successfully complicates this problematic conclusion.

The notion that in America race is commonly understood to be restricted to two-dimensional, narrow, and rigid categories—black and white—pervades the text, on the narrative and the metanarrative levels. Baldwin, however, illuminates the risks of racial thinking, showing that the distinction between black and white very rarely remains based on biological explanations and almost inevitably shifts into the socially dangerous stereotypification of one group by the other. There are numerous incidents of this in the novel, each illustrating how firmly racial myths have taken root in American society and how they poison people's experience. In the scene described above, the barrier separating Vivaldo's musicality and that of Ida and the black musicians has become real, one that is preserved firmly by both characters. Both Vivaldo and Ida are aware of the distance between them, but neither is willing to act in order to lessen that distance. The narrative tone in this passage depicts a combative and cold atmosphere that cannot even be relieved by bodily warmth.

Baldwin clearly shows that many of the popular ideas on racial binarism (i.e., homogenous black or homogenous white) are learned social reactions. The differences between the cultures, as illustrated above through music, are transformed into artificial constructs—rigid masks that the characters expect themselves and the others to adopt and represent. Hence, it follows that while the characters in the novel assume the socially preconstructed identities, they rarely do so comfortably, battling within themselves when these predetermined roles conflict with their own identities. When Cass is introduced into the novel, she seems initially to slip easily into a preconfigured category of white middle-class mother and wife. But this is immediately dispelled by Rufus himself who cannot quite locate her in this map of roles. She is a mystery to him: "He could never quite place her in the white world to which she seemed to belong" (45). Cass does not quite fit into the mold that Rufus has been taught to expect. This is one reason that she is both a source of solace and comfort for him and an upsetting, unsettling quandary. He needs her in order to define himself; indeed she herself says that every time she sees him she realizes how similar they are. If she is not what he expects, then his own understanding of himself, in relation, shifts: "[Cass] smiled at him. He longed to do something to prolong that smile, that moment, but he did not smile back, only nodded his head" (87). Rufus cannot afford to recognize the depth of Cass's character because it might reflect on his own. And as Leona repeatedly remarked, "Rufus, . . . ain't nothing wrong in being coloured" (60). He, more than any of the other characters in the novel, has adopted the two-dimensional, socially constructed identity laid out for him. His is a violent internal conflict to reconcile the inherent inferiority that society and experience have taught him are his with his own natural, instinctive resistance to that inferiority.

The battle between the racially nonspecific individuality and the racialized masks imposed on the individual is nowhere more apparent than in the relationship between Rufus and Leona. As seen in Ida and Vivaldo's relationship,

Baldwin focuses on the point at which ethnic identities meet in order to understand the nature of the boundaries separating them. This focus clearly situates Baldwin's text in the historical moment of bebop, which was simultaneously experimenting with precisely the same boundaries—both in terms of the racial politics of the musical practice and in terms of the music itself and its relation to the various ancestries available to it.

When they first meet, Rufus is conscious of Leona's whiteness but is not consumed by it: "Something touched his imagination for a moment, suggesting that Leona was a person . . . But he shook the suggestion off" (23). There are little lapses in his hatred of her whiteness, and she ceases to be the receptacle of his revenge and becomes a lover who will love him and whom he can love. But these moments are rare. The first sexual encounter between Rufus and Leona has little to do with her; rather, it is Rufus enacting his fantasy of overpowering and violating the white community:

> He wanted her to remember him the longest day she lived. And, shortly, nothing could have stopped him, not the white God himself nor a lynch mob arriving on wings. Under his breath he cursed the milk-white bitch and . . . rode his weapon between her thighs . . . A moan and a curse tore through him while he beat her with all the strength he had and felt the venom shoot out of him, enough for a hundred black-white babies. (31)

His consciousness of their racial and ethnic difference escalates until he is eventually blind to everything but the racial landscape. In this context, his violence toward her seems inevitable. He either hates her for her whiteness or despises her for loving him, despite his blackness. Baldwin demonstrates that this inevitable extension of a descent-based ideology is destructive, slowly eating away at Rufus. He becomes isolated in his self-hatred when he stops playing the drums—his only source of survival, both figuratively and practically. His violence against Leona climaxes, and he himself is beaten. This graphic image linking race with violence and sexuality is repeated many times in *Another Country*, evoking the primitivist imagery historically inextricable from racist imagination. The extreme consequences of this divisive racial thinking are depicted in the scene of Rufus's suicide where he sees the black waters of the Hudson River: "He was black and the water was black" (93). The blackness of the water is an illusion. It is a reflection of the darkness around it. This perception mirrors his own blackness—in the qualitative sense of the word. They are both illusions, but nevertheless they are his truth.

In Ida and Vivaldo's relationship, the traditional meaning of race and the possibilities of change are explored in depth. Ida, repeatedly described by various voices in the text in terms of a link to Africa and her own Africanness,

struggles with the conflict of her ideological racism, the necessity of succumbing to racial stereotypes (in her relationship with Ellis, for example), and
her reluctant love for Vivaldo. Vivaldo wrestles with comparable difficulties.
His ideas about blackness are the exact opposite of Ida's. Whereas she makes
a sweeping and generalized distinction between black and white, he tries to
convince himself that there is no difference whatsoever—a seemingly liberal-minded view, but one that tries to escape the burden of American history
(and one that he himself cannot uphold uniformly throughout). Ida recognizes this escape and resents it. It is this disparity that spells the eventual
dissipation of their relationship, though the very attempt to overcome their
differences and the true love they share indicate the hope of the future.

In *Jazz*, written almost thirty years after *Another Country*, Toni
Morrison's exploration into the experience of blackness reflects the passing
of time and can afford to adopt a somewhat more subtle approach. Where
Baldwin focuses on the interaction between black and white, investigating
the meaning of either category at the junction, Morrison seems to exclude
white Americans from the space of her book, except to preserve their role
as a traumatizing other by which blackness is defined. For Morrison, jazz
links the different ways of being black, and for Baldwin it stretches the very
category itself. Just as bebop explores existing categories in the process of
exploding the boundaries they impose, so does Baldwin's aesthetic force a
new role for and understanding of the categories that can accommodate the
trauma Morrison seeks to reformulate.

Focusing on the model of performativity highlights the distinction
between the explorations of racial and ethnic identity in the two novels. In
Jazz the element of performance takes on new dimensions and new implications. If in *Another Country* Rufus, Vivaldo, and Ida struggled with the
masks and masquerades that consistently conflicted with their own senses of
self, in *Jazz* the characters are faced with their own multiple self-identities
that reflect against one another and begin to belie the very existence of any
true self (racial, ethnic, gendered, or individual) lying at the core of human
experience. The central characters in *Jazz* are each described in terms of
their many selves, each watching the performance of the other. Violet,
called Violent by some after her disruption of Dorcas's funeral, sits in the
drugstore "sucking malt through a straw wondering who on earth that other
Violet was that walked about the City in her skin; peeped out through her
eyes and saw other things" (89). As she tries to explain to Felice about "having another you inside that isn't anything like you," Felice asks:

"How did you get rid of her?"
"Killed her. Then I killed the me that killed her."
"Who's left?"
"Me." (208–209)

This is not the self-effacing conflict of identity that eventually overpowered Rufus in the earlier text, but a living, breathing, acting character that inhabits the same body and, because of the perceived division, poses a violent threat. Joe, Violet's husband, describes a parallel split in identity when he relates how he hunted and finally shot Dorcas, his lover, after she had abandoned him.

> I tracked Dorcas from borough to borough . . . Something else takes over when the track begins to talk to you . . . But if the trail speaks, no matter what's in the way, you can find yourself in a crowded room aiming a bullet at her heart, never mind it's the heart you can't live without . . . I had the gun but it was not the gun—it was my hand I wanted to touch you with. (130–131)

In the retelling of their stories, both Violet and Joe distance themselves from the implications of their own actions by formulating a different self from which they are alienated and yet to whom they are intimately related: thus, there is the storyteller, the one self, and the *other* self, each reflecting and watching the performance of the other. This division inevitably results in destruction in the novel, highlighting the potent dangers of this kind of categorization, of this conception of a cast of roles enacted on the stage of a character that stands in contrast to some essential core.

The kind of divisive danger Morrison points to here is rather different from the alienating racial constructs superimposed on Baldwin's characters, a difference made clearer through its relation to bebop. Morrison is much more immediately focused on her readers, and by extension, on the audience of the beboppers—an interest made explicit not least in the direct address of the narrative voice. The early audience responses to bebop were hardly welcoming. Having come prepared for the dancing entertainment of swing, many audiences were alienated by the intellectualized explorations of bebop. Whereas the blues, in all its manifestations, was an inclusive musical form that included elements of virtually every kind of African American experience, and swing was, at the very least, universal dance music, bebop was one of the first kinds of jazz that could be seen as exclusive, even divisive, within African American communities.[8]

In addition to its relation to the possibly alienating effect the music had on the audiences, the focus on the divided sense of self shared by many of the characters in *Jazz* points to the potential for disintegration within the music itself. Structurally, bebop threw new emphasis on the role of the solo in the musical process. Each musician (usually excluding the rhythm section) was given the space to pursue his or her own musical ideas, extending the solos to unprecedented lengths. The stress on individuality, manifest in the solo, potentially weakened the cohesive force of a musical piece and demanded a concentrated collective effort to avoid the possible fragmentation. One method used to maintain the logic of the piece was the characteristically steady rhythm set by the bass or drum that ran through the work—a beat that, as will be shown presently, has a crucial role in *Jazz*.[9]

In *Jazz*, the volatile implications of this kind of division become evident in the repeated image of the self as disengaged from the body. Violet watches *that* Violet interrupt a funeral to defile the dead Dorcas's face and fight off the men attempting to stop her with a physical strength *this* Violet has long lost. Thus, here, the body is not simply a vessel for the self but changes in response to the role being played. This scene is not only telling in relation to Violet's divided sense of self, it also illuminates the underlying importance of the body and the dangers inherent in a racialized perspective that focuses on the body. As will be shown below, it also illuminates the potentially redeeming factors of a more unifying view. Violet knows that Dorcas is dead but feels she must destroy her face as well, for therein lies a threat equal to the live girl herself. Both Joe and Violet are in the business of appearances, spending their days helping people change or maintain their faces and their appearances, and so it is not surprising that they both become captivated by Dorcas's visage. The face of the dead girl becomes the focal point of their pain as her photograph sits on their mantelpiece, variously drawing the one or the other from their sleepless bed. The photograph offers a literal manifestation of that epidermalizing process so prevalent in the novel. While the face looking out at them cannot satisfactorily capture the dead girl, its presence in their home keeps her, and their hunger for her, alive. Joe explains the power of her face over him as he describes her bad skin: "Little half moons clustered underneath her cheekbones, like faint hoofmarks . . . I bought the stuff she told me to, but glad none of it ever worked. Take my little hoof marks away? Leave me with no tracks at all?" (130). The tracks take hold of him as he hunts her down.

But Morrison adds a new dimension to this destructive divisiveness, complicating the alienating exteriority of the body. Dorcas's face becomes more than the mask that pulls Joe in and pulls Violet apart (splitting her into the two Violets), or a visage that with the props of skin bleach, curling iron, cosmetics, and tonics represents the stage for a masquerade in which Dorcas becomes prey, Joe becomes the hunter, and Violet turns wild. Through Morrison's language, the tracks on her skin become mingled with the tracks of music that saturate the narrative: "[Joe] is bound to the track. It pulls him like a needle through the groove of a Bluebird record. Round and round about the town. That's the way the City spins you" (120). By aligning Joe's response to Dorcas with a musical experience that emanates from and encompasses the City itself, Morrison introduces a redeeming link between the individual and the community.[10] The characters cease being puppeteered by an alienating force that directs the roles they act out. Through music a community is formed that resists the inherent danger of two-dimensionality inextricable from the model of performativity. This link is made more explicit in the description of Alice Manfred, Dorcas's aunt, and the effect a march protesting those who were killed in the East St. Louis riots has on her.

Alice lives in fear, threatened by the realities of racial hatred and ignorance but also by the possibilities of sexuality and creativity, epitomized in the "lowdown music": "[S]ongs that used to start in the head and fill the heart had dropped on down, down to places below the sash and the buckled belts"(56). Watching the march, she watches the "tide of cold black faces"; listens to the beat of their drums and clutches the hand of Dorcas, her orphaned niece; and feels the gap between the angers and the appetites represented by the marchers and her own need to contain and protect her niece from them widening.

> Then suddenly, like a rope cast for rescue, the drums spanned the distance, gathering them all up and connected them: Alice, Dorcas, her sister and her brother-in-law, the Boy Scouts and the frozen black faces, the watchers on the pavement and those in the windows above. (58)

Here, as above, music becomes a unifying force. The fear Alice describes consumes her experience, transforming all other kinds of existence into a direct threat, effectively isolating her. Although she secretly admired the glamorous coats that are so suggestive in her mind, she keeps her sentiment hidden, masked as the contempt with which she speaks of them. It is the rhythm beat out by the drums that dissipates her fears: "The drums and the freezing faces hurt her, but hurt was better than fear" (54). Alice was isolated and insulated by her fears, but the power of pain forces her to actively participate in her experiences. The beat of the drums, echoing the driving rhythms of bebop, forms a community of the many different African American responses to the pain of experience, one that Alice can no longer shy away from. She clings tightly to the rope so that it will protect her from the kind of music that "made her hold her hand in the pocket of her apron to keep from smashing it through the glass pane to snatch the world in her fist and squeeze the life out of it for doing what it did and did and did to her and everybody else she knew or knew about" (59). And yet, it is precisely that rope which links her to the music that—through that underlying rhythm—becomes the organizing principle of the world in *Jazz*.[11]

In *Another Country*, Baldwin explores the implications of positing race as a performed identity. In *Jazz*, Morrison complicates the model of performativity by focusing on the notion of separateness inherent in this model, where some essential self takes on or takes off a particular role. Morrison points to this process' relation to the parallel process of biophysical racism, in that it stresses division and separation. The emphasis of each bop musician on solo improvisation contains the parallel potential for divisiveness. Instead, Morrison offers a model of unity in which the divisive forces are not homogenized but reconciled. As I will demonstrate below, the element of performance is still paramount through the very act of narration that frames and pervades the numerous narratives of Morrison's novel. And it is the recurring thematic and structural motif of storytelling that further links Morrison's text with bebop.

Consonance: Ethnic Harmonies—Consent and the City

As discussed above, Baldwin draws clear distinctions between the white and the African American characters in *Another Country*. However, he makes equally clear the proximity between them. Using definitions of race laid out by Audrey Smedley in *Race in North America* (1993) as a conceptual guideline, it is important to realize that in many ways Rufus, Ida, Vivaldo, Eric, and Cass are united in cultural-historical and—I would argue—ethnic senses. They all coexist in the text and struggle to communicate in intimately related fashions. It is through their struggles and through the active communicative efforts—generally evident in musical expression—that the characters offer a new model for identity-making processes based on ethnicity. Vivaldo realizes that the sets of symbols historically used to identify and categorize people in America have become an intermeshed, interconnected jumble of empty signs. This discovery leaves him temporarily paralyzed:

> [S]omething in him was breaking; he was, briefly and horribly, in a region where there were no definitions of any kind, neither of color, nor of male and female. There was only the leap and the rending and the terror and the surrender. And the terror: which all seemed to begin and end and begin again—forever—in a cavern behind the eye . . . Order. Order. *Set thine house in order* . . . When people no longer knew that a mystery could only be approached through form, people became—what the people of this time and place had become, what he had become. They perished within their despised clay tenements, in isolation, passively, or actively together, in mobs, thirsting and seeking for, and eventually reeking of blood. (297)

This terrifying realm of no definitions marks the birth pangs of an America that accepts the blood ties between black and white citizens. The distinctions so long adamantly preserved are beginning to crumble, revealing "the terror and the surrender" that had created them. Vivaldo must resee things; he

must relearn his surroundings and how to interact with them without succumbing to chaos; and, significantly, he must first make the choice to do
these things. Baldwin uses terms such as *chaos, void,* and *abyss* to describe
the terrifying leap involved in abandoning the racial ideology around
which much of American history revolved. Baldwin explored these ideas
in an earlier nonfiction work, published as "Everybody's Protest Novel"
(1949):

> Society is held together by our need; we bind it together with legend, myth,
> coercion, fearing that without it we will be hurled into that void, within
> which, like the earth before the Word was spoken, the foundations of soci-
> ety are hidden . . . it is only this void, our unknown selves, demanding, for-
> ever, a new act of creation, which can save us—from the evil that is in the
> world. (20–21)

This discovery can be either a deliverance or a devastation. Bebop, too, was
a "new act of creation"—the aesthetic location where racial boundaries were
stretched, consciously incorporating elements of a racially mixed heritage and
acknowledging the vital role played by these "unknown selves." Rufus, on
the other hand, failed to engage with his "unknown self," and by abandoning his music he rejected the act of creation that could have saved him from
being destroyed. The novel opens with Rufus as an observer, external to his
surroundings. Completely alienated, he takes a journey outside of his identity. The focalizing narrative occasionally slips out of focalization and into an
omniscient narrative voice, freezing a moment and looking around. When
he walks uptown into the jazz club at the beginning of the novel, he is able
to see people without their masks, interacting with one another as individuals. Rufus's relationship with Leona offered to mirror the new kind of harmony evident in the jazz clubs in the novel and in bebop itself, but Rufus
was unable to contend with the new reality that knowledge of her entailed.
Instead of reinvesting the energy of his self-discovery into his music, reen-
tering society and thus completing the cycle of growth, he abandoned it
completely, remaining helplessly and angrily in exile. It is crucial to recognize that in Baldwin's construction Rufus has a measure of control over his
fate. This is no longer the tyrannical incontrovertibility of race but a more
flexible and consensual ethnic identity.

The prevalent theme of knowledge, the recognition of ignorance, and
the desire to rectify ignorance are closely associated with sexuality in
Another Country, particularly in the various relationships between Rufus
and Leona, Eric and Vivaldo, Eric and Cass, and Ida and Vivaldo.
Appropriately, the familiar biblical trope linking sexuality with knowledge
is completed with Ida's snake ring. Ida's ring—a "ruby-eyed snake ring"

she received as a gift from Rufus—is repeatedly alluded to and points to the omnipresent theme of sexuality. The recurring references to the story of the Garden of Eden and the concomitant motifs of sexuality, knowledge, and ultimately death reveal Baldwin's delicate reformulation of the tale of origin. Instead of portraying Eden as the paradise of innocence, familiar in Western mythology, Baldwin transforms it into the static haven of ignorance that lies at the foundation of American racial history. Instead of the depraved land implicit in Adam and Eve's exile, Baldwin envisions a productive collective that stands in contrast to the exclusivity of the Garden. His reconfiguration requires a fierce break with a past in search of a new way of social interaction. This relation to the past, as well as the resulting focus on social harmony, begins to emerge in the explorations of the boppers and is later extended in the experimentation of the avant-garde free jazz musicians. By experimenting with the relationship between the notes, the bop musicians delved into the very structure of harmony. Unlike melody, which describes the progression of notes through time, harmonic improvisation played with notions of dissonance and consonance between notes sounded—or absent from—the same moment. Furthermore, the motif of knowledge inextricable from this biblical trope resonates in the very deliberate, intellectualized approach to music, found in bebop.

As in the biblical tale, the novel arguably suggests that sexuality evokes knowledge: Eric and Vivaldo, Vivaldo and Ida, and Eric and Cass all learn about themselves through these relationships. Rufus and Leona represent the sinister alternative: their inability to bear the burden of knowledge left them both in darkness and brought about their destruction. The implicit fall from Eden derived from this imagery resembles the danger of chaos that Vivaldo senses. While the racialized bipolarity of American society is hardly Edenic, it had become a defining, fully institutionalized, and static force. Shaking the foundations of the racial divide causes upheaval in both black and white communities, forcing each to reevaluate themselves and the other, a process that can lead either to destruction or to salvation.

In *Jazz*, there is a parallel stress on behavior that strives toward knowledge, a knowledge that is thematically linked to sexuality and the Garden of Eden, and through which racial and ethnic identifications are ultimately brought to bear. This complex formulation is made unambiguously clear as Joe testifies his love for Dorcas:

> Anything just for you. To bite down hard, chew up the core and have the taste of red apple skin to carry around for the rest of my life . . . I would strut out the Garden, strut! as long as you held on to my hand, girl . . . I talk about being new seven times before I met you, but back then, back there, if you was or claimed to be colored, you had to be new and stay the same every

day the sun rose and every night it dropped. And let me tell you, baby, in those days it was more than a state of mind. (134–135)

Here, Joe is willing to make any sacrifice for the knowledge of her, the experience of her, and the love of her. As in *Another Country*, the fruit of knowledge becomes intrinsically related to the positive experience of an other, forcing a shift from the racialized othering gaze of African American history. Furthermore, in both texts the Garden of Eden is reconfigured as a protected, stagnant seat of ignorance that must be shattered despite the cost of destruction, which inevitably follows. The implications of this dramatic reconfiguration and its relation to ethnicity become clearer through Morrison's subtle reference to an important essay by LeRoi Jones, "The Changing Same" (1968), hinted at in the penultimate sentence of the quoted passage.

In his article, Jones writes about the "new music" that emerged and gained momentum in the 1960s and about the avant-garde explorations of John Coltrane, Albert Ayler, Ornette Coleman, and Sun-Ra, among others, and he compares them with the growing popularity of R&B in America. Jones argues that in contrast to the increasing "whitening" impulse of R&B, the New Black Music transports the musicians and the audience to another place, "a place where Black People live." Thus, Jones identifies jazz as a physical space, a region inhabited by African Americans, not unlike the uniquely black space of the city depicted in *Jazz*. Jones makes a direct link between the developments of bebop and the explorations of free jazz, suggesting that they are intimately linked in the process of self-conscious identification: "And that's what it's about; consciousness. What are you *with* (the word Con-With/Scio-Know). The 'new' musicians are self-conscious. Just as the boppers were" (188). In other words, Jones envisages a new space, created through music, in which African Americans can learn to know themselves: "What is presented is a consciously proposed learning experience" (188). The envisioned end of this process is "[a] really new, really all inclusive music. The whole people" (188). Thus, in *Jazz*, through his relationship with Dorcas, Joe undergoes a process that anticipates the move from bebop to free jazz. The seven transformations he undergoes are resonant of bebop's "rhythm changes," whereby the musicians improvise harmonically on the chords underscoring the melody, rather than on the notes of the melody themselves. Joe shifts between various African American experiences creating a harmony of voices that feed into his narrative (the reader encounters many of Joe's faces: he is the man women feel safe around; he is the adulterer who seduces and then kills his mistress; and he is the hunter, the lost orphan, the masculine worker, and the devastated shell of a man).

The suggestion of the phrase already quoted—"Back then . . . if you was or claimed to be colored, you had to be new and stay the same every day"—is that this changing same encloses an increasingly confining space that must be broken out of. Dorcas learns to recognize the implications of their relationship as she lies dying, sending Joe the message that "[t]here's only one apple" (213). Refusing to betray her lover, even though she is shot by him, Dorcas realizes that love is the key, which recalls another passage in the Jones's essay:

> What is the *object* of John Coltrane's "Love" . . . There is none. It is for the sake of Loving, Trane speaks of. As Ra's "When Angels Speak of Love." . . . The change to Love. The freedom to (of) Love. And in this constant evocation of Love, its need, its demands, its birth, its death, there is a morality that shapes such a sensibility, and a sensibility shaped by such moralizing. (200)

In other words, through love, through constructive relationships with others that concentrate on a unified sensibility of self, rather than on the alienating roles stipulated by racializing social and cultural history, a new musical and moral aesthetic emerges that lays the foundation for a new community.[12]

This appeal to love echoes the haunting plea of the saxophone player in an early scene of *Another Country:* "He had a lot to say. He stood there, wide-legged, humping the air, filling his barrel chest, shivering in the rags of his twenty-odd years, and screaming through the horn *Do you love me? Do you love me? Do you love me?*" (18; italics in the original). The raw, sexualized image that characterizes the music is mingled with the musician's stark loneliness, a human hunger that is satisfied by the musician's ability to transcend his isolation and—through the music—to communicate with the other band members: "Each man knew that the boy was blowing for every one of them" (18).

In *Jazz*, the death of Dorcas at the hands of her newly transformed and—in Morrison's reconfiguration of the Fall—implicitly redeemed lover would seem to contradict this focus on love and community as the key to ethnic reformulation. However, hers is the death that, as in the story of the Old Testament, seals the fate of those displaced—a term resonant of the history of African American experience, as well as of the recurring metaphor linking space and jazz.

Conceptualizing jazz in spatial terms offers new insights into the ethnic formulations and ethnicizing processes that take place both in *Another Country* and in *Jazz*. In these novels, the city itself is perceived in musical terms. As he wanders uptown, in the opening of *Another Country*, Rufus describes the rhythm of the city as encompassing all of African American experience: "*A nigger*, said his father, *lives his whole life, lives and dies accord-ing to a beat* . . . The beat— in Harlem in the summertime one could almost see it, shaking above the pavements and the roof" (16; italics in the origi-nal). He grasps his own state of alienation when he realizes that "he had fled . . . from the beat of Harlem, which was simply the beat of his own heart" (16–17). Thus, Baldwin establishes a direct link between music, eth-nic self-identification, and space. As a drummer, Rufus lays down the beat, but by abandoning his music, he effectively rejects the beating of his own heart, becoming increasingly alienated from his sense of self and from his surroundings. The physicality of this image both anticipates his own suicide and is later taken up in *Jazz* where Morrison considers the destructive implications of focusing on the body as an essentializing manifestation. This increasingly threatening loss drives Rufus to wander through Manhattan seeking oases where a sociomusical haven can be temporarily recaptured. The drumbeat that runs through bebop is lost to Rufus but reappears in *Jazz*. The drums of the protest marchers beat out a rhythm that articulates different kinds of black experiences, resounding in Alice's ears as both urgent and comforting. While in *Another Country* Rufus seeks music as an escape from the crushing power of the city, in *Jazz* the city becomes home precisely through the music.

This difference is related to a distinct difference between the city-space constructed in the two novels, which is already set out early on in each. In the opening pages of Baldwin's novel, Rufus crosses all of Manhattan, start-ing at Times Square, going uptown, then down to Greenwich Village to visit Vivaldo, and finally up to Harlem; the novel is populated by both black and white characters. In contrast, in *Jazz*, Morrison locates her cen-tral narrative around "Lenox Avenue safe from fays and the things they think up" (11) and "Up there, in that part of the City [where] the right tune whistled in a doorway or lifting up from the circles and grooves of a record can change the weather. From freezing to hot to cool" (51). Whiteness becomes an alien other that haunts the periphery of the charac-ters' lives and imaginations. Morrison excludes the white population that has historically dominated Western literature and focuses on the African American processes of ethnic self-identification, thus complicating the con-ception of blackness as biological or even as performed. These processes culminate in the exchange between Golden Gray and his father, Henry Lestory (also called Hunters Hunter). Brought up by his white mother and her slave/servant, True Belle (Violet's grandmother), it is only on reaching adulthood that Golden Gray discovers that his father was a slave. The con-frontation between the white-skinned son and the black father offers an alternative way of conceiving of blackness, not unlike that suggested in *Another Country*: "Look. Be what you want—white or black. Choose. But if you choose black, you got to act black, meaning draw your manhood up—quicklike" (173). Faced with the biological fact of his racial makeup, Golden Gray is summoned to disregard the weight of implications that ancestry imposes and to make a choice and to then be the man he chooses to be. Making a similar argument, Violet laments having "messed up [her] life": "'Forgot it was mine. My life.' . . . 'What's the world for if you can't make it up the way you want it?'" (208). Echoing the construction of ethnic identity Sollors presents in *Beyond Ethnicity,* Morrison stresses consent and choice as defining components of ethnic identity making processes. While the reader never learns which choice Golden Gray makes, it is implied in the text that he has chosen to become Lestory. The narrator reveals that he undergoes a change of mind, perhaps hinting that the transformation was both extensive and dramatic. The implications of Hunters Hunter's surname, Lestory, are self-evident and point to the centrality of storytelling in the novel, which I will elaborate on in the final section of this chapter. The theme of storytelling echoes the central motifs of the novel, both in its self-conscious aesthetic concerns and in the urgent link it makes between the past being narrated and the present of narration, a formulation also recalling the structure of bebop and embodying a unifying social force.

Rhythm Changes: Bebop and Narrative Structure

Another Country is a recognizably racialized text in terms of its structure as well as its content, in that ideas of race and ethnicity are explored in virtually every formal element within the novel (i.e., the language, the central themes, the characters, and the narrative). The jazz tradition of improvisation has informed the narrative structure of Baldwin's novel. Despite a popular misconception, improvisation is far from unique to jazz or African American music in general and is an important characteristic in numerous other musical traditions. In *Jazz in American Culture* (2000), Peter Townsend comments that "[o]ne of the peculiar features of Western music during the last 200 years has been its exclusion of improvisation . . . European 'serious' music of the nineteenth and twentieth centuries is an ethnomusicological exception in its complete severance from improvisatory methods" (8). Thus, in relation to the European music alongside which jazz has developed, improvisation is one of the key identifying features of jazz. One of the main differences between jazz and other musical traditions is in what Bruno Nettl calls density: the number and frequency of reference points within musical structures. In jazz a point of reference is, for example, chord changes. Nettl identifies models of jazz as having a relatively high density, in contrast to "those of Persian music of medium density, and those of an Arabic taqsim or an Indian alap relatively lacking in density" (qtd. in Townsend 13).

Another Country has numerous parallel points of reference: there are as many as fifteen different shifts in narrative focalization between the five focalized characters: Rufus, Vivaldo, Eric, Cass, and Yves. The narrative structure of *Another Country* can be reconstructed in jazz terms as follows: Rufus introduces the central motifs of the story, transforming very standard traditional elements—love, passion, growth, loneliness, pain, and death— into a new and racialized story. These motifs are then adopted and reworked by the different characters, each taking a portion, making it his or her own, and then passing it on. Rufus's fate described concisely in the first ninety pages of the novel is a microcosm of the experiences that Vivaldo, Cass, and Eric all go through. As the focalization jumps from Vivaldo to Eric, back to Vivaldo, on to Cass, and so forth, it grows and takes on a new quality and meaning. The novel ends with the brief but hopeful new voice of Eric's French lover, Yves, who arrives to join Eric in New York. Much like the "rhythm changes" pursued by the boppers, whereby they improvised on standardized chord sequences, changing a standardized melody into a harmonic experience, Baldwin's characters have transformed the central melody into this new configuration of Rufus's tale.

In light of the performative discourse that illuminates Baldwin's novel and is further complicated in Morrison's text, the centrality of jazz to each becomes paramount. Baldwin constructs a performativity quite explicitly linked to jazz (in particular, as shown, to bebop), which complicates the racial binaries. Through his references to bebop in *Another Country,* Baldwin insists that the ethnic identity making processes be reconsidered, making room for positive interracial interdependence, a relationship that consciously redresses the often destructive interdependence which charac- terized American history.

The function of bebop in *Jazz* and its application to constructs of eth- nicity in the novel point less to the interracial community Baldwin envi- sions than they do to a more introspective cohesiveness within African American experience. The narrative technique in *Jazz* is a self-conscious reflection on the act of narration itself. The narrative structure explores how sense is created and sustained and how communication is ensured, reflecting on the significance of the very act of aesthetic production. As seen above, these central themes run through the narrative content and also inform the structural aspects of the novel.

The novel's narrative trajectory weaves in and out of countless stories, anecdotes, and accounts, often seeming only loosely related to the central narrative. The narrative structure of *Jazz,* not entirely unlike that of

Another Country, is ordered along a series of solo narrative voices. Perhaps the main difference between the two novels is in the nature of the central-ized, controlling narrator. In Baldwin's novel, this authoritative voice is a third-person omniscient narrator distanced from the events being related, observing them from outside. In contrast, Morrison's narrator is quite obvi-ously intimately engaged with the characters, the community, and the events depicted. Hers is a first-person, fallible narrative voice that is impli-cated in the narrative itself: "I thought I knew them . . . And when I was feeling most invisible, being tight-lipped, silent and unobservable, they were whispering about me to each other . . . [W]hen I invented stories about them ... I was completely in their hands" (220). The self-conscious narrative technique creates a collage of voices that implicate one another in a process whereby the narrative authority emerges from the collective itself, rather than from any one single voice. This inclusive structure mirrors the characteristic intimacy of bebop. Precisely because of its potentially alien-ating quality, bebop required a much more concentrated engagement—on the parts of the musicians and of the audience—for it to communicate suc-cessfully. As the jazz bands became smaller, the intimacy of the jam sessions grew, with the musicians often sitting in a circle facing one another, enhancing the insider-outsider divide but simultaneously suggesting that this divide was surmounted through the collective musical output. This formulation is echoed in the self-conscious storytelling technique that char-acterizes Morrison's novel.

In *The Story of Jazz: Toni Morrison's Dialogic Imagination,* Justine Tally explores the significance of storytelling in *Jazz* and suggests that it is part of a healing process that will enable African American collective imagina-tion (social, political, and creative) to move beyond the trauma of African American historical experience. In *Another Country,* storytelling becomes the creative act envisioned by Baldwin in the relationship of Ida and Vivaldo, so caught up in the implications of racializing mythologies and narratives, and in the passage already quoted, describing the saxophone player's vital effort to communicate, reconciling the divisive forces of racialized thinking. Thus, in both novels, the process of narration, which is by definition a collaborative exercise, becomes paramount.

Conclusion

Through their emphases on performativity and creative impulses, both Baldwin and Morrison explore the implications of perceiving blackness as a process that relies on consent. Ethnicity as consensus carries with it many potentially destructive as well as productive possibilities. Viewing ethnic identity as a collaborative process rather than as an inherited identity opens exciting new avenues for cultural production and the development of a communal aesthetic. However, it is problematic because it suggests a rejection of both the history of racial thought, which has for centuries been central in defining the experiences of blacks and whites, and the residues of this history in the present cultural landscape.[13] On the other hand, focusing cultural production solely on a backward gaze, even one that crucially rewrites the narrative of history, will eventually become stagnant. Both possible outcomes influence the developments of bebop. Toni Morrison's later novel, *Paradise*, pushes the consequences of both historical perspectives further, examining the aesthetic repercussions of this radical collaborative reconception of ethnic identity. In this novel, Morrison represents a community that begins to disintegrate from within—morally, socially, and physically—because of a self-defining principle that has been frozen in time. She does this using a literary aesthetic that rejects racial identification and thus explores the implications of a postracial notion of self for a contemporary ethnic community. Already foreshadowed in *Jazz*, one way she reclaims a communally unifying principle is by incorporating elements of free jazz into the structural fabric of the novel. Thus, Baldwin's and Morrison's novels can be seen as part of a larger project that, by refusing to be bound by categories of creative impulses and by introducing jazz into the defining literary aesthetic, begins to destabilize and undermine the divisive borders of social, racialized construals, offering instead a much more complex and diverse cultural model.

NOTES

1. As will be demonstrated below, although *race* (as I am using it) is insistently founded on genetics, it lends itself to artificial constructs based on the biological explanation, which, in turn, shifts often and imperceptibly into racism.

2. I am basing my definitions on those made by Audrey Smedley in her book *Race in North America: Origin and Evolution of a Worldview* (1993). There, she defines ethnicity as composed of "all those traditions, customs, activities, beliefs, and practices that pertain to a particular group of people who see themselves and are seen by others as having distinct cultural features, a separate history, and a specific sociocultural identity." Moreover, she makes an explicit distinction between race and ethnicity: "Race signifies rigidity and permanences of position/status within a ranking order that is based on what is believed to be the unalterable reality of innate biological differences. Ethnicity is conditional, temporal, even volitional, and not amenable to biology or biological processes" (31–32).

3. James Baldwin, *Another Country* (1962; London: Penguin Books, 1990); Toni Morrison, *Jazz* (1992; London: Pan Books, 1993). Further references are to

these editions, respectively, and will be made parenthetically in the text. The bebop aesthetic is central to additional works by these and other authors, not least of which are Baldwin's short story "Sonny's Blues" (1957) and Ralph Ellison's *Invisible Man* (1952). Many of the implications of bebop, which I go on to describe below, are crucial thematic, structural, and narrative elements of these texts. Moreover, the conscious intertextual resonances between the works themselves begin to reflect a bebop aesthetic. Because of limitations of space and for the sake of clarity, however, I have chosen to concentrate my discussion on the two novels by Baldwin and Morrison.

4. Somewhat paradoxically, it was precisely the perceived genetic inflexibility of racial categorization that lent itself to the parody of minstrelsy. In other words, it is through the definition of race as a generally inflexible, biologically based category that the minstrel performers were able to safely reduce race to the two-dimensionality of a mask, without implicating their own identity. The role and implications of performance and performativity become much more complex as the configuration of blackness shifts to a predominantly ethnic one. For the role of minstrelsy and parody in African American culture, see, for example, Houston A. Baker, Jr., *Blues, Ideology, and African-American Literature: A Vernacular Theory* (1984); Ralph Ellison, "Change the Joke and Slip the Yoke," in *Shadow and Act* (1995 ed., 45–59); Henry Louis Gates, Jr., *The Signifying Monkey: A Theory of African-American Literary Criticism* (1988); LeRoi Jones (Amiri Imamu Baraka), *Blues People: The Negro Experience in White America and the Music that Developed From It* (1963); Lawrence Levine, *Black Culture and Black Consciousness* (1977).

5. In fact, "rhythm changes," which became a staple feature of bebop, denotes an improvisation on the chord sequence of Gershwin's "I Got Rhythm." (See DeVeaux 203, 326, 328, 421 for details on how this was used.)

6. DeVeaux surveys the use of the revolutionary trope and the links between bebop and race in his introductory chapter (1–31).

7. Vivaldo's ethnic status is complicated by the fact that he is Italian American and is thus subject to the othering process of racist attitudes. Nevertheless, in the racial dynamics of the text, Rufus and Ida perceive him as unambiguously white.

8. Arguably, the blues was associated with a vernacular culture rejected by many middle-class African Americans. However, it was often rejected precisely because it stood for such a significant part of black American history.

9. This description of a steady beat characteristically underlying bebop is not meant to overlook the new and defining complexities of bebop's rhythmic backdrop. Nevertheless, most of bop (particularly in its earlier stages) is characterized by a sustained driving rhythm.

10. This passage also alludes to a repeated link between music and motion: Joe follows a trail into the music of the city. I will elaborate on the implications of this link and its relation to *Another Country*.

11. The unifying power of jazz is made even more explicit in Baldwin's "Sonny's Blues" where the estranged brothers are only truly reconciled through music. In *Invisible Man*, Ellison explores this theme as the fragmented episodes of the

protagonist's experiences become a cohesive narrative when he "slips into the breaks [of the music] and looks around" (8). Morrison picks up this theme in *Paradise* but, much as free jazz moves away from the rhythmic explication of bebop, she focuses more on the resulting collective impulse and less on the initial cause.

12. The collaborative and consensual process of self-identification is embedded into the very structure of Morrison's later novel, *Paradise,* where she extrapolates this configuration to an extreme end, exploring some of its potentially harmful implications. In her latest novel, *Love,* Morrison returns to this theme again, where Love personified becomes a central unifying force.

13. As discussed above, the tension between Vivaldo and Ida, for example, illustrates the liberating and confining implications of this construct.

WORKS CITED

Baker, Houston A., Jr. *Blues, Ideology, and African-American Literature: A Vernacular Theory.* Chicago: University of Chicago Press, 1984.

Baldwin, James. *Another Country.* 1962. London: Penguin Books, 1990.

————. "Everybody's Protest Novel." In *Notes of a Native Son.* 1949. Boston: Beacon, 1984. 13–23.

————. "Sonny's Blues." 1957. In *The Granta Book of the American Short Story.* Ed. Richard Ford. London: Granta, 1998. 170–199.

DeVeaux, Scott. *The Birth of Bebop: A Social and Musical History.* 1997. London: Picador, 1999.

Ellison, Ralph. "Change the Joke and Slip the Yoke." In *Shadow and Act.* 1958. New York: Vintage International, 1995. 45–59.

————. *Invisible Man.* 1952. 2nd ed. New York: Vintage International, 1995.

Favor, J. Martin. *Authentic Blackness: The Folk in the New Negro Renaissance.* Durham, NC: Duke University Press, 1999.

Gates, Henry Louis, Jr. *The Signifying Monkey: A Theory of African-American Literary Criticism.* Oxford: Oxford University Press, 1988.

Gilroy, Paul. *The Black Atlantic: Modernity and Double Consciousness.* London: Verso, 1993.

Jones, LeRoi (Amiri Imamu Baraka). *Blues People: The Negro Experience in White America and the Music that Developed From It.* 1963. Edinburgh: Payback Press, 1995.

————. "The Changing Same (R&B and New Black Music)." In *Black Music.* 1968. New York: Da Capo Press, 1998.

Levine, Lawrence. *Black Culture and Black Consciousness.* New York: Oxford University Press, 1977.

Morrison, Toni. *Jazz.* 1992. London: Pan Books, 1993.

————. "Life in His Language." In *James Baldwin: The Legacy.* Ed. Quincy Troupe. London: Simon & Schuster, 1989. 75–78.

————. *Paradise.* New York: Alfred A. Knopf, 1998.

Smedley, Audrey. *Race in North America: Origin and Evolution of a Worldview.* Oxford: Westview Press, 1993.

Sollors, Werner. *Beyond Ethnicity: Consent and Descent in American Culture.* Oxford: Oxford University Press, 1986.

Tally, Justine. *The Story of Jazz: Toni Morrison's Dialogic Imagination,* vol. 7, *Forum for European Contributions in African American Studies.* Hamburg: LIT Verlag, 2001.

Townsend, Peter. *Jazz in American Culture.* Edinburgh: Edinburgh University Press, 2000.

NARRATING THE BEAT OF THE HEART, JAZZING THE TEXT OF DESIRE: A COMPARATIVE INTERFACE OF JAMES BALDWIN'S *ANOTHER COUNTRY* AND TONI MORRISON'S *JAZZ*

ANNA KÉRCHY

Writing Subversion, Desire and Jazz: An Introduction[1]

In 1962 James Baldwin writes *Another Country,* which narrates the tragic life and impossible loves of a bisexual jazz drummer, Rufus Scott, who—confused by jealousy, sexual disorientation, and racial inhibitions—tortures and maddens his white beloved, Leona; then, half-mad himself, he commits suicide. Thirty years later Toni Morrison's *Jazz* tells the sinister story of a love triangle in which middle-aged, married Joe Trace, bewildered by his neurotic wife, Violet, and a never-ending nostalgia for his long-lost mother, falls in love with eighteen-year-old Dorcas and murders her so as not to lose her. In *Another Country* the horn of a terrific saxophone player keeps screaming: "Do you love me? Do you love me? Do you love me?" (16), and characters wonder: "How can you live if you can't love? And how can you live if you do?" (327), while the crucial question[2] of *Jazz* remains: "Who is the Beloved?" (Naylor 208). For Baldwin and Morrison alike musing to the tune of jazz, longing itself seems to predominate over the potential for fulfillment. Both novels are tales of love, jealousy, and death that take place in the symbolic City—place of (re)birth and death, source of the jazz music inciting, fueling, and soothing all inherently unappeasable and unspeakable loves and fugitive desires constantly displaced in narratives of quest for the self, the other, and love. However, the aim of this chapter is not so much to analyze the thematic points of intersection between the two texts, but rather to highlight the stylistic parallels in their ingeniously subversive language.

Scholars devoted to the study of women's writing and gender studies, like myself, are likely to praise Morrison for her unique female voice, her sincere depiction of women's experience, and the rare verbal sensitivity of her *écriture féminine*,[3] comparable only to the poetic genius of Virginia Woolf, who was certainly admired by Morrison herself.[4] These readers may share my surprise when reading Morrison's eulogy on Baldwin: "You gave me a language to dwell in, a gift so perfect it seems my own invention. I have been thinking your spoken and written thoughts for so long I believed they were mine. I have been seeing the world through your eyes for so long, I believed that clear, clear view was my own" (Troupe 76). Following the track opened by these lines, this chapter proposes to unveil Baldwin's potential influence on Morrison's writing by—keeping the original chronology of my personal reading experience—providing readings of *Jazz* and tracing backwards the linguistic inspiration, the intertextual roots, and the stylistic heritage this novel has gained from *Another Country*. This chapter also highlights how versions of subversive language use may transcend and problematize the gendered concepts of *écriture féminine* and "phallogocentric language."

My aim is to examine the subversive potentials of a writing style capable of disrupting conventional language use as well as the traditional narrative forms and literary norms of the patriarchal canon, while shattering the illusory concept of the homogeneous, rational ego and questioning the seemingly self-evident, naturalized, gender, sexual orientation, and race of the social subject. A discourse vibrated by black jazz music, an embodied voice of corporeality, an erotic text of desire, and a language of loss and melancholy fuse in Baldwin's and Morrison's stories of death and desire. Collectively, they narrate the transverbal experience of impossible loves in a language waved by jazz melodies—the language of heartbeats, a language beyond all words. The process of the "jazzing of the text" will be examined by revealing the influence of African American oral and musical traditions—jazz, blues, spirituals, and race music—on a writing style that turns text into music and music into a text, becoming increasingly jazzy, subversive, and poetic. The chapter also provides a complex analysis of the body in the text and of the text on the body. The polymorphously perverse, blissful, painful, or mad desiring body, a crucial leitmotif on a thematic level, also directs the structure, organizes the plot, and destabilizes and infects language by the subversive potentials of the unspeakable materiality of the body. The workings of the language of desire will be revealed by highlighting how the text combines the language of corporeality, the language of the lost mother, and the language of mourning. The analysis— relying on poststructuralist and French feminist theories—argues that the two texts, moved by the nostalgic yearning for the missing (m)other, recall Julia Kristeva's theory of "revolutionary poetic language" by providing the preverbal, bodily bliss of the lost maternal realm to the reader. The conclusion claims that the destabilization and disintegration of identity caused by the dynamics of desire is reflected in the defaced portrait of the writing-reading subject. The language of the novel is the language of the post-modern as well: it allows the Book itself to speak up, to interact, and to make love and jazz with its readers in texts turned into melodies of love.

Jazzing the Text, Narrating the Beat, Having the True Blues

Jazz is set in the black capital, Harlem, in the Roaring Twenties of the Jazz Age, while *Another Country* takes place mostly in Greenwich Village of the late 1950s or early 1960s. In both novels jazz music seems to penetrate the entire City, filling streets, hearts, and souls alike. On the avenues, in clubs, or on rooftops, jazz music is associated with sensuality, desire, yearning and pain, rage, violence, provocation, excitement, risk, excess, and fever.

At the very beginning of *Another Country,* Baldwin's jazz drummer, Rufus, designates the beat as the metaphor of his life; in a chain of associations the beat becomes synonymous with the most beloved and the most hated. For Rufus to remember the beat was also

> to remember Leona [that] was also—somehow—to remember the eyes of his mother, the rage of his father, the beauty of his sister. It was to remember the streets of Harlem, the boys on the stoops, the girls behind the stairs and on the roofs, the white policeman who had taught him how to hate, the stickball games in the streets, the women leaning out of windows and the number they played daily, hoping for the hit his father never made. It was to remember the juke box, the teasing, the dancing, the hard-on, the gang fights and gang bangs, his first set of drums—bought him by his father—his first taste of marijuana, his first snort of horse. (14)

Rufus's sister, Ida, embodies the quintessence of irresistible, sensuous fem-ininity, performing the femme fatale par excellence when she sings jazz. Couples love, hate, betray, abuse, and adore each other while listening to jazz melodies. À la Marcel Proust, each love has its special "anthem," a small tune standing in a metonymic relation with the tremendous passion inciting all senses.[5] At Rufus's funeral the mourners' grieving is accompa-nied by blues music, which aptly expresses their pain.

In *Jazz* (which clearly reflects Baldwin's influence) girls go to clubs to become women, having been seduced by jazz music, this sensual "lowdown stuff," by "songs that used to start in the head and fill the heart [dropping] on down, down to places below the sash and the buckled belts" (56). This "dirty, get-on-down music the women sang and the men played and both danced to, close and shameless or apart and wild" (58) may also frighten listeners. The drums accompanying riots and marches express rage. Dorcas dances to jazz when she is shot by the jealous Joe, while "the music bends, falls to its knees to embrace them all, encourage them all to live a little, why don't you? since this is the it you've been looking for" (188). As a violent and disruptive erotic element, jazz appears on the structural and linguistic level of the texts as well, perhaps even more predominantly than on the thematic level.

In an interview with a telling title, "I Come from People Who Sang All the Time," Morrison characterizes jazz music as having an improvisational, unanticipated nature, as egalitarian, as a coherent melody constructed with dissolves, returns, and repetitions, as music located in a historical framework, and as related to love. These features of jazz music can be discerned not only in Morrison's textual strategies but in Baldwin's as well.

Neither of the texts is linear, chronological, or teleological. In multilayered narratives that jump in time and space and from consciousness to consciousness, multiple narrative voices give their improvisatory, open-ended versions of the original melody, which is the summary of the plot. The solos of various characters repeat, reformulate, and complement each other with their varying perspectives of the same song of love, adding up to the tune of the ethos of the black city experience and the quest for selves and for love. In *Another Country* Rufus's friends and relatives try to re-member their beloved Rufus by recalling their memories of him, reconstructing from different perspectives the potential reasons for his suicide. This constitutes the base melody of the first chapter. Similarly, in *Jazz*, characters repeatedly re- and deconstruct the narrative of their mutual hunt for the lost object of love, an impossible quest materialized in the tragic events leading to Dorcas's murder, Violet's madness, and Joe's incurable melancholy. By means of an unusual narrative strategy, or in a postmodern gesture, the main story is summarized at the very beginning of both novels: in the first book of *Another Country* and, more radically, in the first powerful sentences of *Jazz*.[6]

As the narratives are presented in a seemingly omniscient narrator's words, the reader is not likely to look forward to unexpected turns, tensions, mysteries, or final surprises. The novel repeats, reformulates, and amplifies this basic story, and presents variations of the same plot again and again from different perspectives, reinforcing the postmodern notion of the relativity of truth. However, it is exactly through the text's repetitive, improvisatory, variable nature, coupled with an unusually poetic, musical, violent, erotic, and overall subversive language, that both novels surpass the banal love story of a traditional blues song and become masterworks.

The listener of jazz music has to take an active part in the construction and interpretation of the experience. The two novels analyzed function in the same way: enigmas, holes, and uncertainties are left open (we never learn what happens with Baldwin's Leona or Morrison's Wild), the texts leave the readers their imaginative freedom and encourage creativity, and with this the pleasure of a shared music, a communal experience.[7] Critics of jazz in *Jazz*—such as Nicholas F. Pici, Eusebio L. Rodrigues, and Roberta Rubenstein—underline the importance of group experience, of audience participation and interplay as mutual provocation, inspiration, and energization in jazz. Accordingly, Morrison herself claims that her writing demands emotive, participatory reading as the involved reader is invited into the holes and spaces left open in the text (Tate 125). And just as jazz music always lacks a final chord, the fragments of the text are left unended, as if echoing Baldwin's musical heritage's mastertext or Morrison's definition of jazz: "It doesn't wholly satisfy, it kind of leaves you a little bit on the edge at the end, a little hungry" (Morrison 1996, 4).

As Pici describes, the multiinstrumental, polyrhythmic nature of jazz music is mirrored by the multivocal, polyphonic characteristic of the narrative. The "head and riffs method" of jazz (main distinctive melody and repetition of brief patterns) is inscribed in the text by repetitions (375). These are renarrations of the same symbolic object or scene from different perspectives (Ida's earrings or song/ Dorcas's death), corrected renarrations of the same scene by the same narrator (Vivaldo's struggle with writing/ Golden Gray's arrival), descriptions of persons from different viewpoints (Rufus is brother, lover, torturer, son, musician/ Dorcas is mother, sweetheart, never-had child, fake friend), contradicting definitions of the same concept (in both novels jazz is threatening, seducing, loving, and maddening)—all related to and reframing the main plot, the base melody. As Morrison's critics agree, the "call and response strategy" of jazz (question and answer of instruments, of musician and audience) appears on a structural level: a leitmotif at the end of one chapter (love, music, the City) is repeated in the opening sentence of the succeeding chapter, or an idea left unended at the end of one chapter is elaborated on in the next. This strategy may also be revealed in Baldwin's novel in the constant displacement of desire and the complex web of intimate relationships that change from chapter to chapter, as the focus shifts from one love to another and on to another: Rufus was a lover of Eric, who has an affair with Cass, who is married to Richard. Readers see the characters as they are reflected in one another's eyes. A cubist-style, multifaceted, changing portrait is drawn of each of the characters who are depicted from multiple, subjective perspectives, which are all distorted or embellished by passions, as the text slides from one stream of thought to another.

The most poetic features of Morrison's text are clearly rooted in Baldwin's writing, especially in the brilliantly dynamic, tense, and tightly written first part of his novel. "The effusive legato-like flow of a liquid syntax" and "the staccato of non-standard comma use" (Pici 380), as well as

the lack of punctuation marks and the overabundance of repetitions, variations, rhythmic enumerations, internal rhymes, and alliterations, all contribute to the exceptional musicality and "jazzing" of both texts.

> The beat: hands, feet, tambourines, drums, pianos, laughter, curses, razor
> blades; the man stiffening with a laugh and a growl and a purr and the
> woman moistening and softening with a whisper and a sigh and a cry. The
> beat—in Harlem in the summertime one could almost see it, shaking above
> the pavements and the roof. (*AC* 14)

> The City is smart at this: smelling and good and looking raunchy, sending
> secret messages disguised as public signs: this way, open here, danger to let col-
> ored only single men on sale woman wanted private room stop dog on prem-
> ises absolutely no money down fresh chicken free delivery fast. And good at
> opening locks, dimming stairways. Covering your moans with its own. (*J* 64)

The subversive style reinforces and echoes the rhythm of the excited lover's
heartbeats and the rhythm of the city, birthplace of jazz and of passion. In
the long run it creates a piece of writing that transforms jazz music into
written language, or language into jazz music fueled by desire.

As Pici underlines, jazz is a hybrid creole genre, a fusion of heterogeneous
dialogues and folk traditions (398)—it is no wonder that traces of blues music
are embedded in jazz music and in jazzy texts. Blues originated in songs of
lament that were sung in the days of slavery to keep alive, repeat, and perform
the memories of brutal experiences and lost loves so as to transcend their pain
by lyricism.[8] Baldwin's and Morrison's texts perform the blues by singing of
impossible loves (Rufus-Leona, Eric-Cass, Rufus-Vivaldo, Dorcas-Joe), dead
beloveds (Rufus and Dorcas substitute the lost other for almost every character), and melancholic moods (Vivaldo smoking marijuana, Violet drinking).
Blues and the color blue—the color of unspeakable infinity and fugitive
desires—have a symbolic significance in both novels: in *Another Country* blue
may stand for homosocial bonding and queer desires, and in *Jazz* for the
never-ending quest for the blue bird of happiness. But most importantly,
being blue (or having the blues) signifies being sorrowful, or sad.

> When my bed get empty, make me feel awful mean and blue,
> "Oh, sing it, Bessie," Vivaldo muttered.
> My springs is getting rusty, sleeping single like I do. (*AC* 56)

> Blues man. Black and bluesman. Black therefore blue man.
> Everybody knows your name.
> Where-did-she-go-and-why man. So lonesome-I-could-die man.
> Everybody knows your name. (*J* 119)

Black love (and in Baldwin's case interracial love too) is always blue: it is the longing for a heart that you can neither live with nor without, a faithlessly faithful passion, sung both in jazz music and in the blues, vibrating both texts.

The two novels can be interpreted as funeral songs in memory of a dead beloved, the stories being recollections of events leading to Rufus's suicide and Dorcas's murder, with musical fragments remembering and mourning them. In traditional blues songs, grieving leads to spiritual healing and to a settling of accounts with the past; however, in *Another Country* and *Jazz*, yearning never stops. Neither private pains nor communal loss can be healed. The "cultural mourning" (Rubenstein 147) for lost lives and possibilities—inherent in the collective memory of African American experience—is explicitly political for Baldwin's nihilistic and skeptical (anti)heroes, disillusioned by the injustice of racism, sexism, and homophobia and by the impossibility of an immaculate love; its atmosphere also penetrates Morrison's mournful and melancholic novel, making every day a gloomy Sunday.

The long list of parallels between Morrison's and Baldwin's writing styles and traditional black forms of artistic expression does not end here. The rhythms of both texts recall the tam-tam drums of African tribes, slave work songs, black sermons, and contemporary rap music. The other stories hidden behind the base plot, the (inter)play of multiple meanings, and the frequent biblical allusions (Moses, Bridegroom, Lord, and Bethlehem in Baldwin; apple, Eve, Adam, and paradise in Morrison) remind us of the coded language of slaves, and of gospels and spirituals. The performative, repetitive, interactive, and open-ended nature of spirituals is echoed throughout the novels' stylistic and textual composition. The violence in the language recalls toasts, ritual insults, and "the signifying monkey" tradition. As Rodrigues stresses, in *Jazz* Morrison combines black vernacular with standard English, jazz jargon, purified tribe dialect, and the language that women use among themselves to invent a new language of her own in a dynamic, audible text with an oral quality (736–737). The same multilayered, polyphonic quality can be found in *Another Country* as well: Baldwin combines metropolitan black slang, obscene street words, the jargon of jazz musicians, sensitive, allegoric-melodic lines in a lyrical mode, subtle vibrations of a textualized subconscious, and the "other text" of queer desire, producing a personal voice that speaks for all. Most importantly, in Morrison's and Baldwin's texts, jazz is not only a musical form but also a fundamental expression of black experience, reverberating Nina Simone's assertion that "jazz is not just music, it's a way of life, it's a way of being, a way of thinking . . . The Negro in America is jazz" (Ryan and Conwill Majozo 130).

Jazz is not just music. It is a definition of Morrison's and Baldwin's subversive language as well—open, complicated, experimental, provocative, playful, and passionate.

Somatized Text and Semioticized Body in the Revolutionary Poetic Language of Desire

The verbalization of desire and the extreme musicality embedded in the analyzed texts are major characteristics of "revolutionary poetic language," defined by Julia Kristeva in her *La révolution du langage poétique* as a discourse vibrated by transverbal practices, repetition, rhythm, music (alliteration, onomatopoeia, etc.), the transformation of language, playful linguistic subversions of other meanings, and the breaking loose of passions. These linguistic maneuvers lend Baldwin and Morrison a subversive poeticity that can express transitive sensations condensed; synesthetic, almost palpable, flashes of momentary passions; and drops of streams of consciousness—even of less central characters such as Eric or Dorcas.

And just as the speeding rain distorted, blurred, blunted, all the familiar outlines of walls, windows, doors, parked cars, lamp posts, hydrants, trees, so Eric, now, in his silent watching, sought to blur and blunt and flee from all the conundrums which crowded in on him. (*AC* 376)

Dorcas lay on a chenille bedspread, tickled and happy knowing that there was no place to be where somewhere, close by, somebody was not licking his licorice stick, tickling the ivories, beating his skins, blowing off his horn while a knowing woman sang ain't nobody going to keep me down you got the right key baby but the wrong keyhole you got to get it bring it and put it right here, or else. (*J* 60)

According to Kristeva the revolutionary poetic language speaks in an embodied physical voice; it is a "body-talk" that gains its energy from a transverbal corporeality implanted in the text. The unspeakable materiality of the body destabilizes Morrison's and Baldwin's texts on both thematic and stylistic levels: it directs the structure, organizes the plot, and "infects" language by the subversive potential of its materiality. Words stumble; conventional language turns into poetic melody, excessive, delirious raving or a telling, polysemic silence; and both readers and narrations become confused as the desiring, ecstatic, suffering, mad body becomes the source of the subversive voice, as well as the site, motor, and major leitmotif of the texts. In Peter Brooks's words, the semioticization (the narrativization) of the body in the text and the *soma*tization of the text on the body are intertwined, resulting in the destabilizing dynamics of the "body-text" (xii).

Desiring bodies lie at the heart of multiply subversive texts that combine a jazz music aimed at awakening its listeners' sexual hunger with an *écriture féminine* fueled by libidinal energies and a stream of consciousness echoing subconscious erotic drives. Yearning, jealousy, sexual excitement, hunger, and frustration are equally incorporated in a poetic and eroticized text vibrated by jazz music. The body in the text and the text on the body turn equally transgressive, excited by desire. Baldwin's sexually explicit lines perform the striptease of lovers to the tunes of a blue love song in a catatonically pulsating text echoing the rhythmic heartbeats of a sexually excited body. In Morrison, conventional language use is transcended by long, breathless, waving, vibrating narrative solos addressing all the senses, by a poetic text filled with sexual metaphors, allusions, and alliterations, resounding (and becoming itself) a flow of desire.

If it were the girl, the movement would be sighing and halting—sighing because of need, halting because of hostility. If it were the boy, the movement would be harshly or softly brutal: he would lunge over the girl as though rape were in his mind, or he would try to arouse her lust by means of feathery kisses, meant to be burning, which he had seen in the movies. Friction and fantasy could not fail to produce a physiological heat and hardness, and this sheathed pressure between her thighs would be the girl's signal to moan. She would toss her head a little and hold the boy more tightly and they would begin their descent into confusion. Off would come the cap—as the bed sighed and the grey light stared. Then his jacket would come off. His hands would push up the sweater and unlock the brassiere . . . Then the record on the hi-fi came to an end, or, on the radio, a commercial replaced the love song. He pulled up her skirt. (*AC* 131–132)

Take her to Indigo on Saturday and sit way back so they could hear the music wide and be in the dark at the same time, at one of those round tables with a slick black top and a tablecloth of pure white on it, drinking rough gin with that sweet red stuff in it so it looked like soda pop, which a girl like her ought to have ordered instead of liquor she could sip from the edge of a glass wider at the mouth than at its base, with a tiny stem like a flower in between while her hand, the one that wasn't holding the glass shaped like a flower, was under the table drumming out the rhythm on the inside of his thigh, his thigh, his thigh, thigh, thigh, and he bought her underwear with stitching done to look like rosebuds and violets, VIOLETS, don't you know, and she wore it for him thin as it was and too cold for a room that couldn't count on a radiator to work through the afternoon while I was where? (*J* 95)

As the heat rises in nightclubs of Baldwin's and Morrison's city, the body is marked by the longing of jazz, music becomes the voice of the flesh, and the dancer cannot be told from the dance. The narrative on the body dancing to the tune of desire becomes in its turn melodic poetry, music, dance. Dancing is a mode of communication[9] transmitting seduction, violence, and despair—just like the "energetic, balanced, fluid" text of a writer dancing beyond gravity (LeClair 120).

Like pleasure, pain is written in texts on bodies, that throb with bitter memories of lost, sweet loves. At the beginning of Baldwin's novel the reader encounters Rufus's abject, wretched body, ruined by impossible desires[10] and tormented by corporeal needs and urges: Rufus sweats, faints of hunger, retches, cries of the need to urinate, and trembles from nausea at the fringe of prostitution, on the verge of a total mental and physical breakdown. The language, which depicts the violent presence of the shameful body and the abjection of the subject, combines vulgar slang ("take a leak") with poeticity ("caterpillar fingers between his thighs") and with embodied voice filling the text with the growling of Rufus's empty stomach (11, 13, 47) to culminate in the beat of the loud and empty music eliciting Rufus's memories of the past (constituting an important part of the first book), re-membering his abject, desiring body. Wandering at night in the streets of New York, like a shadow from Dante's *Inferno*, the disillusioned Rufus, blackest of all blacks, bleeding from multiple wounds, hunting for love yet unable to love himself, embodies "a generation of bitterness" (64) and a ruined race. A bar fight, after which Rufus, brutalized by the punch of a fist, is blinded with blood and flies in the air, prophesies his final annihilation, his deadly flight from the bridge into nothingness.

Similarly, in *Jazz* unfulfilled longings mark the pained body and the poetic text alike. Morrison never names explicitly the heartbreaking traumas, yet she succeeds in narrating the beat of the heart with "words that become active boils in the heart" (51). Neola's "clutch of arm to breast" seems to express a wish to "hold the pieces of her heart in her hand" (63) a hand that was paralyzed when her treacherous lover left her. Traces on Dorcas's bad skin indirectly testify to the traumas of her childhood and the loss of her parents (Paquet 226), and recall the empty tracks of Joe's lost mother. Violet's violent expression of love, the cut on dead Dorcas's face opens the way to remembering, that is the reconstruction of the beloved's body in the reweaving of the text. Joe's two-color eyes and Violet's "wayward mouth" (24) signify their heterogeneous, neurotic identities, destabilized by desire. The never-ending, aching search for (self-)love and self-definition of the racialized body can be revealed in the light-skinned Golden Gray's quest for his "nigger" father, "the blackest man in the world" (157, 172), in Joe's hunt for the nauseatingly black and naked, absent-present Wild, and in Violet's fixation with Dorcas's shiny skin and straightened hair (signifying the stylized black body) (Bell 225). However, this attempt to learn to love the blackness and the heterogeneity of the other (and thus accept one's own black self) turns unsuccessful for the black subject destabilized by its schizophrenic desire for the light body, which, via its inaccessibility, stands in (even if as a simulacrum) for the lost primary object of love. The black characters' painful search for the light bodies (of Dorcas and of Golden Gray) marks the impossibility of desire.

The language of corporeality taints the text in the tongue of the mad body as well. In Morrison, Violet's madness is reflected discursively in her "renegade tongue" and in the verbal "collapses" (24) that let her unconscious speak up, disturbing language and mind alike. The uncontrollable slips of her tongue, her wild, delirious monologues, and her hysteric outbursts, varied by her incomprehensible and melancholic silences, infect the narrative voice as well. It claims to be omnipresent and objective, but it is unreliable and influenced by personal feelings. The narrative is full of gaps, silences, and uncertainties; it is also repetitive, loquacious, and full of maniac, endlessly flowing monologues. While trying to remember Joe's and Violet's going to the city, "nothing comes to mind"; nevertheless, immediately after this statement the forgetful voice recalls memories of this journey for seven pages (29–36). The schizophrenic, polyphonic language is spoken by Violet and the *other* Violet, "*that* Violet [who] is me" (96)—a violent double, a neurotic "other" who cuts a dead girl's face. The other Violet embodies unconscious, repressed drives and desires: she is a Woolfian Septimus speaking with trees (216) in the revolutionary poetic language of the madwoman in the text. Morrison's borderline narrative stumbles through "innarable cracks" (Jones 486) and gaps, splitting life, identity, and language alike with the aim to project the self into language with "space between words, as though the self were really a twin or a thirst or a friend or something that sits right next to you and watches you" (Naylor 208). The "nerve-wracking," "visceral," "emotional and intellectual" jazz music becomes a trope of nervous breakdown and mental disorder (Morrison 1992, viii). The uncanny melody of jazz vibrating through Violet's lunatic language can embrace the *other* Violet and unite with the repressed and haunting *other* within the self, the "not-me" within the "me," and can speak the unspeakable desires of the split self.

In *Another Country* madness is explicitly verbalized[11] in the scene of Rufus's final breakdown. The last thoughts and events leading to the suicide, narrated in the third-person singular, seem to represent Rufus's own paranoid stream of consciousness flowing from a destabilized mind and a disembodied body. Rufus reflecting on himself is no longer Rufus Scott—"I"—but a "baby," a "rag doll," he, he, he, a madman already half-dead. The body is paradoxically experienced as a foreign entity when it experiences the most private sensations as he smells, freezes, cries, hurts, and dies. It is only a language turned poetic, a language that is metaphoric (cars write an endless message, the city is on fire), musical, and painfully pure, that can go against Wittgenstein's private language argument and communicate the self's personal experience of the real.[12] The "I" returns only at the very last moment of uniting with death, with "you" becoming "one," abolishing all differences of beings, all difficulties of desire, and all displacements in language.

The emphatic Vivaldo, haunted by resurging memories of his friend, reexperiences Rufus's paranoid breakdown in his drunken deliriums and passionate dreams (like before his lovemaking with Eric, a small death itself). Only the sensitive writer has the damned and divine potential to feel and narrate the pain, rage, and madness of the other, to name mental and corporeal annihilation in a shattered, subversive language. Only the subtle poetic vision may speak the unspeakable Death in a "sweet and overwhelming embrace" beyond all words.

> There was only the leap and the rending and the terror and the surrender. And the terror: which all seemed to begin and to end and begin again—forever—in a cavern behind the eye. And whatever stalked there *saw*, and spread the news of what it saw throughout the entire kingdom of whomever, though the eye itself might perish. What order could prevail against so grim a privacy? And yet, without order, of what value was the mystery? Order. Order. *Set thine house in order.* (290)

Among the bodies in the text disrupting the text on the body, the writing body plays a significant role in Baldwin. Vivaldo is the trope of the writer (*Another Country* can be considered as the story of his coming to text, of his birth as an author) whose corporeal reality invades the narrative. In the process of textual composition—"his buttocks sticking to the chair, sweat rolling down his armpits and behind his ears and dripping into his eyes and the sheets of paper sticking to each other and to his finger"—Vivaldo realizes a veritable writing from the body. Even the typewriter seems to become flesh of his flesh as the keys move "with a dull, wet sound" (305). "The sound of Vivaldo's typewriter, the sound of Ida's voice, the sound of the record player" (307) fill the text, combining the voiced body with the embodied voice, addressing all senses. Preverbal sounds, moans, cries, and sighs of the embodied voice intertwine with synesthetic poeticity in unforgettable, rhythmically pulsating, rhyming, musically alliterating language: "They listened to the footfalls and voices in the street: someone was singing, someone called, someone was cursing. Someone ran. Then silence, again." (328) Similar sentences keep echoing in the destabilized and enchanted reader's ears for a lifetime.

In *Jazz*, the narrative voice, musing over the incompetencies of her writerly strategy and realizing the impossibility of naming desires, invites Joe's wild mother into her text: "She hugs me. Understands me. Has given

me her hand. I am touched by her. Released in secret. Now I know"
(221). Metaphorically touched by the mother, the text is infected by the
preverbal song, laughter, moan, and cry of Wild, realizing Morrison's
primary goal to "remove the print quality of language to put back the oral
quality, where intonation, volume, gesture are all there" (Tate 126). As the
voice embodied in the touch invades the narrative, meanings are disseminated and the text is turned into a rhythmic, repetitive, musical flow, the
language of the (m)other. On its very first page, *Jazz* begins with the preverbal sound "Sth" instead of a word, associated with the word "woman"
("Sth, I know that woman" [3]). In the epigraph the Goddess of Thunder
speaks up, identifying herself as the "name of the sound" and "the sound
of the name," "the sign of the letter" and the "designation of the division."
This suggests that the text is shattered, exploded from within via a thun-
derlike, sensual, female voice—perhaps that of a goddess, a dead girl, a jazz
diseuse, or a mother. In the following section my aim is to unveil the
embodied maternal voice as a primary engine of the two texts.

Melancholy and Melody: The (M)other Text

Kristeva claims that the semioticized body language of the revolutionary
poetic language subverts conventional language from within. It liberates
corporeality, libidinal energies, drives, and desires by recuperating the
"good vibration" of the Semiotic, which is a preverbal, presymbolic, pre-
Oedipal *maternal* realm of primary perfect symbiosis marked by the blissful
materiality of the *mother*'s body. The Semiotic is characterized by rhythmic
corporeal energies, music of the waves of the amniotic fluid, the rhythm of
the mother's heartbeat, and the womb's repetitive, caressing convulsions.
These illuminating moments of the lost sensual pleasures of preverbal corporeality may be regained via poetic maneuvers that subvert our conventional language from within. Kristeva's revolutionary poetic language
waved by the desire of (m)other's body; Hélène Cixous's corporeal, volcanic pleasure text of gift; and Luce Irigaray's libidinal, maternally fecund,
sensible, fluctuating body-talk are all versions of *écriture féminine*, defined by
French psychoanalytical feminist theory as a "volcanic," "heterogeneous"
writing from an endless body without end, "writing in [the] white ink" of
mother's milk (see Marks and De Courtivron).

   However—as the major poststructuralist psychoanalytical theoreticians
Jacques Lacan and Kristeva highlight—the Semiotic bliss gained from with-
in the prisonhouse of language cannot be but momentary, as the constitu-
tion of the speaking and writing subject is originally based on primary loss.
Faced with the traumas of socialization (Territorialization of the body,
Mirror Stage, Symbolization, Oedipalization) the subject must renounce

the preverbal Semiotic jouissance and exchange mother's body for the repressive, substitutive, Symbolic language of the Father. The entry into the realm of representation—the constitution of the autonomous individual—signifies the loss of the primary object of love through a symbolic matricide. Therefore language use, no matter how subversive, is always a compensatory activity, an impossible attempt to recuperate the lost beloved, the waving vibration of the maternal body, by the pleasure of the text, the rhythmic, repetitive, musical poeticity of the literary language. Thus the literary text is at the same time a "rape-text" and a "mother-text" (Cixous 120), "matricide" and "incest" (Klein 188), intertwining the "Symbolic" language of the Father with (the longing for) the maternal body's blissful, preverbal, "Semiotic" realm (Kristeva 22). According to poststructuralist theory, desire vibrates every literary text. The nostalgia for the maternal body and a melancholic longing for the missed primal jouissance become engines of the text.

As I have argued, *Jazz* and *Another Country* are like jazz masterpieces, melodic texts of blues composed in the language of desire about unfulfilled longing, insatiable hunger, and desire incited by its own impossibility. Desiring infiltrates the city and becomes a veritable symptom of the spirit of Jazz Age. In *Jazz* married, middle-aged Joe Trace is in love with the young and beautiful Dorcas, who loves someone else, while Violet's desire is fueled by the memory of a never-had golden child and the longing for the long-lost loving man her husband had once been. *Another Country* overabounds in impossible loves, "neither with nor without you" passions. Rufus loves but tortures Leona, his liaison with Eric remains a bittersweet memory, and his longing for latent homosexual Vivaldo is never fully appeased. Eric loves Yves but cheats on him with Cass, who is married to and supposedly in love with Richard. Ida and Vivaldo never cease fighting and loving each other: moreover, Ida is the mistress of Richard's manager, and Vivaldo submits himself to the seduction of Eric. In the meantime, all the characters are tormented by the absence of the beloved Rufus. The never-ending quest for something lost and the melancholic memory of the missing beloved become repeated leitmotifs in both novels, written in a language combining yearning and corporeality, poetry and madness, mourning and jouissance. However, in my reading, the most important among the impossible loves is the longing for the lost maternal, narrated in a language moved by the desire of the (m)other. The nostalgia for the lost primary object of love can be revealed as a more explicit, fully developed metaphor and textual engine in Morrison's *Jazz;* however, it is perhaps even more interesting to detect how the attentive reader can trace the origins of this metaphor to Baldwin's *Another Country,* where it is present in a more subconscious, latent manner.

(M)other Text in *Jazz*

In *Jazz* the beloved always proves to be a displacement of the original object of love; love turns impossible, ending in murder, disillusionment, loss, or a bittersweet, nostalgic melancholy at best. Joe is hunting for Dorcas in the same way that he tracked Wild, the uncivilized, naked madwoman sneaking in forests, his never-seen mother who abandoned him. Joe loves Dorcas because he associates her with Wild. Dorcas fills the "empty nothing" (37) in Joe's heart that was left behind by his lost mother. The hoofmarks on her face substitute for Wild's tracks, the honey of her body and the candies she eats correspond to Wild's honeycomb, and her bleeding shoulder displaces the birds with red wings accompanying and signifying Wild; moreover, Dorcas (as Violet) is referred to as "wild" (153, 182). Dorcas and Wild fuse in Joe's imagination, as indicated by the use of the same personal pronoun to refer to the two women: "But where is she?" refers to Wild, while in the next sentence "There she is" designates Dorcas (184, 187). The dying Dorcas utters the sentence: "I know his name but Mama won't tell" (193), and hence becomes completely one with Wild, the lost primary object of Joe's desire. Her death repeats his primary loss and reveals the impossibility of desire: when desire is fulfilled, it must die. In a crooked kind of love, Joe can only touch his beloved, his mother-substitute, by killing her; his gun is the caressing hand of the Freudian "double bind" when his arm reaches her. In the Bible Dorcas is an early Christian seamstress who dies suddenly and is resurrected by the apostle Peter (see Ryan and Conwill Majozo 137); hence Dorcas could symbolize the resurrected mother, lost again.

Violet, in an inner monologue, thinks that Joe searches in Dorcas for somebody else, her (Violet's) younger self or "somebody golden, like my own golden boy" (97). The target of Violet's longing is Golden Gray, "who I never saw but who tore up my girlhood as surely as if we'd been the best of lovers" (97). Violet was "made crazy about" the golden boy by her grandmother's, True Belle's, stories of the illegitimate mulatto child with the golden hair, an eternal child, an imaginary lover Violet holds on to when she embraces Joe. Violet recognizes the fugitive, displaced, impossible nature of desire when she says, "Standing in the cane, he [Joe] was trying to catch a girl he was yet to see, but his heart knew all about [Dorcas, Wild?], and me, holding on to him but wishing he was the golden boy I never saw either. Which means from the very beginning I was a substitute and so was he" (97). However, as the chain of substitutions does not end with Dorcas substituting Violet, but from Dorcas it leads to Wild, so the reader must recognize that the primary object of Violet's desire is someone "beyond," who is substituted by Golden Gray, just as Golden Gray is displaced by Joe.

A central passage of the text, repeated and reformulated twice by the narrative voice, tells of Golden Gray's arrival at Hunter's Hunter Les*tory*'s house carrying the pregnant, unconscious Wild on his horse. Allegorical figures of desire are juxtaposed in this highly symbolic scene, bearing considerable significance on a metatextual level as well, hiding the emblematic "coming to text," the birth of the text as ultimate object of desire. Golden Gray is imagined standing next to a well that appears as the enigmatic source and target of the text, the Omphalos, the center of the labyrinth, the bull's eye of all tracking and desiring:

> I want him to stand next to a well dug quite clear from trees so twigs and leaves will not fall into the deep water, and while standing there in shapely light, his fingertips on the rim of the stone, his gaze at no one thing, his mind soaked and sodden with sorrow, or dry and brittle with the hopelessness that comes from knowing too little and feeling too much (so brittle, so dry he is in danger of the reverse: feeling nothing and knowing everything). (161)

This sorrowful and hopeless well, mirroring Golden Gray and Wild, may be interpreted as the very same one into which Rose Dear, Violet's mother, plunged when she committed suicide (102). Thus, the recurring motif of the well can serve as a clue that leads (also) to Violet's primary object of desire, to *her* lost mother.

The narrative voice, associating the beloved with the well, reflects on the language of the text of desire:

> I want to dream a nice dream for him, and another of him. Lie down next to him, a wrinkle in the sheet, and contemplate his pain and by doing so ease it, diminish it. I want to be the language that wishes him well, speaks his name, wakes him when his eyes need to be open. I want him to stand next to a well . . . (161)

A "language wishing well," calming and soothing, is associated with the "well," the maternal metaphor of the text: the pleasure of the literary text signifies a momentary return to mother. This hypothesis is reinforced by a close reading revealing that the "language wishing him" and the narrative voice "want[ing] him" express a desire for the lost mother in Golden Gray. Similarly, lying down next to him, contemplating his pain, and diminishing it by doing so is an allegory of "incest and matricide" in the literary text, trying to heal symbolically in vain the primary loss, implanting never-ending desire into the text.

Unlike most critics,[13] I think that the final seemingly idyllic and happy-end-like passages prove that longing does not stop, desire cannot be satisfied or pacified, and that Joe and Violet keep on yearning for the impossible, for the lost object of love or for desiring itself. "Lying next to her, his head turned toward the window, he sees through the glass darkness taking the shape of a shoulder with a thin line of blood. Slowly, slowly it forms itself into a bird with a blade of red on the wing. Meanwhile Violet rests her hand on his chest as though it were the sunlit rim of a well . . ." (224–225). Joe and Violet are lying side by side in their bed under the symbolically blue blanket and the blues of desire recalls in Joe the bleeding shoulder of Dorcas associated with the redwinged birds signifying Wild, while Violet yearns for the sunshine of a golden boy's hair and for the well, a symbol shared by Rose Dear and Golden Gray. The signifieds of desire keep fleeing yet seducing, and it is only the substitutive displacement that one can hold in one's arm. In my reading the fugitive nature, and constant displacement of the couple's desires, and the impossibility of a final fulfillment (that would put an end to desire), echo the quest for happiness in the artificial, imaginary Paradise of the city and the vibrating instability of the era, as well as the infinite longing of jazz music and the functioning of the literary text itself.

By the end of the novel the narrative voice confesses to have believed that desiring flesh "hangs on to wells and a boy's golden hair, would just as soon inhale sweet fire caused by a burning girl as hold a maybe-yes maybe-no hand." The voice continues by saying "I don't believe that anymore," hence playing down the validity of the substitutive objects of desire. According to the voice, "Something is missing there. Something rogue. Something else you have to figure in before you can figure it out" (228). This missing part, desired, never successfully displaced, and never reached can be interpreted as the "nowhere-everywhere" mother, the desire of the mother that is experienced ("figure in") preverbally ("before figure it out"), to become in language a rogue absence blasting and blessing the text, vibrating wild words. The fugitive characteristic of desire coincides with the inherent insufficiency of a language: substitutive objects can never stand in for the lost primary object of love, floating signifiers never succeed in touching the sliding signified in the prisonhouse of language, and the narrative of desire—oscillating between matricide and incest, shallow words and elusive silences—never reaches a satisfactory end. This paradoxical impossibility of language and the longing for the preverbal bliss is voiced ingeniously: "Violet had the same thought: *Mama. Mama?* Is this where you got to and couldn't do it no more? The place of shade without trees where you know *you are not and never again will be loved by anybody who can choose to do it? Where everything is over but the talking?*" (110). Accordingly, the passage describing Joe and Violet, lying (in both senses of the word) in each other's arms, thinking of lost beloved mothers, ends with the phrase: "And down there somebody is gathering *gifts* (*lead pencils,* Bull Durham, Jap Rose Soap) to distribute to them all" (225; emphasis mine). By recalling the expression "to put lead in one's pencil," which is a male slang for a full erection, the text suggests that the mother's body is not only exchanged for the language of the Father, but that symbolic discourse and corporeal energies fuse in the vibrating text of desire. The melancholy of desiring and missing the mother is compensated for by gifts of pencil, that is, by the coming to text, by the birth of the literary text itself. Nevertheless, the noun "das Gift" means "poison" in German, while pencils are made of poisonous lead: they can only lead to a text that is bittersweet substitution, forever painful-pleasurable displacement, and never-ending desire.

(M)other Text in *Another Country*

The yearning for the lost maternal as engine of all desires and major motif of the text is less explicit in *Another Country,* and it is very likely that on the first reading the reader immersed in the pleasures of the text does not recognize the importance of the minor yet fundamental passage to be analyzed below. The final pages of the first book describe the events and, primarily, the feelings last experienced by Rufus before his suicide. Rufus's maddening vertigo, which, leads to his tragic death, is incited on a subway platform by a disturbing memory:

> *Something he had not thought of for many years, something he had never ceased to think of,* came back to him as he walked behind the crowd. The subway platform was a dangerous place—so he had always thought, it sloped downward toward the waiting tracks, and *when he had been a little boy and stood on the platform beside his mother he had not dared let go her hand. He stood on the platform now, alone* with all these people, who were each of them alone, and waited in acquired calmness, for the train. (88; emphasis mine)

The first stumble in Rufus's stream of thoughts is his traumatic re-recognition of the primary loss, of being alone, separated, and divided. He is both attracted and frightened by the emptiness left behind by the missing beloved. Instead of the mother, it is a mad train that emerges from the blackness of the womb-like tunnel. In Rufus's vision this is a murderous train "splashing in blood, with joy—for the first time, joy, joy, after such a long sentence in chains," a train with "people screaming at windows and doors and turning on each other," a train filled with violent waves discovering secrecies, a train that never stops. Rufus would like to "get off here and go home," yet he knows "that he [is] never going home any more" (88–89). In my reading this is a train of desire that never stops to write a soothing, substitutive text, aiming to escape from the long sentence of the Symbolic sentence through a revolutionary poeticity (like polysemy, repetition, rhythm, word play), bringing an ephemeral joy that can stand in the space left painfully empty by the lost home of Semiotic bliss. It is a text combining matricide (murder, blood) with incest (joy, waves), Thanatos with Eros, aggression with longing. An elemental passion is recalled as the train of text, fueled by ungendered desire, rushes on the vulva-like "great scar of tracks" with "a phallic abandon into the blackness which opened to receive it, opened, opened, the whole world shook with their coupling" (89). The groaning, lurching, gasping, and moaning, the tearing sound of the (text) train, echo the embodied voice of the revolutionary poetic language of desire—which is all the more interesting as the allegorical image of the rushing train is described in the very language, the rhythmic, repetitive, rushing text, it symbolizes; theme and style coincide.

The fugitive nature of desire and the impossibility of language (forever displacing the presence, the truth, of reality to subjective experience's distortion, and further on, to an imperfect linguistic-symbolic representation of the original, authentic presence) are reflected in the rushing of the train and in the fast, dense sentences in Rufus's stream of consciousness, suggesting movement, the passing of time, the loss of the pleasures of a childhood when representation was unnecessary:

A fence, a farmhouse, a tree, seen from a train window: coming closer and closer, the details changing every instant as the eye picked them out, then pressing against the window with the urgency of a messenger or a child, then dropping away, diminishing, vanished, gone forever. *That fence is falling down,* he might have thought as the train rushed toward it, or *That house needs paint,* or *The tree is dead.* In an instant, gone in an instant—it was not his fence, his farmhouse, or his tree. As now, passing, he recognised faces, bodies, postures, and thought. *That's Ruth.* Or *There's Old Lennie. Son of a bitch is stoned again.* It was very silent. (87)

In a final, highly symbolic scene, Rufus—shaking like a "rag doll" and cursing God ("Ain't I your baby too?")—commits suicide by throwing himself off "the bridge built to honour the father of his country," while car lights on the highway seem to be writing "an endless message, writing with awful speed in a fine, unreadable script." The wind takes him, and he flies into the black water below, feeling himself "going over, head down, the wind, the stars, the lights, the water, all rolled together, *all right* [. . . thinking . . .] *all right, you motherfucking Godalmighty bastard, I'm coming to You*" (90–91). The bridge marked by the Name of the Father is left behind for the feminine entity of the water, to return to the blissful, homogeneous, Semiotic symbiosis that can only be reexperienced in death. The deathly, mothering waves are black, hence the journey back to the mother is also a return to the other. (The frustration felt over the loss of the maternal is reinforced by the traumas caused by a homophobic, racist society: "The train as though . . . protesting the proximity of white buttock to black knee, groaned" [89]. Thus, the impossible wish to go home can signify in Rufus's vision a reconciliation with the mother intertwined with a reconciliation with the (racial or sexual) other. Rufus can come to the (m)other only by flying, or resisting gravitation, recalling Cixous's definition of the subversive writing of *écriture féminine:* "stealing words and making them fly" (Cixous 1991, 343).

Traditional African American conviction (which reverberates in Alice Walker's womanism and black womanist theology) imagines God to be supremely personal, just, loving, and caring toward everyone alike, as a mothering black woman.[14] Thus Rufus, associated with a baby, a doll, the icon of a child, attacks with his curse words mother and God in one, performing the Freudian double bind—like Joe Trace in *Jazz*—hitting instead of caressing the most beloved, who was unable to maintain the primary paradise of omnipotent love. Rufus's question to his God must be: "Mother, Mother why did you love, leave, give birth, death, and language to me?" The endless message and unreadable script of car lights is this very epiphanic vision of the drama of the constitution of the writing subject and the impossibility of desire revealed to Rufus before his death.

Rufus remembering the loss of his beloved mother before his suicide seems to be an episode of central importance in the text, since characters in the remaining three hundred pages of the novel try to reconstruct, renarrate, and analyze this never-seen scene that remains a black hole, a gap, a textual absence that they know nothing about but that keeps haunting them, becoming an obsession, an enigmatic leitmotif governing their lives, longings, and narratives, like an unspeakable loss vibrating every text on desire.

Subverting Subjects Endlessly: The Book's Lovesong

Although my subjective reading argued for the significance of this episode in Baldwin, it is clear that the memory of the lost mother as a text-organizing principle is much more explicit and consciously exploited in Morrison. It would be tempting to account for this dissimilarity by the two genders' different psychosexual development: in the Freudian Oedipal scenario men are obliged to renounce the primary object of love, alienating and symbolizing it, while women are marked with proximity to the mother, identifying with the primary caretaker and her body. According to Nancy Chodorow, gender identity becomes "internalized" through the mother–child relationship: the mother signifies object and difference from the boy's view, but self and sameness for the girl.

Nevertheless, it seems to me that the explicit nature of the text on the mother is not so much due to the author's femalehood or femininity, but rather to Morrison's novel being closer to a postmodern metatext than her predecessor's novel, written thirty years before hers. However, it is remarkable to note that Morrison's constant reflections on the drama of the writing subject, as well as her musings on the incompetencies of communication intertwined with the impossibility of desire, may have been inspired by Baldwin's Vivaldo, the archetype of the author struggling with his text, which could be, in the long run, the very book in the reader's hands. Thus, it can be argued that both texts contain the deconstructed, defaced portrait of the emblematic writer, who is destabilized by his/her poetic text of desire. Accordingly, the gendered terms *écriture féminine* and of phallogocentric language lose their validity, as the subversive writing style internally transgressing the common obstacle of language is available to anyone with a sense of poetry, regardless of gender.

The linguistic subversion of the revolutionary poetic language goes hand in hand with the subversion of the ideologically interpellated, homogenized, racially othered, engendered subject position on a thematic level. The novels illustrate Gilles Deleuze and Félix Guattari's argument on the convergence of content and style, namely, that "there is no difference between what a book is about and how it is made" (10; translation mine). Both in *Jazz* and in *Another Country* the subject is troubled, split by adulterous, incestuous, sexual, and murderous drives and desires, becoming a Kristevian heterogeneous subject in process / on trial.[15] The desire for the dead mother signifies, in a psychopathological sense, matricide, incest, and even necrophilia. The heteronormative, monogamous, reproductive economy of the disciplined subject is questioned by the sterility of Violet, the adultery of Cass, and the multiple queer liaisons of Rufus, Vivaldo, Eric, and Yves. Traditional femininity—the ideologically prescribed passive feminine sexuality governed by hierarchical gender oppositions—is challenged by excessive, risky, dispersed, wild female desires—especially in Morrison—echoing the rage of the oppressed African American women (Mbalia 625) along with the threatening yet tempting, unspeakable female sexuality (Wild's absent presence, Ida's tuneless song) haunting the texts. The rationality of the homogenized subject is threatened by Violet's and Leona's madness, Rufus's final ecstatic epiphany, and Joe's confusion. In Baldwin's interracial relationships desires and racial prejudice are interchangeable between black and white; thus, the process of racial othering is problematized and relativized. The perversions, deconstructions, and destabilizations of the subject play a crucial role beyond the thematic level: as I tried to demonstrate, on a metaphoric, stylistic, and linguistic level they symbolize, narrate, and address poetically the desiring writing subject. For Morrison's and Baldwin's revolutionary poetic language destabilizes the reading subject as well.

James Baldwin's *Another Country* and Toni Morrison's *Jazz* challenge their readers to participate actively in the composition of the jazz story and text, filling in gaps, musing over mysteries, tracking disseminated meanings, tracing floating signifiers, playing with open possibilities at the numerous entrances and exits of the self-deconstructive texts, vibrating sensitive chords, and voicing written melodies. In Roland Barthes's terms, these are "writerly texts of jouissance," inciting the reader's cooperation and providing the "bliss of a text," not simply that of real literature but also of true love. The reader ready to take up the rhythm of jazz is involved in the text and cannot help being ravished, excited, or deranged, feeling touched and marked by a unique language that is at the same time yearning and violent, a language tainted by desire and sensual corporeality, by melancholy and mourning, by silence, madness, and music. The texts transgress conventional discourse, show ways of flight from the prisonhouse of language, and provide heterogeneous, alternative identifications (with the desiring subject-in-process or the polyphonic, choral narrative voice[s]) beyond the ideologically prescribed subject position. The liberated reading subject can embrace—beyond (yet within) conventional representation—subversive languages of the "other." A Semiotic, renegade mother tongue; body-talk; languages of madness; revolutionary, rhythmic poetry; and melodious music weave the text, functioning as a "desire machine," narrating (on the thematic level), echoing (on the stylistic, linguistic level), exciting (on the receptive level), and operated by (on the level of the plot and of the deeper motor of text) the yearning body.

Talking about love is a verbalized displacement of lovemaking. Reading about love can be very close to an amorous, affectionate encounter. Reading, making the text, making (and disseminating) meanings equals making love with the text, in a dangerous liaison infected by desire, madness, mourning, sex, wild beat, and jazz. The reader's touch can remake the text, interpreting its embrace varyingly according to fugitive desires, past loves and intertextual background, and can produce a new jazzing text of desire, a new narrative of the beat of a heart, a fruit, a memento of this love between Book and Reader, a new r(ead)ing in the endless chain of interpretations, an answer to the invitation to dance, a playful performance to the rhythm of the beat of free jazz.

NOTES

1. I would like to thank Vik Doyen of Katholieke Universiteit Leuven as well as Nóra Séllei and Peter Doherty of the University of Debrecen for their inspiring remarks.
2. This very question governs Morrison's trilogy on impossibly excessive, horrifying, awry loves. *Jazz* tells the story of a bloody, oedipal love triangle,

while *Beloved* narrates a mother's murderous, "too thick" love for her child, and *Paradise* reflects on a community's distorted love for God and tradition.
3. *Écriture féminine* is a metaphorically feminine (that is, transgendered) linguistic subversion available to both sexes, all of mother born.
4. It is interesting to note that Baldwin too suggests that he is an admirer of Virginia Woolf by naming his married couple in *Another Country* Cass and Richard, presumably after Clarissa and Richard Dalloway of Woolf's *Mrs Dalloway* (1925).
5. While in Marcel Proust's *A la recherche du temps perdu*, Odette and Swan made Vinteuil's sonata the anthem of their love, in Baldwin the love of Rufus and Leona is heralded by the beat of the drums, Vivaldo and Ida listen to Bessie Smith and *Porgy and Bess*, Eric and Yves have Beethoven for their hymn of passion, and Eric and Cass are intimately linked by the music of Shostakovich.
6. "Sth, I know that woman. She used to live with a flock of birds on Lenox Avenue. Know her husband, too. He fell for an eighteen-year-old girl with one of those deepdown, spooky loves that made him so sad and happy he shot her just to keep the feeling going. When the woman, her name is Violet, went to the funeral to see the girl and to cut her dead face they threw her to the floor and out of the church. She ran, then, through all that snow, and when she got back to her apartment she took the birds from their cages and set them out the windows to freeze or fly, including the parrot that said, 'I love you.'" (3)
7. "Collective authorship," the reconstruction of a common "site of memory" (Ryan and Conwill Majozo 132), underlies traditional African American folk literature, black sermons, and spirituals as well.
8. On blues music and black literature see Michael G. Cooke, *Afro-American Literature in the 20th Century: The Achievement of Intimacy* (New Haven and London: Yale University Press, 1984).
9. In Baldwin "they danced with a concentration at once effortless and tremendous, sometimes very close to one another, sometimes swinging far apart, but always joined, each body making way for, responding to, and commenting on the other" (341), while Morrison writes about dancers touching beyond words, becoming one body, "sharing a partner's pulse like a second jugular" (65).
10. Apparently Rufus's impossible desires are displaced onto his sister's, Ida's, body: the handcuffs given to him by Eric are "transformed on the body of his sister" into Ida's barbaric earrings, which attract Vivaldo's attention; Rufus's beat is recalled by Ida "drumming fingernails" (241); while Ida's seducing yet disharmonic and harsh voice sings the blues of her brother's and a whole generation's wasted life and tainted loves.
11. *Another Country*'s madwoman in the text, Leona, is almost entirely silenced, traumatized by the cruel love of Rufus, and speaks only a few insignificant lines. She is a woman without a man, a mother without a child, a being without words, whose body and mind alike are wounded by her silent absence, leading her to the asylum. Her loss (of hope, stability, reason, and self), her absent words, and her silent omnipresence emblematize pain as a Zeitgeist.

12. Wittgenstein in his theory of the "private language argument" outlined in his *Philosophical Investigations* (1953) challenges the notion of discourse as a transparent, direct, unproblematic means of communication, as he suggests that reality is multiply distorted in/via all our utterances, since reality is filtered through our subjective experiences, which are displaced further by the conventional, limited sign-system substituting a linguistic representation for reality's presence. Accordingly, an individual's words refer to what can only be known to the person speaking, to his version of reality, to his immediate private sensations, so another person will not be able to fully understand him. Verbalized feelings, moods, sensations (such as pain or love) are particularly prone to be misunderstood and fail to be communicated. (No one else shall feel my pain when I say I am hurt.)

13. I disagree with most of the critics, who claim that Violet's cutting of Dorcas's face, her "rebirth" as a new Violet, and her reunion with Joe after Dorcas's death represents a reassuring reunion (Ryan and Conwill Majozo 138), a celebration of the power of subjectivity (Cannon 246), an adult, mature love (Peach 127), or a final, soothing release (Otten 664).

14. On loving, caring, and mothering black women see Brown (1989) and Burrow (1998).

15. Kristeva's term *sujet en procès* (*subject-and meaning in process/on trial*) intertwines her tenets on subjectivity and meaning-formation, both conceived as heterogeneous, dynamic, metamorphic fluxes in a self-subverting system, where to be imprisoned in meaning signifies taking into account the trials of meaning, and to be walled into the transcendental ego implies outlining the course of the ego in crisis.

WORKS CITED

Baldwin, James. *Another Country*. 1962. London: Michael Joseph, 1979.

Barthes, Roland. *Le Plaisir du Texte*. Paris: Seuil, 1973.

Bell, Vikki. "Passing and Narrative in Toni Morrison's *Jazz*." *Social Identities*, June 1996: 221–237.

Brooks, Peter. *Body Work. Objects of Desire in Modern Narrative*. Cambridge: Harvard University Press, 1993.

Brown, Kelly Delaine. "God Is as Christ Does: Toward a Womanist Theology." *Journal of Religious Thought*, Summer–Fall 1989: 7–16.

Burrow, Rufus. "Enter Womanist Theology and Ethics." *The Western Journal of Black Studies* 22 (1998): 19–29.

Cannon, Elizabeth M. "Following the Traces of Female Desire in Toni Morrison's *Jazz*." *African American Review*, Summer 1997: 235–248.

Chodorow, Nancy. *The Reproduction of Mothering*. Berkeley: California University Press, 1978.

Cixous, Hélène. *La venue à l'écriture*. Paris: UGE, 1975.

————. "The Laugh of Medusa." In. *Feminisms: An Anthology of Literary Theory and Criticism.* Ed. Robyn R. Warhol and Diane Price Herndl. New Brunswick: Rutgers University Press, 1991. 334–350.

Cooke, Michael G. *Afro-American Literature in the 20th Century. The Achievement of Intimacy.* New Haven, CT: Yale University Press, 1984.

Deleuze, Gilles, and Félix Guattari. "Rhizome." In *Mille plateaux.* Paris: Minuit, 1976. 9–37.

Jones, Carolyn M. "Traces and Cracks: Identity and Narrative in Toni Morrison's *Jazz.*" *African American Review,* Fall 1997: 481–496.

Klein, Melanie. "Réflexions sur l'*Orestie.*" *Envie et gratitude et autre essais.* Paris: Gallimard, 1997: 188–219.

Kristeva, Julia. *La révolution du langage poétique.* Paris: Seuil, 1985.

Lacan, Jacques. "The Mirror Stage as Formative of the Function of the I as Revealed in Psychoanalytic Experience." In *Modern Literary Theory. A Reader.* Ed. Philip Rice and Patricia Waugh. London: Edward Arnold, 1992.

LeClair, Thomas. "The Language Must Not Sweat: A Conversation with Toni Morrison." In *Conversations with Toni Morrison.* Ed. Danille Taylor-Guthrie. Jackson: University Press of Mississippi, 1994. 119–129.

Marks, Elaine, and Isabelle de Courtivron, eds. *New French Feminisms: An Anthology.* Amherst: Massachusetts University Press, 1980.

Mbalia, Doreatha Drummond. "Women Who Run With Wild: The Need for Sisterhood in *Jazz.*" *Modern Fiction Studies,* Fall-Winter 1993: 623–646.

Morrison, Toni. *Beloved.* London: Picador, 1987.

————. *Playing in the Dark. Whiteness and Literary Imagination.* Cambridge, MA: Harvard University Press, 1992

————. *Jazz.* London: Picador, 1993.

————. "'I Come from People who Sang All the Time.' A Conversation with Toni Morrison." *Humanities,* March-April 1996: 4–13.

————. *Paradise.* New York: Knopf, 1998.

Naylor, Gloria. "A Conversation: Gloria Naylor and Toni Morrison." In *Conversations with Toni Morrison.* Ed. Danille Taylor-Guthrie. Jackson: University Press of Mississippi, 1994. 188–218.

Otten, Terry. "Horrific Love in Toni Morrison's Fiction." *Modern Fiction Studies,* Fall-Winter 1993: 651–667.

Paquet, Marie Anne Deyris. "Toni Morrison's Jazz and the City." *African American Review 2,* Summer 2001: 219–232.

Peach, Linden. *Toni Morrison.* London: Macmillan Modern Novelists, 1995.

Pici, Nicholas F. "Trading Meanings, the Breath of Music in Toni Morrison's Jazz." *Connotations* 3 (1997–98): 372–398.

Rodrigues, Eusebio L. "Experiencing Jazz." *Modern Fiction Studies,* Fall-Winter 1993: 733–754.

Rubenstein, Roberta. "Singing the Blues, Reclaiming Jazz: Toni Morrison and Cultural Mourning." *Mosaic,* June 1998: 147–164.

Ryan, Judylyn S. and Estella Conwill Majozo. "Jazz…On the Site of Memory." *Studies in the Literary Imagination,* Fall 1998: 125–153.

Tate, Claudia. "Toni Morrison." *Black Women Writers at Work*. Harpenden: Oldcastle Books, 1989.

Troupe, Quincy ed. *James Baldwin: The Legacy*. New York: Simon & Schuster, 1989.

Walker, Alice. *In Search of Our Mothers' Gardens. Womanist Prose*. London: Harvest, 1983.

REVISING REVISION: METHODOLOGIES OF LOVE, DESIRE, AND RESISTANCE IN *BELOVED* AND *IF BEALE STREET COULD TALK*

MICHELLE H. PHILLIPS

Revisionary approaches have become increasingly apparent in contemporary literary criticism, so much so that *New Literary History* dedicated an issue to the topic in 1998. Among the articles featured therein is Miguel Tamen's "Phenomenology of the Ghost: Revision in Literary History," which traces the popularity of the term "revisionism" to Harold Bloom, who described it as a combative need for the poet or reader "to usurp" from the text or tradition "a place, a stance, a fullness, an illusion of identification or possession" (Bloom 17). However, both Tamen and Bloom recognize that although revisionism produces the illusion of truth as well as the prospect for novelty, it inherently denies either possibility (Tamen 302). While the text seeks to demystify the pre-text, revisionism, by definition, turns in on itself. "All of us," writes Bloom, "despite our overt desires, are doomed to become the subjects of our own need for demystification" (16). Another of the issue's articles is a report from a focus group led by Norman Holland on the topic of revisionism, consisting of experts from the fields of psychology, literary studies, writing, and science. The report attributes to revisionism a threefold functionality: it is a means of rejecting past literary theories (of which New Criticism arose as a primary candidate), of responding to and rebelling against "political marginalization," and of "asserting the role and situation of the subject" (178–179).

All of these characteristics of revision, theoretical and practical, are visible within African American literary theory's identification and affirmation of "revision as an important trope in black fiction" (Jablon 136). At the forefront of this theoretical approach are the works of Robert B. Stepto, Houston A. Baker, Jr., and Henry Louis Gates, Jr. In his *From Behind the Veil: A Study of Afro-American Narrative* (1979), Stepto argues that the history of African American narrative is one of revision, of dialectical call and response. Arising from the founding models of slave narratives, which inextricably bind the "quest for freedom" with literacy acquisition, modern African American narratives seek to continue or complete this "pregeneric myth for Afro-America" through advanced literacies and expanded authorial control (xv). Unlike Stepto, Baker and Gates identify the locus for African American signifying not with the written but with the black vernacular tradition. In his "Belief, Theory, and Blues: Notes for a Post-Structuralist Criticism of Afro-American Literature" (1986), Baker argues that the "blues matrix" is an amalgam, "combining work songs, group seculars, field hollers, sacred harmonies, proverbial wisdom . . . and much more," which "as a code radically condition[s] Afro-America's cultural signifying" (231). One of the dominant codes to which Baker is referring is what he sees as the "cultural mimesis" of the blues, the way in which the music imitates the "*train-wheels-over-track-junctures.*" As such, the blues not only repeats the "desire and absence" that the performer feels but also provides, through the metaphor of mobility, for the "amelioration of such conditions" (233). Arguably, the most prominent African American theory of revision, however, is that proposed by Gates in *The Signifying Monkey: A Theory of African-American Literary Criticism* (1988). "Signifyin(g)," according to Gates, is "the figurative difference between the literal and the metaphorical, between surface and latent meaning" (82). It is the "figure of the double-voiced" or the linguistic incarnation of double consciousness, offering, on the one hand, a literal, publicly accessible meaning and presenting, on the other, a figurative meaning, often contrary to the first (xxvii).

Despite the differences between these three theories of revision, some of which have been articulated by the theorists themselves, there are at least two significant points of convergence. First, though they do not all share Bloom's sense that revision is combative in nature, they do share the view that revision is fundamentally guided by a dynamic of and a desire for power. Second, and most important for the purposes of this chapter, Stepto, Baker, and Gates propose similar methods for achieving this end. Whether they use the terminology of the "veil," the "code," or "signifyin(g)," they all demonstrate a preference for the figurative as a tool for countering and overcoming the literal circumstances of existence. Despite the political and aesthetic potential of these theories, this affirmation of a highly intellectual and rational empowerment achieved through the negation of the literal body and practical experience has sparked significant criticism. Deborah McDowell, Michael Awkward, Valerie Smith, and Joyce A. Joyce (among others) have all critiqued the patriarchal and poststructuralist tendencies of Baker and Gates especially. Of these critiques, Joyce's is both the most detailed and the most unrelenting, arguing that the emphasis on metaphor, and more specifically the association of race with metaphor, forms a significant rift between the black community and the creative writer, on the one hand, who seek to recognize and represent "hundreds of years of disenfranchisement," and the black poststructuralist theorist, on the other, who views language (and hence experience) as "merely a system of codes or as mere play" (295). Adding a feminist slant to Joyce's theoretical criticism of Gates and Baker, Margaret Homans argues that by consciously advocating the superiority of the figurative, Gates and Baker, like their Western counterparts, construct a binary opposition equivalent to that between the mind (figurative) and the body (literal), a rift that has long plagued Western feminist thought (78).

Taken together, these critiques are significant indicators of revisionism's negligent stance toward concrete existence and experience. Their validity should not be perceived as a repudiation of the concept of revisionism in general, however. Revisionism as a theory is remarkably resilient and, in fact, denotatively demands its own correction. Revising revision is, therefore, a crucial task; however, such a project need be neither futuristic nor utterly theoretical in nature. As Barbara Christian passionately argues in her essay "A Race for Theory," the creative works of African Americans, especially those by women, are always already theoretical, meaning in part that a study of literature can yield as much as, if not more than, concepts situated in abstraction (281). With this in mind, I turn to two specific works by James Baldwin and Toni Morrison that I believe offer insight into the alternative revisionist possibilities suggested by criticism and theory alike. Though the texts of Morrison and Baldwin have themselves been inscribed within the standard revisionist context, to step outside of this stance is to see, ironically, that some of their most powerful transformative efforts apply to the process of revision itself. A detailed examination of Morrison's *Beloved* (1987) and Baldwin's *If Beale Street Could Talk* (1974) reveals that their theoretically subtle approaches to resistance are made even more so by their insistence on the centrality of love and desire. In *Beloved* the quest for humanizing love leads Morrison to engage in signifying at the same time that she ultimately deconstructs and reconstitutes the application and form of that system. Baldwin, however, in *If Beale Street Could Talk*, largely refuses the independently powerful methodology of revision in favor of the dependently loving process of translation.

The critical flaws within the system of revision, and signifying in particular, are problematic for none more than they are for black women, whose "other"ness in Western society has always been a function of a degraded and degrading ideology of the body. During slavery, two pervasive constructs of black womanhood were the mammy and the "loose woman," both of which served as contrasting caricatures of the body. The loose woman was licentiousness incarnate who, unlike the white lady, "craved sex inordinately"

(Christian, *Black Women*, 13–14). The mammy, on the other hand, embodied the maternal, wishing to nurture "the children of the world" (11). The narratives of black women during slavery were written on the body as it were. Not only were black women imprisoned within Western constructs of a body believed, in the hierarchy of reason, to be inferior, but their oppression was circuitously justified by their own corporeal form. The mammy was "enduring, strong, and calm . . . black in color as well as race and fat, with enormous breasts"; she was, unlike the loose woman, also perceived as "sexless," a direct result of her unattractiveness (11–12). The physical depiction of the loose woman, on the contrary, matched her perceived carnal nature. Sarah Bartmann, otherwise known as the "Hottentot Venus," became the icon of such beliefs in the nineteenth century. Her "primitive" genitalia, "a hypertrophy of the labia and nymphae" known as the "Hottentot apron," and her "protruding buttocks" were seen as signs of her "'primitive' sexual appetite" (Gilman 232). Despite these apparent differences, the mammy and the loose black woman were united in their ultimate opposition to the white lady, who was pure, chaste, and beautiful (unlike the loose woman) (Christian, *Black Women*, 15) and who was also completely fragile and helpless (unlike the mammy) (10–11).

Since this period, the history of black women's sexuality in literature has been a process of refuting these negative images, which ultimately equate black women with the unrefined and the primitive. However, this history of revision has been problematized by a disproportionately antagonistic reaction to expressive sexuality. Character types such as the "proper mulatta," the matriarch, and the sapphire reveal the primary revisionist preference for the attributes of the sexless mammy over those of the loose woman (77). Even within the realm of literary criticism, "the restrictive, repressive, and dangerous aspects of black female sexuality have been emphasized . . . while pleasure, exploration, and agency have gone under-analyzed" (Hammonds 134). The impetus in *Beloved,* therefore, to rehumanize the black body and to do so through a system of signification characterizes the dual movement of the novel: first, to revise or "rememory" the history of African American experience and second, to reimagine the process of revision itself.

Like many of her predecessors, Morrison revisits in *Beloved* the foundational stereotypes that have plagued black women: the mammy and the loose woman. However, unlike those who have aligned their characters more closely with the figure of the mammy, choosing her asexual strength over the libido-driven loose woman, Morrison creates a complex amalgamation of the two. Her central protagonist, Sethe, combines the strength and maternal drive of the mammy with the pleasureful pursuits of the loose woman. Even within the first chapter of the novel, the former is clearly portrayed through the eyes of Denver, who describes her mother as a "quiet, queenly woman" who "when the baby's spirit picked up Here Boy and slammed him into the wall hard enough to break two of his legs and dislocate his eye . . . had not looked away; rather, Sethe had taken a hammer, knocked the dog unconscious, wiped away the blood and saliva, pushed his eye back in his head and set his leg bones" (12–13). In this moment, Sethe's compassion and determination to preserve life, a derivation of her maternal drive, are matched and even masked by her emotional strength. This dual need is undoubtedly a result of Sethe's experiences with slavery, where both strength and maternity were essential elements of survival. During her harrowing, solitary escape from Sweet Home, for example, Sethe is literally compelled forward by her unborn child, the "little antelope" who "rammed her with horns and pawed the ground of her womb" whenever she tried to stop (32). Psychologically, Sethe is driven by a far deeper maternal instinct to get her milk to yet another of her children, already across the Ohio River. Indeed, when Sethe remembers the episode years later, she does so in language remarkably similar to that used by Barbara Christian to define the mammy stereotype. She remembers triumphantly that when she finally arrived at 124 Bluestone Road, "sure enough, she had milk enough for all" (106).

Unlike the traditional image of the mammy or the subsequent historical portrayals of strong women, however, Sethe's strength and her maternal instinct do not preclude her capacity for desire. Not only does Sethe feel completely comfortable with her hair down and her feet bare in front of the newly returned Paul D, but she readily has sex with him soon thereafter. Sethe also has no problem with combining the traditionally separate, though rationally linked, concepts of maternity and sexual pleasure. When to cover up his affair with Beloved Paul D deceptively tells her that he wants to get her pregnant, Sethe "quickly" thinks "of how good the sex would be if that is what he wanted" (138). More important, however, is Sethe's ability to combine and even enhance her sexuality with her strength. It is Sethe's scarred back, for example, symbolic of her ability to survive the severest physical and psychological obstacles that provides the spark for their initial sexual encounter.

Morrison's balanced treatment and transformation of black female sexuality is indicative of the novel's greater thematic concern with the dangers of excess, epitomized for Morrison by two historical moments. The first and primary source of inspiration for the novel was the story of Margaret Garner, a fugitive slave who in 1856 committed infanticide because "she was unwilling to have her children suffer as she had done" (Plasa 40). The second came from a photograph taken by Van der Zee of a young Harlem girl's funeral. The description explained that the woman was apparently shot at a party by an ex-boyfriend. However, in the moments after being attacked, she refused to reveal her assailant's identity, saying only to those who inquired, "I'll tell you tomorrow" (qtd. in Rushdy 143). What connected both of these stories for Morrison was the paradox with which black women in particular are faced. "The whole problem," says Morrison, "was trying to do two things: to love something bigger than yourself, to nurture something; and also not to sabotage yourself, not to murder yourself" (qtd. in Taylor-Guthrie 253–254). In a society structured on binaries, the negotiations between self and other, between past and present, are especially difficult. But where love is concerned, love that "demands" more of us "intellectually" and "morally," it is an essential process (267–268).

Like Margaret Garner and the girl in Van der Zee's photograph, both of whom paid for their love with their very selves, Sethe makes the mistake of loving unconditionally. In this regard, Morrison echoes Paul D's belief that Sethe's love, love that leads to infanticide, is "too thick" (173). On her own, without Halle, without a partner to mitigate her love, Morrison says that Sethe "merges into [the] role" of mother completely. Her love is then "unleashed and it's fierce." When she kills Beloved, Morrison argues that Sethe "almost steps over into what she was terrified of being regarded as, which is an animal. It's an excess of maternal feeling, a total surrender to that commitment, and, you know, such excesses are not good. She has stepped across the line, so to speak. It's understandable, but it is excessive" (qtd. in Taylor-Guthrie 252). The dangers of excessive love reverberate throughout Beloved; in fact, such is what makes Beloved, reincarnate, an ultimately destructive presence. Contrary to the way the community portrays her, as a "devil-child" (275), the narrator continually emphasizes that Beloved's life is one of sorrow and unfulfilled desire—a persistent compulsion to be-loved. However, while Beloved's motives are at least ambiguous, her threat is not. Her "clamor for a kiss" is ultimately as narcissistic as Sethe's is altruistic and is consequently as great a source of potential destruction.

The same dangers rendered in Beloved also mark the traditional process of revision, itself a method of excess. Even though primary meaning is initially sustained as repetition, revision, as it is primarily emphasized by Bloom, Stepto, Baker, and Gates, almost always requires a choice to be made. Whether it be depth over surface, figurative over literal, or present over past, one form of meaning is sacrificed for another. Morrison's modification of revision is a direct response to this construct. In general, many scholars have noted Morrison's interest in alternative vantage points. Barbara Schapiro discusses the relationship between self and other in Beloved in terms of boundaries and balance (170); Deborah Sitter, focusing on the narrative and metaphoric aspects of the novel, characterizes Morrison's approach as dialogic (201); and Mae Henderson, in her own unique terminology, argues that Morrison occupies the "borders" between inside and outside (36). While the terminology differs, these various approaches to *Beloved* are united by the recognition that Morrison seeks to maintain difference at the same time that she wishes to inspire unity. With regard to revision, therefore, the effects of this paradoxical approach are demonstrated best by Morrison's own revisionist practice. The novel is itself a figurative re-creation of literal events. If Morrison had written *Beloved* as nonfiction, it would be a very different and far more devastating text. That the life of the Harlem girl ended tragically is apparent, but the same was true for Margaret Garner, who was recaptured and returned to slavery. The changes Morrison makes between these true stories and the novel she produced are all directed toward balance and ultimately toward a potentially more-fulfilling future. Specifically, Morrison adds to these images of boundless, destructive love visions of conditional love, which, unlike the former, hold the promise of reconciliation and survival. Rememory is one example of how this process occurs. When Sethe thinks about Sweet Home, she does not remember it in all of its monstrosity. She cannot. As Morrison says, "it is not possible to survive" the past of slavery and the Middle Passage "and dwell on it" (qtd. in Taylor-Guthrie 247). Nonetheless, Morrison also argues for the responsibility of remembering and passing on one's history "in a manner in which it can be digested, in a manner in which the memory is not destructive" (247–248). The only way Sethe can survive on any genuine level is to find a balance between the past and the present, a solution she finds in rememory. Sethe remembers Sweet Home, for example, "rolling out before her eyes . . . in shameless beauty. It never looked as terrible as it was . . . Boys hanging from the most beautiful sycamores in the world. It shamed her—remembering the wonderful soughing trees rather than the boys" (6). Sethe finds something in her memories of the past to love. In this moment it is the natural setting rather than either the masters who occupied it or the slaves who suffered as a result. The focus of her own revision is significant in that it allows her to place the blame for her past where it rightfully belongs—on the individuals responsible—while leaving her a landscape on which to found a new life.

Morrison's form of revision, demonstrated here through Sethe, is as realistic as it is imaginary, achieving an equilibrium absent from traditional modes of revision. In fact, the combination of the literal and the figurative not only defines rememory but also characterizes Morrison's most dramatic and optimistic alteration of the "true" account of Margaret Garner: the addition of romantic love. Sethe's relationship with Paul D is one of the few portraits of productive love in a novel driven by the hope of such an entity. Their love, however, does not correlate with any contemporary Western definition of the term. It is not "that desperate need to love only one person"; it is not "romantic-love-eternal" (qtd. in Taylor-Guthrie 73).

On the contrary, they experience normalcy in all of its flawed, human splendor. Both Paul D and Sethe begin with romanticized notions about what sex with the other will be like. Climbing "white stairs," Paul D "dropped twenty-five years from his recent memory" at the "certainty of giving her his sex" (21), and Sethe saw something "blessed" in the "manner" of Paul D and thought of his body as "an arc of kindness" (18). When the sex is over, "before they could get their clothes off," however, both feel a sense of disappointment. Morrison writes of Paul D that "his dreaming of her had been too long and too long ago," and of Sethe that "her deprivation had been not having any dreams of her own at all" (21). Their disappointment, in other words, stems from excess. Where Paul D's perception of romantic fulfillment was excessively figurative, with no practical foundation, Sethe's was too literal, with no extension into the figurative and imaginative realm. Gradually, however, their feelings begin to change and both start to settle into an extraordinary ordinary love. Sethe goes from thinking that Paul D is a "dog," "nothing but a man" after all, to realizing that her own stereotypes of manhood, passed down to her in part from Baby Suggs (whom she is quoting), are flawed (23). Sethe feels Paul D's gaze on her and, though the typical male would be critical of her for "how bad she looked," she can tell "there was no mockery coming from his eyes." In fact, his gaze, as Sethe describes it, is almost feminine. It is "soft" and "waiting" (27). Paul D undergoes a similar process of change. He smiles at "his foolishness," examining Sethe with her eyes closed, "her hair a mess," and thinks, "Looked at this way, minus the polished eyes, her face was not so attractive. So it must have been her eyes that kept him both guarded and stirred up. Without them her face was manageable—a face he could handle. Maybe if she could keep them closed like that . . . But no, there was her mouth. Nice. Halle never knew what he had" (26). In this tumultuous moment, Paul D is faced with all of the stereotypes he has been taught—of traditional beauty and desire—all of which are contradicted here by Sethe's "unmanageable" appearance. The fact that Paul D works his way to a deeper appreciation of Sethe demonstrates the extent to which he has come to appreciate the ordinary, the taken for granted (Sethe), as the extraordinary.

More important than Sethe and Paul D's movement away from excess, either figurative or literal, is their movement toward a space that simultaneously unites and transcends these concepts. The inciting moment of their first sexual encounter, when Paul D discovers the "tree" on Sethe's back, is itself a romantic revision of two previous moments. Though it is schoolteacher and his nephews who first see (and create) the marks on Sethe's back, it is Amy Denver who first revises them, identifying the lashes as a "chokecherry tree . . . red and split wide open, full of sap" (83). The image she creates is paradoxically beautiful and horrific, juxtaposing vibrant natural imagery alongside the recognition that the tree, like Sethe, has been ravished; both have been "split wide open." In contrast, Paul D's revision of Sethe's scars is both less vibrant and more hopeful. He sees the "tree," as Sethe now calls it, as a "sculpture . . . like the decorative work of an ironsmith too passionate for display" (18). In viewing Sethe's scars as art, Paul D adds communicative depth to superficial flesh. As art, her back, her body, now has a story to tell; it, like rememory, is the imaginative mitigation of her experience. For Morrison, who views black writing as more than "the language, the dropping of g's," as "something so much more earthbound . . . much more in touch with the magic and the mystery and things of the body" (qtd. in Taylor-Guthrie 78), Sethe's back epitomizes the communicative connection between the literal and the figurative. This conjunction is further solidified in this moment of romantic revision by the juxtaposition of the sexual alongside the artistic. By seeing Sethe's back in both artistic and sexual terms, both of which are intersubjective in nature, Paul D gives himself a role to play—he becomes interpreter and lover. He "learn[s]" of "her sorrow" through the feel of "his cheek on her back"; he supports her by holding "her breasts in the palms of his hands" (18). He makes of his body "an arc of kindness," and for the first time Sethe feels the weight of her trauma lifted, along with the possibility for rest and peace and feeling (19).

This ironically silent dialogue between Sethe and Paul D leads to dialectical fulfillment in the ensuing sexual encounter. Though the sex act itself is initially disappointing, Sethe and Paul D find fulfillment in a silent exchange of memories, where the thoughts of each fill in the gaps of the other. The fact that sex leads to such a plethora of shared memories, mutual and separate, liberates it from its associations with the merely physical while simultaneously altering the traditional, Western notions of physicality altogether. Considering the crucial role that rememory plays in the novel, the fact that sex can produce communication through memory demonstrates its importance as a tool for working through a separatist past and moving toward a unified future. By the end of the chapter, there is a moment of shared memory that encapsulates this change. As both are remembering Sethe and Halle's sexual misadventure in the cornfield and of the corn they subsequently ate that night, one or both think, "How loose the silk. How jailed-down the juice," a line that is repeated with some variation to close out the chapter: "How loose the silk. How fine and loose and free" (28–29). The act of eating the corn was for Paul D, especially, a way of sublimating his sexual desire at Sweet Home. He remembers, for example, "parting the hair to get to the tip, the edge of his fingernail just under, so as not to graze a single kernel." Now, as shared memory, the eating of the corn actually becomes the long-awaited sexual climax between Paul D and Sethe—psychological union and fulfillment made possible by the physical act of sex. It is also a rewriting of the past, the consummation of a moment that provided neither real fulfillment nor the freedom to be "loose."

In some ways *Beloved* is an extremely complex romance novel. It is filled with characters suffering from a narrative of abandonment wrought by loved ones who ultimately could not find a balance between loving themselves and nurturing others. When Paul D returns to 124 Bluestone Road, he effectively revises this narrative for Sethe with his own. His is a love that runs counter to the Western romantic notions of eternal consumption, affirming instead what Morrison has termed "comradeship," in which the individual and the collective find mutual support (qtd. in Taylor-Guthrie 73). Paul D recognizes in Sethe "a friend of [his] mind," and he wishes to put "his story next to hers" (287). In the end, it is this—their conditional love for each other—that frames the novel and gives it its strength as well as its hope for the future. Unlike many other applications of revision as resistance, *Beloved* does not shy away from this love on any level. On the contrary, it revises the association of the physical with the inferior and instead creates an alternate vision of love and sexuality as intimately human, affecting us physically and metaphysically by opening doors to and away from a traumatizing past.

Like Morrison, James Baldwin is devoted to a project of resistance that bears "witness" to the dehumanization of the African American body at the same time that it envisions, via an aesthetic commitment to authentic love and desire, a movement away from this "mortification of the flesh" (qtd. in Standley and Pratt 55). Unlike Morrison, however, Baldwin's form of testimony does not arise from a theoretical attachment to the ambiguous. Where there is little more terrifying than a past of unmitigated suffering in *Beloved,* for Baldwin a holistic recognition and understanding of one's past is the only saving grace in present American society. Here, where false consciousness is a racial epidemic, Baldwin argues that individuals and the nation as a whole have "modified and suppressed and lied about all the darker forces in our history" ("Creative" 672). The import of such an absence or false presence cannot be overestimated for Baldwin, whose philosophical vision aligns past with present identity formation. That the past is "contained in all of us" (qtd. in Standley and Pratt 27) is an assertion repeatedly made by Baldwin and passionately stated in his essay "The White Man's Guilt" (1965), in which he commands: "White man, hear me! History, as nearly no one seems to know, is not merely something to be read . . . On the contrary, the great force of history comes from the fact that we carry it within us, are unconsciously controlled by it in many ways, and history is literally *present* in all that we do" (722–723). To deny one's past, therefore, is to void oneself not only of authentic being in the present but of all existential possibilities for the future.

While Baldwin, like Morrison and other African American writers and theorists, is clearly driven by a desire to transform humankind's present state, he refuses the standard approach of revision as his means of resistance. Though Morrison and others have deftly illustrated the adaptability of revisionism, Baldwin's work appears to attempt no such adaptation. Indeed, Baldwin's difference may be due to his perhaps limited perception of revision as oppositional in nature. In "Everybody's Protest Novel" (1949), for example, Baldwin specifically critiques the process of revision on these grounds. Using the examples of Harriet Beecher Stowe's *Uncle Tom's Cabin* (1852) and Richard Wright's *Native Son*, (1940) Baldwin argues that while wishing to counter the Uncle Tom image provided by Stowe, Wright offers only "a continuation, a complement, of that monstrous legend it was written to destroy" (18). Binary oppositions are problematic for Baldwin because they maintain and even validate a disingenuous past. The aspect of revision that repeats the past in order to change it or to oppose it altogether poses a problem for Baldwin, who believes that to do so is to acknowledge the past and to cement it as something real and actual and true. Even the aspect of revision that seeks to move beyond repetition into the realm of change is problematic for Baldwin if that transformation is not substantively consistent with its origins. As with repetition, the essential flaw here is in the validation of a fundamentally Western notion of creation and invention in which "the temptation to invent" is consistent with "the temptation to evade" (qtd. in Standley and Pratt 279).

In contrast to the standard methodologies of revision, Baldwin seeks to maintain and affirm authentic history and experience. Baldwin, who chooses his terminology meticulously, repeatedly refers to this process of "excavation" and deliverance as "translation." In an interview for *The Black Scholar*, Baldwin, speaking of the ways in which African Americans have survived in the twentieth century, states that "we were able to raise our children because we had a real sense of the past . . . All you have is your history, and you had to translate that through everything that you did, so the kid would live. That is called love, too" (qtd. in Standley and Pratt 151). Baldwin's immediate association of translation with love is, I believe, critical, particularly as it connects what many critics see as two disparate factions in his work. Baldwin's thematic concerns with love or the lack thereof in his fiction have long been noted as the source either of an individual's survival and maturation or of his respective destruction and death. Many of these same critics, however, have been troubled by what they see as a conflict between this personal pursuit and Baldwin's openly political agenda. Baldwin, however, as is apparent in the interview mentioned above, evinces no such anxiety. In this same interview, in fact, Baldwin seamlessly juxtaposes the responsibility of the black family for its children with his responsibility as an artist for the community at large. Art, he says, is "a very violent and terrifying act of love . . . If I love you, I have to make you conscious of the things you don't see. Insofar as that is true, in that effort, I become conscious of the things that I don't see . . . The only way you can get through it is to accept that two-way street which I call love" (qtd. in Standley and Pratt 156).

Coincidently, Baldwin gave this interview in October 1973, the exact month and year when he finished writing *If Beale Street Could Talk,* a novel that many see as his most successful attempt to reveal the interrelatedness and interdependence of the drive toward love and personal fulfillment with the project of public and political resistance. Though the novel received mixed reviews—some seeing it as too repetitive of Baldwin's earlier work or lacking the complexity thereof—a number of critics have recognized its subtle attributes. Lynn Orilla Scott, for example, has argued that though "Baldwin appears to be 'repeating' certain characters or stories from his own or other works of fiction" in this novel, "he does so with a difference . . . that many of the negative reviews, in particular, failed to perceive" (113). Here, Scott is making an argument for *If Beale Street Could Talk* as a text that signifies on the protest novel by imagining the love and commitment of family as revolutionary force. Similarly, Houston A. Baker makes a claim for *If Beale Street Could Talk* as a novel in which Baldwin's artistic concerns merge with his desire for revolution through the relationship of Fonny, "the embattled craftsman," with the Rivers family (1988, 75–76). And Emmanuel S. Nelson claims that the personal and the political, the private and the public, conjoin as well through the figures of the community (represented by the Rivers family) and the individual (represented by Fonny), each of which achieves fulfillment through the other (124). Whether they use Baldwin's terminology or not, these critics, among others, are implicitly engaging in a study of translation, which, as Baldwin's language reveals, is critical to any form of development and progress, individual or societal. What remains to be explicitly examined are the precise dynamics of Baldwin's philosophy of translation and the relationship between this methodology of resistance and the process of revision.

The first suggestion of translation within Baldwin's penultimate novel comes from the title itself. Immediately the novel announces itself as translation—as the articulation of the unspoken and invisible experience of the struggling black community, symbolically represented by Beale Street. Within the text as well, one finds two explicit references to the term. The first occurs when Tish is describing Fonny's strained relationship with his mother, Alice Hunt. What Fonny has found with Tish is a love that he was never able to find from his mother, but Tish knows "how much [Fonny] loved her: how much he wanted to love her, to be allowed to love her, to have that translation read" (Baldwin 16). The second is used to describe Joseph Rivers, Tish's father, as he is waiting for the news of Tish's pregnancy to be revealed. Tish says that "his face became as definite as stone, every line and angle suddenly seemed chiseled, and his eyes turned a blacker black. He was waiting—suddenly, helplessly—for what was already known to be translated, to enter reality, to be born" (37). The current, standard definition of translation as linguistic conversion bears little relationship to Baldwin's use of the term in these instances. Largely, this is due to Baldwin's disavowal of current approaches to language as a series of meaningless signs in favor of the belief that vocabulary and experience are irrevocably conjoined. He argues, for example, in his essay "If Black English Isn't a Language, Then Tell me, What Is?" (1979) that even people with a "common" language speak differently because they have different experiences. "A French man living in Paris," Baldwin asserts, "speaks a subtly and crucially different language from that of a man living in Marseilles . . . and they would all have great difficulty in apprehending what the man from Guadeloupe, or Martinique, is saying." In the end, "although the 'common' language of all these areas is French," the fact is that these different people "are not saying, and cannot be saying, the same things: They each have very different realities to articulate, or control" (780).

A closer look at the etymology of "translate" reveals that Baldwin's use of the term recalls its history. The term has Latin origins in the prefix *trans,* meaning "across," and in the root words *latus,* meaning "to carry," and *ferre* (e.g., transfer), meaning "to bear," as in a burden or even a child (Claiborne 67, 243). Like Baldwin's use of the term, its history suggests experiential application. The earlier meaning—"to carry or bear something across"—conveys a sense of weight and distance not found in current standard usage. From this basis in experience, the sheer difficulty of the process, as well as the recognition of translation as *process,* with no fixed beginning or end, is also clarified. Baldwin's usage places a similar emphasis on process; however, unlike the traditional understanding of experience, his is decidedly internal. The result is that translation for Baldwin, rather than occurring across space or across languages, is always a movement from the inside out. Such is the case in *If Beale Street Could Talk.* The narrative itself, for example, by articulating the experiences of the oppressed black community, demonstrates the extent to which the journey *into* language, let alone *across* languages, is always already one of translation. Similarly, the instances in which the term is explicitly used within the novel, with regard to Fonny and Joseph, are also moments that demonstrate the difficulty, the heft, and the process of translation as a movement from latency to manifestation—both men are waiting for what is already known or felt to achieve external realization.

Baldwin's philosophy of translation, is even further distinguished from present and past uses of the term not only by his altered perceptions of language and experience but also by his similarly complex understanding of self. While traditional notions of translation (those past and present) imply that it is the result of individual agency, in *If Beale Street Could Talk* translation is always the result of a dialectical process with another. Not surprisingly, the two artists in the novel, Tish and Fonny, best exemplify this aspect of what is for Baldwin an aesthetically centered task. At the end of the novel, for example, Fonny denounces the title "artist" in favor of "artisan," a change indicative of Baldwin's aesthetic philosophy overall. Unlike an artist, in the Western sense, Fonny does not create art—he reveals it. His process is remarkably similar to that of ancient craftsmen, intended as purposeful and revelatory. Though the extent of Baldwin's interest in existentialist literature is unclear, his concept of art is strikingly similar to Martin Heidegger's. Heidegger, like Baldwin, was invested in transforming contemporary Western ways of being in the world. Like Baldwin, as well, Heidegger's focus was on revealing connections. Focusing particularly on modern technology's destructive, androcentric treatment of the natural world, Heidegger harkened back to the time of ancient Greece, when *technē* (ancient craftsmanship) was an interactive process between material and artist in which it was the craftsman's particular task to reveal the essence of the medium at hand, a process Heidegger termed "bringing-forth" (Heidegger 295). A closer examination of Fonny's artistry suggests a similar philosophy. Not only is his medium alive and "breathing," but Fonny envisions himself learning about his productions only as he releases them (64). Indeed, Fonny's role as revealer transforms into liberator after his own imprisonment. He dreams of working on a bust of Tish, "terrified" because his creation is tied to the medium. He must wait "for the wood to speak. Until it speaks, he cannot move. [Tish] is imprisoned somewhere in the silence of that wood, and so is he" (149). For Fonny, artistry is dialectical. As he translates or "brings-forth" the essence of the wood from latency to manifestation, he creates the means for his own liberation.

While Fonny is the only explicit artist in the novel, Tish is equally deserving of that title. Not only is she the narrator of the story, but she is also a prospective mother. Although pregnancy would not normally be construed as art, considering Baldwin's frequent association of his own work with childbirth (Leeming 325) as well as the etymological application of the Latin *ferre* to pregnancy, such an association is fitting in this case. Like Fonny's art, Tish's pregnancy is representative of the dialectical necessity for renewed life. Just as the latent essence of the wood and stone must be brought forth by the artist, so too Fonny and Tish's child depends on Tish to nurture and deliver him into the world. As with Fonny's artistry, translation, for Tish, requires recognition. In fact, it is worth noting that the novel, though centered on Tish's pregnancy, does not begin where it logically might—with conception or with Tish's personal discovery of her condition. Rather, it begins with the moment Tish first shares her knowledge, implying that Fonny and the family's acceptance and support are crucial not only to her but also to the health and future of her unborn child.

More than the pregnancy itself, Baldwin's narrative treatment thereof also emphasizes the critical role of another in the process of transformation. By ending the novel with the relentless cries of Fonny and Tish's newborn child, Baldwin leaves Fonny's prison narrative unresolved. Whether the child's cries imply anguish and the continuing struggle toward freedom or whether they serve to connect the birth of the child with the rebirth of Fonny, thereby suggesting his imminent release, is left undetermined. There is a reason, however, behind the novel's implicit question, which is that Baldwin alone cannot answer it. By the end, the central focus of the novel has been translated; the latency of the child, announced at the beginning of the novel and consciously carried throughout by Tish as a literal and symbolic burden, is made manifest. The next generation is delivered, and now it is up to them (Baldwin's readers in part) to recognize the translation that has occurred, to remember their histories and the burdens that were carried in their names, and to honor those memories with action.

In a time and a society where protest and progress were dominated by ideologies of power, Baldwin's belief in the dependence of translative reform on external recognition and understanding led him to reject such approaches in favor of a nearly antithetical, and seemingly oxymoronic, ideology of love. For Baldwin, love is a dynamic tool of recognition because it, like little else in life, can actually make us see differently. Upon falling in love, Baldwin writes, "the world changes then, and it changes forever. Because you love one human being, you see everyone else differently than you saw them before—perhaps I only mean to say that you begin to *see*." Ironically, some of the most important aspects of this newfound sight are located in blindness. Baldwin writes, for example, that love is powerful in part because people "do not fall in love according to color," which means that they cannot "on any level whatever, use color as a weapon" (*No Name* 365–366).

Similarly, in *If Beale Street Could Talk*, Tish's sense of perception is drastically altered and expanded when she falls in love with Fonny. Strikingly, what she sees is absence. In addition to viewing this land as a "kingdom of the blind," Tish is also able to see that beneath the masks worn by society is an institutionalized world devoid of love (23). She remembers the days spent in the city with her sister and her father when she was younger, eating "ice cream and hot dogs," as "great days," but now Tish says that she and

Ernestine felt happiness "because we knew our father loved us. Now, I can say, because I certainly know it now, the city didn't" (8). Tish's ability, now that she has found love, to see where love is not, reveals itself in church as well, where she and Fonny are awakened to the knowledge that they know who loves them and that "whoever loved [them] was not here" (22). The church, as a symbol of the institutional negation of true identity formation, reappears in other similarly loveless contexts. For example, walking into the prison where Fonny is kept, appropriately dubbed the "Tombs," is for Tish "just like walking into church" (22). Tish emphasizes the sterility, which is to say the lovelessness, of this image by comparing this same journey to the Sahara desert, where if you fall, "by and by vultures [will] circle around you, smelling, sensing, your death . . . They know exactly when the flesh is ready, when the spirit cannot fight back" (6).

Implicit here is the direct correlation between the absence of love and the absence of resistance. Concomitantly, the presence of love, in addition to invoking internal change, provides a powerful source for external reform. "Love" according to Baldwin is not "passive"; rather, it is "something active, something more like fire, like the wind, something which can change you"; it is "a passionate belief, a passionate knowledge of what a human being can do, and become, what a human being can do to change the world in which he finds himself" (qtd. in Standley and Pratt 48). In this light, the driving force of *If Beale Street Could Talk,* Tish's pregnancy, takes on further import as a unified symbol of translation and the productive and reproductive forces of love. Tish's pregnancy, like translation as a whole, is produced out of love. After Fonny's imprisonment, it is Tish's mother who reminds her of this fact: "You got that child beneath your heart and we're all counting on you, Fonny's counting on *you,* to bring that child here safe and well . . . remember, love brought you here. If you trusted love this far, don't panic now" (94). Without love, Tish would undoubtedly be tempted to abandon the arduous path of translative resistance; with love, there is no such option. Indeed, Tish appears to be a voice for Baldwin himself. Theirs is the work of the artist "trying to . . . bear witness to the endless possibilities of the human spirit," "always working in an utterly hostile climate" (qtd. in Standley and Pratt 186). Being an artist and engaging in this process of translation, for Baldwin, as for Tish, is never a choice because it is "an act of love" (187), and "if you do love somebody, you honor the necessity endlessly, and being at the mercy of that love, you try to correct the person whom you love" (155).

Love's productive capacity, therefore, is essential as a catalyst for translation, but it is love's ability to reproduce itself that allows first for communal recognition and ultimately for societal transformation. Tish's pregnancy embodies this crucial aspect of translative resistance as well. Though the child is the product of Tish and Fonny's love for each other as individuals, this type of productive translation, promising hope for the future, assuring that "what gets worse can also get better," transcends the interpersonal, inspiring familial and communal love, acceptance, and support (102). In *If Beale Street Could Talk,* the entire Rivers family, along with Fonny's father, are united by their loving recognition of the journey Tish and Fonny have begun toward a better future, and each family member contributes something invaluable to this process. While Ernestine uses her connections to locate a lawyer who will join them in their loving commitment to Fonny's liberation, Sharon transforms herself into a private investigator in an attempt to repair the damage done by a corrupt and perverse justice system. And all the while, Frank and Joseph work tirelessly to pay for the high price of such justice. In the end, whatever success Tish and Fonny gain is founded as much in familial strength as it is in personal endurance. Tish's continued visitations with Fonny in prison, for example, are more than a sign of her love for him; they are a sign that "others love him, too, love him so much that they have set [her] free to be there" (135).

As in *Beloved,* love in *If Beale Street Could Talk* has the invaluable capacity of "bearing witness" to circumstances removed from sight. In both novels, therefore, love produces the intersubjective recognition and commitment necessary for a promising future. However, in both novels, love is only as powerful as the philosophy that frames it. Within a Western construct, love, for Morrison, is "full of possession, distortion, and corruption" (qtd. in Standley and Pratt 162), and for Baldwin it is the equivalent of institutionalized desire. It is perverse, taking the form in *If Beale Street Could Talk* of the masturbatory and the ravishing. Consequently, for both authors, authentic and productive love is a liberating force. Unfortunately, escaping the Western frame and achieving this form of love also means altering African Americans' predominant mode of theoretical resistance. Morrison revises revision by advocating conditional love, a love that both occupies and transcends an ambiguous space, balanced between the literal and the figurative, the superficial and the profound. Baldwin, on the other hand, offers a subtly yet vastly different approach to revision, as he himself conceives it. For him the "form is the content" (*Perspectives* 115), and the extent to which society has established a distinction and, in fact, an opposition between surface and depth, external and internal, is precisely equivalent to the degree of its inauthenticity. This is not to say, however, that either Baldwin or Morrison offers a quintessential answer to the problems of revision. The value of their work arises, instead, from the possibilities they reveal. Indeed, both Morrison and Baldwin are attracted to love as a foundation for change because of its capacity to open the mind and the heart. Their goal is less didactic than it is emotional—theirs is a desire to engender desire.

WORK CITED

Awkward, Michael. *Inspiriting Influences: Tradition, Revision, and Afro-American Women's Novels.* New York: Columbia University Press, 1989.

Baker, Houston A., Jr. "Belief, Theory, and Blues: Notes for a Post-Structuralist Criticism of Afro-American Literature." In *African American Literary Theory: A Reader.* Ed. Winston Napier. New York: New York University Press, 2000. 224–241.

————. "The Embattled Craftsman: An Essay on James Baldwin." In *Critical Essays on James Baldwin.* Ed. Fred L. Standley and Nancy V. Burt. Boston: G. K. Hall, 1988. 62–77.

Baldwin, James. "The Creative Process." 1962. Rpt. in *Baldwin: Collected Essays.* Ed. Toni Morrison. New York: Library of America, 1998. 669–672.

————. "Everybody's Protest Novel." 1949. Rpt. in *Baldwin: Collected Essays.* Ed. Toni Morrison. New York: Library of America, 1998. 11–18.

————. *If Beale Street Could Talk.* New York: Dell, 1974.

————. "If Black English Isn't a Language, Then Tell Me, What Is?" 1979. Rpt. in *Baldwin: Collected Essays.* Ed. Toni Morrison. New York: Library of America, 1998. 780–783.

————. *No Name in the Street.* 1972. Rpt. in *Baldwin: Collected Essays.* Ed. Toni Morrison. New York: Library of America, 1998. 353–475.

———— et al. *Perspectives: Angles on African Art.* New York: Center for African Art and Harry N. Abrams, 1987.

————. "The White Man's Guilt." 1965. Rpt. in *Baldwin: Collected Essays.* Ed. Toni Morrison. New York: Library of America, 1998. 722–727.

Bloom, Harold. *Agon: Towards a Theory of Revisionism.* New York: Oxford University Press, 1982.

Christian, Barbara. *Black Women Novelists: The Development of a Tradition, 1892–1976.* Westport, CT: Greenwood Press, 1980.

————. "The Race for Theory." 1987. Rpt. in *African American Literary Theory: A Reader.* Ed. Winston Napier. New York: New York University Press, 2000. 280–289.

Claiborne, Robert. *The Roots of English: A Reader's Handbook of Word Origins.* New York: Times Books, 1989.

Gates, Henry Louis, Jr. *The Signifying Monkey: A Theory of African-American Literary Criticism.* New York: Oxford University Press, 1988.

Gilman, Sander L. "Black Bodies, White Bodies: Toward an Iconography of Female Sexuality in Late Nineteenth-Century Art, Medicine, and Literature." *"Race," Writing, and Difference.* Ed. Henry Louis Gates, Jr. Chicago: University of Chicago Press, 1986. 223–261.

Hammonds, Evelynn. "Black (W)holes and the Geometry of Black Female Sexuality." *Differences* 6, nos. 2–3 (1994): 126–145.

Heidegger, Martin. "The Question Concerning Technology." *Basic Writings.* Ed. David Farrell Krell. San Francisco: Harper San Francisco, 1977. 287–317.

Henderson, Mae Gwendolyn. "Speaking in Tongues: Dialogics, Dialectics, and the Black Woman Writer's Literary Tradition." In *Changing Our Own Words: Essays on Criticism, Theory, and Writing by Black Women*. Ed. Cheryl A. Wall. New Brunswick, NJ: Rutgers University Press, 1989. 16–37.

Holland, Norman N. "Report: Focus Group on Revisionism." *New Literary History* 29, no. 2 (1998): 173–196.

Homans, Margaret. "'Racial Composition' Metaphor and the Body in the Writing of Race." In *Female Subjects in Black and White: Race, Psychoanalysis, Feminism*. Ed. Elizabeth Abel, Barbara Christian, and Helene Moglen. Berkeley: University of California Press, 1997. 77–101.

Jablon, Madelyn. "Rememory, Dream Memory, and Revision in Toni Morrison's *Beloved* and Alice Walker's *The Temple of My Familiar*." *CLA Journal* 37, no. 2 (1993): 136–144.

Joyce, Joyce A. "The Black Canon: Reconstructing Black American Literary Criticism." *African American Literary Theory: A Reader*. Ed. Winston Napier. New York: New York University Press, 2000. 290–297.

Leeming, David. *James Baldwin: A Biography*. New York: Alfred A. Knopf, 1994.

McDowell, Deborah E. "New Directions for Black Feminist Criticism." In *African American Literary Theory: A Reader*. Ed. Winston Napier. New York: New York University Press, 2000. 167–178.

Morrison, Toni. *Beloved*. New York: Plume, 1987.

Nelson, Emmanuel S. "James Baldwin's Vision of Otherness and Community." In *Critical Essays on James Baldwin*. Ed. Fred L. Standley and Nancy V. Burt. Boston: G. K. Hall, 1988. 121–125.

Plasa, Carl, ed. *Columbia Critical Guides: Toni Morrison, "Beloved."* New York: Columbia University Press, 1998.

Rushdy, Ashraf H. A. "Daughters Signifyin(g) History: The Example of Toni Morrison's '*Beloved*.'" In *New Casebooks: Toni Morrison*. New York: St. Martin's Press, 1998. 140–153.

Schapiro, Barbara. "The Bonds of Love and the Boundaries of Self in Toni Morrison's *Beloved*." In *Understanding Toni Morrison's "Beloved" and "Sula": Selected Essays and Criticisms of the Works by the Nobel Prize-winning Author*. Ed. Solomon O. Iyasere and Marla W. Iyasere. Troy, NY: Whitston, 2000. 155–172.

Scott, Lynn Orilla. *Witness to the Journey: James Baldwin's Later Fiction*. East Lansing: Michigan State University Press, 2002.

Sitter, Deborah Ayer. "The Making of a Man: Dialogic Meaning in *Beloved*." In *Critical Essays on Toni Morrison's "Beloved."* Ed. Barbara H. Solomon. New York: G. K. Hall, 1998. 189–204.

Smith, Valerie. "Black Feminist Theory and the Representation of the 'Other.'" In *African American Literary Theory: A Reader*. Ed. Winston Napier. New York: New York University Press, 2000. 369–384.

Standley, Fred L., and Louis H. Pratt, eds. *Conversations with James Baldwin*. Jackson: University Press of Mississippi, 1989.

Stepto, Robert B. *From Behind the Veil: A Study of Afro-American Narrative*. 2nd ed. Chicago: University of Illinois Press, 1991.

Tamen, Miguel. "Phenomenology of the Ghost: Revision in Literary History." *New Literary History* 29, no. 2 (1998): 295–304.

Taylor-Guthrie, Danille, ed. *Conversations with Toni Morrison*. Jackson: University Press of Mississippi, 1994.

REVISING THE INCEST STORY: TONI MORRISON'S *THE BLUEST EYE* AND JAMES BALDWIN'S *JUST ABOVE MY HEAD*

LYNN ORILLA SCOTT

The great interdiction against incest
is an invention of the intellectuals.

Foucault (302)

When the act of incest is signified or engaged in, it
takes place in the context of a specific cultural setting,
so that a symbolic meaning is also at issue.

W. Arens (106)

Incest stories and incest themes have provided specific challenges and opportunities for African American writers, because incest has long been associated with the poor and with people of color. As Elizabeth Wilson has argued, the "official domestic ideology of the white middle class" is that "incest does not take place in the white middle class family; it is a vice of class and racial others who lack the rationality necessary to control their impulses. Suspicions that others engage in incestuous practices have long been part of the arsenal of moral prejudice that has been used to justify the social and political hegemony of the white middle class" (38).[1] Given this ideological function of incest discourse—to reinforce and justify white supremacy—one might suspect that African American writers concerned with the politics of racial representation have historically avoided the subject. Trudier Harris made this argument in her 1982 essay on Alice Walker's short story "The Child Who Favored Daughter." Harris claimed that the subject of "incest [in African American literature] is especially taboo" and that "the trend among black writers has been to leave the subject of incest alone" (495). Black writers who have treated the subject have done so with caution, "tiptoeing," so to speak. For example, she argues that in *The Bluest Eye* (1970), "the horror of [incest] is toned down" and that incest is only "a brief part of the novel" (496–497). The one exception that Harris finds to this tendency of African American writers to tiptoe through the subject of incest is James Baldwin's *Just Above My Head* (1979). She argues that "through his blatant treatment of incest, Baldwin moved into another realm of what black writers in this country have been willing to do" (497).[2]

More significant, however, than the issue of blatancy are the symbolic and ideological uses of incest stories and themes in African American writing. Indeed, a number of notable African American writers have *not* avoided the subject. In addition to *The Bluest Eye* and *Just Above My Head*, incest or incestlike relationships are important in the Trueblood episode of Ralph Ellison's *Invisible Man* (1952), in Maya Angelou's *I Know Why the Caged Bird Sings* (1970), in Gayl Jones' *Corregidora* (1975), in Alice Walker's *The Color Purple* (1982), in Carolivia Herron's *Thereafter Johnnie* (1991), and in Sapphire's *Push* (1996). In fact, one can argue that the incest story and theme has been a very important site for cultural interpretation and critical revision in novels by African American writers at least since the mid-twentieth century. The stories of father–daughter incest in *The Bluest Eye* and *Just Above My Head*, in particular, reveal the ideological uses to which incest stories have been put to mark subjects as racially and sexually other. The representation of incest in both novels contributes to what has been a significant shift in the discourse of incest and the incest taboo over the past thirty years. Furthermore, in his last novel, *Just Above My Head*, Baldwin revises key aspects of the incest story in Morrison's *The Bluest Eye*, published nine years earlier. Both Morrison and Baldwin explore ways in which a discourse of incest obscures other "tabooed" subjects that are, in fact, more "unspeakable" than incest. For Morrison that subject is racial self-loathing, and for Baldwin it is internalized homophobia.

Although *Just Above My Head* is unique in its dramatic representation of father–daughter incest, Baldwin had been using incest motifs throughout his writing.[3] In his work through the 1960s, one important function of the incest theme was to illustrate the illusion of racial and sexual boundaries. In a 1961 interview with Studs Terkel, Baldwin stated that

> no matter who says what, Negroes and whites in this country are related to each other. Half of the black families in the South are related, you know, to the judges and the lawyers and the white families of the South. They are cousins, and kissing cousins at that—at least kissing cousins. Now, this is a terrible depth of involvement. (rpt. in Standley and Pratt 7)

Here Baldwin points to the hidden history of interracial kinship. Southern whites' denial of their blood ties with Southern blacks becomes a metaphor for their denial of equal membership to blacks in the American nation and is key to Baldwin's understanding of American racism as a "family" problem. Thus, in Baldwin's fiction, the recognition of the hidden truth of incest or of incestlike relationships, or desires is a reoccurring motif that is often linked to a project of deconstructing racial (and gender) differences. Indeed, incestlike relationships carry a positive valence in most of Baldwin's fiction, where lovers are often described as being "like" brother and sister or "like" brother and brother. For example, in *Tell Me How Long the Train's Been Gone* (1968), the protagonist, Leo Proudhammer, and his lover, Barbara King, refer to themselves as brother and sister, connoting a relationship based on deep affection and equal partnership. Barbara, a white girl from a wealthy Kentucky family, falls in love with Leo, a bisexual, poor black boy from Harlem. Being aspiring young actors, both are acutely aware of the way in which American racial and sexual ideologies threaten to define and circumscribe their relationship. After confessing their love to each other, Barbara says to Leo, "Well I hope you like having a sister—a white, incestuous sister. Doesn't that sound like part of the American dream?" (211).

Baldwin's use of the incest motif to represent interracial love as key to interpreting the dreams (and nightmares) of American racial history signifies on the "longstanding tradition of fusing the representation of incest and miscegenation" in American literature and law (Sollors 287). Werner Sollors's study of interracial literature, *Neither Black Nor White Yet Both* (1997), is particularly useful in understanding the nineteenth-century discourse of race and incest that twentieth-century American writers such as Baldwin and Morrison have inherited. At first glance the conflation of incest and miscegenation seems illogical, since incest is extreme endogamy and miscegenation is extreme exogamy. Yet the sexual practices of some slave owners, as well as the laws that defined race and citizenship and prohibited black and white intermarriage, brought these apparently opposite concepts together as both historical fact and contested discourse. Sollors argues that the linked miscegenation/incest theme was used by a wide variety of authors with "heterogeneous ideological motives" (314). Pro-slavery and white supremacist writers identified both miscegenation and incest as forms of "blood sin." In this way they found "the perfect metaphor for expressing their horror" of interracial sexual alliances and a way to consolidate their own group consciousness (320). Literature by liberal antislavery writers made the less-metaphorical and more-"realistic" argument that unacknowledged miscegenation (particularly between the white slave master and his black slave) can lead to unwitting incest when the slave master's black and white offspring fall in love, not knowing they are siblings. Yet another group of novels written by white antislavery writers portrayed interracial sibling incest as a justifiable response to patriarchal tyranny. This group, according to Sollors, seems to argue on the basis of a universalist ideal of brotherhood that all human beings are siblings and that there is "no such thing as miscegenation, only a form of universal incest that is weakened, however, by being so universal. Sibling incest can thus be represented as the victory of revolutionary *fraternité* over the tyrannical father" (319). In much of his work, Baldwin seems to deploy incest themes in this last tradition. Sibling incest, in particular, becomes a metaphor for a universalist, humanist ideal that is associated with the breaking down of racial and gender hierarchies.

In *Just Above My Head,* however, Baldwin tells a brutal story of intraracial father-daughter incest, and in *Tell Me How Long the Train's Been Gone,* he makes a brief foray into the topic of intraracial incest by depicting Leo Proudhammer's sexual experience with his brother, Caleb.[4] Neither of these stories involves crossing racial boundaries, although the contexts of both suggest an investigation into the problems of African American identity formation within a racist society. On a rhetorical level, Baldwin continues to express a universalist theme: "Someone said that all love is incest," states the narrator of *Just Above My Head* (377). But his depiction of Joel Miller's rape of his daughter, Julia, suggests that his use of the incest story in his last novel departs from his earlier universalist theme and bears a signifyin(g) relationship to the work of two African American predecessors, Ralph Ellison and Toni Morrison.[5] Morrison's *The Bluest Eye* (1970) would prefigure a major shift in the discourse of incest, a shift from theorizing an incest taboo to documenting and interpreting the problem of father-daughter incest.

For much of the twentieth century, psychoanalytic, sociological, and anthropological disciplines theorized a universal incest taboo to explain the origins and functions of culture. This taboo was believed to "[set] in motion social and cultural systems" and "set humanity off from the animal world" (Arens 44). Violations of the taboo against incestuous acts were thought to be rare, but when they did occur, they were characterized as threatening social collapse and marking a descent into the nonhuman. However, by the early 1980s, most notably with the publication of Judith Herman's *Father-Daughter Incest* (1981), a major shift occurred in the discourse of incest. Through studies in feminist psychology and sociology, it was "discovered" that father-daughter incest, in particular, was neither rare nor a practice confined to the abnormal, the poor, or those deemed racially other. As a result, there was a shift in the discourse of incest from theorizing a supposedly universal incest taboo to disclosing the actual practice of incest as a significant social problem.[6] As violations of the incest taboo were discovered to be less uncommon than was previously believed, social scientists also began to recognize that the incest taboo is not universal and that the definition of incest and the prohibitions against marriage and sex between related individuals vary from one society to another. Moreover, it has been argued that the very obsession with theorizing a universal incest taboo was deeply implicated in masking the actual abusive practice of incest.[7] The feminist analysis of incest that emerged by the early 1980s reverses the notion that incest leads to social collapse and claims, instead, that father-daughter incest reflects and maintains patriarchal power.[8]

This shift in the sociological and philosophical interpretation of incest has its literary counterpart. The theory that a universal incest taboo is constitutive of human culture and that its violation brings about social collapse is evident in the genre of the (white) Southern romance (e.g., William Faulkner's *Absalom, Absalom!* [1936]), while the more recent genre of incest survivor stories (e.g., Dorothy Allison's *Bastard Out of Carolina* [1992]) reflects the feminist discourse of incest as an abusive practice that maintains patriarchy. Critics who have addressed the incest theme in Morrison's *The Bluest Eye* have generally read the novel in relationship to a feminist discourse of incest; yet, as I shall argue, the novel should also be understood in relationship to the discourse of the universal incest taboo, especially as that discourse constructed race and power.

The Bluest Eye has been given credit for enabling "the explosion of women's writing and speaking about incestuous abuse" that began in the late 1970s (Gwin 67). Critics Doane and Hodges read the novel as groundbreaking because it "made the incest narrative available to many other writers, such as white feminists, who use accounts of incest to articulate a history of subjugation" (331). Morrison's remarks during her appearance on the *The Oprah Winfrey Show* (2000) support this aspect of the book's reception: "A lot of white women write to me about *The Bluest Eye because of* the incest, a lot of white females who are interested in the book because of *that,* not the other level of meaning." But without diminishing the importance of the novel to subsequent narratives of incest, Morrison's comment also suggests that she does not see the book as primarily "about" incest. Moreover, the novel itself does not support a particularly feminist understanding of incest. Judith Herman views father-daughter incest as a "consequence of male socialization within the patriarchal family" (56), and she and other psychologists and case workers "have pointed to the 'normality' of the offenders, their families and their lives" (Bell 3). However, Cholly Breedlove, the incestuous father in *The Bluest Eye,* has had no such socialization. The novel represents father-daughter incest as a consequence of the disempowerment of the black male, who because of racism is not able to fulfill the role of father.[9] Morrison uses the incest story not to indict patriarchy, but to expose a system of racial othering in which the father is as much a victim as the daughter.[10] What

The Bluest Eye does share with a feminist discourse of incest is the idea that incest can produce power rather than bring about social collapse. And because incest is used in *The Bluest Eye* to show how racial hierarchies are established and maintained, the novel also signifies on the earlier representations of incest in the interracial literature that Sollors has described. *The Bluest Eye* rewrites the Southern romance in which incest brings about the social decay and destruction of a "white" family. In it, incest completes the destruction of a black family, while reconstituting a system of white hegemony.

Morrison demonstrates her engagement with the disciplinary power of incest discourse by the way she introduces the incest plot at the beginning of the novel as a site of interpretation, or, more to the point, as a site of misinterpretation. In the italicized preface to the novel, the narrator, Claudia McTeer, now grown up, says,

> Quiet as it's kept, there were no marigolds in the fall of 1941. We thought, at the time, that it was because Pecola was having her father's baby that the marigolds did not grow. A little examination and much less melancholy would have proved to us that our seeds were not the only ones that did not sprout; nobody's did. (5)

In this opening passage, Morrison deflates the explanatory power of the incest taboo and its violation. She signals her readers that they are not to interpret Cholly's rape of his daughter as the primary cause for natural and social dysfunction, or even for the destruction of Pecola herself. In order to interpret Pecola's destruction the novel asks that we understand the relationship between an ideology of white supremacy and a discourse of incest that promotes and maintains that ideology. Claudia makes this connection when she compares her and her sister's act of planting the marigolds to Cholly's act of impregnating his daughter. She says, "We had dropped our seeds in our own little plot of black dirt just as Pecola's father had dropped his seeds in his own plot of black dirt. Our innocence and faith were no more productive than his lust or despair" (5–6). By changing the signification of "black dirt" from a rich, growing medium to a racial slur, Claudia demonstrates how Pecola became the depository not only of her father's seed, but of a racist discourse that equates black skin with moral degeneracy. The community's act of scapegoating Pecola as a racial and moral other functions to maintain notions of white superiority and seriously compromises the "innocence and faith" of the girls wishing to grow flowers in black earth. Metaphorically joining Claudia's act with Cholly's, the narrator suggests the pervasive and unacknowledged damage caused by racism and implicates the larger community in the problem. The secret, signified by the opening phrase, "quiet as it's kept," becomes not the story of incest, which is, after all, known to the community and put to predictable use, but the story of racial self-loathing, a story more problematic and difficult to tell. The story of racial self-loathing is told through Pecola's quest for blue eyes, a quest that originates in the violation of Pecola's black body by a white gaze. The logic of Pecola's desire is undeniable, born as it is from the daily experience of being told directly and indirectly that her blackness makes her "ugly," unlovable. The white gaze is ubiquitous. It is in Rosemary Villanucci's "fascinated eyes in a dough-white face" (30). It is in the coveted Shirley Temple cup, in the "blue-eyed, yellow-haired, pink-skinned doll[s] that every girl child treasured" (20), and in the Mary Jane candy wrappers. It is in the distaste of the shopkeeper who does not want to touch Pecola's hand (49); in the group of black boys who circle Pecola and chant, "Black e mo. Back e mo. Yadaddsleepsnekked" (65); in the scream of the high yellow girl, Maureen Peal, "I am cute! And you ugly! Black and ugly" (73); in the words of Geraldine, "You nasty little black bitch. Get out of my house" (92). It is in the eyes of Pecola's mother, Pauline, who describes her newborn as "a right smart baby . . . But I knowed she was ugly. Head full of pretty hair, but Lord she was ugly" (126). And it is in the very device Morrison uses to structure the novel: the public school primer, the Dick and Jane Reader, which introduces Pecola to what it means to be part of a "normal" American family, circa 1944.

Metaphorically speaking, Pecola has been raped by "whiteness," long before her father enters her. The great irony of the father-daughter incest is that unlike the previous "rapes," the incest represents not just another violation but also an act of love. The actual incest scene occurs at the end of the chapter describing the father's life and is rendered entirely from the father's point of view. The reader views the father's act not as an assertion of power, but as the culmination of his tortured experiences with love and intimacy—experiences that in many respects parallel his daughter's. Cholly was abandoned from infancy by both of his parents, the grandmother who raises him dies when he is fourteen, his sexual initiation is marked by a humiliating encounter with white hunters who make him "perform" at gun point, and his search for his father ends in brutal rejection. Yet Cholly also falls in love with Pauline, Pecola's mother. Morrison makes it clear that while that relationship has deteriorated into grotesque violent encounters, it originated as a love match. Cholly's rape of his daughter is infused with his memory of the affection and tenderness he felt for Pauline. His motivations are contradictory. In the moments before the rape, as Cholly watches Pecola washing dishes in the kitchen, "the sequence of his emotions [is] revulsion, guilt, pity, then love" (161). "He want[s] to fuck her— tenderly" (163). At the end of the novel, the narrator says that Cholly "was the one who loved [Pecola] enough to touch her . . . . But his touch was

fatal" (206). Morrison ironically suggests that Cholly's incestuous act is the
one affirmation of her blackness that Pecola experiences. Incest, in this
novel, thus both reinforces and exposes the taboo of blackness.

While the narrator demands that we view Cholly's motives as hidden
and complex, the rape's effect on Pecola and the community's use of
the incest are predictable. For Pecola, "the damage done was total" (204).
Increasingly desperate to have blue eyes, she eventually loses her grip on
sanity, she becomes silent, speaking only to an imaginary friend, and haunts
the outskirts of town like "a winged but grounded bird" (204). The
rape/incest merely completes the dehumanizing and scapegoating of Pecola
that the reader has been viewing from the novel's opening pages, confirming for the community her status as an "other" marked by immorality, ugliness, and blackness. In this role she is useful to the community that not only
avoids her, but that also "[feels] so wholesome after we cleaned ourselves
on her" (205). By making the cause of Pecola's demise bigger than an act
of incest and by placing the responsibility for it beyond her father's act, the
novel exposes the way that a discourse of incest has been used to reinforce
a system of racial gazing. The incest makes Pecola a taboo figure in the
community, and as such, she is used to uphold a system of white dominance and black racial self-loathing that we understand to be the very cause
of the rape/incest in the first place. Thus, incest (and its taboo) circulates as
a form of social control.

The Bluest Eye allegorizes an idea that is central to Baldwin's work from
his early essay "Everybody's Protest Novel" (1949)—the idea that even
well-intentioned "protest" literature reifies racial oppression through a
"theology" of whiteness that denies the complexity of black experience,
demonizes darkness, and associates blackness with sin. By exposing the
damaging effects of internalizing white standards of beauty, The Bluest Eye
reveals what Baldwin had described as the hidden and unchallenged ideology of white supremacy at the core of protest fiction from Uncle Tom's
Cabin to Native Son. Yet in its very affirmation of his idea, The Bluest Eye
must have given Baldwin pause. The unrelenting destruction of Pecola
gives Morrison's novel a determinism that Baldwin resisted throughout his
own work. In addition, Baldwin often objected to depictions of black characters as either victims or monsters. While Morrison carefully avoids
depicting Cholly as a monster, she makes Pecola one of the most poignant
victims in all of American literature. The mixture of admiration and reser-
vation that Baldwin had for Morrison's work is captured in his last interview with Quincy Troupe, where he refers to Morrison as a writer whose
"gift is allegory" and who is "very painful to read . . . because it's always,
or most times, a horrifying allegory; but you recognize that it works. But
you don't really want to march through it. Sometimes people have a

lot against Toni, but she's got the most believing story of everybody" (Troupe 203).

As mentioned earlier, the depiction of father-daughter incest in *Just Above My Head* marks a departure from Baldwin's typical use of the incest motif to suggest themes of kinship and universal brotherhood. Given Baldwin's engagement with Morrison's work, it is appropriate to read the incest story of Baldwin's last novel as a revisionary response to the "horrifying allegory" of *The Bluest Eye*. While in Morrison's novel the force of allegory creates a unified vision of a destructive social order, Baldwin's capacious book (over 550 pages) seems to open up that vision, suggesting different possible outcomes for the character of the incest victim, as well as different uses of the incest story, in a novel that probes identity formation in a hostile (read "racist" and "homophobic") environment. Baldwin's revision occurs on a number of levels, including characterization, theme, and symbol, all of which are intertwined.

In both novels, the incested daughter's experience is tied to the theme of African American identity formation. In many respects Baldwin's powerful and articulate Julia Miller is drawn in stark contrast to the whipped Pecola Breedlove; however, as children, both characters are responding to the cultural conditions of black life in the 1940s. They come of age before the black power movement and its articulation that black was beautiful, and before the era of identity politics. Julia Miller's religious conversion at nine years of age to a fundamentalist Christian theology is Baldwin's narrative equivalent to Pecola Breedlove's desire for blue eyes. Both are flawed quests for acceptance that reinforce the values of a dominant white culture equating blackness with that which is ugly or sinful. Both quests are born from personal deprivation and rooted in family relationships that have been damaged by poverty and racism. Like Pecola, Julia is emotionally abandoned by her parents as a young child and sees in her role as child preacher a way to keep her parents together and secure their love. In direct contrast to Pecola, however, Julia Miller is a survivor who eventually becomes stronger and wiser because of her suffering. After her father rapes her, Julia "[falls] into a silence far more real than the silence of a grave" (172); but unlike the fatally damaged Pecola, who remains silenced and who flails "like a winged but grounded bird" in a "grotesquely futile effort to fly" (204), Julia, the phoenix, "recover[s] with astonishing speed" (336). From child preacher to adult "obeah" woman, it is Julia's *voice* rather than her silence that characterizes her central role in the novel.

Both novels are retrospective and span a generation beginning and ending in the period following the civil rights and black power movements. In *The Bluest Eye*, Claudia's ability to interpret Pecola's life develops as a result of the social changes that have occurred; yet Pecola's life is truncated, frozen in time. In *Just Above My Head,* Julia's life is represented within a changing social context and is described as a long journey toward coherence (523). Part of that journey takes her to Africa in search of a new racial and gender identity. In an effort to "undo" the emotional and physical damage that her father has caused her, Julia meets and marries an African tribal leader who is old enough to be her father, but who is "black in a way [her] father never was" (527). Julia's search for a black father is thus figured as another type of incest; she has "walk[ed] out of one trap into another" (527). While in Africa, she discovers "another definition of what it meant to be a woman, and especially a black woman [,] . . . [but] it did not appear to be a role that she could play" (504). Moreover, Julia, who is sterile because of a miscarriage induced by her father, discovers that "not even Africa had been able to make her fertile" (504–505). Here Baldwin criticizes an overly romanticized view of Africa as the motherland for black Americans. Through Julia's unsuccessful journey to Africa, he shows his distance from some elements of the black power movement that viewed black identity in essentialist terms. Julia's experience suggests that individual identity exceeds racial and national categories. Africa does, however, become an important part of Julia's journey toward coherence. Her African American identity is symbolized near the beginning of the novel, when she is described as living in a white suburb of New York in a home that is adorned with "genuine African sculpture," including a "wooden African deity" (35, 38). Barbecuing in her backyard, she wears "a vaguely African robe" and "one talismanic bronze earring" (34). Thus, Julia's African journey becomes a part of her complex and evolving identity from child (Christian) preacher to adult (African) "griot."

It can be argued that Baldwin presents the incest story more realistically and less allegorically than Morrison, because he suggests both psychological and economic causes for the incestuous relationship that develops between Julia and her father, Joel. Joel expects Julia to support and serve him, while Julia's mother, Amy, believes that her daughter has a direct link to God. Both of Julia's parents are responsible for reversing the normal parent-child relationship. "You both scared of that child. And you both done let something happen to that child—that ain't supposed to happen to a child," says Paul Montana, the narrator's father (127). Hall Montana says that "without Julia's notoriety, and her earning power Brother Joel Miller would have long ago split the scene . . . [for] Joel did not love his wife so much as he loved his daughter because she put bread on the table" (102). Joel abdicates parental authority, allowing Julia to make disastrous decisions for the family. Believing in her divine powers to heal, Julia refuses to let Amy, who is dying of cancer, see a doctor. On her deathbed, Amy, now disillusioned, "looks at her daughter . . . with something very close to hatred" (166), accuses her of fakery, and tells her that the only way she will "get the Lord's forgiveness" is if she takes care of her brother, Jimmy (167). Shortly after his wife's death, Joel rapes his fourteen-year-old daughter when she refuses to return to the pulpit to support him. In *Just Above My Head* rape/incest is depicted not as a tortured expression of love, as it is in Morrison's novel, but as the father's crass exploitation of the daughter—economically, emotionally, and finally, sexually. In what appears to be a signifying move on the narrator's claim at the end of *The Bluest Eye* that Cholly loved Pecola (206), Baldwin has Joel try to justify his behavior by saying, "Love is a beautiful thing, darling; something in every man, I believe, wants to turn his daughter into a woman" (171). While the narrator of *The Bluest Eye* concludes that "love is never better than the lover" (206), Baldwin, through his character's jiving language, insists that some things are not love.

Baldwin reframes the question of the incestuous father's guilt and responsibility. As argued earlier, the narrator of *The Bluest Eye* presents Cholly's act of incest as a consequence of his own victimization and complex experiences. While Morrison is not trying to "excuse" Cholly's behavior, she is trying, as she explains in her "afterword," "to avoid complicity in the demonization process Pecola was subjected to" by "not . . . dehumaniz[ing] the characters who trashed Pecola" (211). In fact, Cholly, the outlaw, the "dangerously free" man, gains an almost tragic aura in *The Bluest Eye* (159).[11] Baldwin's Joel Miller, on the other hand, is more pathetic than tragic or romantic. Probably the most unsympathetic male character in all of Baldwin's fiction, Joel is depicted as a selfish and weak man who has seriously deceived himself. Significantly, Baldwin puts Joel's defense not into the voice of an omniscient narrator (as Morrison does with Cholly), but into the words of the incested daughter, whose point of view is "corrected" by the narrator. Several years after the incest/rape, Julia asks Hall if he has seen her father, who seems to have disappeared. She goes on to say that she does not "have anything against him. Nothing at all" (346). She worries that he is "alone and afraid." She goes on to claim, "He's not the only guilty party!" (347). Hall responds firmly: "He *is* the guilty party. That's why you ain't heard from him. *You* can't take on his responsibility. How you going to take on a responsibility when there wasn't no possible way for you to have *understood* it, or even to know what a responsibility was? And you going to try to assume all that now?" (347; emphasis in original). By bracketing Morrison's "defense"of Cholly in this way, Baldwin reopens the question of guilt and responsibility that Claudia probes from the beginning to the end of *The Bluest Eye*. While Claudia concludes that "it [Pecola's demise] was the fault of the earth, the land, of our town" (206), Baldwin seems to place responsibility on the shoulders of the incestuous father and views the community's response to incest in less totalizing terms. Unlike Pecola, Julia does receive support and compassion, especially from the Montana family.[12]

Baldwin's purpose in revising the figures of the incested daughter and incestuous father, however, goes beyond empowering the victim and holding the victimizer responsible. Like Morrison, Baldwin uses a father-daughter incest story as a site of interpretation for a subject more "tabooed" than incest. In spite of her prominence in *Just Above My Head*, Julia Miller is not the stated focus of Hall Montana's narrative. Rather it is Arthur Montana, the narrator's homosexual brother, who has died alone in a men's room in a London pub two years before Hall's narrative begins. Arthur's position in the novel as an other, despised for his homosexuality, substitutes for the position of Pecola, who is despised for her blackness in Morrison's novel. This substitution allows Baldwin to shift the symbolic significance of the incest story. Playing on the idea of incest as the ultimate taboo, both Morrison and Baldwin use a father-daughter incest story symbolically as a site of interpretation for what they view as a subject less representable than incest. In Baldwin's case, however, the less-representable subject is not racial self-loathing, but homophobia within the (black) family and community.[13] In a key revision of Morrison's text, Baldwin uses the story of father-daughter incest as a foil for a story of black male homosexual love. This move challenges the taboo against homosexuality and suggests that homosexuality remains a less-tellable tale than father-daughter incest, a thesis supported not only by Julia's survival, but also by her prominent role in the narrative, which appears at times to displace that of the subject, Arthur Montana. Thus, on a metafictional level, *Just Above My Head* suggests the way in which incest stories maintain a heteronormative ideology and cast homosexuality as other or abnormal.

Julia Miller represents the very idea of incest in its Freudian psychoanalytic formulation as a universal (always heterosexual) desire of the child toward the parent of the opposite sex, a desire that is repressed by a universal taboo against incestuous behavior. In this formulation, homosexuality is explained as the abnormal outcome of an unresolved Oedipus complex. In Hall's narrative, Julia becomes the displaced object of his Oedipal desire (a point made explicit when Hall, while making love to Julia, says, "All love is incest" [377]). Hall's strongly ambivalent feelings toward Julia and his view of her as powerful, mysterious, and intimately connected with his destiny suggest Julia's symbolic role. She has the status of an ancient tragic heroine who inspires horror, love and pity in Hall (130). Hall depicts Julia as a timeless figure of preternatural power. As a child preacher, Julia is described as a "witch," "a sorceress," an "adolescent high priestess" (70, 105). Although Julia is thirty-nine years old at the present time of the novel, Hall says, "If she looked her real age, whatever it is, she'd turn to dust" (34). Julia is the vehicle through which Hall achieves his (heterosexual) manhood as he comes to understand his relationship with her as preparation for his marriage to Ruth and a life of domestic happiness. Hall says, "Julia was a part of me, forever; and, precisely because she was a part of me, she was part of a mystery I would never unlock" (527). Julia is the nexus of relationships between the novel's two central families, the Millers and the Montanas. She is "sister," "lover," "daughter," and, for the homosexual Arthur, a sexual competitor. At one point she becomes the female lover of Arthur Montana's first homosexual lover, Crunch. Later she becomes Hall Montana's lover, and she is the sister of Arthur's long-time lover, Jimmy Miller. Hall's mother treats Julia as if she were a daughter coming to her rescue after Julia's father almost kills her in a drunken, jealous rage. Thus, given Julia's central and symbolic role, it is not surprising that Hall Montana relies on her to help him remember and interpret Arthur's story. It is in Julia's house—symbolically, the house of the heteronormative narrative—that the novel begins as Hall starts to speak about his brother to his wife and children.

Yet if Julia seems to represent a psychoanalytic formulation of incest as desire and taboo (especially in her relationship with the narrator), Baldwin's depiction of her as an exploited daughter undercuts this symbolic role and thus calls into question Freud's theory of incest as a foundational discourse. A striking image early in the novel demonstrates that while Julia sincerely believes in her powers of (religious) interpretation, her position and her authority are, in fact, inauthentic. As a child preacher, Julia is carried around by her father and placed on a special collapsible platform that he has constructed. The platform "makes her appearance in the pulpit seem mystical" (70). This deus ex machina image links Julia to the gods of Greek tragedy (and thus to the source and name of Freud's incest theory), while at the same time exposing her performance as staged by her father, whom Hall suspects of "jiving the public" (69). Baldwin elevates the figure of the incested daughter to mythical proportions, but the irony is unmistakable. Her authority is clearly not divine; rather it is manipulated by her earthly father for his selfish gain. On a symbolic level, Baldwin may be calling into question the very formulation of the Oedipus (Electra) complex—suggesting that the psychoanalytic discourse of incest as desire and taboo is a patriarchal construction, a collapsible platform, built to serve the father.

Hall Montana sets out to tell the story of his dead homosexual brother, Arthur Montana, whom he loved, but whose life made him so uncomfortable that he was unable to mourn his brother's death or talk about him to his family for two years; however, Julia's story of surviving incest takes center stage in Hall's long narrative, both framing and eclipsing Arthur's story. Why are these two stories side by side, and what is their relationship to each other? To the extent that Julia's story appears to displace Arthur's, Baldwin's novel gives narrative form to Judith Butler's argument that heterosexuality is created by the incest taboo and that a taboo against incest implies a prior taboo against homosexuality:

> Although Freud does not explicitly argue in its favor, it would appear that the taboo against homosexuality must precede the heterosexual incest taboo; the taboo against homosexuality in effect creates the heterosexual "disposition" by which the Oedipal conflict becomes possible . . . The dispositions that Freud assumes to be primary or constitutive facts of sexual life are effects of a law which, internalized, produces and regulates discrete gender identity and heterosexuality.
>
> Far from foundational, these dispositions are the result of a process whose aim is to disguise its own genealogy. In other words, "dispositions" are traces of a history of enforced sexual prohibitions which is untold and which the-prohibitions seek to render untellable. (Butler 64)

By framing the story of a homosexual male with the story of an incested daughter, the very form of *Just Above My Head* suggests the difficulty of representing the homosexual's story outside of a heteronormative framework.

Even Arthur comes to interpret his situation as a homosexual through Julia's incest story. Arthur's first homosexual love affair runs parallel to Julia's incestuous relationship with her father. Both Julia and Arthur are adolescents (fourteen and sixteen years old, respectively) who are keeping their tabooed sexual relationships secret. Their secrets create a bond of suffering. When Arthur looks at Julia, even before he knows her story, he feels that he is "staring, in a way, into his mirror" (227). Yet Arthur's identification with Julia is problematic, because Arthur's and Julia's situations are only parallel in terms of the social judgment that the two face, a judgment that silences and shames them. The love affair between Arthur and Crunch is mutual, passionate, and caring—quite the opposite of Julia's desperate situation with her father. By paralleling Arthur's and Julia's stories, Baldwin shows the lack of equivalence between the socially tabooed behaviors of incest and homosexuality. In this novel, therefore, homosexuality as an act of love is sharply juxtaposed with incest as an act of exploitation and abuse. Through this juxtaposition Baldwin challenges the moral basis for the taboo against homosexuality. The fact that Arthur finds his "mirror" in Julia's situation suggests the problem of representing homosexuality within a (heterosexual) discourse that condemns it. Furthermore, Arthur's absence from the novel, his death in contrast to Julia's survival, and the gaps in his story as told by a heterosexual brother who is clearly struggling to understand Arthur's homosexuality, all point to the problem of representation when the story of homosexual manhood is reflected through a heteronormative narrative structure.

Baldwin makes this problem explicit near the end of the novel, when he switches the point of view to a character who bears his own name. Unable to answer questions about his brother's death, Hall turns the story over to Arthur's lover, saying, "Perhaps I must now do what I have most feared to do: surrender my brother to Jimmy, give Jimmy's piano the ultimate solo" (550). Jimmy's words provide unequivocal testimony to the homophobia that threatened their relationship and destroyed Arthur:

> I am scared, and I'd like to be safe, and nobody likes being despised. And, quiet as it's kept, you can't bear for anyone you love to be despised. I can't break faith with Arthur, I can't ride and hide away somewhere, and treat my love, and let the world treat my lover, like shit. I really cannot do that. And the world doesn't have any morality. Look at the world. What the world calls morality is nothing but the dream of safety. That's how the world gets to be so fucking moral. The only way to know that you are safe is to see somebody else in danger—otherwise you can't be sure you're safe. (551)

In this passage, Baldwin, speaking through Jimmy, echoes and revises *The Bluest Eye's* rhetoric and thematic concerns. The phrase "quiet as it's kept" opens Morrison's novel, making her readers privy to a "secret" that, as I have argued, is hidden by a discourse of incest. The real secret in Morrison's novel is that of a community's complicity in racial self-loathing. By repeating the phrase "quiet as it's kept" toward the conclusion of *Just Above My Head*, Baldwin signifies on Morrison's project, but changes the focus from racial self-loathing to internalized homophobia. Both authors indict the "moral" discourses that create outsiders and victims. Jimmy speaks for the "despised" Arthur as Claudia speaks for Pecola. In doing so, both Jimmy and Claudia charge the other characters, and by extension the readers, with unacknowledged complicity in Arthur's death and Pecola's destruction. Complicity for both authors occurs when one's sense of well-being requires a scapegoat. Jimmy's statement, "The only way to know that you are safe is to see somebody else in danger," reformulates Claudia's words near the end of *The Bluest Eye*: "All of our waste which we dumped on her and which she absorbed. And all of our beauty, which was hers first and which she gave to us. All of us—all who knew her—felt so wholesome after we cleaned ourselves on her" (205). Significant in Baldwin's reformulation, however, is the difference in pronouns. Through her use of the first-person plural (us/we), Morrison's narrator, Claudia, includes herself in the indictment she makes of her community's role in destroying Pecola. Thus, while Claudia holds herself partially responsible for Pecola's fate, by figuring herself inside the community that destroyed Pecola, she also reveals her distance from it. However, in *Just Above My Head*, Jimmy uses the first-person singular and the second-person "you," metaphorically maintaining a point outside of the novel—that is, Hall's narrative—from which to indict others of homophobia and reveal his identification with the "despised" subject, Arthur ("I am scared"). Jimmy's words expose the heteronormative nature of Hall's narrative when he explicitly says to Hall, "And you, too, motherfucker, you!" (553), thus including Hall in the long list of people whom Arthur feared he had shamed. By contextualizing Hall's narrative voice through Jimmy's brief "solo," Baldwin points to the potential complicity of narrative itself in reconstituting the very systems of racial and sexual gazing that it may seek to disrupt, a move that critiques the ("horrifying") allegorical mode of *The Bluest Eye*.

In conclusion both *The Bluest Eye* and *Just Above My Head* expose the ideological uses of incest stories to normalize cultural scripts about race and sex and to render other subjects and stories "unspeakable." Claudia McTeer puzzles over what destroyed Pecola and who was responsible. "The *Thing* to fear," says Claudia, "was the *Thing* that made *her* [the light-skinned Maureen Peals of the world] beautiful and not us" (74; emphasis in the original). The unnameable "thing" is the total force of cultural assumption that links beauty to being white, an assumption that maintains white power and is enforced by the attitudes and actions of the white and black communities. These racial attitudes are exposed in the novel through the scapegoating of an incested African American daughter, who becomes the vehicle through which the community denies its own racial self-loathing. In *Just Above My Head* Jimmy, Arthur's lover, promises to tell Hall about "whatever had hurt us so. Whatever had smashed him" (55). The unnameable "whatever" is the force of the cultural assumption that homosexuality is an abnormal and illicit expression of love. The way in which this assumption is maintained and hidden through a psychoanalytic discourse of incest as desire and taboo is given form in the story of an incested African American daughter as told by a heterosexual African American son.

NOTES

1. Such classist and racist assumptions about where incest occurs continued to be reflected in sociological and psychological research through the end of the 1970s. According to Elizabeth Wilson, however, recent research has not confirmed these prejudices, and "while it may be premature to say that incest is actually more prevalent in the white middle class than in other class or racial groups, it does seem that incest in the middle class is no less prevalent than it is elsewhere" (41).

2. Harris is not alone in characterizing incest as a particularly taboo topic for African American writers, who are afraid of confirming white stereotypes and alienating black readership. In the introduction to her *Crossing the Boundary: Black Women Survive Incest* (1993), journalist Melba Wilson says:

> The fear that I have about saying this publicly is considerable. I worry that this book will be misconstrued and misinterpreted by many in our black communities. Some may feel that I have breached an even greater taboo, crossed a bigger boundary (in their eyes) than incest. By airing publicly some of the uncool stuff that goes on in our communities, I and the other women whose stories are included are exposing the dirty linen that we all know and keep quiet about. (1)

3. Trudier Harris has written about the frequency of incestuous overtones in Baldwin's fiction. See her *Black Women in the Fiction of James Baldwin* (1985) (esp. 193–200). She views *Just Above My Head* as the culmination of Baldwin's thesis about "incestuous biological and extended family relationships," pointing out that "Julia's and Joel's relationship is the only one in the novel that fits the definition of incest as sexual contact between blood relatives; practically every other relationship in the novel, though, is 'incestuous'" (193).

4. For a discussion of the significance of the incestuous relationship between Caleb and Leo in *Tell Me How Long the Train's Been Gone*, especially for Leo's transition to manhood and for Baldwin's implicit criticism of both the homophobia of the black nationalist movement and mainstream cultural, psychological, and literary discourses on homosexuality of the time, see Lynn Orilla Scott's *James Baldwin's Later Fiction: Witness to the Journey* (2002) (58–61).

5. It is not in the purview of this essay to trace the intertextual relationship between Morrison's and Ellison's incest stories, which has been done most notably by Michael Awkward in "Roadblocks and Relatives: Critical Revision in Toni Morrison's *The Bluest Eye*" (1988) Awkward notes the "parodic relation" in the names of the incestuous fathers, Trueblood and Breedlove, and argues that Morrison provides a feminist revision of the Trueblood episode:

> So while the victims of incest in both novels ultimately occupy similarly asocial, silent positions in their respective communities, Morrison explicitly details Pecola's tragic and painful journey, while Ellison in confining Matty Lou to the periphery, suggests that her perspective contains for him 'no compelling significance. (66)

To extend Awkward's reasoning to Baldwin's text, one could argue a further feminist progression. Baldwin's incest victim does not occupy a silent or asocial position; on the contrary she becomes an important voice in the text. A preacher, turned griot, she is the source of much of the narrator's understanding.

Janice Doane and Devon Hodges also see Morrison as revising Ellison's story, particularly in her depiction of Cholly's humiliation by the white hunters. In contrast to Trueblood, "the novel's narration of the white men's voyeuristic pleasure at compelling Cholly's sexual performance makes it clear that Cholly is not rewarded for providing this entertainment, but rather disabled and disempowered. In this way, Morrison makes the black perpetrator's story less assimilable to white pleasure and even more linked to the abused victim than is Trueblood's" (43).

In exploring the intertextual relationship between Baldwin's and Morrison's incest stories, it is clear that Ellison's story is the common ancestor.

6. In *Interrogating Incest: Feminism, Foucault and the Law* (1993), Vikki Bell discusses the changes that occurred in the 1980s in regard to incest discourse:

> Over the past decade or so, many media discussions have highlighted the issue, and in the academic arena social science no longer proffers theories of the incest prohibition. Where incest is discussed it tends to be as a social problem . . . Thus incest seems to have changed or be in the process of changing discourse within social science. It no longer finds its place as a social rule requiring explanation as to its origin and function, but has been identified as an abusive practice, located as a social problem to be uncovered and measured. (2)

7. In *The Original Sin: Incest and Its Meanings* (1986), W. Arens argues that "the very concept [of an incest taboo] is culture-bound" (5–6) and that the "massive amount of attention paid . . . to the [putative] incest taboo has meant a denial of incest. Thought has been controlled by discourse" (4). In direct contrast to the formulations of Freud and Levi-Strauss, Arens argues that humans innately outbreed and avoid incest, but social arrangements can countermand incest avoidance; "The occurrence of incest is cultural in origin, rather than an expression of our animal nature or primal heritage" (152).

8. See Vikki Bell's discussion of the ways in which feminism reversed commonly held ideas about incest and social order. "Sociologists and anthropologists have traditionally regarded incest as disruptive of the family and as, therefore, disruptive of social order. By contrast feminism has suggested that, paradoxical as it may seem, incest is actually reproduced and maintained by social order: the order of a male-dominated society" (57).

9. Also see Morrison's discussion of Cholly in her 1977 interview with Jane Bakerman:

> In *The Bluest Eye*, Cholly, Pecola's father, is a broken man chained by poverty and circumstance, so "he might love her in the worst of all possible ways because he can't do this and he can't do that. He can't do it normally, healthily and so on. So it might end up this way [in the rape]. I want here to talk about how painful it is and what the painful consequences are of distortion, of love that isn't fructified, is held in, not expressed." (rpt. in Taylor-Guthrie 41)

10. Minrose Gwin also understands Cholly's rape of Pecola as a consequence of "race and class disempowerment" (75). However, in Gwin's reading whiteness becomes a metaphor for patriarchy. "We see the force field of whiteness exert itself in the black community. In this sense whiteness becomes the abusive father" (78). She argues that the novel is about the power dynamics of incest, while I am arguing that *The Bluest Eye* is about the power dynamics of racism and the way in which incest is read as a form of social and racial control.

11. I am thinking of the eloquent passage that immediately precedes the rape, where Morrison summarizes Cholly's life, a life so full of pain and complexity that it "could become coherent only in the head of a musician" (159). Here Cholly becomes the very embodiment of the black blues life.

12. The community response to incest is important to thematic development in both novels. In *The Bluest Eye,* the incest solidifies Pecola's role as a scapegoat for the community's own racial self-loathing. Baldwin, on the other hand, represents a variety of responses to Julia's incestuous relationship with her father in *Just Above My Head.* After the "accident," Julia goes to New Orleans to live with her grandmother and brother. There she is treated, like Pecola, with "brooding distrustful curiosity . . . It was as though she had been marked by the devil" (344). In New York, among those who don't know Julia and her father, the incest story is denied altogether. Joel's story— that he beat Julia because she had been turning tricks with white men—is "the one that got sold "(299).But for the Montanas and others who know Julia, the incest is a "revelation," threatening their gender identity and calling into question their notions of womanhood and manhood. Mama Montana and Hall's girl friend, Martha, are "appalled by Julia's bloody passage into womanhood. Their eyes were all fixed on something which, perhaps, no man could see" (317). Hall says that Joel "appalled the man in me, he made me sick with shame" (317), and for Jimmy, his father's treatment of his sister "made his manhood an embattled, a bloodstained thing" (342). Through these responses, Baldwin does repeat Morrison's theme of the incest victim as social scapegoat but, more importantly to his novel, he develops a connection between incest and a painful initiation into gender identity.

13. In his first novel, *Go Tell It on the Mountain* (1953), Baldwin explores the theme of racial self-loathing through the character of Gabriel Grimes, who embraces the values of a flesh- and sex-denying Christianity. Homosexuality is a subtext of this first novel, but it's not until *Just Above My Head* that Baldwin explicitly explores the experience of a black homosexual character within his family and community. Significantly, Baldwin gives Arthur, the homosexual son, a family that is not ambivalent about its racial identity. The father, Paul, a blues performer, identifies with a cultural and historical black experience. Thus, Baldwin seems to carefully separate the problem of racial self-loathing from the problem of homophobia: even within this "ideal" black family, Arthur suffers from internalized homophobia.

WORKS CITED

Arens, W. *The Original Sin: Incest and Its Meaning*. New York: Oxford University Press, 1986.

Awkward, Michael. "Roadblocks and Relatives: Critical Revision in Toni Morrison's *The Bluest Eye*." In *Critical Essays on Toni Morrison*. Ed. Nellie Y. McKay. Boston: G.K. Hall, 1988. 57–67.

Baldwin, James. "Everybody's Protest Novel." 1949. In *Notes of a Native Son*. Boston: Beacon Press, 1955. 13–23. 1984 edition.

————. *Just Above My Head*. New York: Dell. 1979. Laurel ed., 1990.

————. *Tell Me How Long the Train's Been Gone*. New York: Dell, 1968.

Bell, Vikki. *Interrogating Incest: Feminism Foucault and the Law*. London: Routledge, 1993.

Butler, Judith. *Gender Trouble: Feminism and the Subversion of Identity*. New York: Routledge, 1990.

Doane, Janice, and Devon Hodges. *Telling Incest: Narratives of Dangerous Remembering from Stein to Sapphire*. Ann Arbor: University of Michigan Press, 2001.

Foucault, Michel. *Politics, Philosophy, Culture: Interviews and Other Writings, 1977–1984*. Trans. Alan Sheridan and others. Ed. Lawrence D. Kritzman. New York: Routledge, 1988.

Gwin, Minrose C. *The Woman in the Red Dress: Gender, Space, and Reading*. Urbana: University of Illinois Press, 2002.

Harris, Trudier. *Black Women in the Fiction of James Baldwin*. Knoxville: University of Tennessee Press, 1985.

————. "Tiptoeing Through Taboo: Incest in the 'Child Who Favored Daughter.'" *Modern Fiction Studies* 28, no.3 (1982): 495–505.

Herman, Judith Lewis with Lisa Hirschman. *Father-Daughter Incest*. Cambridge, MA: Harvard University Press, 1981.

Morrison, Toni. *The Bluest Eye*. New York: Penguin, 1970. Plume Ed. 1994.

————. Discussion with Oprah Winfrey. "Oprah's Book Club." *The Oprah Winfrey Show*, ABC 53, May 26, 2000.

Scott, Lynn Orilla. *James Baldwin's Later Fiction: Witness to the Journey*. East Lansing, MI: Michigan State University Press, 2002.

Sollors, Werner. *Neither Black Nor White Yet Both: Thematic Explorations of Interracial Literature*. New York: Oxford University Press, 1997.

Standley, Fred L. and Louis H. Pratt. *Conversations with James Baldwin*. Jackson: University Press of Mississippi, 1989.

Taylor-Guthrie, Danille, ed. *Conversations with Toni Morrison*. Jackson: University Press of Mississippi, 1994.

Troupe, Quincy, ed. *James Baldwin: The Legacy*. New York: Simon and Schuster/Touchstone, 1989.

Wilson, Elizabeth. "Not in This House: Incest, Denial, and Doubt in the White Middle Class Family." *Yale Journal of Criticism* 8 (1995): 35–58.

Wilson, Melba. *Crossing the Boundary: Black Women Survive Incest*. London: Virago, 1993.

WATCHERS WATCHING WATCHERS: POSITIONING CHARACTERS AND READERS IN BALDWIN'S "SONNY'S BLUES" AND MORRISON'S "RECITATIF"

TRUDIER HARRIS

In James Baldwin's "Sonny's Blues" (1957),[1] Sonny's mother narrates a story about the death of Sonny's uncle. She tells the story to Sonny's brother, the unnamed narrator, in an effort to stress to him the importance of "being there" for Sonny. In a rural area in some unidentified southern state, Sonny's father and uncle had gone to a dance one Saturday night and were on their way home, when some young white roughnecks decided to make sport of the uncle just as he stepped onto the highway after urinating behind a tree. With deliberate malice, the whites ran down Sonny's uncle and sped away. In the silence and darkness following the incident, Sonny's father experiences the worst loneliness and helplessness he has ever felt. There, in the moonlit blackness, on a lonely highway a long ways from home, with an injured and dying brother bleeding his life onto the ground, with echoes of the splintering wood of a guitar ringing in his ears, with rage against calculated racism, and with the helplessness of knowing that he will never know the identities of those who killed his brother, Sonny's father is left in the almost unimaginable position of carrying throughout his life the burden of events surrounding his brother's death. Having sight, but not being able to see. Being on the scene of destruction, but being kept from knowledge of it. Knowing that something horrible has happened, but not being able to know the details. Shut out by geography and light from the very things that matter, but permanently locked into them by the biology that labels one human being brother to another. It is indeed the stuff of which the blues are made.

The scene of Sonny's uncle's death provides an apt microcosmic metaphor for reading the larger narrative events in "Sonny's Blues" as well as for contemplating the action of Toni Morrison's "Recitatif" (1983).[2] Characters in each text join readers in being placed in positions that border upon voyeurism. We watch characters being shut out of one another's lives even as we are titillated by the events of those lives. Characters reach out for one another in the darkness of drug oblivion or racial ignorance and just barely miss one another. Readers of "Recitatif" reach again and again for the racial markers that will enable them to familiarize characters into the racial pigeonholes with which they are most comfortable, while those characters keep slipping, like that elusive car on the country road, just out of our grasp.

How characters are positioned in these texts mirrors how readers are positioned in reading them. What we think we know, or what we may want to know, may guide our reading responses, but an elusive, unknowable quality still holds sway. We read over the shoulders of the narrators, longing for clarity, understanding, or clear markers of reconciliation. Through speculation or hope or wishful thinking, perhaps we get some of those things, but not all of them in any given instance.

Just outside the Funkiness of the Blues

Baldwin's story is about the blues—the blues of the uncle's death and the burdens borne by the father and the mother, the blues of Sonny's brother not having "been there" for Sonny, the blues inspired by Sonny's drug use and jail time, the blues of the death of the narrator's daughter, Grace, the blues of the religious experience that drives the little troupe of converts to sing their praises in Sonny's and the narrator's hearing. The story is built upon layers and layers of watching as spectator readers and characters feast upon the troubles of others in the stories. In the blues analogy, listeners can only empathize with the blues singer telling of his trouble; they can never really know or experience it. The medium of song is designed to approximate the feeling associated with whatever is troubling the musician. Similarly, the narrator of Sonny's blues is positioned as the listener, the outsider, even as he is simultaneously positioned as a character who has a song, for the narrative is indeed his. However, it is a song—so he would have us believe—more about other people's troubles than his own. It will take the better part of the narrative before the narrator comes to understand that Sonny's blues are indeed his blues and that Sonny's blues mirror his own set of blues-inducing circumstances, particularly the death of his young daughter.

Initially, however, the narrator is a watcher, a spectator, an outsider to the circumstances of Sonny's life. His very geographical positioning accounts for that in the early historical part of the narrative. The narrator, who is in the military following his mother's death and during the time that Sonny is banging the life out of the piano at Isabel's house, can only watch, through layers of reports, what is happening with his brother. The geographical distance that defines their relationship becomes a class issue once the narrator is back in town. Sonny goes the way of drugs, whereas the narrator goes the way of educational, middle-class escape from the ghetto. It will be some time before the narrator realizes that he and Sonny are kindred as well in their attempts to escape; they are both singers of the blues. In the meantime, he merely watches Sonny's life.

The extent to which the narrator has become a spectator to his brother's life is evident from the first few sentences of the text:

> I read about it in the paper, in the subway, on my way to work. I read it, and I couldn't believe it, and I read it again. Then perhaps I just stared at it, at the newsprint spelling out his name, spelling out the story. I stared at it in the swinging lights of the subway car, and in the faces and bodies of the people, and in my own face, trapped in the darkness which roared outside. (86)

In this first paragraph of the story, readers know that something traumatic has occurred, but they may be surprised, later, to discover that this is a brother speaking of his brother's arrest for drug use. He is so detached from Sonny that he can speculate, "I wondered what he looked like now" (86), and he will note a few pages later that he has not seen Sonny "for over a year" (89). The distance between brothers is captured in the newspaper article: the medium of print, which is so antithetical to the reality of drug use, highlights the wedge between the narrator and Sonny. The narrator has been watching his brother from a distance just as readers are forced to watch and wait while the narrator reveals what the problem is. The narrator refuses, in these first few sentences, to claim complete ownership of the problem by linking it to himself; it is merely a horrible problem, hanging in the air. Through language and a leisurely approach to the story, the narrator delays his own emotional confrontation with what he has learned and delays our knowledge of whatever the situation is. We watch him go through his rejecting antics and are kept in the dark until his emotional state is again secure enough for him to reveal the truth.

Strikingly, images of light and darkness, seeing and not seeing, are introduced in the first few sentences of the story. The relational darkness that positions the narrator as an outsider to his only living kin is mirrored by the darkness against which the subway lights reflect. The possibility for connection might be there, as are the subway lights, but it is not a connection that the narrator has cultivated.[3] Reading about Sonny in the paper effectively means that the narrator has washed his hands of him. He has, in other words, cleaned himself up from Sonny's funkiness and has become the watcher from the lofty height of middleclassness of what goes on in his brother's life.

The newspaper account of Sonny's arrest and the narrator's detachment from it is the present counterpart to another incident from the past, the one in which Sonny banged himself into ostracism within Isabel's household and finally into the military. The narrator hears of the incident and attempts to imagine the effect of Sonny's piano playing. Geographical distance again mirrors psychological distance, as the narrator pictures the problem more from Isabel's and her "dicty" parents' point of view (annoying disturbance) than from Sonny's (true pain): "Well, I really don't know how they stood it. Isabel finally confessed that it wasn't like living with a person at all, it was like living with sound. And the sound didn't make any sense to her, didn't make any sense to any of them—*naturally*" (107; my italics). The narrator privileges the class perspective in his evaluation of what is appropriate (Isabel's family's peace of mind) or not (Sonny's jazzy piano playing.). We watch his estrangement and his lack of understanding, and we may wonder at this point whether he will ever move from watcher to empathizer. Music is the site on which potential bonding *could* occur, but it will be until the street scene and later in the jazz club before the narrator truly merges his perspective with Sonny's and his life with Sonny's woes.

Like Geraldine in Toni Morrison's *The Bluest Eye* (1970) or like Mr. Davis in Baldwin's "Come Out the Wilderness" (1964), the narrator of "Sonny's Blues" is a man who wants to get rid of the funkiness and who does not want flies on him.[4] As long as Sonny is into drug use, he is one of the flies, so the narrator distances himself from him. His attitude toward Sonny the drug user can be read in part in his attitude toward the young man who comes to tell him about Sonny's arrest. He expresses disgust at the sight of the young man, hates him, and does not want to hear his "sad story." To hear the story is to know the extenuating circumstances, to give validity to the possibility of lawlessness, which the narrator is too straitlaced ever to consider.

The narrator is a willful and understandable outsider to Sonny's drug use. This restraint, however, does not make him any less curious about what it means to be a drug addict. This space of Sonny's life provides the potential voyeuristic site on which the narrator and readers can view Sonny. What is it like to take a hit of "horse"? How can that experience be achieved without the possibility of addiction? What is the attraction of drugs? What is that "deep, real deep and funky hole" (92) that Sonny describes really like? With his questions and ours, the narrator can only watch and wait until Sonny decides to attempt to reveal the funkiness. That revelation positions us to watch over the narrator's shoulder as he is watching Sonny relate his experience.

The scene leading up to the one in which Sonny tries to explain to the narrator what it feels like to use drugs is another microcosmic setting for viewing reader, narrator, and characters. The narrator is standing at his apartment window, which is up from the street level, *looking down* on Sonny as Sonny in turn watches a religious group of three women and a man singing and praying. "It was strange, suddenly, to *watch,* though I had been seeing these street meetings all my life. So, of course, had everybody else down there. Yet, they paused and *watched* and listened and I stood still at the window" (111; my italics). Readers are figuratively positioned behind the narrator, looking over his shoulder and through his interpretations. What we see is detached observation from the narrator toward the whole scene, empathetic involvement from Sonny toward the singers, and the unvarnished, bluesy pain of life and suffering in the revivalists' voices. In these levels of watching, metaphors of knowing and not knowing, and of light and darkness, again surface.

From his Hawthornian vantage point, the narrator can observe and record—indeed, he can guide our interpretations, but he cannot know, definitively, if what he is witnessing is actually what he is witnessing. He can see that Sonny and one of the women are bonding at some level, but Sonny's unmediated words put the final interpretation on his part in the scene. And since the narrator does not know the women's stories, or, as with Sonny's friend, does not give validity to the fact that they *have* stories, what he provides us is mediated through history and the knowledge of African American cultural forms that we bring to the text. Our awareness of the place of song to the religiously work-worn and weary in black communities enables us to substantiate the superficial observation of the women's suffering. Our knowledge to this point in the story of Sonny's addiction to drugs enables us to link his suffering to the suffering of the women.

In the street scene, the secular and the sacred traditions in African American culture merge into drugs and church practices. Heroin to Sonny is just as addictive and potentially escapist as is the religion in which the women are vested. Both are crutches; both allow the "users" to transcend suffering and try to survive in this world. Sonny comments about the singer: "While I was downstairs before, on my way here, listening to that woman sing, it struck me all of a sudden how much suffering she must have had to go through—to sing like that. It's *repulsive* to think you have to suffer that much" (114; italics in original). The irony is that drugs are not a socially acceptable panacea for suffering, whereas religion is. Sonny must free himself from his drug addiction and turn to the more acceptable "music as addiction" path of transcendence. The women are socially and morally locked into the drug of religion and can only hope that the afterlife will truly make it worth their temporary transcendence on earth.

Shut out from the pain of the women, the narrator can only observe superficially and offer once-removed commentary on them by picturing them through Sonny's eyes. And we in turn can only know the twice-removed "truth"—imagined through Sonny and then the narrator. The darkness of the country highway and the city subway invokes its lack of knowing in these layered representations as well.

When Sonny leaves the street and tries to articulate for the narrator the truth of his experience as it has been evoked by the singers, the wall of not-knowing is lowered a bit. Sonny describes his past drug usage: "I was all by myself at the bottom of something, stinking and sweating and crying and shaking, and I smelled it, you know? *my* stink, and I thought I'd die if I couldn't get away from it and yet, all the same, I knew that everything I was doing was just locking me in with it" (116–117; italics in original). As with the mother's narration of the uncle's death, however, the "real deep and funky hole" (92) is not one into which the narrator can enter, at least not yet.

At the beginning of the nightclub scene, the narrator is still detached from Sonny. He watches as the other musicians tease Sonny and incorporate him into the world from which the narrator is effectively excluded.

> Here, I was in Sonny's world. Or, rather: his kingdom. Here, it was not even a question that his veins bore royal blood . . . Then I *watched* them, Creole, and the little black man, and Sonny, and the others, while they horsed around, standing just below the bandstand. The light from the bandstand spilled just a little short of them and, *watching* them laughing and gesturing and moving about, I had the feeling that they, nevertheless, were being most careful not to step into that circle of light too suddenly . . . I just *watched* Sonny's face. (118, 119; my italics)

It is only when he gives himself over *completely* to the music, when he *truly* listens, that the narrator can begin to close the gap between himself and the musicians as well as between Sonny and himself. Only through listening to the music does he begin to realize that his loss of little Grace is his father's loss of his brother is Sonny's loss of potential in his own life by succumbing to the "death" of drug addiction; only at this moment is he allowed the empathetic union of past and present experiences. As he listens to Sonny and the group play, he thinks:

> I saw my mother's face again, and felt, *for the first time,* how the stones of the road she had walked on must have bruised her feet. I saw the moonlit road where my father's brother died. And it brought something else back to me, and carried me past it. I saw my little girl again and felt Isabel's tears again, and I felt my own tears begin to rise. (122; my italics)

Earlier, the narrator had said of Sonny after Grace's death, "My trouble made his real" (110), but there is little follow-up empathy that we might expect to flow from such a statement (though he does begin to write to Sonny). Here, at this moment in the nightclub, the narrator takes a drop into that "real deep and funky hole" and becomes Sonny and his father—that is, he is no longer an outsider to their suffering. As the watcher turned participant in familial, historical, and racial suffering, the narrator moves us to soften toward him, to be less detached in our assessments of him. From the haughtiness of not wanting to recognize that the "poor bastard," Sonny's friend, *had* a story, the narrator is now, finally, caught in his own story. His "conversion" breaks down the barriers of class and profession, religion and drugs, and college and ghetto and places him on the street with the singers, on the country road with his father, on the road that his burden-bearing mother walked throughout her life, and with Sonny in all of his lapses. The narrator is finally *humanized* for us, which in turn closes the gap between empathy and detachment that readers may have evinced at various points in their readings.

To think of the narrator's transformation as a conversion is to recognize, once again, the integral blending of the secular and the sacred in African American culture. The jazz club becomes a church, and the musicians and listeners its congregation. A church, by definition, has a mission of incorporation, of turning watchers into participants and of bringing the lost into the fold of salvation, even if only temporarily. No better literary example of this exists than Helga Crane's temporary conversion from scarlet woman to saint in Nella Larsen's *Quicksand* (1928). In the nightclub scene in "Sonny's Blues," the narrator is the Helga Crane outsider. He goes to support Sonny, to watch, only to find himself moved to a different space as a result of the "service" rendered by the musicians, who are in turn preacher, congregation, and Amen Corner. Sonny's desire to have his brother *see* what he does becomes a rite of incorporation for the narrator into *feeling* what Sonny does, believing in the power of music, and meeting Sonny on a common ground of human experience. Finally, the height separating them is leveled.

For Baldwin, suffering is external, internal, and collective. No one escapes. To believe that one has escaped, as the narrator tries so desperately to cloak himself in middle-class superiority, is but the staging ground for and the invitation to catastrophe. The message is ultimately surprisingly Christian, for Baldwin posits that every man's suffering is every man's suffering; it is the price one pays for being human. Certainly there are times when we can be the gawking spectators to someone else's pain, as in passing a fatal accident on a freeway, but a time will come when something in our own experiences will put us back on that freeway, howling out our anguish in concert with the relatives of the accident victims. No class aspirations, media coverage, narrative detachment, or readerly noninvolvement will spare us from that destiny with life.

Thwarting Expectations, Reinscribing Prejudices

James Baldwin and Toni Morrison, as African American writers, are heirs to a tradition of expectation. Just as students of European American literature strive to achieve competency in the expectations of "received traditions," so too do readers of African American literary texts bring with them assumptions about what black writers will treat, the perspective(s) from which they will treat it, and the depictions of characters within that treatment. If blacks suffer in African American texts, it is more than likely that whites will cause that suffering. If excessive burdens are borne, it is more than likely that blacks will bear them. To deviate from such expectations, therefore, and a host of others, is to upset readers, to defamiliarize their assumptions, and to place them in the uncomfortable position of not being able to stand on recognizable solid ground. For example, when Zora Neale Hurston focused primarily on poor white characters in *Seraph on the Suwanee* (1948), readers, especially African American readers, were confused and set adrift by this thwarting of expectations. Why would Hurston, such a talented black writer, spend one iota of her talent limning white characters who are not only *not* villainous but who are not even sensational? But what if Hurston, following the trail Frances Ellen Watkins Harper blazed, had simply refused to mark her characters racially? Would the response to the novel have been the same? And what if an African American writer who would later win the Nobel Prize for Literature picked up the experiment almost one hundred years after Harper? That is precisely what Morrison does in "Recitatif," the only short story she has published to date.

Morrison deliberately sets out to upset the comfort level of readers who want racial clarity of entry into literary texts. She creates characters not easily identifiable as black or white. In fact, she wrote the story as an experiment; in *Playing in the Dark: Whiteness and the Literary Imagination* (1992), she comments: "The only short story I have ever written, 'Recitatif,' was an experiment in the removal of all racial codes from a narrative about two characters of different races for whom racial identity is crucial."[5] By so doing, Morrison unseats the received expectations we have of African American literature and African American writers. She thereby positions readers with a racial discomfort that they either overcome, entering the text by the rules she creates, or that they consistently try to overcome by probing the text for blackness or whiteness, eagerly waiting and watching for the disguise to slip and the racial markers to reassert themselves.[6] Morrison's experiment heightens engagement for readers conditioned by a racially constructed American social system. This intensification of reader involvement parallels the readers' desire and the narrator's quest in "Sonny's Blues" to know the "deep and funky hole" of drug use.

Throughout "Recitatif," Morrison has her readers watching and waiting as they hope that Twyla, the narrator, will provide some clue to her racial identity. And we enter the story like eager detectives, for we believe that our received tradition of knowledge about racial markers will allow us to uncover what Twyla and Morrison are so intent upon hiding. So we ask questions: Is Twyla a name usually assigned to black girls or white girls? It *sounds* black, but . . . a dancing white woman *could* name her daughter Twyla, because there would be a less-than-sticking-to-white traditions attached to her. And what about Twyla's dancing mother? Is being a potential stripper more a black occupation than a white occupation? Or has class reduced a white woman to such an occupation? And the illness attached to Roberta's mother—is it not just like a white woman to be "sick" and allow her daughter to spend time in a shelter? The cultural/racial stereotypes keep coming at us, and we keep reading, watching, and working hard to uncover the *real* racial identities.

This work continues with the name Roberta. Black? White? Are black people or white people more inclined toward nicknames? If black, then perhaps Twyla is black, because she gives the nickname "the Big Bozo" to the matron at St. Bonny's shelter. Or is Roberta black, because her last name is Fisk and Morrison may be evoking the historically black Fisk University?[7] What about the size of the mothers? Is Roberta black because of the following description: "I looked up it seemed for miles. She [Roberta's mother] was big. Bigger than any man and on her chest was the biggest cross I'd ever seen. I swear it was six inches long each way. And in the crook of her arm was the biggest Bible ever made" (247). Is this description one we stereotypically associate with large, strong black women? Would that be true as well of the symbols of Christianity, the cross and the Bible? More black than white?

When the mothers appear at the shelter and food is mentioned, is the description of "chicken legs and ham sandwiches" (248) designed to evoke soul food and thus identify Roberta's mother as black? But then, the meat is neutralized by the inclusion of "oranges and a whole box of chocolate-covered grahams" (248). Potential racial stereotyping is also questioned by whose mother snatches her daughter from whom. Upon being introduced to Twyla and her mother, "Roberta's mother looked down at me and then looked down at Mary [Twyla's mother] too. She didn't say anything, just grabbed Roberta with her Bible-free hand and stepped out of line, walking quickly to the rear of it" (247). Have we been socialized to believe that a white mother would be more upset than a black mother about her daughter having a roommate of the other race? Which one would be inclined to be so utterly uncivil? Would a black child or a white child be more inclined to use the formal "Mother," and would a black woman or a white woman be more inclined, when slighted, to refer to the other one as "That bitch!" (247). Can we imagine a black child, given the sacredness of mothers in black communities, uttering about the one who gave her birth, "All I could think of was that she really needed to be killed" or "I could have killed her" (248)?

As the two women move through the years, do we think that Twyla is black because she becomes a waitress and evinces a stereotypically black motherly attitude toward food: "Things are not right. The wrong food is always with the wrong people. Maybe that's why I got into waitress work later—to match up the right people with the right food" (248)? Do we think that Roberta is black because she goes to track down Jimi Hendrix, or white because we think more frequently of white girl groupies? Is Twyla black because she is so woefully socially ignorant and because that is a stereotype we associate with the so-called nonreading black working class? Or is a lower-class white stereotype at work?

Morrison relegates us to racial stereotyping hell, and we keep trying to wiggle our way out of it without rejecting what we have come to know. It is this refusal or reluctance to start anew that keeps us in such hot water during the course of the text and that simultaneously keeps us so unabashedly engaged. The possibility exists for us to learn a lot about our prejudices during the course of the narrative. Only our racial assumptions stand in the way of that education. So, as we do with the narrator in "Sonny's Blues," we peep over Twyla's shoulder waiting for the revelation. "Slip up," we whisper. "Give us a hint. Let us know."

As one of the scholarly readers of Morrison's text, I am forced to dredge up, replay, and engage the very stereotypes that Morrison is trying to steer me away from, even as I am trying to make sense of the narrative she has constructed. It is a peculiar position in which to find oneself, but nonetheless necessary to the ultimate understanding of what is being protested, if something is indeed being protested. Where I end up, and where many readers end up, is shifting focus, temporarily, from Twyla and Roberta to the text's parallel site on which ugly racial tensions get played out. That site is Maggie.

Who is Maggie, and what does she mean to the text of "Recitatif" and to Twyla and Roberta? Maggie is just as racially unknowable, finally, as are Twyla and Roberta. Early on, however, many *believe* she is black, and that belief assigns her value for them. Maggie is the ugly outcast, the rejectable blackness, the communally disconnected, the diseased, the deformed. In other words, she is the scapegoat toward whom everyone can feel superior. Though Twyla and Roberta are temporarily orphaned, they can feel superior to Maggie because they do not have parentheses legs and do not have clothes and hats that instantly classify them as outsiders. Maggie is the character about whom Twyla and Roberta can believe no one cares, for even they, in the union they form at the shelter, are not as isolated as she appears to be. To them and the "gar girls," Maggie can suffer their insults and cruelty because she somehow deserves it. Not unlike Pecola Breedlove, Maggie serves as the character of rejection for Twyla and, through her, the other characters we encounter in the story.

Maggie is the site on which Twyla and Roberta can exercise their mob psychology, their desperation to belong in the same positions of power and favoritism as the gar girls (although the very name "gar" and the actions Twyla and Roberta witness from the girls are just as ugly as their name).[8] Like Pecola, Maggie enables powerless people to feel powerful, and who can be more powerless than children abandoned to a shelter? Maggie's size and muteness are key to the power play, for triumph over her, an adult, is fairly easy because she is the size of a child. Also, the muteness effectively prevents her from screaming for help during the attack—though she can certainly "tell" later.

In beating and kicking Maggie, the gar girls act out what they believe is a racial drama—if we can trust Roberta's version of the incident:

> "Maybe I am different now, Twyla. But you're not. You're the same little
> state kid who kicked a poor old black lady when she was down on the
> ground. You kicked a black lady and you have the nerve to call me a bigot."
> The coupons were everywhere and the guts of my purse were bunched
> under the dashboard. What was she saying? Black? Maggie wasn't black.
> "She wasn't black," I said.
> "Like hell she wasn't, and you kicked her. We both did. You kicked a
> black lady who couldn't even scream."
> "Liar!"
> "You're the liar! Why don't you just go on home and leave us alone,
> huh?" (257–258)

In Twyla's shock that Maggie *could* have been black is the reiteration of Morrison's thesis about racial markers. Twyla muses:

> I know I didn't do that, I couldn't do that. But I was puzzled by her telling
> me Maggie was black. When I thought about it I actually couldn't be
> certain. She wasn't pitch-black, I knew, or I would have remembered
> that. What I remember was the kiddie hat, and the semicircle legs. I tried to
> reassure myself about the race thing for a long time until it dawned on
> me that the truth was already there, and Roberta knew it. I didn't kick her;
> I didn't join in with the gar girls and kick that lady, but I sure did want
> to. We *watched* and never tried to help her and never called for help.
> (259; my italics)

We can never know the truth of Maggie's identity, but Twyla's and Roberta's versions of what happened to Maggie finally merge in Roberta's last long speech in the story:

> "Listen to me. I really did think she was black. I didn't make that up. I really thought so. But now I can't be sure. I just remember her as old, so old. And because she couldn't talk—well, you know, I thought she was crazy. She'd been brought up in an institution like my mother was and like I thought I would be too. And you were right. We didn't kick her. It was the gar girls. Only them. But, well, I wanted to. I really wanted them to hurt her. I said we did it, too. You and me, but that's not true. And I don't want you to carry that around. It was just that I wanted to do it so bad that day—*wanting to is doing it.*" (261; my italics)

Roberta's rationale is not unlike the one Eva Peace uses with Nel in asserting that Nel is as guilty as Sula of having killed Chicken Little. Nel's initial shock, like Roberta's, gives way to self-awareness:

> All these years she had been secretly proud of her calm, controlled behavior when Sula was uncontrollable, her compassion for Sula's frightened and shamed eyes. Now it seemed that what she had thought was maturity, serenity and compassion was only the tranquillity [*sic*] that follows a joyful stimulation. Just as the water closed peacefully over the turbulence of Chicken Little's body, so had contentment washed over her enjoyment.[9]

In explaining her role in the scene with the gar girls, Roberta makes it clear that she *believed* Maggie was black; that is sufficient for their prejudiced desires. And it is sufficient that both girls wanted in on the scapegoating ritual, which they perhaps envisioned as a kind of rite of passage of recognition from the gar girls.[10]

Whether Maggie was black or not, both Twyla and Roberta were intent upon denying her humanity by stepping over her body into another state of being. And perhaps that is one of Morrison's points. If people can treat each other so cruelly at such an early age, whether they are certain of their racial identity or not, then what difference does race make? The violence was the constant. On the other hand, if Roberta thought that Maggie was black and still wanted to kick her, then what does that suggest about *intra*racial prejudice, if Roberta is the black character? And if Twyla is the black character, what does her desire to kick Maggie suggest about her conscious denial of her own blackness? If Twyla is the white character, what does it suggest about her willingness to deny the humanity of kindred?

Although we are consistently thwarted in our efforts to assign stable racial identities to Twyla and Roberta, another pattern develops in the story that makes our efforts moot. Twyla and Roberta are busily *reinscribing* the very racial differences and prejudices the existence of which the story seeks to deny. Over a period of three decades, Twyla and Roberta move from being girls who slept in beds one after the other to adult women whose fangs of prejudice show clearly around a school desegregation. Their conflict amounts to a small racial war that is preceded by eye-opening declarations from each woman: "'I wonder what made me think you were different.' 'I wonder what made me think you were different'" (256). "'I used to curl your hair.' 'I hated your hands in my hair'" (257). Despite the aspirations to violence that both Twyla and Roberta expressed in reaction to Maggie, their relationship has been founded on exceptionalism, on politeness, on the superficial exchanges across racial lines in which neither of the so-called friends dares to move beyond surface interactions to true communication. Now that they have become mothers and have children to protect, the ferocity of the tiger of racism is unleashed. We watch the women become banshees intent upon hurting each other under the guise of marching about mothers' and children's rights. And other women at the march also watch the developments between Roberta and Twyla:

> The women were moving. Our [Twyla's and Roberta's] faces looked mean to them of course and they looked as though they could not wait to throw themselves in front of a police car, or better yet, into my car and drag me away by my ankles. Now they surrounded my car and gently, gently began to rock it. I swayed back and forth like a sideways yo-yo. Automatically I reached for Roberta, like the old days in the orchard when they saw us watching them and we had to get out of there, and if one of us fell the other pulled her up and if one of us was caught the other stayed to kick and scratch, and neither would leave the other behind. My arm shot out of the car window but no receiving hand was there. Roberta was looking at me sway from side to side in the car and her face was still. (257)

Thus publicly bared in front of the marching/watching women, Twyla and Roberta cannot forgive each other for who they are (a black woman and a white woman) or for what they have done (refused to forge a *true* interracial friendship in spite of the shared suffering of their lives). Yet they miss and need each other, as is reflected in Twyla's peeking around corners to see if Roberta is there.

By baring the women's racial prejudices during the school desegregation incident, Morrison debunks her initial thesis that race does not matter—or at least she severely calls it into question. Absence of racial markers aside, black and white human beings on American soil seem incapable of peaceful coexistence without tension based on race. *It is the norm*, and everyone seeks after the norm. Twyla and Roberta *need* each other, *need* to know that the other one exists in order to define themselves. As George S. Schuyler posits in *Black No More* (1931), if racism and prejudice did not exist in America, it would have to be invented. After a scientist creates a formula for turning all the black folks white in *Black No More*, it is discovered that the newly minted white folks are a shade paler than those biologically produced, so tanning becomes all the rage. Twyla and Roberta move from their peaceful coexistence as children to reinventing prejudice during the marching scenes. They *need* the conflict to know who they are. In this context, on American soil, racism is just as natural as breathing. As Gwendolyn Brooks asserts of the whites who stoned little black children in Little Rock, Arkansas, in 1957, racists are not two-headed monsters: "They are like people everywhere."[11] Twyla and Roberta are like people, especially Americans, everywhere.

By centering conflict upon school desegregation, Morrison underscores the lack of educational development in her readers as well as in her characters. Just as readers of Morrison's story have consistently refused to move to another level of encountering difference, so too have Twyla and Roberta. Morrison places additional pressure on her characters to grow, however, because, unlike the readers, *Twyla and Roberta know each other's racial identities.* Yet their experiences in the shelter and beyond have not educated them. Their encounter with Maggie has not educated them. And their experience of having children and being responsible for children has not educated them. Maggie remains their deep, dark little secret, hidden between them in the spaces where human beings always like to hide the things that make it difficult for them to face themselves in the mirror. Instead of growing intellectually, Twyla and Roberta devolve, and it is this unfortunate devolution that marks them, and the country in which they live, as irreparably, irrecoverably racist. This ugly fact makes clear Twyla and Roberta's need for each other, a need manifested in the length of their relationship.

Twyla and Roberta's relationship lasts as long as it does in part because it takes them so long to confront truth and speak it. Time is also important in highlighting the women's need for each other, or at least Twyla's need for Roberta. Twyla cannot let her childhood acquaintance go. The need reflected in normative racism is paralleled in normative self-development. Roberta mirrors Twyla in so many ways that she is like a part of her. For Twyla to reject Roberta, or vice versa, is to deny the validity of her own experience. Roberta was there with Twyla in St. Bonny's and was obviously one of the better things about the place. For Twyla to deny that connection, that integral part of her self-formation, would be comparable to cutting off her nose to spite her face.

The sad truth of Morrison's experiment is that it undoes itself. We are witness to this process of undoing just as Twyla and Roberta are witness to the ugly unraveling in their own lives. What Morrison achieves at one carefully constructed level of language (the thoughtfulness of narrative reflection that precludes racial marking) is undone at another (the rawness of immediate conversation in the heat of passionate racist encounters). The seepage for which we watched and waited occurs in a deluge of insults. It will take the women years to even speak to each other again, and there will be absolutely no recovery. Roberta's final question to Twyla, which is also the last line of the story, is, "What the hell happened to Maggie?" (261). Haunted and hounded by the forces of racial shaping to which they have both been heir, Roberta and Twyla can only return to the site of racial conflict, to power and domination, to an ugly reality that will never be smoothed over by the beauty of language.

The Satisfaction of Detective Work

In "Sonny's Blues" and "Recitatif," James Baldwin and Toni Morrison create investigative narrators who are intent upon solving puzzles surrounding other characters. We in turn are shadow detectives, following along the paths those narrators have carved out for us or deviating when it seems most appropriate to our desires. Both narrators create a tension in us, one that is almost sexual in nature and that begs for relief. We are finally "converted" to a belief in the possibility of Sonny's survival, for the narrator and Sonny finally meet on some ground that transcends suffering. We are finally brought to a peaceful pause, if not calm resolution, in the troubled tale of Twyla and Roberta.

When we reflect upon the title of Morrison's story, we can see another way in which the two stories are connected. In the musical contexts of the stories, the word "recitatif," with its beautiful sound and sometimes awkward pronunciation, evokes comparison to the blues. A beautiful word applied to a story about the ugly, troubled interracial relationship of two women, recitatif is a long way from its pristine, classical origins. In the ugliness of racial strife, it can serve as an indicator of the blues-like existence of both of Morrison's characters. Twyla and Roberta may be considered to have the blues because their loved ones, in this instance their mothers, "done gone." A blues condition exists when they are deposited at St. Bonny's, for they have essentially been abandoned by those loved ones. A blues condition continues to define their relationship as Twyla starts to parallel a lover in the blues song mode. From the perspective of the blues, therefore, both women are black.

As with Ellison's narrator in *Invisible Man* (1952), the conditions of "blackness" and "blueness" inform the lives of both women. Twyla is not happy when Roberta is around, but she longs for her when Roberta is not present. Twyla is just as absorbed with Roberta's life as the unnamed narrator of "Sonny's Blues" is with Sonny's. An emptiness exists that only the absent loved one can fill. The pause that occurs at the end of "Recitatif" occurs *only* because Roberta grants an explanation and eases the pain that Twyla is in. As with any blues condition, however, the cathartic moment is only temporary. As the narrator of "Sonny's Blues" asserts, even after he very healthily recognizes his spiritual kinship to Sonny, "And I was yet aware that this was only a moment, that the world waited outside, as hungry as a tiger, and that trouble stretched above us, longer than the sky" (122). The musical tradition thus makes clear that release from the pain of drugs or the pain of racism is indeed but a pause.[12]

Therefore, as we watch both sets of characters reach significant points in their journeys, we as readers are astute enough to know that we are caught in another of our received traditions about African American literature: most of it does not end "happily ever after." As with Ellison's *Invisible Man*, Lorraine Hansberry's *A Raisin in the Sun* (1959), Baldwin's *Go Tell It on the Mountain* (1953), or Morrison's *Beloved* (1987), the struggles continue. It is in part this defining characteristic of African American literature that keeps us reflectively engaged long after Sonny's ceremonially Christian jazz set and Roberta's provocatively lingering question.

NOTES

1. James Baldwin, "Sonny's Blues," in *Going to Meet the Man* (New York: Dell, 1964), 86–122. References to this source will be enclosed in parentheses in the text.

2. Toni Morrison, "Recitatif," in *Confirmation: An Anthology of African American Women,* ed. Amiri Baraka (LeRoi Jones) and Amina Baraka (New York: Quill, 1983), 243–261. References to this text will be enclosed in parentheses in the text.

3. For other commentary on lightness and darkness in the text, see Donald C. Murray, "James Baldwin's 'Sonny's Blues': Complicated and Simple," *Studies in Short Fiction* 14 (1977): 353–357.

4. Morrison, *The Bluest Eye* (New York: Holt, Rinehart, and Winston, 1970); Baldwin, "Come Out the Wilderness," in *Going to Meet the Man.* Sarah, the disturbed black woman who is trapped in a destructive relationship with a white man, observes of her fellow office worker, a black man by the name of Mr. Davis: "From the crown of [his] rakishly tilted, deafeningly conservative hat to the tips of his astutely dulled shoes, he glowed with a very nearly vindictive sharpness. There were no flies on Mr. Davis. He would always be the best-dressed man in *any*body's lobby" (188).

5. Morrison, *Playing in the Dark: Whiteness and the Literary Imagination* (Cambridge, MA: Harvard University Press, 1992), xi.
6. Morrison employs a comparable device in *Paradise* (New York: Knopf, 1998). The first sentence, "They shoot the white girl first," leads to endless speculation about who the white girl is. That quest for clarity is a quest for the societal status quo, a quest to reseat familiarity and make the world right again.
7. David Goldstein-Shirley also makes this connection, as do others discussing the text. Goldstein-Shirley and I share some points in our attempts to break the racial stereotyping codes, but we diverge on other points. See his "Race and Response: Toni Morrison's 'Recitatif,'" *Short Story* 5 (Spring 1997): 77–86. See also Ann Rayson, who approaches the racial identities with more certainty in "Decoding for Race: Toni Morrison's 'Recitatif' and Being White, Teaching Black," in *Changing Representations of Minorities East and West*, ed. Larry E. Smith and John Rieder (Honolulu: University of Hawaii, 1996), 41–46 and Elizabeth Abel, "Black Writing, White Reading: Race and the Politics of Feminist Interpretation," *Critical Inquiry* 19 (Spring 1993): 470–498, in which she is also more committed to claiming the racial identities for the characters in "Recitatif."
8. Kathryn Nicol suggests that the phrase "gar girls" is a childish corruption of "gargoyles." See "Visible Differences: Viewing Racial Identity in Toni Morrison's *Paradise* and 'Recitatif,'" in *Literature and Racial Ambiguity*, ed. Teresa Hubel and Neil Brooks (Amsterdam, Netherlands: Rodopi, 2002), 217.
9. Morrison, *Sula* (New York: Knopf, 1974), 170.
10. Rayson argues that Maggie represents both girls' negligent mothers: "Each girl saw the sandy-colored, racially indeterminate Maggie as a mother figure; to Twyla Maggie was white, to Roberta she was black. The story's epiphany is that each girl wanted to hurt Maggie because each wanted to punish her own mother for being unable to care for her" (45). Abel shares this position by commenting: "'Recitatif' ends with parallel recognitions by Twyla and Roberta that each perceived the mute Maggie as her own unresponsive, rejecting mother, and therefore hated and wanted to harm her" (495).
11. Gwendolyn Brooks, "*The Chicago Defender* Sends a Man to Little Rock," in *Selected Poems of Gwendolyn Brooks* (1963; rpt. New York: Perennial Classics, 1999), 89.
12. Goldstein-Shirley also comments, briefly, on the musical significance of "Recitatif" (84–85).

WORKS CITED/CONSULTED

Abel, Elizabeth. "Black Writing, White Reading: Race and the Politics of Feminist Interpretation." *Critical Inquiry* 19 (Spring 1993): 470–498.

Baldwin, James. "Sonny's Blues." In *Going to Meet the Man*. New York: Dell, 1964. 86–122.

———. "Come Out the Wilderness." In *Going to Meet the Man*. New York: Dell, 1964. 170–197.

Brooks, Gwendolyn. "*The Chicago Defender* Sends a Man to Little Rock." In *Selected Poems of Gwendolyn Brooks*. 1963. New York: Perennial Classics, 1999. 89.

Byerman, Keith E. "Words and Music: Narrative Ambiguity in 'Sonny's Blues.'" *Studies in Short Fiction*, 19, no.4 (Fall 1982): 367–372.

Goldstein-Shirley, David. "Race and Response: Toni Morrison's 'Recitatif.'" *Short Story* 5 (Spring 1997): 77–86.

Morrison, Toni. *The Bluest Eye*. New York: Holt, Rinehart, and Winston, 1970.

———. *Paradise*. New York: Knopf, 1998.

———. *Playing in the Dark: Whiteness and the Literary Imagination*. Cambridge, MA: Harvard University Press, 1992).

———. "Recitatif." In *Confirmation: An Anthology of African American Women*. Ed. Amiri Baraka (LeRoi Jones) and Amina Baraka. New York: Quill, 1983. 243–261.

———. *Sula*. New York: Knopf, 1974.

Murray, Donald C. "James Baldwin's 'Sonny's Blues': Complicated and Simple." *Studies in Short Fiction* 14 (1977): 353–357.

Nicol, Kathryn. "Visible Differences: Viewing Racial Identity in Toni Morrison's *Paradise* and 'Recitatif.'" In *Literature and Racial Ambiguity*. Ed. Teresa Hubel and Neil Brooks. Amsterdam, Netherlands: Rodopi, 2002. 209–231.

Rayson, Ann. "Decoding for Race: Toni Morrison's 'Recitatif' and Being White, Teaching Black." In *Changing Representations of Minorities East and West*. Ed. Larry E. Smith and John Rieder. Honolulu: University of Hawaii Press, 1996. 41–46.

Reid, Robert. "The Powers of Darkness in 'Sonny's Blues.'" *CLA Journal* 43, no.4 (June 2000): 443–453.

Reilly, John M. "'Sonny's Blues': James Baldwin's Image of Community." *Negro American Literature Forum* 4, no.2 (July 1970): 56–60.

Schuyler, George. *Black No More*. New York: Macaulay, 1931.

PLAYING A MEAN GUITAR: THE LEGACY OF STAGGERLEE IN BALDWIN AND MORRISON

D. QUENTIN MILLER

" Staggerlee was a bad man." So begins Mississippi John Hurt in a spoken preface to a live recording of "Staggerlee Blues" at Oberlin
College in 1965. This assessment sums up Staggerlee's story in a succinct
way, but it also opens it up to interpretation. The familiar figure of the bad
black man (also known as "baaadman," or "bad nigger") is an ambiguous
one, and Staggerlee is one of its most enduring incarnations. Daryl Cumber
Dance has defined the "bad nigger" as "tough and violent. He kills without blinking an eye. He courts death constantly and doesn't fear dying"
(224). "Bad" can mean lawless, feared, or respected in this context. "Bad"
can mean all three at the same time, and in the ultimate resistance to fixed
meaning in language, what Henry Louis Gates, Jr., would call "Signifyin'"
(46), it can even mean "good." Staggerlee, made famous in popular song
and oral narrative and recently explored in detail in Cecil Brown's 2003
study *Stagolee Shot Billy,* is an ambiguous figure of resistance and fierce individualism. He is bad in his lawlessness and his will to commit cold-blooded
murder, but perhaps good insofar as his story can inspire rebellion against
injustice, as it frequently did during the civil rights and black power movements. Houston Baker notes, "Stackolee represents the badman hero who
stands outside the law; he is the rebel who uses any means necessary to get
what he wants" (37). The fiction and drama of James Baldwin and Toni
Morrison preserve the "rebel" aspect of this definition, but treat Staggerlee
less as a "hero" than as an influence on heroes who are expected to grow
into complete humans capable of love as well as rage.

Brown's study traces the origins of the Staggerlee legend to 1895, when
the historical event that spawned it took place: Lee Shelton (who becomes
Stagolee, Stack Lee, or Staggerlee in various versions) shot one William
Lyons (who becomes Billy Lyons, Billy DeLyon, Bully, or Lion). The dis-
pute took place in a barroom and escalated to murder when Billy grabbed

Lee's Stetson hat. This tragic but not monumental event grew into a full-blown legend as it was passed along through oral narrative and blues songs. Staggerlee became an archetype of a man so powerful and fear-inspiring that he even conquers the devil and takes over hell in some versions of the tale. Brown discusses how the legend has influenced not only narrative and song, but also American literature, dwelling on works by Richard Wright and Sterling Brown and pausing a little longer on James Baldwin, particularly Baldwin's poem "Staggerlee Wonders" (1985). In this essay I will pick up where Brown leaves off, for Staggerlee runs deeper in Baldwin's other works than in this poem, informing his play *Blues for Mister Charlie* (1964) and his novel *Tell Me How Long the Train's Been Gone* (1968). Brown's study leaps from the Black Panther and black power movements of the 1960s to contemporary rap music, but Staggerlee remained a powerful force in the literature of the 1970s, the decade in which he appeared as Superfly and Shaft on the silver screen, two characters on opposite sides of the law. Staggerlee surfaces in Toni Morrison's *Song of Solomon* (1977) in the figure of Guitar, whom critics of this novel have frequently overlooked because of his disturbing implications. These three works by Baldwin and Morrison have in common an ambivalence toward the violent black militancy of the mid-1960s, and Staggerlee is an appropriate archetype to examine in this context because he embodies the same ambivalence.

It is difficult to embrace Baldwin's Richard Henry and Black Christopher and Morrison's Guitar Bains as heroes, or even to understand them in the context of their larger narratives, because of their attraction to guns and their will to murder white people. In fact they are not heroes, no more than Staggerlee is; yet they are not simply antiheroes either. The evident flaw in Brown's insightful study is that he is overly willing to allow Staggerlee to become a culture hero in the book's final pages, glorifying a character who is at heart an impulsive thug. Mark Schone concurs: "When it comes to the meaning of the song, Brown has a nostalgic allegiance to what Stagger Lee signified in the '60s, and an inability to see that his hero is more tragic than revolutionary" (2).[1] Brown's interpretation of "Staggerlee Blues" leads him to a similar interpretation of literature. There is a danger in applying Brown's conclusion to Baldwin and Morrison, whose nuanced narratives are meant to challenge readers rather than to represent archetypes. Brown uses Staggerlee to yoke Baldwin and Wright together in a problematic way, given that Baldwin's career essentially began with his argument with Wright's *Native Son* (1940) as a prototype of the black protest novel; Brown concludes that "Baldwin and Wright saw Stagolee as a defiant, angry revolutionary, a figure consistent with his reputation from the St. Louis streets of the last century. These authors recognized the essential character of Stagolee as a symbol of protest" (220). In

Baldwin's case, one has to qualify this association, especially if one considers "Staggerlee Wonders" a companion to *Native Son*, for it is difficult to see Wright's antihero and Baldwin's speaker in the same light. Wright's Bigger Thomas is far from eloquent and is completely deprived of his voice in the lengthy last section of the novel, as his lawyer takes over the narrative. Baldwin's Staggerlee is a cultural critic who uses his pent-up anger to probe the depths of racism in his country. Early in his career, Baldwin saw Bigger as a helpless victim of that racism and strove throughout his career to represent African Americans with grace, subtlety, and human dimensions that Bigger did not exhibit.[2] H. Nigel Thomas, in a study that includes *Uncle Tom's Children* (1938) as well as *Native Son*, concludes that "Wright, somewhat deliberately, points to the limitations of a Bad Nigger existence—especially since white oppression is crucial to its genesis" (164). Baldwin and Morrison are well aware of these limitations, which is one of the reasons their Staggerlee figures are not the central foci of their works. Their writings represent a departure from Wright and other African American writers whose primary concern is protest; and Staggerlee, though an important figure in their works, carries a different meaning.

Brown is right in asserting that Staggerlee is for Baldwin a "defiant, angry revolutionary," and I will argue that Morrison casts him the same way. Yet for both Baldwin and Morrison, Staggerlee is more than a "symbol of protest." He is an *agent* of protest as well as a thoughtful speaker who has been damaged by racism to the point of revenge. Moreover, the Staggerlee characters in Baldwin's and Morrison's works have not been undone by racism as Wright's Bigger has, and they seek to be leaders rather than angry young men who act individually. Refusing to reduce their characters to symbols, Baldwin and Morrison appropriate Staggerlee not as a hero of a protest movement, but rather as a figure ancillary to the heroes of their works, one who can clarify the dangers of uncontrolled anger and at the same time provide a path to salvation for the actual heroes. These authors continue a tradition that Thomas traces in other black writers who "find in the behaviors of Bad Niggers vehicles to successfully explore in fiction the ongoing struggle by African Americans to liberate themselves from white oppression" (149). Staggerlee is an important figure in *Blues for Mister Charlie*, *Tell Me How Long the Train's Been Gone*, and *Song of Solomon*, but he is not the central one. Meridian, Leo, or Milkman can run from, ignore, befriend, or fight with Staggerlee, but they are not meant to become him as they develop and change over the course of their narratives. In short, Baldwin and Morrison recognize the importance and power of Staggerlee within the context of black social protest of the 1960s, but they refuse to glorify him. They interpret Staggerlee's story as a cautionary tale. His lawlessness, anger, and skewed sense of justice are options for Baldwin's and Morrison's protagonists, but not solutions.

The Song and the Legend

Blues for Mister Charlie, Tell Me How Long the Train's Been Gone, and *Song of Solomon* have more in common than the fact that they are informed by the violent history of the civil rights movement of the 1950s and early 1960s. In their titles, they all explicitly refer to music. Music is of supreme importance to both Baldwin and Morrison, and a good deal of criticism has been devoted to this subject.³ (The titles of their works alone underscore this theme: Baldwin's most famous story is "Sonny's Blues" [1957], his collection of poetry is titled *Jimmy's Blues* [1983], and his fifth novel, *If Beale Street Could Talk* [1974], alludes to the birthplace of the blues. Morrison's fifth novel is *Jazz* [1992], and her only short story is "Recitatif" [1994]). Other critics have explored and will undoubtedly continue to explore the profound influence of music on these writers, especially musical form and rhythm; but one of the most important aspects of music in their works is song lyrics. Four of Baldwin's novel's titles—*Go Tell It on the Mountain* (1953), *Tell Me How Long the Train's Been Gone,* If Beale Street Could Talk and *Just Above My Head* (1979)—*are* song lyrics, and Baldwin infuses liberal doses of gospel, blues, and soul song lyrics into his nonfiction and fiction, especially his last three novels. *Song of Solomon* is on one level a novel about trying to peel back the layers of the blues song that Pilate sings as Robert Smith jumps off a roof: "O Sugarman done fly away / Sugarman done gone / Sugarman cut across the sky / Sugarman gone home" (6). Like Staggerlee's name and his legend, the meaning and the actual words of Pilate's song change and grow according to context and region: Sugarman is a version of Solomon, a name that bends to become Shalimar, Charlemagne, and so on.

All of this demonstrates that figures such as Staggerlee, whose story was passed down through song, are of supreme importance to Baldwin and Morrison, both of whom share the goal of preserving African American oral tradition in their written works. Houston Baker has traced the way "black literary artists have employed the black folk base in their work" to communicate a "theme of repudiation" (14). An awareness of this connection thoroughly informs the criticism of Baldwin and especially of Morrison. However, as the writers of some of the richest and most challenging American fiction and drama published in the latter half of the twentieth century, Baldwin and Morrison are not content to merely preserve or represent figures like Staggerlee without questioning these characters' morality. Their shared primary goal is to produce highly complex narratives with an eye to history, mythology, and the tough reality of racism and other divisions in the United States.

In accordance with the history of the 1960s, the anger associated with Staggerlee figures in Baldwin and Morrison is directed at white people.

However, the historical facts of Staggerlee and most of the ensuing mythology surrounding him do not denote an incident of racism. Although the murder of Billy DeLyon took place in the Jim Crow South, it was an example of what we have come to call a black-on-black crime. Yet something about the protean nature of Staggerlee allowed him to transcend the actual nature of his crime to become symbolic. Trudier Harris writes:

> The ultimate destroyer of values, Stagolee nonetheless reaps the approbation of the hero because the values are not those of his community, but those of the larger society. Tellers of Stagolee's exploits believe that those values, often antithetical to the life and health of the black community, deserve to be upset; they therefore side with Stagolee in his temporary triumph over the almost unbeatable foe of white power. This victory seems to outweigh in the tellers' minds the fact that Stagolee's aggression is initially turned against his own community. (129)

Brown notes that Staggerlee *was* a symbol of protest when he was reborn in the supercharged atmosphere of the 1960s. Yet Baldwin and Morrison were neither as reactionary nor as revolutionary as some of the figures who framed this protest in the 1960s, and they never completely side with their Staggerlee characters. As a symbol of protest in this context, Staggerlee was also potentially a symbol of hatred. In *Song of Solomon,* Guitar tries to convince Milkman that his will to murder is inspired not by hatred, but rather by love; he says, "What I'm doing ain't about hating white people. It's about loving us. About loving you. My whole life is love" (159). But Guitar does murder people, white people, who may not be racists and who become, then, victims of racism. The obvious moral center and guide in Morrison's novel is Pilate, who states succinctly, "Life is life. Precious" (208). Caleb, the voice of conventional Christian morality in *Tell Me How Long the Train's Been Gone,* expresses a similar sentiment: "The body just turns into garbage when the gift of life has left it. What a mystery. We have no right to kill. I know that" (300).

At its core, the story of Staggerlee is a story of cold-blooded murder. Moreover, it is murder that takes place over a material object, a Stetson hat. As Brown points out, in nearly all versions of the story, Billy DeLyon begs and pleads for his life, and he almost always asks for mercy because of his wife and either two or three children. Staggerlee shoots him anyway. Baldwin and especially Morrison often incorporate violence and even murder into their works; yet neither can be said to celebrate it, as versions of the Staggerlee ballad often do. The interpretive danger is that the reader or listener may become desensitized to violence or murder if he or she hears about it enough: this is presumably how Richard, Guitar, and Christopher develop their militancy. The listener should be revolted or chilled upon hearing the Staggerlee story; we should react the same way to the murder of innocents in Morrison's work—Chicken Little in *Sula* (1974), Beloved in *Beloved* (1987), the four girls in the Birmingham church in *Song of Solomon*, and so forth. At the same time, there is something seductive and powerful about Staggerlee; as Black Panther leader Bobby Seale said when his wife asked him why they should name their son Stagolee, "Stagolee was a bad nigger off the block and didn't take shit from nobody" (Brown 214). Such defiance and independence can easily be associated with pure power.

To regard Staggerlee as a hero is to limit the choices that young black males have in contemporary America. Brown seems almost desperate to put a positive spin on the Staggerlee legend when he says, "Stagolee is a metaphor that structures the life of black males from childhood through maturity" (2), and adds, "We Americans love our folk heroes and the ballads made about their lives. Yet we are reluctant to admit that many of those heroes come from the lowest levels of society" (12). There is some truth in both of these statements, but they reduce their subject considerably. In the three works under consideration, the Staggerlee characters are only one possible model for the characters, and the authors regard their Staggerlee characters with suspicion. Without condemning or endorsing Staggerlee, Baldwin and Morrison place him in their works as a legitimate possibility, a legend that can influence the contemporary black male, but certainly not as a metaphor that automatically structures anyone's life. To choose to become Staggerlee is to choose not to become oneself. This, Morrison and Baldwin would argue, is much more dangerous than any barroom brawl.

Baldwin and Staggerlee: Rage on Stage

Baldwin's first overt reference to Staggerlee is his introduction to Bobby Seale's autobiography, *A Lonely Rage: The Autobiography of Bobby Seale* (1978). From this moment Baldwin associates Staggerlee with a black militancy that refuses to be intimidated by white oppression. Unlike the classic versions of Staggerlee, though, Seale is a man of passionate intensity in Baldwin's eyes, not a man of impulsive action. Baldwin describes Seale as "tense and quiet as the air becomes when a storm is about to break" and as possessing "a kind of intelligence of anguish" ("Stagolee" ix). Baldwin had great admiration for Seale even as he was conflicted about the proper response to racism in America, the poles represented by his friends Martin Luther King, Jr., and Malcolm X, who called for nonviolent resistance and resistance by any means necessary (even armed self-defense), respectively. Seale, like Malcolm X, was clearly a Staggerlee figure in Baldwin's mind; yet since both Malcolm X and King were assassinated, Baldwin joined many of his countrymen in a period of great disillusionment about the tragic outcome of the struggle for civil rights, and militancy became a more potent and attractive option, as is evident in *No Name in the Street* (1972). Even Eldridge Cleaver's vicious ad hominem, homophobic attack on Baldwin in his memoir, *Soul on Ice* (1967), did not turn Baldwin completely against black militancy. It is clear from his introduction to Seale's autobiography that Baldwin admired and respected the rage that would serve as a kind of support for the black community. But it is also clear that he would not have titled his own autobiography "Stagolee." Throughout his career, he blended the call to militancy with the call to preach King's gospel of love in a secular context, and binding it all together was a call for respect of self and others. In fact, Baldwin does not mention violence in his introduction to Seale's book; rather, he defines the civil rights movement, beginning with Rosa Parks, as the historical period that "helped Stagolee, the black folk hero Bobby takes for his model, to achieve his manhood. For, it is that tremendous journey which Bobby's book is about: the act of assuming and becoming oneself" (x). For Baldwin, there were no easy answers to the problem of racism, and he used Staggerlee to illustrate what for him would always be a debate about the proper response to it. For embracing Staggerlee's rage and personal sense of justice would not protect young black men from winding up in jail, or getting shot, as Seale and Malcolm X illustrate. Baldwin is cautious about Staggerlee, entertaining the legendary figure's potential as a victim, a martyr, or an inspiration, but never as an unmitigated hero.

Baldwin generally keeps his Staggerlee figures in the margins of his works, but he does make Staggerlee the central figure in "Staggerlee Wonders," the long opening poem of his collection *Jimmy's Blues*.[4] The speaker of Baldwin's poem is a prophetic, protean trickster who deliberately addresses white America on behalf of black America. Unlike the legendary Staggerlee, Baldwin's speaker is not hot-tempered or immediately dangerous. He is cool and intellectual in his approach to the problem of race, and he presents "snapshots" of contemporary America "with a satiric humor that belongs to the marketplace" (Brown 210). Baldwin's Staggerlee is a witness to the crimes of the latter half of the twentieth century, and he sees his role as reporting the impending apocalypse—the rage that seethes not beneath his brow, but beneath the brows of all of the "niggers" who "are calculating" (23), and who are also angry, because "the niggers are aware that no one has discussed / anything at all with the niggers" (16). Staggerlee uses his voice to communicate the rage of the oppressed to the naive oppressors who refuse to see the consequences of their crimes. This is a Staggerlee who is not quick to use his gun, yet one who clearly understands why someone would be. He is the Staggerlee who has tempted Baldwin and infused his rhetoric with righteous anger.

It is a slightly different Staggerlee who takes the form of Richard in *Blues for Mister Charlie* and Christopher in *Tell Me How Long the Train's Been Gone*. In both cases, Staggerlee inspires but does not offer easy solutions to the terribly complex problems faced by the main characters, who are trying, as Baldwin said of Stagolee while discussing Seale, to achieve their manhood. Staggerlee's role in all of these cases is to raise awareness, whether it is an individual's awareness of the meaning (or possible form) of his anger or the white public's awareness of the explosive potential of black anger.

Blues for Mister Charlie is one of the more complex pieces of the Baldwin puzzle. It was written at a crucial time in his career, just after the publication of his most famous essay, "Down at the Cross" (the main essay in *The Fire Next Time* [1963]); in the same year he appeared on the cover of *Time* magazine (May 17) and was invited to speak with Attorney General Robert Kennedy on the racial tension affecting the country, especially in the South. Baldwin's second play was also his first critical failure where there had been until that point nearly universal praise, and he suffered a "near-breakdown" during the play's production (Leeming 234). Baldwin first traveled to the American South in 1957 to write a series of journalistic essays and, according to David Leeming, after seeing "something of the South for himself, he wondered if nonviolence would be enough" (145). By the time he returned to the South in 1963, he had begun to embrace some of the violent indignation that was affecting many of his black countrymen. Baldwin met civil rights leader Medgar Evers in January of that explosive year—five months before Evers was assassinated—and the two of them investigated the racially motivated murder of a young black man, most likely at the hands of a white storekeeper. This event—with echoes of the murder of Emmett Till—becomes the basis for Baldwin's play, and he imagines the victim as a version of Staggerlee. As in the poem, the black man's rage "grows . . . from the white man's 'sleeping terror' [and] the white man's insistence on his own superiority" (*Time* 26). Thus, the blues Baldwin sings in this play are for Mister Charlie—that is, for white Americans. Richard's death is not tragic for Mister Charlie according to Richard's own father, Meridian, who says to the judge at the murder trial, "For you, it would have been tragic if he had lived" (135). In many versions of the Staggerlee legend, the judge and jury elect to kill Staggerlee because they fear someone so cruel that he would commit murder over a hat. Richard, however, is alive throughout the play, though he dies in the opening scene. He returns to the stage repeatedly as the action flashes back to what happened before the murder. Like the legend of Staggerlee, Richard does not die; rather, he is preserved through the memories of those he intimidated as well as of those he inspired.

Baldwin's play is hardly conventional, though it embodies ancient conventions such as a chorus (actually a chorus split into two known as "Blacktown" and "Whitetown") as well as modern conventions such as on-stage scene changes meant to reflect a character's subjectivity or memory, in the tradition of Arthur Miller or Tennessee Williams. The absence of a clear protagonist is what makes Baldwin's play so complex. If Blacktown and Whitetown represent the stereotypical responses to a racist murder, and if Lyle Britten is clearly the antagonist we are meant to hate, then all of the other characters are possible protagonists; Leeming observes that, "in a sense, each of the characters gives voice to an aspect of—sings a stanza of—the blues parable" (236). The play's structure is similar to that of Baldwin's *Another Country* (1962), which also begins with the death of a black man damaged by discrimination and follows with the effect his death has on his friends and family. Richard is denied the status of a tragic figure, but his legacy lives on through his gun.

In an inversion of typical tragic (especially Oedipal) models, in this play the son passes something along to his father that will potentially address the conflict in the future: a gun. Yet the play ends in tremendous ambiguity: Meridian has placed Richard's gun "under the Bible. Like the pilgrims of old" (158) and has warned with Baldwinian prophecy, "You know, for us it all began with the Bible and the gun. Maybe it will end with the Bible and the gun" (156). The twist on the Staggerlee story is that Richard never uses his gun, and yet he is shot in cold blood for his tough Staggerlee talk. Moreover, Chekov's dictum that a gun mounted on the wall in the first act of a play must be fired in the third act is not fulfilled here: the gun is still loaded at the play's conclusion. Staggerlee's anger has gotten him killed in the mid-twentieth-century racist South; but the source of the play's tension is its ominous ending, as his gun may be fired yet.

Richard is evidently a Staggerlee character not only through his association with his gun, but also because he has grown to trust only his own instincts and to prefer a personal sense of justice to the flawed judicial system. His fierce individualism is first revealed through his conversation with his grandmother, Mother Henry, in the play's first act when he says of his trip to the North, "I was just a green country boy and they ain't got no signs up, dig, saying you can't go here or you can't go there. No, you got to find that out all by your lonesome" (34). Like Guitar in *Song of Solomon*, Richard expresses pent-up rage at the death of one of his parents at the hands of white people, and he has not forgiven his father for failing to seek revenge: "I just wish, that day that Mama died, he'd took a pistol and gone through that damn white man's hotel and shot every son of a bitch in the place. That's right. I wish he'd shot them dead. I been dreaming of that day ever since I left here" (35). Richard's anger has grown not only into cancerous hatred but also into self-loathing, which explains why he can only self-destruct, like Rufus in *Another Country* or Roy in *Go Tell It on the Mountain* (1953), both of whom contain enough rage and bravado to become versions of Staggerlee. Like these other characters, Richard has lost perspective; he says,

> I'm going to treat [all white people] as though they were responsible for all the crimes that ever happened in the history of the world—oh, yes! They're responsible for all the misery *I've* ever seen, and that's good enough for me. It's because my Daddy's got no power because he's *black*. And the only way the black man's going to *get* any power is to drive all the white men into the sea. (35)

He then proclaims that he is going to "get well" by drinking a little of his own poisonous hatred each day, and he produces his gun, which he claims "is all that the man understands. He don't understand nothing else. *Nothing else!*" (37). Like Staggerlee, all Richard has is a gun, a taste for revenge, and the belief that the former is the only cure for the latter. It is fittingly ironic that he is shot by Lyle Britten, a man no less infected with racial hatred and no less stubborn in his own quest for vengeance.

Part of the Staggerlee legend is Staggerlee's status as a tremendous lover, occasionally even a pimp. Baldwin emphasizes Lyle's sexual anxiety over black men—a familiar motif in Baldwin's works that is especially prominent in the short story "Going to Meet the Man" (1965)—and part of Richard's persona is the swaggering braggart who crows about his conquests of white women in the North: "Every one of them's got some piss-assed, faggoty white boy on a string somewhere. They go home and marry him, dig, when they can't make it with me no more—but when they want some *loving*, funky, down-home, bring-it-on-here-and-put-it-on-the-table style . . . " Juanita interrupts him to say how sad these exploits sound, but he refuses to let down his guard: "Well, I want *them* to be sad, baby, I want to screw up *their* minds *forever*. But why should *I* be so sad?" (42). He is almost too angry to be sad; there is really nothing left for him but his final grand drama, his version of Staggerlee's barroom brawl, which he initiates with Lyle Britten first in Papa D.'s store, then in Lyle's. The animosity between them is due to their possessiveness not of a Stetson hat, but rather of women: Jo and Juanita. Despite his claim that "this gun goes everywhere I go" (37), Richard deliberately gives it away so that his confrontation with Lyle becomes more like suicide than a brawl. His tough talk, his revenge, and his gun are meant not for him but for another, the protagonist toward whom the play reaches.

The four most likely candidates for protagonist represent four distinct groups, all of whom would have been among Baldwin's intended audience: Lorenzo, the young black militant in training; Parnell, the aging white liberal; Juanita, the enraged black woman who has loved and lost the victim, Richard; and finally Meridian, who represents the older black generation and who doubts the efficacy of Christianity. It is Meridian who is poised to receive Richard's message most directly because, like Leo in *Tell Me How Long the Train's Been Gone* and Milkman in *Song of Solomon*, the Staggerlee figure perceives Meridian to be insufficiently angry about racial injustice. From Richard's point of view Meridian is blinded to the truth because of his devotion to Christianity. Meridian falls into a long line of similarly blinded characters in Baldwin's work, including Gabriel in *Go Tell It on the Mountain*, Sister Margaret in *The Amen Corner* (1955), and Mrs. Hunt in *If Beale Street Could Talk* (1974). Like the speaker of "Staggerlee Wonders," Richard's role is to illuminate the blind and to infuse them with a sense of righteous anger to complicate their sense of forgiveness. I should emphasize that Richard and Staggerlee are only personae of Baldwin, who writes in his introduction to the published play that

> with one part of my mind at least, I hate [racists like Lyle] and would be willing to kill them. Yet with another part of my mind, I am aware that no man is a villain in his own eyes . . . What is ghastly and really almost hopeless in our racial situation now is that the crimes we have committed are so great and so unspeakable that the acceptance of this knowledge would lead, literally, to madness. The human being, then, in order to protect himself, closes his eyes, compulsively repeats his crimes, and enters a spiritual darkness which no one can describe. (6)

The fact that Richard relinquishes his gun and his murderous anger demonstrates that he, like Baldwin, admits to having "another part of his mind" that realizes how futile the other half is. Baldwin points out in "Many Thousands Gone" that "no American Negro exists who does not have his private Bigger Thomas living in the skull . . . This dark and dangerous and unloved stranger is part of himself forever. Only this recognition sets him in any wise free" (*Notes* 42). Yet Richard has no outlet for the other part of his mind, the part that would balance the murderous rage within him. His only recourse is the kind of suicide that will carry a heavy message for his father, not unlike the situation of Olunde and Elesin in Wole Soyinka's play *Death and the King's Horseman* (1975). Baldwin and Soyinka are artists, though, whose frustrations with their societies turn a suicidal or homicidal rage into drama that can elicit a response both onstage and in the audience. Baldwin concludes his introduction with: "We are walking in terrible darkness here, and this is one man's attempt to bear witness to the reality and the power of light" (8). Richard, like Baldwin and like the speaker of "Staggerlee Wonders," chooses to illuminate Meridian's "spiritual darkness" while passing along some of his anger before dying.

In their final conversation, Richard asks Meridian if he has thought about marrying Juanita and says, "I'm a man now, Daddy, and I can ask you to tell me the truth. I'm making up for lost time. Maybe you should try to make up for lost time too" (52). He moves quickly to the heart of the issue with regard to truth: "Why didn't you tell me the truth way back there? Why didn't you tell me my mother was murdered?" (53). Meridian's response is that of someone who has closed his eyes "in order to protect himself":

> Richard, your mother's dead. People die in all kinds of ways. They die when their times comes [sic] to die. Your mother loved you and she was gone—there was nothing more I could do for her. I had to think of you. I didn't want you to be—poisoned—by useless and terrible suspicions. I didn't want to wreck your life. I know your life was going to be hard enough. (53)

Of course, Richard has discovered the truth no less from his father's evasions than from the rumors he has heard. Meridian's attempts to protect Richard backfire, and Richard sacrifices his own life to awaken in his father the anger that he has so long buried. He hands his father the gun with no instructions except, "When I ask you for it, you got to give it to me" (54).

The effect of this gesture is almost immediate. When Meridian speaks with Parnell after Richard's death, he says, "Maybe I was wrong not to let the people arm" (55). When Parnell points out the dangers of this position, Meridian persists: "Maybe they'll find a leader who can lead them someplace." Parnell responds: "Somebody with a gun? Is that what you mean?" and Meridian delivers an anguished speech that demonstrates his wavering faith in Christianity and gradual contact with his own fury against God and against his own response to his wife's death. He concludes it with, "The eyes of God—maybe those eyes are blind—I never let myself think of that before" (57). Parnell remarks, "There's something in your tone I've never heard before—rage—maybe hatred." Meridian shows how complete his transformation is: "You've heard it before. You just never recognized it before. You've heard it in all those blues and spirituals and gospel songs you claim to love so much" (59). These blues are for Mister Charlie, as Meridian tells Parnell, passing along some of his dead son's anger, the anger that is also passed along through songs like the "Stagolee Blues." Meridian has taken on at least the visionary quality, and some of the rage, of Baldwin's poetic persona Staggerlee, who bears witness: "I have seen a veil come down, / leaving myself, and the other, / alone in that cave / which every soul remembers, and / out of which, desperately afraid, / I turn, turn, stagger, stumble out, / into the healing air" ("Staggerlee" 12).

Parnell reacts to Meridian's newfound anger with the shock of the white liberal who feels betrayed by it: "You sound more and more like your son, do you know that? A lot of the colored people here didn't approve of him, but he said things they longed to say—said right out loud, for all the world to hear, how much he despised white people!" Meridian responds, "He didn't say things *I* longed to say" (59). Meridian's growth is positive because he has clung to his individual identity, refusing to become an archetype or a caricature of single-minded rage, as his son had become. Whether he will or ought to use the gun that Richard has given him after the play's conclusion is left for the audience to decide. David Leeming writes that *"Blues for Mister Charlie* opened on April 23 [1964] to an audience of highly appreciative blacks and sometimes angry and often shocked whites" (238). The white audience's reaction aligns them with Parnell and is probably explained by their fear of the gun that Meridian hides under his Bible. Yet the gun is not in Staggerlee's hands anymore, and it is not likely to be fired indiscriminately. Meridian has matured and developed in the way his son was never allowed to; as he says in court, "I am a man. A *man! I tried to help my son become a man. But manhood is a dangerous pursuit, here. And that pursuit undid him because of *your* guns, *your* hoses, *your* dogs, *your* judges, *your* law-makers, *your* folly, *your* pride, *your* cruelty, *your* cowardice, *your* money, *your* chain gangs, and *your* churches!" (137). When the court asks him, "And you are a minister?" he responds, "I think I may be beginning to become one" (139). The gun under Meridian's Bible has less power than his new rhetoric, and there is no question that by the end of the play his perspective is aligned with that of his author, also a former minister in the church, who later discovered his calling as a secular preacher whose gospel was the bitter truth about American racism.

Baldwin's experience with the theater in the production of *Blues for Mister Charlie* was a traumatic one not only because of the play's poor reviews, but also because of his perceived loss of creative control to the actors, directors, and producers of the play. He went into a period of exile to write his next novel, and his alter ego, who suffers a heart attack after a performance, shows up on the first page of *Tell Me How Long the Train's Been Gone.* Leo Proudhammer's near-fatal collapse demonstrates not only Baldwin's disillusionment with the theater, but also his weariness at becoming a player on the national stage for the civil rights movement, which had begun to resemble civil war by the late 1960s. Baldwin bitterly titles the first section of the book "The House Nigger," alluding to Leo's status as someone who has betrayed the downtrodden of his race for the approval of the rich and powerful whites. His salvation comes in the third section of the book titled "Black Christopher" after the black militant Staggerlee figure who awakens the righteous anger that had been buried in Leo. As in *Blues for Mister Charlie,* the hero of this novel is not meant to become Staggerlee, but rather to follow him in a certain direction on the path to growth. Christopher's militancy at the end of the novel might again shock white audiences, as it seems as though Baldwin is advocating a race war: "'Guns,' said Christopher. 'We need guns'" (369). But Leo's response is, "I said nothing" (369). Though sympathetic to Christopher's position, Leo, like Baldwin, does not accept it as his own. The novel is again about Leo's development from someone whose anger is turned inward to someone whose anger can find the proper outlet. Christopher-as-Staggerlee leads Leo toward that outlet, but Leo (like Baldwin) is not someone who sees guns as the solution to injustice. As Lynn Orilla Scott observes, "Those critics who read *Tell Me How Long the Train's Been Gone* as a simple endorsement of black militancy missed the ways that the novel speaks to and signifies on the black power movement of the 1960s" (32).

Before the final few pages of the novel, Leo tells us precious little about the significance of Black Christopher in his life. Very early on, though, he says something reminiscent of Baldwin's introduction to *Blues for Mister Charlie:* "My life, that desperately treacherous labyrinth, seemed for a moment to be opening out behind me; a light seemed to fall where there had been no light before. I began to see myself in others. I began for a moment to apprehend how Christopher must sometimes have felt" (7). Leo's admission that he has begun to identify with others, including the angry Christopher, is evidence of his maturity, not unlike Meridian's suspicion that his pacifist/Christian message might have been irresponsible. These are not necessarily endorsements of the militant mindset, though they could be; but they are evidence that the protagonists of these works have grown skeptical of the ways of thinking to which they had devoted their lives. Baldwin is consistently skeptical of the notion of safety, and it could be said that Leo attempts to hide in the theater behind various faces just as Meridian would hide in the church. The speaker of "Staggerlee Wonders," Richard, and Black Christopher all have the ability to lead these characters and Baldwin's audience out of their respective caves—a "labyrinth," in Leo's words—and into the light.

Leo's crisis is precipitated by his response to fame, and it reflects Baldwin's return to exile (in Istanbul) following his period of high exposure after the publication of "Down at the Cross" (1962), the riots in Birmingham, and the production of *Blues for Mister Charlie.* Leo's collapse is more significantly an identity crisis related to his latent feelings that he has neglected the anguish of his race in favor of artistic safety. After he collapses, he is taken to his dressing room and observes that his makeup is still on; as he says, "I had not got my own face back" (9). His thoughts are drawn outward: "Something happened to me, deep in me. I thought of Africa" (10). Throughout the 1960s, black Americans frequently associated their racial identity with Africa, the land of their distant ancestry, and

Baldwin visited Senegal, Guinea, and Sierra Leone in 1962 despite the fact that he was "frankly skeptical of the interest among American blacks at the time in their African 'homeland'" (Leeming 207). Leo's associations with Africa are not nostalgic: rather, he feels buried anger at the injustice of slavery, at what might be called his "previous condition":

> I remembered that Africans believed that death was a return to one's ancestors, a reunion with those one loved. They had hurled themselves off slave ships, grateful to the enveloping water and even grateful to the teeth of sharks for making the journey home so swift. And I thought of a very great and very beautiful man whom I had known and loved, a black man shot down within hearing of his wife and children in the streets of a miserable Deep South town (10).

This obvious allusion to Medgar Evers connects recent racial outrage to the history of slavery and the seething rage of this novel to *Blues for Mister Charlie*. Leo's collapse comes less from the stress of his career than from his perception of himself as a "house nigger," someone who has not yet spoken or acted on behalf of the victims of racism.

Part of the reason that Leo has repressed his anger is that he has seen his father do the same. He recalls how his father allowed himself to become a victim by refusing to indulge the rage within him. Observing how he is being cheated at the market, he tells his sons, Leo and Caleb, "You got to watch them all the time. But our people ain't never going to learn. I don't know what's wrong with our people. We need a prophet to straighten out our minds and lead us out of this hell" (18). Caleb and Leo interpret the word "prophet" differently: Caleb becomes a self-righteous minister; and Leo takes refuge in his acting, yet eventually understands that the "prophet" his father refers to might be someone more like Black Christopher, whose savior status ("Black Christ") is inextricably linked to his race and his rage, pointedly *not* to religion. Leo says, "Black Christopher: because he was black in so many ways—black in color, black in pride, black in rage" (56). Both Leo and Caleb have witnessed their father's repression, and as children they responded to it the same way. When they are mistreated by their landlord, Caleb and Leo both wish that their father would assault him:

> Our father was younger than Mr. Rabinowitz, leaner, stronger, and bigger. With one blow into that monstrous gut, he could have turned Rabinowitz purple, brought him to his knees, he could have hurled him down the stairs. And we knew how much he hated Rabinowitz . . . we would have been happy to see our proud father kill him. We would have been glad to help. But our father did nothing of the sort. He stood before Rabinowitz, scarcely looking at him, swaying before the spittle and the tirade, sweating—looking unutterably weary. (12–13)

Like Meridian and Milkman, Leo's father is flawed not because he refuses to kill someone for mistreating him, but because he refuses to release the power of his own rage in any way, and thus allows it to weaken him.

Throughout most of the novel—made up of flashbacks that Leo pieces together during his recovery in the hospital—Leo is someone who exists between the poles of a Staggerlee-like unbridled anger and his father's (or brother's) tremendous capacity to suppress such anger. Over the course of the narrative we see both elements surface, and Leo can be seen as a "double-minded man," calling to mind, as Lynn Orilla Scott points out, DuBois's concept of the painful double consciousness of black Americans (36), and also Baldwin himself in the introduction to *Blues for Mister Charlie*. Leo experiences discrimination both firsthand and secondhand. His own experiences include the fact that he is stereotyped during his first meeting with the San-Marquands; during his painful walk with Barbara through the New Jersey town that houses the theater, when they are taunted by the racists there; and by the police harassment he faces after his affair with Madeleine. Yet all of these experiences pale in comparison with the book's most painful racist incident: Caleb's imprisonment and subsequent emotional and sexual torture in prison. Caleb's arrest had been foreshadowed first when his friend Arthur leads Leo to him and later when Caleb leads Leo home. In both cases, the murderous rage against white policemen is unmistakable, and it connects to countless other depictions of police racism in Baldwin's works; Arthur mutters, "You white cock-suckers. I wish all of you were dead" (38). After a similar incident, Caleb says under his breath, "Thanks, you white cock-sucking dog-shit miserable white mother-fuckers. Thanks, all you scum-bag Christians" (45). He explains to Leo that they were harassed "because I'm black and they *paid* to beat on black asses . . . All black people are shit to them. You remember that. You black like me and they going to hate you as long as you live just because you're black. There's something wrong with them. They got some kind of disease. I hope to God it kills them soon" (46). Caleb, Leo, and their father bond over their anger directly after this incident; yet their father has already buried his rage, and Caleb's will be converted to Christianity after his prison experience. Leo's father says to him, "Don't let them make you afraid," but he admits, "I knew that I was already afraid" (50). This fear goes a long way toward explaining how Leo deals with his emotions. In a later meeting with Saul and Lola San-Marquand, he makes a sarcastic joke at the expense of his race and walks away from them; he admits, "I was bitter, I was twisted out of shape with rage," but "[I am] trying to bring myself to some reasonable, fixed place, to turn off the motor which was running away with me" (74). Acting becomes a way of turning off this motor, one of the many possible "gimmicks" Baldwin describes in "Down at the

Cross" that will help him to survive his plight: "Every Negro boy—in my situation during those years, at least—who reaches this point realizes, at once, profoundly, because he wants to live, that he stands in great peril and must find, with speed, a 'thing,' a gimmick, to lift him out, to start him on his way. *And it does not matter what the gimmick is*" (*Fire* 38).

Although it may not matter what the original gimmick is to start a young black boy on his way, Baldwin becomes increasingly suspicious of religion as that gimmick. *Tell Me How Long the Train's Been Gone* was written in between the assassinations of Malcolm X and Martin Luther King, the representatives of black vengeance and Christian forgiveness, respectively. Leo is also divided between these poles, as I have said, and his sympathy for Caleb demonstrates a capacity for love so deep that it causes him to break one of the most entrenched taboos and engage in incestuous love with his brother as a way of healing his wounds. Within the novel's world, Christopher and Caleb represent the two opposite responses to racism represented by King and Malcolm X. In the mode of Staggerlee, Christopher relies only on his own actions for justice and places himself in a position to disrupt the cosmos: "Christopher did not believe that deliverance would ever come—he was going to drag it down from heaven or raise it up from hell" (85). Caleb, perhaps sharing his younger brother's fear inspired by routine police harassment, relies on religious deliverance. When he is about to be arrested for a crime he did not commit, Caleb tells the police, "You don't need those guns. I've never shot nobody in my life." The police officer's response is enough to kindle Leo's rage; the officer says, "'You're a very inquisitive bunch of niggers. Here's what for,' and he suddenly grabbed Caleb and smashed the pistol butt against the side of his head" (96). The young Leo is ineffective in his attempts to kick, punch, even bite as a way of responding to his injustice, and the older Leo's silence in response to Christopher's "We need guns" probably resonates with a chord of vengeance buried deep within Leo from the moment of Caleb's arrest.

The sexual event between Caleb and Leo is born of Leo's hatred, in solidarity with his brother, for the way Caleb had been treated in prison. Just before they make love, Leo thinks,

Never, never, never, I swore it, with Caleb's breath in my face, his tears drying on my neck, my arms around him, would I ever forgive this world. Never. Never. Never. I would find some way to make them pay. I would do something one day to at least one bland, stupid, happy white face which would change that face forever. If they thought that Caleb was black, and if they thought that I was black, I would show them, yes, I would, one day, exactly what blackness was! I swore it. I swore it. (162)

After hearing Caleb's entire narrative later, he uses words almost identical to Richard's in *Blues for Mister Charlie:* "I realized I could hate. And I realized that I would feed my hatred, feed it every day and every hour. I would keep it healthy, I would make it strong, and I would find a use for it one day" (184). Leo's intensified rage, building on the mistreatment of his father and the police harassment he faced in his youth, suggests the same kind of anger that Richard develops in *Blues for Mister Charlie* and that Guitar develops in *Song of Solomon,* also in response to racial discrimination inflicted upon a loved one. Leo is the novel's protagonist, though, and Baldwin displaces this rage onto Christopher, who more closely resembles Richard and Guitar. Part of the reason Leo does not allow this rage to dominate him is that he is, like Meridian or Milkman, a character who spends time with black and white people and who has developed empathy for both. Baldwin and Morrison would agree that the heart of the race problem in the United States is segregation, the post–Civil War heir to slavery, and the problem of legal or de facto segregation would not be addressed if Leo were to nurture his rage until it grew into murder. Although Christopher does not kill anyone (unlike Guitar or Richard, each of whom, in a sense, murders himself), his willingness to do so is clear; yet the fact that Leo does not fully adopt Christopher's anger indicates Baldwin's skepticism toward the kind of anger that could either lead to self-destruction or become ideology, as is clear from his conclusions about the Black Muslim movement in "Down at the Cross": "I could have hoped that the Muslim movement had been able to inculcate in the demoralized Negro population a truer and more individual sense of its own worth" (Baldwin, *Fire* 95). As is consistently true in Baldwin's work, the emphasis of this novel is on the individual learning to love, not on a pre-scribed way of thinking.

Even so, Caleb's response to racism—a Christian conversion that subsumes his life—is even less acceptable to Leo than Christopher's militancy is. This difference has to do with Baldwin's (and Leo's) belief that in order to be free in contemporary America, "one needed a handle, a lever, a means of inspiring fear" (35); to Baldwin, the Christian church was decidedly *not* that. Rejecting Caleb's solution for Christopher's, Leo says, "God's batting average failing to inspire confidence, I committed myself to Christopher's possibilities. Perhaps God would join us later, when He was convinced that we were on the winning side" (255). Leo clearly feels forsaken by a God who has failed to protect his people, and his bitter rejection of his brother testifies to the depth of his pain. In an imagined conversation with Caleb, he says,

What a slimy gang of creeps and cowards those old church fathers must have been; and remained; and what was my brother doing in that company? Where else should a man's breath be, Caleb, I asked, but in his nostrils? Have you forgotten, have you forgotten, the flesh of our fathers which burned in that fire, the bones of our men broken by that wrath, the privacy of our women made foul by that conquest, and our children turned into orphans, into less than dogs, by that universal righteousness? Oh, yes, yes, yes, forgive them, let them rot, let them live or die; but how can you stand in the company of our murderers, how can you kiss that monstrous cross, how can you kiss them with the kiss of love? How can you? I asked of Caleb, who moaned and thundered at me from the fire. I had not talked to Caleb for years, for many years had cultivated an inability to think of him. (258)

Leo's preference for Christopher's "possibilities" and his rejection of Caleb's capacity for forgiveness has much to do with his distrust of religion. The intense love that had existed between the brothers is replaced by physical violence as Caleb repeatedly slaps Leo after exhorting him to lead a moral life. Leo responds with a newfound strength: "I curse your God, Caleb, I curse Him, from the bottom of my heart I *curse* Him. And now let Him strike me down. Like you just tried to do" (326). Caleb fails to inspire either his brother or his father to repent, and, like Leo, their father chooses Christopher as his savior: "He and Christopher would spend hours together, reconstructing the black empires of the past, and plotting the demolition of the white empires of the present" (335).

Christopher appeals to Leo for different reasons. His words, for one thing, sound free to Leo, "a way I'd never sounded; a way I'd never been" (339). He is also fearless; Leo observes, "If I was afraid of society's judgment, he was not: 'Fuck these sick people. I do what I like'" (339). This self-determination and defiance is what makes Christopher, like Staggerlee, so attractive; his credo is, "I was born in the streets, baby, and I take nobody's word for *nothing*" (345). And although Christopher is not as aggressive as Lee Shelton, or as any of the mythical variations of Staggerlee, he is not going to be pushed around: "'We are not going to walk to the gas ovens,' Christopher said, 'and we are not going to march to the concentration camps. We have to make the mothers know that'" (349). Although at the novel's conclusion, Christopher repeatedly tries to get Leo to admit that they "need guns," and although Leo feels "a terrible weight on [his] heart" (370) when he does admit it, Christopher's message is not really about guns so much as it is about defiance. Christopher is a thinker and a spokesman as well as a leader, and Leo develops in Christopher's direction not when he embraces the need for guns—which he never fully does—but when he lectures Barbara's family about race while Christopher watches approvingly. Leo's impulse is to drink too much and avoid the topic, but he eventually speaks: "The point is that the Negroes of this country are treated as none of you would dream of treating a dog or a cat. What Christopher's trying to tell you is perfectly true. If you don't want to believe it, well, that's your problem. And I don't feel like talking about it anymore, and I won't" (358). During his time with Christopher, Leo has clearly gained a voice with which to express his anger; and even though he concludes his narrative "standing in the wings again, waiting for my cue" (370), he is much better prepared than he has ever been to control his destiny. Leo's father and Christopher nearly merge in the book's concluding paragraph: "They looked very much like each other, both big, both black, both laughing" (370). Here the anger and passion of the young Staggerlee and the impotent anger of the older black man merge, just as they did in *Blues for Mister Charlie*. Yet Leo leaves them behind and travels alone to Europe, keeping black militancy at a distance and at the same time carrying its power within him.

Morrison and Staggerlee: Guitar/Solo

The person that Leo Proudhammer is becoming at the conclusion of *Tell Me How Long the Train's Been Gone* sounds like the person that James Baldwin became, at least in the words of Toni Morrison, who says in a tribute just after Baldwin's death, "Yours was the courage to live life in and from its belly as well as beyond its edges, to see and say what it was, to recognize and identify evil but never fear or stand in awe of it" (Morrison, "Life" 77). These same words could also be applied to Pilate, Milkman's wise aunt in *Song of Solomon*, whose courage in the face of evil make her the strongest and most positive role model in Milkman's life. What renders the novel tremendously complex is that Guitar, Pilate's killer, might also be described using these same words. Guitar and Pilate are equally courageous, and although each might have separate definitions of evil, neither of them fears it. Like Baldwin's Staggerlee characters, Guitar is capable of both murder and self-sacrifice: "Would you save my life or would you take it? Guitar was exceptional. To both questions he could answer yes" (331). It is true enough that the people closest to Milkman—his parents and his lover Hagar—have done nothing but take from or actually try to take his life. In contrast, Pilate sacrifices her life for Milkman. Guitar is exceptional in his capacity for both; yet Guitar's potential for self-sacrifice is obscured because he is so driven in his quest for Milkman's life that he comes across as deranged, like Hagar, rather than influential, like Pilate. The conclusion makes it seem as if Pilate and Guitar are battling for Milkman's soul, and if Pilate is good, Guitar must be evil. As is always the case in Morrison's work, good and evil are never quite so conveniently divided; as she notes in a 1983 interview, "The people in [my] novels are complex. Some are good and some are bad, but most of them are bits of both" (Taylor-Guthrie 165). Both Pilate and Guitar serve to encourage Milkman's growth, and even though they are not allies, they are allied in that singular purpose.

Indeed, in the novel's opening chapter, "The cat-eyed boy [Guitar] listened to the musical performance [Pilate's song] with at least as much interest as he devoted to the man flapping his wings on top of the hospital" (8). Despite Guitar's prominence in the narrative, most of the novel's critics all but ignore him in favor of Pilate, Macon, Ruth, Hagar, and Milkman himself.[5] They overlook Guitar partially because of the difficulty he presents. He is poisoned by his hatred and (unlike Baldwin's Staggerlee figures) he actually does commit murder in the name of the Seven Days, the secretive black society dedicated to racial revenge. Moreover, his allegiance to Milkman dissolves in favor of his obsession with gold, making him seem crassly materialistic, like Staggerlee in his obsession with his Stetson hat. Yet Guitar desires Milkman's gold to support his crusade, not to indulge in the materialism he has rejected. He essentially shares Black Christopher's affinity for guns, but he lays down his gun in his final battle with Milkman. Guitar's meanness and his terrifying sense of justice discourage readers from seeing him as anything more than a "bad nigger" to be feared. Yet in his mind, his self-proclaimed mission has everything to do with love, and his killing embrace of Milkman in the novel's final scene is the culmination of his lifelong attempt to educate his younger friend: "My main man" (337), he murmurs as they careen into each other's arms. This whispered phrase proves that throughout the book, Guitar's goal, no less than Pilate's, is to guide Milkman into maturity, to ensure that he becomes a man as Leo and Meridian do. Milkman's growth had been stunted not only by his mother's selfish nursing, but also by his father's insensitivity to the plight of his race. Pilate seeks to eradicate Ruth's influence on Milkman by teaching him that love involves giving as well as taking, a lesson that he learns too late to save Hagar's life. Guitar, on the other hand, seeks to eradicate Macon's influence on Milkman by teaching him that black people suffer because of the materialistic values Milkman inherits. The fact that Hagar, Pilate, and either Guitar or Milkman must die after these lessons are imparted is troubling, but it underscores the novel's definition of love as the willingness to give and to take even something as precious as life. Ultimately, life itself is not as important as growth, and Milkman's flight at the novel's conclusion indicates his growth as it connects him to his ancestors and to Pilate, whose written name is borne away in a bird's beak as her life ebbs from her (336).

Naming is, of course, one of the most important motifs in the novel,[6] and Milkman's growth is inextricably tied to his understanding of the significance of names and oral history. After his eventual realization of the Solomon song's meaning, he closes his eyes and meditates on the significance of names: "Names they got from yearnings, gestures, flaws, events, mistakes, weaknesses. Names that bore witness" (330). The list includes his name and that of virtually everyone in the book, but also "Staggerlee, Jim the Devil, Fuck-Up, and *Dat* Nigger." Angling out from these thoughts of names was one more—the one that whispered in the spinning wheels of the bus: "Guitar is biding his time" (330). Milkman's connection with and understanding of the meaning of naming in his culture links Staggerlee with Guitar here: their names contain history ("events") and desires ("yearnings"). Both men are guided by their need to establish justice in a world that would take their possessions away from them. Staggerlee murders a man who tries to take his hat; emphasizing the same possessiveness, Railroad Tommy lectures Guitar extensively about all of the things Guitar cannot have (59–61). In fact, the name Guitar was given to him because of something he desired and could not have: a guitar. The central damage in his life is revealed through something else he cannot have—candy— because it reminds him of the unwanted gift of candy a white man gave him after his father's death. Guitar's rage is directly connected to something he has lost and cannot recover.

Even readers who understand Guitar are not likely to sympathize with him. He inspires fear because, as he says to Milkman, "I was never afraid to kill. Anything" (85). Unlike Milkman, he understands that the source of his pain is connected to race; when Milkman seeks him out as "the one person left whose clarity never failed him" (79), Guitar tries to explain why Milkman hit his father:

> Listen, baby, people do funny things. Specially us. The cards are stacked against us and just trying to stay in the game, stay alive and in the game, makes us do funny things. Things we can't help. Things that make us hurt one another. We don't even know why. But look here, don't carry it inside and don't give it to nobody else. Try to understand it, but if you can't, just forget it and keep yourself strong, man. (87–88)

This lecture follows Milkman's first gleanings of the seething anger of the Seven Days, who discuss the murder of Emmett Till in the barbershop. Yet Milkman is in no way aware of his connection to this anger or to this murdered boy, and his complacency is something that Guitar feels he must address if Milkman is ever to become a true man.

What separates Guitar from Milkman is not merely class, but also their opposite responses to the restive racial situation that develops from their class positions. Milkman accuses Guitar of romanticizing black poverty: "You mad at every Negro who ain't scrubbing floors and picking cotton. This ain't Montgomery, Alabama." Milkman isn't aware of the political implications of his reference to the town at the center of so much racial tension, and when Guitar points it out and asks him what he would do if he were in Montgomery, Milkman answers, "Buy a plane ticket" (104). Guitar interprets this statement carefully: "You're not a serious person," he tells Milkman (104). During the same conversation, when Milkman spontaneously tells Guitar about his dream about his mother Guitar again interprets it in terms of Milkman's lack of empathy: "Why didn't you go help her?" (105). Guitar sees Milkman as a copy of Macon: neither man would help someone else because each is concerned only with gratifying his own needs. The sense of justice that emerges from Guitar's contact with the Seven Days is not meant to encourage Milkman to sympathize with their cause. Instead it is meant to awaken Milkman from his complacency about the suffering of others.

It is evident that Morrison does not advocate the actions of either Guitar or the Seven Days as the proper response to racial injustice and violence. Her focus is on Milkman's growth—his development of a conscience that connects him to his heritage. Milkman's gradual understanding of the songs and stories that constitute his past is the most evident and positive development in his growth. But Morrison also questions Milkman's complacency about current events, such as the murder of Emmett Till. When Milkman thinks, "The racial problems that consumed Guitar were the most boring of all" (107), Morrison reveals her concern for him, and although she would not have him become "consumed" with such problems, she *would* have him admit that they are problems and react with an appropriate measure of outrage. Freddie, the character who names Milkman and thus represents the link to his ancestral past, is "incredulous" (111) that Milkman cannot recall the date of Emmett Till's murder. Guitar's role is thus to reveal the potency of black anger to Milkman.

Straddling the line between trickster and badman, Guitar repeatedly instructs Milkman, subtly trying to awaken within his friend any kind of sympathy or awareness of the intensifying racial animosity around him. Jerry H. Bryant agrees that Guitar shares some traits of the badman, but is a somewhat altered version: "In Guitar some of the traits of the traditional badman remain, but while no pure badman would ever join a black nationalist moral crusade, Morrison suggests that Guitar illustrates how, by the late sixties and early seventies, the Black Power movement might plausibly legitimize 'bad niggers' (185). Guitar jokingly leads Milkman through a clever discussion of geography, tea, and eggs, and then "change[s] the air" with the line, "Somebody got to bust your shell" (116). Although this metaphor connects directly to the flight and bird imagery that dominates the novel, it does so in a violent way. Guitar reveals his violence at every turn. In their oft-analyzed discussion of the peacock and the "jewelry [that] weighs it down. Like vanity," Guitar's impulse is to chase the bird down and "eat him!" (179). His willingness to kill is commensurate with his awakening cry to Milkman: "You listen! You got a life? Live it! Live the motherfuckin life! Live it!" (183). Pilate emphasizes birth and assesses life as "precious," but both Pilate and Guitar, to different degrees and in different contexts, witness death and face it directly, which is necessary if one is to feel alive. Milkman jokes that he is "already Dead" throughout the novel, and Pilate and Guitar are together responsible for guiding him away from the Dead household that has prevented his growth. Pilate may be the one who points Milkman in the direction of his ancestors, but it is Guitar who initiates his adventure and introduces Milkman to Pilate in the first place.

Still, Milkman is right to regard Guitar with suspicion; he sees Guitar as "the one sane and constant person he knew [who] had flipped, had ripped open and was spilling blood and foolishness instead of conversation" (165). Here Morrison's own wariness of Guitar's twisted brand of militancy is evident. Guitar, like Staggerlee, has come to believe too much in the idea that "young dudes are subject to change the rules" (161). If Macon, Ruth, and Hagar represent lovesickness, Guitar and the Seven Days have turned that lovesickness into justice-sickness. Milkman is in no way encouraged by Guitar's description of the Seven Days; he feels "tight, shriveled, and cold" upon hearing it (155). Morrison's essential humanism rejects Guitar's ideology, especially when he reveals the logical flaw in the Seven Days' belief system, that "there are no innocent white people, because every one of them is a potential nigger-killer" (155). Guitar attempts to be rational and eloquent like Baldwin's Staggerlee characters, and he is similarly willing to sacrifice himself for his notion of justice: "How I die or when doesn't interest me. What I die *for* does. It's the same as what I live for" (159). When Milkman compares Guitar to Malcolm X, Guitar rejects the association: "Guitar is *my* name. Bains is the slave master's name. And I'm all of that. Slave names don't bother me; but slave status does." Milkman argues that "knocking off white folks" will not change the "slave status" of either one of them and concludes, "Guitar, none of that shit is going to change how I live or how any other Negro lives" (160). In taking this ethical stance, Milkman proves that he is not "already Dead" and that Guitar's anger and response to injustice are not his own. The point is that Milkman must learn to fly on his own wings; Guitar has succeeded in busting his shell, but Guitar cannot manufacture Milkman's wings for him.

Guitar's problem is that he has accepted the ideology of the Seven Days, and it is ideology that Morrison distrusts, especially when it threatens to obscure the individual. As Wahneema Lubiano says of *Song of Solomon*, "I do not think that identity in this novel can be conceived simply in opposition to an oppressive force (with its genesis in the dominant culture) that balks the emergence of a self" (96–97). Milkman is able to separate Guitar's essentially violent tendencies from his involvement with the Seven Days; he realizes, "Guitar could kill, would kill, and probably had killed. The Seven Days was the consequence of this ability, but not its origin" (210). Although Milkman ostensibly travels south to search for gold, the object of his quest quickly turns to familial identity. When he hears the story of his grandfather's death, he feels anger for the first time: "Milkman wondered at his own anger. He hadn't felt angry when he first heard about it" (232). Reverend Cooper wonders whether Milkman's purpose for coming south is to "even things up," and Milkman finds himself in an awkward position: "Milkman couldn't answer except in Guitar's words, so he said nothing" (233). It is significant that Milkman experiences some of Guitar's rage and just as significant that he refuses to express that rage in Guitar's language. His friend has influenced him, clearly, but he has made his own decision about how thoroughly to internalize this influence.

Milkman discovers another kind of rage within him, too, and it is also linked to Guitar. As he watches the children chant what is still for him "some meaningless rhyme," he recalls a buried memory from his own youth when he was repeatedly attacked for his wealth. Guitar was his savior in the ensuing fights: "Milkman smiled, remembering how Guitar grinned and whooped as the four boys turned on him. It was the first time Milkman saw anybody really enjoy a fight. Afterward Guitar had taken off his baseball cap and handed it to Milkman, telling him to wipe the blood from his nose. Milkman bloodied the cap, returned it, and Guitar slapped it back on his head" (264). This ritual connects them and initiates Milkman into a world where violence can be power. It also prefigures the Staggerlee-like brawl that immediately follows Milkman's memory of his youth, a brawl that is, again, over Milkman's opulent clothing, not unlike the brawl over Shelton's Stetson hat. He escapes the fight alive, though significantly wounded. But the most significant result of the fight is that something has been awakened within him: "Milkman was frozen with anger. If he'd had a weapon, he would have slaughtered everybody in sight" (269). Perhaps this is why Trudier Harris associates Milkman, not Guitar, with Staggerlee; she writes, "We can applaud Milkman even when he is immoral because we have so many masculine models for the individual resisting the pressures of community. We can see traits of Stagolee in Milkman" (128). The distance between Milkman and Guitar has decreased: Milkman feels anger both at his grandfather's death and at his own mistreatment. Like Guitar, he realizes that he is capable of murder in response to such mistreatment.

This capacity is part of what makes the conclusion of Song of Solomon so ambiguous, for now Milkman can kill. He has changed from the days when he would passively await Hagar's attacks on him, and his battle with Guitar is evidence of his willingness to fight for life even as he risks it, declaring to Guitar, "You want my life?" (337). Like Meridian and Leo in Baldwin's works, Milkman has recovered from a spiritual paralysis; in all three cases, characters with Staggerlee's violent and individualistic sense of justice have aided in this recovery.

Yet it would be a mistake to suggest that Baldwin and Morrison celebrate Staggerlee while ignoring his disturbing implications. Insofar as he is associated with black militancy, Staggerlee in these fictions is a powerful figure who can inspire and awaken the type of anger needed for social change. Baldwin and Morrison are concerned immediately with individual change, and although their protagonists might grow in the direction of Staggerlee's anger, Meridian, Leo, and Milkman become more mature versions of themselves, not replicas of Staggerlee. As Guitar says, "Everybody wants the life of a black man" (222). That "everybody" includes the Staggerlees of the world who would seduce black men like Meridian, Leo, and Milkman and become, as Brown says, "a metaphor that structures the life of black males from childhood through maturity" (2). All of these characters finally do what has always been done to legends like Staggerlee or to any version of the blues: they play their own version, modifying what they have heard and making it their own.

NOTES

1. Schone takes his critique of Brown's study a bit further: "But *Stagolee Shot Billy* is flawed by the author's need to romanticize his subject, and by his strained efforts to prove that the real Stagolee was a pimp. When it comes to the life and career of the man behind the song, the book is an object lesson in what happens when a writer starts with a theory and then forces the facts to fit" (2).
2. See "Many Thousands Gone" in *Notes of a Native Son* (1955) (24–45) and "Alas, Poor Richard" in *Nobody Knows My Name* (1961) (146–170).
3. See, for example, Cat Moses, "The Blues Aesthetic in Toni Morrison's *The Bluest Eye*" (1999); and Saadi Simawe, "What Is in a Sound?: The Metaphysics and Politics of Music in *The Amen Corner*" (in Miller 12–33), or Simawe's book *Black Orpheus: Music in African American Fiction from the Harlem Renaissance to Toni Morrison* (2000).
4. I analyze this poem at length in my essay "James Baldwin, Poet," (in Miller 233–255), and Brown also discusses it in *Stagolee Shot Billy*, so rather than analyzing it in depth here, I will use it as a starting point for a discussion of Staggerlee in Baldwin's dramatic and narrative work of the mid-1960s.
5. There are, of course, exceptions; Wahneema Lubiano, for instance, states, "Guitar's identity is as important to this text as Milkman's" (108), and Ralph Story treats the Seven Days in depth in his essay "An Excursion into the Black World: The 'Seven Days' in Toni Morrison's *Song of Solomon*" (1989).
6. See Marianne Hirsch, "Knowing Their Names."

WORKS CITED

Baker, Houston A. *Long Black Song*. Charlottesville: University Press of Virginia, 1972.

Baldwin, James. *The Amen Corner*. New York: Dell, 1968.

————. *Blues for Mister Charlie*. New York: Laurel, 1964.

————. *The Fire Next Time*. New York: Dell, 1963.

————. *If Beale Street Could Talk*. New York: Dell, 1974.

————. *Jimmy's Blues*. New York: St. Martin's, 1983.

————. *Nobody Knows My Name*. New York: Dell, 1961.

————. *No Name in the Street*. New York: Dell, 1972.

————. *Notes of a Native Son*. 1955. Boston: Beacon, 1984.

————. "Stagolee." Introduction to *A Lonely Rage: The Autobiography of Bobby Seale*. New York: Times Books, 1978.

————. *Tell Me How Long the Train's Been Gone*. New York: Laurel, 1968.

Brown, Cecil. *Stagolee Shot Billy*. Cambridge and London: Harvard University Press, 2003.

Bryant, Jerry H. *Born in a Might Bad Land: The Violent Man in African American Folklore and Fiction*. Bloomington and Indianapolis: Indiana University Press, 2003.

Cleaver, Eldridge. *Soul on Ice*. New York: McGraw-Hill, 1967.

Dance, Daryl Cumber. *Shuckin' and Jivin': Folklore from Contemporary Black Americans*. Bloomington: Indiana University Press, 1977.

Gates, Henry Louis, Jr., *The Signifying Monkey*. New York and Oxford: Oxford University Press, 1988.

Harris, Trudier. *Fiction and Folklore: The Novels of Toni Morrison*. Knoxville: University of Tennessee Press, 1991.

Hirsch, Marianne. "Knowing Their Names": Toni Morrison's *Song of Solomon*." *New Essays on Song of Solomon*. Ed. Valerie Smith. Cambridge: Cambridge University Press, 69–92.

Leeming, David. *James Baldwin*. New York: Knopf, 1994.

Lubiano, Wahneema. "The Postmodernist Rag: Political Identity and the Vernacular in *Song of Solomon*." In *New Essays on Song of Solomon*. Ed. Valerie Smith. Cambridge: Cambridge University Press, 1995. 93–116.

Miller, D. Quentin. *Re-Viewing James Baldwin: Things Not Seen*. Philadelphia: Temple University Press, 2000.

Morrison, Toni. "Life in his Language." *James Baldwin: The Legacy*. Ed. Quincy Troupe. New York: Touchstone, 1989.

————. *Song of Solomon*. 1977. New York: Plume, 1987.

Moses, Cat. "The Blues Aesthetic in Toni Morrison's *The Bluest Eye*." *African American Review* 33. no. 4 (1999): 623–637.

Scott, Lynn Orilla. *James Baldwin's Later Fiction: Witness to the Journey*. East Lansing: Michigan State University Press, 2002.

Schone, Mark. "The Original Gangsta." *Boston Sunday Globe,* June 1, 2003, sec. D, 2–3.

Simawe, Saadi. *Black Orpheus: Music in African American Fiction from the Harlem Renaissance to Toni Morrison.* NY: Garland, 2000.

Smith, Valerie, ed. *New Essays on Song of Solomon.* Cambridge: Cambridge University Press, 1995.

Soyinka, Wole. *Death and the King's Horseman.* 1975. New York: Norton, 2002.

Story, Ralph. "An Excursion into the Black World: The 'Seven Days' in Toni Morrison's *Song of Solomon.*" *Black American Literature Forum* 23, no. 1 (Spring 1989): 149–158.

Taylor-Guthrie, Danielle. *Conversations with Toni Morrison.* Jacksonville: University of Mississippi Press, 1994.

Thomas, H. Nigel. "The Bad Nigger Figure in Selected Works of Richard Wright, William Melvin Kelley, and Ernest Gaines." *College Language Association (CLA) Journal* 39, no. 2 (December 1995): 143–164.

Time. "Races: Freedom—Now." May 17, 1963, 23–27.

Wright, Richard. *Native Son.* New York: Harper, 1940.

REFIGURING THE FLESH: THE WORD, THE BODY, AND THE RITUALS OF BEING IN BELOVED AND GO TELL IT ON THE MOUNTAIN

CAROL E. HENDERSON

In the beginning was the Word . . . and the Word was made flesh, and dwelt among us . . .

—*John 1*

The connection between James Baldwin and Toni Morrison may seem unexpected at first. Most mainstream critics of African American and American literature extol the many talents of Morrison, whereas Baldwin has consistently remained at the periphery of literary studies, almost like a "stepchild," critically and systematically eclipsed by his sexuality, his attention to cultural and theological oppression, and his unflinching examination of social and political racism. As Ishmael Reed acknowledges in the epigraph to *Writin' Is Fightin'* (1990), Baldwin was one of the writers "who fought the good fight" for over forty years, boxing on paper with the demons that haunt the collective American memory—a memory shaped by the terrors of history. In recent years, much deserved attention has been given to Morrison's outstanding contribution not only to this history but also to African American and American letters. Her powerful words and profound offerings are monumental in their ability to redirect the reader to the struggles of alienation, fragmentation, self, and identity that Baldwin so eloquently spoke of—struggles so intimately connected with a history that refuses to die.[1]

Morrison's fifth novel, *Beloved* (1987), spiritually explores the illimitable but unresolved history intrinsically tied to the horrors of slavery. For this very reason, it has garnered significant critical acclaim. Her careful examination of not only the generational begetting of wounds but also the memorial haunting that precipitates familial and ancestral recovery of the suppressed narratives of slavery makes palpable the (in)human condition of the enslaved—the immoral and socially sanctioned disassembling of the African American person, body and soul. Morrison is keen in fleshing out the dynamics of human relationships, demonstrating that some wounds cannot heal unless they are *seen,* manifested in the flesh, so that one's spiritual essence can be reconnected with its host's self. Beloved's presence, in particular, facilitates this reconciliation of body and spirit, making public the private longings of a people. For Morrison scholars, the reconstitution of this yearning into an embodied configuration *is* the unspeakable spoken through the flesh.[2] According to John Edgar Wideman, "Past lives in us, through us. Each of us harbors the spirits of people who walked the earth before we did, and those spirits depend on us for continuing existences, just as we depend on their presence to live our lives to the fullest" (7). In "clearing space" for the recovery of this past, Morrison allows herself the room to focus on the interior lives of the enslaved persons whose spirits falter under its weight.

Morrison's consideration of the literal and figurative presence of unhealed wounds in the African American racial memory answers the call of many of her literary predecessors, who similarly explore the devastating effects the past can have on the spirit. One such writer is James Baldwin, whose extraordinary novel *Go Tell It on the Mountain* (1953), calls for a coming together of mind, body, and spirit through the searching of a spiritual self coming to terms with the conflict between its carnal and sacred identities—a self shaped by the racist violence and poverty of the 1930s, a self neglected and bruised by years of abuse at the hands of family members and friends who have internalized these experiences. This devaluation of personal self-worth has left "its toll in the psychic scars and personal wounds now inscribed in the souls of black folk" (West 123). Baldwin's novel foreshadows many of the contemporary considerations of slavery and its aftermath, particularly as it relates to the creative investigations of the spiritual and mental energy that binds the black church together, as well as the contradictions in spirituality it attempts to resolve. Its portrayal of characters such as Deborah, Florence, Gabriel, and John points up the complicated history black people share with fundamentalist versions of spirituality and sexuality. It "clears space" for the reading of such a character as Baby Suggs, whose "unconventional" Protestant theology complicates the narratological landscape of American literary culture. Many of the customs Baldwin critiques are rooted in a Judeo-Christian theology that splinters body from spirit, and for some, spirit from self. These practices bind the African American body to a "racialized" form of religion that is rooted in the Cainan and Hamitic myths—and that leaves African Americans at the edge of salvation and redemption. Morrison and Baldwin, through literary artistry, engage in discursive interplay with the philosophical and cultural aspects of the principles of redemption and salvation, morality and piety, and purity and virtue, bringing to the forefront the innovative ways in which African Americans have sought to circumvent the contradictions of sacred and secular existence.

In fact, both writers use place—Morrison, "the Clearing" and Baldwin, "the threshing floor"—as an avenue for "clearing space" in order to refigure not only the problem of the inheritance of Christianity (and Puritanism), but also the racism associated with that inheritance. Woven into the texture of each novel is the volatile confrontation of the past with a present haunted by these legacies. If, as Gaston Bachelard argues, poetic space assumes the value of expansion, that is, it becomes an articulated extension of the lived experience, then one could rightly assert that the Clearing and the threshing floor are designated places of expression for individuals invested in its images in ways that facilitates our understanding not only of the human experience, but also of the process of being, allowing for a further exploration of the figurative and literal constructions of reality. The ceremonial rituals performed in these places that connect character to space/place in each instance point up the cycle of repression and oppression associated with each character's attempt to reconcile the self with the self. These efforts reinscribe the textures of flesh, unearthing the fundamentalist codes that hinder the process of resolution between mind/body and flesh/spirit. Nowhere is this impulse more evident than on the threshing floor—that sacred space before the altar. Baldwin's novel stages this site as a conversionary space where the secular and the sacred meet as the individual prays for spiritual renewal before God and the congregation.

It is not ironic that Baldwin would make use of the concept of the threshing floor for his climactic exchange between "the father and the son"—in this case, Gabriel and John Grimes. A hard man, Gabriel is unyielding and abrasively strict in the relationships he builds in his church and at home. Gabriel's "holier than thou" attitude toward John, who can never live up to his father's expectations, fuels John's own self-doubt about his status as "rightful" heir to his father's legacy. Implicit in this line of inquiry is John's illegitimate birth—a sore spot for Gabriel, who is obsessed with fathering a holy line of heirs.[3] The biblical undertones of this relationship are quite obvious here, but critics have also pointed to the autobiographical currents that dominate the narrative's second storyline. Trudier Harris, in particular, has pointed to the troubling and complex relationship Baldwin shared with his stepfather, David Baldwin.[4] It may well be taken that Baldwin's literary exorcism of his stepfather's ghost helped to shape his own understanding of John's relationship with Gabriel, for in it Baldwin responds to a familial legacy that finds fathers using religion to abuse their families.

It is this generational begetting of wounds that Baldwin addresses on the threshing floor in *Go Tell It*. Although John's transformation on the threshing floor frames the vantage point from which the reader comes to understand not only the process of redemption but also John's development from child to man, Baldwin also positions the ritual of testifying as the mechanism that makes plain the spiritual pain of the other characters in the narrative, detailing in excruciating fashion the injuries to their souls. Florence, Gabriel, and Elizabeth form a collective triune that reflects upon the racial and gendered subjugation of African American people and allegorizes the journey of self-realization in terms that articulate John's ambivalent relationship with this ancestral and familial past. Baldwin's use of flashbacks is important in setting both the psychological and spiritual conditions for John's experiences on the threshing floor. Here, John enters purgatory, descending into the depths of a psychical and emotional wilderness that will reveal the tenuous relationship between the flesh and the spirit.

When the reader encounters John on the threshing floor, John has lost possession of his body. He is "caught up," "invaded, set at naught, possessed" (193). His embodied experience with the Spirit is not pleasant—he is in anguish, haunted by the "sins" he has committed against himself, "with his hands . . . in the school lavatory, alone, thinking of boys, older, bigger, braver" (19), and against his father, Gabriel, when he had looked "on his father's hideous nakedness" while leaning over the bathtub to scrub his father's back (197). John's spiritual dilemma, brought on by theological and sociological myths that admonish sexual gratification and curse the sons of Noah,[5] points up the pleasures he simultaneously derives from his sin as these acts affirm his physical being. His need for affirmation comes not only from his fear of eternal damnation due to his attraction to other boys, but also from his hatred of a father who finds him morally and physically reprehensible. His encounters with the neighborhood boys and girls, who would yell "Hey, Frog-eyes!" (216) and mock his walk, further condemn him to an emotional and spiritual hell that makes him hate his own body. It is the threshing floor that makes his wounded body visible as his pleas for help are made public in the spiritual realm before the altar:

> And he could never in his life have imagined, how this power had opened him up; had cracked him open, as wood beneath the axe cracks down the middle . . . so that John had not felt the wound, but only the agony, had not felt the fall, but only the fear; and lay here, now, helpless, screaming, at the very bottom of darkness. (193)

Here, John wrestles with the demons that confine his flesh to perpetual purgatory as he struggles to find his way back to his self—a self muted by the language of sin.

Baldwin's use of the concept of sin within the novel's narrative framework is interesting. In some respects, sin becomes a formidable literary device, a metaphor that allows for the active reinvention of the archetypal terms of "blackness"; it also serves as the mechanism that brings "the sinner" before the altar in an act of contrition that subverts the power dynamics of relationships between fathers and sons, mothers and daughters, saints and sinners, and saved and unsaved—relationships that are constantly being produced and reproduced in cultural and familial contexts. In Baldwin's narrative, John does find a sense of purpose on the threshing floor in his "sin," but he does not know how to speak the language of redemption that facilitates his movement from sinnerhood to sainthood: this help comes not only from Elisha, whose "perfect" body (he is easy on the eyes as the narrative relates) and spiritual tongue make him an able-bodied surrogate for John,[6] but also from the "Prayers of the Saints," whose spiritual evocations at the altar reveal the impact of the past on the present and the cultural and social anxieties that inhibit self-love and acceptance.

According to Dolan Hubbard, African Americans have often attempted to redefine themselves, their culture, and their history through the many speech acts that articulate the depths of their suffering (3). Folk cries, hollers and shouts, work songs, and other secular songs, as well as dance rituals and ceremonies, became communal methods not only of expressing these longings but also of resisting racial oppression and spiritual depravity, through a reaffirmation of the flesh. As Morrison and Baldwin both demonstrate, the residue of slavery left a deeply encoded rejection of the body embedded in the African American racial collective. The psychic battles that ensue presuppose a cycle of self-denial that prohibits self-knowledge, so much so that the ritualistic reworking of the bodily codes that silence the body's "voice" (i.e., the spirit of desire so intimately connected with the *essence* of physical and spiritual freedom) becomes refigured as a sort of self-generating language rooted in the bodily experiences of slavery and rearticulated in the linguistic utterances of prayer—a public and private ritual that combines the secular and the sacred, the flesh and the spirit, in a holy dance of submission to a being larger than the human self. In the fictive world Baldwin creates in *Go Tell It,* prayer manifests itself as a dialogue between the "spirit" and one's "memory" as the individual, situated on bended knee, prays for a revival in spirit before God and the congregant. Thus, prayer is a rite of passage—a self-reflexive journey—that allows the "sinner" to reexamine the past in the present in hopes of enjoining others to participate in this act of repentance and facilitate communal and individual healing.

The public recantation of "sin" is something that shadows the philosophical and theoretical discussions of the church in Baldwin's fiction and non-fiction. One cannot help but wonder if Baldwin's closeness to the subject—his knowledge of biblical principles (he was a youth minister) and his emerging sexual identity—presented, in flesh and blood, the warring ideals of the spirit and the flesh. In *The Devil Finds Work*, Baldwin again and again speaks of the "unspeakable fatigue" that accompanies the flesh's yearning for rest and reconciliation with the spirit—a spirit encountering the theatrical ramifications of the spectacle of race and the personal demons of self-rejection. In an effort to reinvest the self with a power generated from within, and the symbols of race with their original energy, African Americans enter a perpetual act of re-creating the self through the ritual of "pleading the blood." In Baldwin's church, this rite occurs "when the sinner [falls] on his face before the altar, the soul . . . locked in a battle with Satan" (137). Although Baldwin does concede that the devil can have many faces and take many forms,[7] his justification that such a journey can take place only when "the saints" who had passed through "the fire" pray and intercede on one's behalf is important.[8] Here, Baldwin points out the need for placing before the community and the nation the internalized wounds of people so that those who cannot speak for themselves find a voice in ancestral "witnessing."

In *Beloved*, prayer operates in a similar fashion but it also becomes an extension of the cultural utterances of Baby Suggs, who, as spiritual leader and cultural medium, stresses the need to reconnect the flesh to the essence of an ancestral soul obliterated under the weight of a collective past. While in *Go Tell It* the flesh is subjected to the conventions of Christian and Protestant theology, Suggs's experiences in chattel bondage give her a different view of the flesh and a distinct perspective on the ghosts that haunt the African American racial memory. As Sethe remembers, the "fixing ceremonies" in the Clearing did more than provide space for collective exhortations; they allowed formerly enslaved persons the opportunity to reclaim themselves "bit by bit" in a gesture of self-reflexivity. This self-examination, as in Baldwin's novel, greatly affects each character's views regarding the Christian ethos. For Baby Suggs, Christianity takes the shape of her mangled flesh as her spirit becomes framed by and affected by a "slave life that had 'busted her legs, back, head, eyes, hands, kidneys, womb and tongue' . . . she had nothing left to make a living with but her heart—which she put to work at once" in the new community she joined in freedom (87). "Uncalled, unrobed, unanointed," Baby Suggs puts her talents to use, preaching a message of hope that

> did not tell them to clean up their lives or to go and sin no more. She did
> not tell them they were the blessed of the earth, its inheriting meek or its

glorybound pure. She told them that the only grace they could have was the grace they could imagine. That if they could not see it, they would not have it. (88)

Suggs's ministry differs in principle from traditional Christian religion, which proposes prohibitive forms of morality and spirituality and a separation of the flesh and the soul.[9] Instead, her philosophies align themselves more readily with the ideals of the fugitive slave Frederick Douglass, who, in his narrative, demonstrates how these forms of theology were manipulated in the past to justify the enslavement of a people. As Douglass explains,

> What I have said respecting and against religion, I mean strictly to apply to the *slaveholding religion* of this land, and with no possible reference to Christianity proper; for, between the Christianity of this land, and the Christianity of Christ, I recognize the widest possible difference—so wide, that to receive the one as good, pure, and holy, is of necessity to reject the other as bad, corrupt, and wicked . . . I therefore hate the corrupt, slaveholding, women-whipping, cradle-plundering, partial and hypocritical Christianity of this land. Indeed, I can see no reason, but the most deceitful one, for calling the religion of this land Christianity. I look upon it as the climax of all misnomers, the boldest of all frauds, and the grossest of all libels. (75)

In rejecting these forms of religion, Douglass, and likewise Baby Suggs, represents an epistemological and philosophical shift that emphasizes the spiritual energy that binds the black community together—an energy that does not favor the autonomous recovery of culture and self, but instead encourages the self-discerning privileges of a form of spiritual practice rooted in personal discovery.

Although the secular portrayal of traditional theology was undergirded with the racist ideology and moral impiety of the nineteenth and twentieth centuries, writers like Douglass and Morrison engage in a discursive literary dialogue that seeks to reconstitute the forum in which such discussions occurred. Spirituality—the inner essence of one's being as supported by the philosophical tenets of one's culture—is the other site from which the epistemological precepts of theology can be dismantled. Baldwin also sought to rend the veil of sacrilege that confused the spiritual with the secular traditions of Christianity. As an author, Baldwin embodies a kind of collective consciousness he was unable to access as the young John Grimes because of his inability to gain access to his family members' prayers, or his own hidden history. This naiveté mirrors, in many respects, the conventional and secularized Christian experience. Thus, the oppressive natu⌐ organized religion and its warring ideals looms large in *Go Tell* ⌐ telling is the manner in which Baldwin uses the ontology of ⌐

comment on each character's inability to resist the degenerative pathos of a volatile and violent history. Both of these affect the relationship each character develops with his or her spirit and flesh.

For Florence, this conflict evolves before the altar as she recollects the events of her life that haunt her. Her inability to forgive her brother, Gabriel, her mother, and herself stands as a moral and spiritual hindrance between her present and her past. Her mother's connection to slavery operates as an ancestral link that demonstrates the lasting effects of chattel bondage on the African American racial memory. Florence's mother was a slave woman who had been raised as a field hand. Her children had been taken from her, one by sickness and two by auction. The third child was raised in the master's house; Florence and Gabriel were the children of her old age. These combined losses cause Florence's mother to favor Gabriel in a way that alienates Florence. Florence's mother felt that because she was a girl and would be married someday and have children of her own, all future preparation should be focused on Gabriel: "He needed the education that Florence desired far more than he . . . it was Gabriel who was slapped and scrubbed each morning and sent off to the one-room schoolhouse," not Florence (73). This resentment caused Florence to leave her mother on her deathbed in her quest for a better life up North so that when she herself became ill with a "burning in her bowels [that] did not cease," Death came to her, "blacker than night . . . watching her with . . . the eyes of a serpent when his head is lifted to strike" (67).

With these visitations came as well Florence's reflections on her past deeds. Many voices came to curse her at her bedside.

> Her mother, in rotting rags and filling the room with the stink of the grave, stood over her to curse the daughter who had denied her on her deathbed. Gabriel came, from all his times and ages, to curse the sister who had held him to scorn and mocked his ministry. Deborah, black, her body as shapeless and hard as iron, looked on with veiled, triumphant eyes, cursing the Florence who had mocked her in her pain and barrenness. Frank came, even he, with that same smile, the same tilt of the head. (68)

It is this symphony of voices that causes Florence to raise "her voice in the only song she could remember that her mother used to sing: 'It's me, it's me, it's me, oh, Lord, standing in the need of prayer'" (66). The private anguish that had brought her so low is made public in this moment as she kneels before her family and the congregation. Her anger does not allow her to achieve full reconciliation; she must rely on the saints to tarry for her as she makes her journey to the other side of forgiveness and redemption.

Florence's attempt at obtaining absolution for herself offers her little solace. But her journey to the centers of her self left void because of unfulfilled dreams gives her a unique perspective at the altar. It allows her to serve as John's intermediary on his journey to self-actualization. At an important juncture during the purification process of the threshing floor, she tells him, "You fight the good fight . . . you here? Don't you get weary, and don't you get scared. Because I *know* the Lord's done laid His hands on you" (208). Her affirmation of John's spiritual purpose and her acknowledgment of his emotional recovery come as a result of her ability to confront directly Gabriel's self-aggrandizing gestures. At the altar, she speaks to him in a tongue only he can decipher, laying before him his own sins:

> When Florence cried, Gabriel was moving outward in fiery darkness, talking to the Lord. Her cry came to him from afar, as from unimaginable depths; and it was not his sister's cry he heard, but the cry of the sinner when he is taken in his sin. This cry he had heard so many days and nights, before so many altars, and he cried tonight, as he had cried before: "Have your way, Lord! Have your way!" (92)

In her position as "sinner," Florence is able to force Gabriel to confront his past as he wrestles with his own personal demons. These ghosts recall Gabriel's nine-day affair with Esther that produced a son, Royal, whose tumultuous life ends the way it began—in chaos. Similarly, Florence's prayer and her subsequent cry allow us entry into Gabriel's marital woes as the current struggles in his marriage to Elizabeth conjure up the ghost of his former wife, Deborah. Gabriel's infidelity to Deborah permits Florence to bring him low as she speaks on Deborah's behalf. As the narrative reveals, Deborah's rape had silenced her and altered the personal voice she had within her own community: "That night had robbed her [Deborah] of the right to be considered a woman. No man would approach her in honor because she was a living reproach, to herself and to all black women and to all black men" (73). Deborah was viewed as a perpetual sinner because no one saw further "than her unlovely and violated body" (73), a body tainted by "white men's milk" (107). At the altar, Florence "calls" on Deborah, crying out in a voice that utters the mysteries of the spirit, giving her a spiritual voice that refigures her violated body, and baring the sins committed against her by her husband and her community. It is here that Gabriel and the others, "transfixed by something in the middle of the air" (92), wait for *that* power, a quickening power that will arrest the flesh and transform former sins into faint memories.

But, as the reader finds out, these characters' journeys are complicated and in principle do not lead to the ritualized conversion so common at the altar or on the threshing floor. As Dolan Hubbard reminds us, the threshing floor, in its metaphoric representation, extends the power of redemptive love for those willing to accept it (98). Gabriel, Florence, and Elizabeth each find it difficult to accept this love. Elizabeth, in particular, struggles with the unresolved issues from her childhood that found her marked by her dark skin and with the social transgression of bearing a child out of wedlock. Elizabeth unwittingly passes these insecurities on to John, who intuitively suffers from his outcast status and his ancestral legacy.[10] Like Sethe's Denver, John is shrouded in the indelible stain of the personal and historical liability that marks the engendered sojourn of African American women. Thus, the threshing floor can also serve as a metaphor for a slave past that alters the ways in which African American people come to terms with their own bodies, their own spirit. That is why, in the Clearing, Baby Suggs encourages a celebration of the cultural elements that acknowledge the wounds of the flesh. In the Clearing, she preaches the redemption of the body —a body numbed by its experiences in slavery.

> "Here" she said, "in this here place, we flesh; flesh that weeps, laughs; flesh that dances on bare feet in grass. Love it. Love it hard. Yonder they do not love your flesh. They despise it . . . *You* got to love it. This is flesh I'm talking about here. Flesh that needs to be loved . . . and all your inside parts that they'd just as soon slop for hogs, you got to love them. The dark, dark liver—love it, love it, and the beat and beating heart, love that too. More than eyes or feet. More than lungs that have yet to draw free air. More than your life-holding womb and your life-giving private parts, hear me now, love your heart. For this is the prize." (88)

In re-membering the body one part at a time, Baby Suggs calls forth a complete being that counters the dismembered self created in chattel bondage. In this way, she creates a shared communal experience for the healing of personal pain, whether self-inflicted or genealogically begotten. "Call and response" becomes a collaborative venture in this instance, as those who have been silenced by social fear or intimidation are empowered to "speak" in a language that allows them to make the emotional transition from seeing themselves as objects to seeing themselves as subjects. Moreover, speech itself is rewritten in this space (as on the threshing floor), for participants laugh, cry, and sing, and these utterances become their form of communication. These gestures are not empty expressions of protest, but they are liberational acts of empowerment that, as bell hooks reminds us, the oppressed and the exploited use as a sign of "defiance that heals, that makes new life and growth possible" (9). Dance also functions as the bridge, I would argue, that speaks the unspeakable in rhyme and rhythm so that flesh and spirit become one. Like Elisha, Ella Mae and others present fervent invocations before the altar of the Temple of Fire Baptized that transform their bodies, their faces, and their voices into something "riding on the air" (*Go Tell It*, 15). Baby Suggs invokes this same tradition in a way that John can only intimate at the end of *Go Tell It*, reinventing the twisted body into which she was parceled under slavery as an instrument of praise and celebration for the reclamation of the self: "Saying no more, she [Baby Suggs] stood up then and danced with her twisted hip the rest of what her heart had to say while the others opened their mouths and gave her the music. Long notes held until the four-part harmony was perfect enough for their deeply loved flesh" (89). The path Baby Suggs takes to free herself from the debilitating language of bondage leads her to embrace certain spiritual forms connected with her African ancestry. Historian Sterling Stuckey speaks of a Congo ancestral ritual found among African slaves that symbolized the "living" African's connection with those who died during the Middle Passage.

> The horizontal line of the cross, referred to as the Kalunga line . . . [is] associated, as in the Congo, with those who lived long and were generous, wise and strong "on a heroic scale." Such people, in the imagination of the Congo people, "die twice . . . once 'here,' and once 'there,' beneath the watery barrier, the line Bakongo call *Kalunga*" . . . When that line, which extends from dawn to sunset, is evoked by the Congo staff-cross, it symbolizes the surface of a body of water beneath which the world of the ancestors is found. (13)

The dances performed by Baby Suggs and the others in her community may well have been a form of this ritual. Like John's apocalyptic visions before the altar in *Go Tell It* that found him struggling with the ghosts of memory—ancestral spirits that mount John up into that sacred, private place above and beneath natural living space—Beloved's subsequent "appearance" may well have been an effect of this spiritual supplication lamenting or celebrating the "freed" ancestors who were able to evade slavery through death.

Alternatively, Beloved's appearance may well be read as a blending of two forms of spiritual expression—African and "Americanized" African traditions—whereupon entry into this spirit world calls forth not only the river spirits but also the other restless spirits, "the people of the broken necks, of firecooked blood and black girls who had lost their ribbons" (181). This is the roaring that Stamp Paid cannot decipher when he tries to knock at the door of 124:

> Over and over again he tried it: made up his mind to visit Sethe; broke through the loud hasty voices to the mumbling beyond it and stopped, trying to figure out what to do at the door. Six times in as many days he abandoned his normal route and tried to knock at 124. But the coldness of the gesture—its sign that he was indeed a stranger at the gate—overwhelmed him. Retracing his steps in the snow, he sighed. Spirit willing; flesh weak. (172)

I would argue that because these spirits have gathered over time, inhabiting various linguistic and cultural spaces, language itself becomes problematic for formerly enslaved persons such as Stamp Paid, whose generous spirit was more than willing to embark on the journey "to the other side" of the door (and the river—Stamp Paid was a conductor on the underground railroad), but whose battered and reformed slave flesh refused to reenter the conundrum of chattel purgatory. To this extent, the women who perform the final exorcism of 124 must engage with these restless spirits in a "call and response" dialogue that privileges neither Western nor African religions.[11] Rather, it acknowledges an origin in the beginning when "there were no words. In the beginning was the sound, and they all knew what that sound sounded like" (259). The sound allows these women to blend the essence of their painful experiences with that of their ancestors, forming, in effect, one united chorus of voices that builds one upon the other "until they found it" (259), the key that would allow them to recover and lay to rest the disembodied spirits of 124. The blending of the geographical spaces of water and land—of Africa and America—through dance serves to link the experiences of two groups as sound becomes the healing ritual that soothes the wounded spirit.

Drawing on Melville J. Herskovits's work *The Myth of the Negro Past* (1958), Stuckey notes that "the river spirits are among the most powerful of those inhabiting the supernatural world, and . . . priests of this cult are among the most powerful members of tribal priestly groups"(15). Stuckey's observations are key to understanding Baby Suggs's role as spiritual priestess in the community that surrounds 124. Her physical death does not limit her ability to return to those who need her in the earthly realm. Denver experiences the ghostly presence of Baby Suggs one day: "Her throat itched; her heart kicked—and then Baby Suggs laughed, clear as anything" (244). Sethe longs for her during the time when she is besieged by the presence of Beloved, and she also feels the presence of Baby Suggs in the keeping room, whispering words to her. Yet this connection does not prove to be enough for Sethe, so in "some fixing ceremony, Sethe decided to go to the Clearing, back where Baby Suggs had danced in sunlight" (86). This journey through rememory, brought on by Beloved's arrival, makes Sethe realize the importance of the spirituality Baby Suggs embodied: "Sethe wanted to be there now. At the least to listen to the spaces that the long-ago singing had left behind. At the most to get a clue from her husband's dead mother as to what she should do with her sword and shield now, dear Jesus" (89). Baby Suggs's words, her creative power, and her spiritual essence offer her believers a supernatural ability to transcend their circumstances. The respect she is afforded by family and friends alike attests to her gifts. And although she "proved herself a liar, dismissed her great heart and lay in the keeping-room bed roused once in a while by a craving for color and not for another thing" (89), her legacy as community activist (her house is a way station for the underground railroad) and spiritual guide is significant, and is not erased by her human foibles.

The need to find a space of her own is what drives Baby Suggs to the Clearing to reclaim herself, and others, from the traumatic effects of slavery. The women in *Go Tell It* suffer from the effects of various forms of racial and sexual slavery that seek to relegate them to the margins of certain Christian religious practices. Yet, in an effort to circumvent these practices, women such as Praying Mother Washington refigure the boundaries that determine their womanhood. As "pillars of the church" (16), these individuals position themselves within the very fabric and foundation of their community. Because they live in the vicinity of their church, their roles in their spiritual community also carry over into their secular lives. Thus, Praying Mother Washington becomes not only a pillar of the church but also a "powerful evangelist [who is] very widely known"(16) within and outside her immediate communal circle, linking her in very convincing ways to the spiritual history of the Temple of Fire Baptized and the African American community as a whole. In these ways, she complicates the formal codes of Christianity in American culture.[12]

Baby Suggs, too, serves as a foil to these misguided notions of spirituality and virtue. She blends the best of the secular and the sacred worlds as a "woman of words," as Trudier Harris puts it (146), and her ability to refigure her position within the community of ex-slaves located on the outskirts of Cincinnati demonstrates black people's reliance on language as a way to fashion a counterdiscourse in a manner that protests their dehumanizing conditions. This impulse to testify, to map out the contours of one's journey from bondage to freedom in some cases, provides the most stimulating view of cultural re-creation, as the quest for dignity and selfhood becomes the impetus for a restructuring of African American subjectivity. Suggs's actions in the Clearing bear witness to this premise. Although marked "when she hurt her hip in Carolina" (139), which caused her marketability as a slave to plummet, Baby Suggs is empowered, in her role as priestess; she has the ability to heal and counter the discourses of enslavement. This power, as Stuckey further explains, involves the community at large: "Since storytellers, or griots, focus mainly on the history of their people, ancestors are usually the principal subjects of a particular chronicle of the past—the ceremony framed, as it were, by the listeners gathered around the storyteller. Depending on the demands of the narration, they either listen or, on signal from the storytellers, become active participants" (14).

The Clearing, for those who might have been "homesick," functions as a site for self-renewal and self-evaluation. As the narrative discloses, "the Clearing . . . [was] a wide-open place cut deep in the woods nobody knew for what at the end of a path known only to deer and whoever cleared the land in the first place" (87). In this space close to nature, created by the hands of those who "cleared the land in the first place," Baby Suggs preaches self-empowerment and stresses the need for self-love. According to Melvin Dixon, images of landscapes, such as the wilderness, the underground, and the mountaintop, often serve as sites for refuge and revitalization (5). The Clearing, when placed in this context, functions as a metaphor for the performance of identity and the celebration of self. It becomes a powerful site that Sethe physically returns to, and that Ella and the rest of the women in the African American community spiritually return to, as they exorcise Beloved from Sethe's house.

Urban decay and economic and educational scarcity make the Temple of the Fire Baptized and its extended spaces—the threshing floor and the altar—communal sites of spiritual regeneration. Because the city offers no refuge for religious reaffirmation, rituals performed in these sites—many of them feeble attempts at reclaiming a self fractured by self-denial and self-deprecation—harken back to the ancestral practices performed by Baby Suggs in the Clearing. John's journey through these extended spaces—a journey that points up the figurations of a cultural impulse to move toward inner freedom and self-fulfillment vis-à-vis the refiguring of the flesh—demonstrates, at once, the quickening power of the Word and the reconstitution of the body within the exigencies of spiritual redemption and memorial confrontation with the past. In the Clearing, too, memories are reinvested with a sense of urgency in the fractured attempt to become whole. The Clearing offers Sethe a direct connection to Africa, as her memories of her mother from early childhood come to life. Her mother, most certainly an African, relives the traditions of her native land with other members of the slave community: they sang and danced the antelope, shifting shapes and demanding that others in attendance follow suit. It is the empowering force of the dance itself that Sethe remembers well. In shifting shapes, these slaves imagine a self unbound and unmarked. Sethe's recollection of this ceremony is significant in that it comes when she is on the run, pregnant with her daughter, Denver. Her swollen feet and disfigured body provide the limitation of her circumstance; the child in her womb, whom she called "the little antelope," signifies the promise of a future she could only imagine and the hope of a future generation born in freedom. In these ways, both novels imagine a reclaimed spiritual past that stands on the edge of time, healing the disfigurements of a tortured soul shaped by the vestiges of history.

NOTES

1. In her eulogy to Baldwin entitled "Life in his Language," Morrison speaks movingly of Baldwin's courageous efforts to appropriate the alien and hostile world of the white supremacist notions of history, and of his ability to inspire others, such as herself, to do the same.
2. Many articles have been written on this aspect of Morrison's work. Some notable discussions include Mae G. Henderson's "Toni Morrison's *Beloved*: Re-Membering the Body as Historical Text" (1999); Rafael Perez-Torres's "Between Presence and Absence: *Beloved*, Postmodernism, and Blackness" (1999); and Linda Krumholz's "The Ghosts of Slavery: Historical Recovery in Toni Morrison's *Beloved*" (1999).
3. Although critics such as Trudier Harris and Shirley S. Allen have pointed to the fact that John is unaware of his status as illegitimate, I feel it is important to note that John knows he is different—and also knows that this difference makes him unacceptable to his stepfather, Gabriel.
4. See Trudier Harris's introduction to *New Essays on James Baldwin's Go Tell It on the Mountain* (1996), especially 3–4.
5. This myth, like the Cainan myth, states that African Americans were descendants of this branch of Noah's family. Baldwin comments further on this myth in *Go Tell It* (197–198).
6. The reader is well aware of the fact that Elisha is not perfect. As we are told very early in the narrative, Elisha had "sinned" with Ella Mae Washington. They had been found "'walking disorderly'; they were in danger of straying from the truth . . . as Father James spoke of the sin that he knew they had not committed yet" (16). This act is made public before the body of the church, but Elisha's ability to circumvent this public humiliation is found in his acceptance of his manliness and his spirituality. That is the strength John seeks from him on the threshing floor.
7. Although in this same text Baldwin notes that he has seen the devil in "you and me, the cop and the sheriff and the deputy, the landlord, the housewife" (147), I feel it is important to point out the complicated history of naming "devils" in our society—a history too voluminous to detail here.
8. Going through "the fire" implies that one has experienced, and successfully overcome in some ways, the battle of spirit and the flesh.
9. The New Testament of the King James Version of the Bible is laden with imagery of the consequences of following the whims of the flesh. Galatians 5:16 admonishes its followers to "walk in the spirit and ye shall not fulfill the lust of the flesh."
10. As critics such as Shirley Allen and Joseph A. Brown have pointed out, only the reader is privy to the prayers of the saints, not John. John himself may have "intuitions" about his origin of birth, but his mother Elizabeth who attempts to shield him from his auspicious beginnings, guards the subject of his birth.
11. As *Beloved* makes clear, African American spirituality is a blended experience, because "some [women] brought what they could and what they believed

would work" to the exorcism. Items were "stuffed in apron pockets, strung around their necks, lying in the space between their breasts. Others brought Christian faith—as shield and sword. Most brought a little of both" (257). This latter point is key to understanding the significance of this scene. And I might point out that Baby Suggs's "theology," which was preached in the Clearing, serves as a precursor to those various forms of religious practices questioned during the Reconstruction era.

12. Here, I am thinking of the cult of true womanhood that, as a practice, influenced or was influenced by the formal codes of Christian theology that considered black people, and black women in particular, nonvirtuous beings. For more discussion, see Hazel Carby's *Reconstructing Womanhood* (1987), 32–33.

WORKS CITED

Allen, Shirley S. "Religious Symbolism and Psychic Reality in Baldwin's *Go Tell It on the Mountain.*" In *Critical Essays on James Baldwin*. Ed. Fred L. Standley and Nancy V. Burt. Boston: G. K. Hall, 1988. 166–188.

Bachelard, Gaston. *The Poetics of Space*. Boston: Beacon Press, 1969.

Baldwin, James. *Go Tell It on the Mountain*. New York: Bantam Doubleday Books, 1953.

———. *Devil Finds Work*. New York: Bantam, 1976.

Carby, Hazel. *Reconstructing Womanhood*. New York: Oxford University Press, 1987.

Dixon, Melvin. *Riding Out the Wilderness: Geography and Identity in Afro-American Literature*. Urbana: University of Illinois Press, 1987.

Douglass, Frederick. *Narrative of the Life Frederick Douglass, An American Slave, Written by Himself*. 1845. Ed. William L. Andrews and William S. McFeely. New York: W. W. Norton, 1997.

Harris, Trudier. "*Beloved*: Woman, Thy Name is Demon." In *Toni Morrison's Beloved: A Casebook*. Ed. William L. Andrews and Nellie Y. McKay. New York: Oxford University Press, 1999. 127–157.

———. Introduction. *New Essays on Go Tell It on the Mountain*. New York: Cambridge University Press, 1996. 1–28.

Henderson, Mae G. "Toni Morrison's *Beloved*: Re-Membering the Body as Historical Text." In *Toni Morrison's Beloved: A Casebook*. Ed. William L. Andrews and Nellie Y. McKay. New York: Oxford University Press, 1999. 79–106.

Herskovits, Melville J. *The Myth of the Negro Past*. Boston: Beacon Press 1958.

hooks, bell. *Talking Back*. Boston: South End Press, 1989.

Hubbard, Dolan. *The Sermon and the African American Literary Imagination*. Columbia: University of Missouri Press, 1994.

Krumholz, Linda. "The Ghosts of Slavery: Historical Recovery in Toni Morrison's *Beloved*." In *Toni Morrison's Beloved: A Casebook*. Ed. William L. Andrews and Nellie Y. McKay. New York: Oxford University Press, 1999. 107–125.

Morrison, Toni. *Beloved*. New York: Penguin Books, 1987.

————. "James Baldwin: His Voice Remembered; Life in His Language." *New York Times*, December 20, 1987, sec. 7.

Perez-Torres, Rafael. "Between Presence and Absence: *Beloved*, Postmodernism, and Blackness." In *Toni Morrison's Beloved: A Casebook*. Ed. William L. Andrews and Nellie Y. McKay. New York: Oxford University Press, 1999. 179–201.

Reed, Ishmael. *Writin' Is Fightin': Thirty-Seven Years of Boxing on Paper*. New York: Atheneum Press, 1990. ix.

Stuckey, Sterling. *Slave Culture: Nationalist Theory and the Foundations of Black America*. New York: Oxford University Press, 1987.

West, Cornel. *Race Matters*. New York: Vintage Books, 1994.

Wideman, John Edgar. *Sent for You Yesterday*. New York: Avon Books, 1983. 7.

RESISTANCE AGAINST
RACIAL, SEXUAL, AND SOCIAL OPPRESSION
IN *GO TELL IT ON THE MOUNTAIN* AND *BELOVED*

BABACAR M'BAYE

Go Tell It on the Mountain (1953) and *Beloved* (1987) explore the effects of slavery and racism on African Americans and European Americans since the period before the Emancipation Proclamation of 1863. Tracing the relations between blacks and whites to slavery, the two novels examine the violence, sexual exploitation, and discrimination that whites have perpetrated on blacks from slavery through the twentieth century on grounds of racial supremacy. This violence has created a double consciousness in the ways in which blacks remember the past and relate to whites. It has also problematized the ways in which whites imagine blackness in racist terms, reinforcing the restiveness in the American psyche and culture that Baldwin and Morrison have traced to the brutality of slavery and racism.

Go Tell It on the Mountain

Go Tell It centers on John Grimes, a black teenager who believes that he sinned on the night of his fourteenth birthday. His stepfather's wrathful condemnation of sin leads him to experience anxieties as he tries to achieve spiritual salvation and understand his relationships with God and his family. The book also focuses on the dilemmas that confront John's stepfather, Gabriel, and his mother, Elizabeth, in Harlem, where they migrated in the early twentieth century. In Harlem, Florence, Gabriel's sister, remembers how their mother lived in a Southern plantation while Elizabeth reminisces about how Richard, John's biological father, lived in a Northern ghetto.

Critics have interpreted Baldwin's writings as either celebrations of American multiculturalism, condemnations of African American religious fundamentalism, or denunciations of rigid forms of African American masculinity. In so doing, they have overlooked the central themes of white oppression and misrepresentation of black people in these works. For example, in their interpretations of *Go Tell It,* Carolyn Wedin Sylvander, James Campbell, and Lawrie Balfour do not emphasize the physical, emotional, and psychological violence, the social invisibility, and the economic alienation that white Americans imposed on African Americans from the Emancipation Proclamation through the twentieth century. In *James Baldwin* (1980), Sylvander describes *Go Tell It* as an analysis of "the impact of history—personal and collective—on an individual [James Baldwin]" (36). In *Talking at the Gates: A Life of James Baldwin* (1991), James Campbell portrays it as an "accomplished novel" that "is informed by deep autobiographical feeling" (77). Finally, in *The Evidence of Things Not Said: James Baldwin and The Promise of American Democracy* (2001), Lawrie Balfour notes that *Go Tell It* "displays his [Baldwin's] understanding of both the appeal and the illusory nature of the idea that it is possible for people simply to rise above the circumstances that made them" (147). Although these assessments compliment the novel for being influenced by Baldwin's personal life and history, they do not comment on the book's radical condemnation of white supremacy, violence, and prejudice toward blacks from slavery through the twentieth century.

Referring to Baldwin's reactions to Harriet Beecher Stowe's controversial novel *Uncle Tom's Cabin* (1852), Porter argues in *Stealing the Fire: The Art and Protest of James Baldwin* (1989) that Baldwin "speaks as a representative of the oppressed black masses. But as quickly as he moves unconsciously in the direction of Stowe, even alluding to the plight of blacks during slavery, he consciously and polemically veers away. He objects to 'categorization' and sees societal definition as a 'trap'" (56). Porter's statement suggests the highly problematic and offensive notion that Baldwin did not care about slavery and that any interpretation of his work as a reflection of African Americans' predicament during or after slavery would be a "categorization" of black people. This viewpoint precludes an exploration of the ongoing traumatic and dehumanizing effects of slavery on African Americans, which are visible in the continuity of racial oppression, social and economic inequalities, and invisibility that Baldwin portrays in *Go Tell It.*

Like Porter, Macebuh steers away from slavery and race. In *James Baldwin: A Critical Study* (1973), he writes,

> *Go Tell* may be seen as a very subtle essay on the effects of social oppression on a minority group, as an attack on the excesses and snares of black inspirational worship, or as a passionate plea for love in relationships. In addition to these perspectives of meaning, the novel can even more significantly be

seen as an eloquent record of Baldwin's struggle to break away from his step-father's God. (53)

Macebuh's rationale removes Baldwin's novel from its locus in white racial exploitation and puts it into the context of black religious subjugation. This strategy places the burden of structural racism, which is rooted in slavery and discrimination, on Baldwin's African American family and community rather than on the white American society that was responsible for it. Baldwin's personal life cannot be separated from the large American context that produced it, because, as Baldwin's biographer David Leeming argues, Baldwin helped "to convey the national anguish and to see that anguish through his personal tragedy" (316).

Macebuh's interpretation of *Go Tell It* as a denunciation of the God of Baldwin's stepfather anticipated the inclination of current scholars to overemphasize Baldwin's condemnation of fundamentalist versions of black Christianity and masculinity. In *James Baldwin's God: Sex, Hope, and Crisis in Black Holiness Culture* (2003), Clarence E. Hardy argues that in Baldwin's work, "the legacy of slavery is most simply expressed as this loss of black manhood" (70). Earlier, Hardy noted that "Baldwin's intense exploration of sex and race is seen most clearly as he grapples throughout his work with the hypereroticized black male body in much of American culture" (70). Although they are central components of Baldwin's writings, the "loss of black manhood" and the "hypereroticizing" of the black male's body are not the most visible effects of slavery represented in Baldwin's work. To understand Baldwin's analysis of the misrepresentation of black sexuality in American culture, one must explore the historical context of the objectification, exploitation, and denial of the sexual and reproductive rights of black women during slavery.

Before the Emancipation Proclamation, blacks lived under the regulations of slave codes that restricted their freedom and their right to own property, carry guns, resist whites, and run away.[1] They were required to wear metal badges and could be beaten or killed for breaking these laws. Between the 1650s and the 1750s, many slave codes were passed in states such as Virginia, Maryland, the Carolinas, and Georgia.[2] In addition to these laws, there was the practice of "concubinage" and separation of slaves from their families.[3] These restrictions show that slavery violated the sanctity of the black family.[4] The impact of slavery on the black family is visible in *Go Tell It* through the tragic experiences of Rachel. This character spent most of her life in Southern plantations, where she worked, without pay or respect, for abusive and cruel slaveholders who raped her and sold her children on auction blocks: "On this plantation she had grown up as one of the field workers, for she was very tall and strong; and by and by she had married and raised children, all of whom had been taken from her, one by sickness and two by auction, and one, whom she had not been allowed to call her own, had been raised in the master's house" (69–70). The planters' expropriation of Rachel's children reflects the injustice done to black women slaves who were victims of white sexual exploitation. In assigning sleeping partners to Rachel, the planters violated the black woman's body, reinforcing the sexism against women in the plantation. The relationship between the sexual oppression of black women and the sexism in the plantation is visible in how Rachel spent her life working for free while she was forced to pay tithes and bear children for both white and black men. Rachel was, then, the prime victim in a system in which black women were positioned at the nexus of race, class, sex, and gender oppression and exploitation.[5]

The physical and sexual abuse against Rachel shows the impact of sexual violence on the relationships between blacks and whites. This impact is noticeable in Rachel's troubled and anxious emotional state, which is her psychological response to being raped. Baldwin depicts this violence as phases of psychological and physical oppression in which whites perpetrated sexual sin and economic injustice against blacks without acknowledging the consequences of such acts. From Baldwin's perspective, the first sexual act that the planter perpetrated against an African American created a trauma in the American psyche, as blacks continued to suffer sexually, physically, socially, and spiritually in an attempt to redeem white oppressors who had never come to terms with their actions. In *Go Tell It*, this ongoing black purgation of white sexual and economic guilt is visible in how Rachel wants to avenge her rape while she, at the same time, nurtures the desire to save the rapist from his sins. Lying on her deathbed, Rachel realizes that "in her tribulations, death, and parting, and the lash, she did not forget that deliverance was promised and would surely come. She had only to endure and trust in God. She knew that the big house, the house of pride where the white folks lived, would come down: it was written in the Word of God" (70). Rachel also told her children, "God was just, and He struck no people without first giving many warnings" (70).

Later, Rachel urges her white oppressors to change their hearts before time runs out. She says, "God gave men time, but all the times were in His hand, and one day the time to forsake evil and do good would all be finished" (70–71). Rachel develops this merciful theology toward the planter until the day when a slave called Bathsheba comes to her room and tells her, "Rise up, rise up, Sister Rachel, and see the Lord's deliverance! He done brought us out of Egypt, just like He promised, and we's free at last!" (71). Rachel's theology conveys Baldwin's attempt to absolve the sins that whites have committed against blacks. Rachel's mercifulness toward the planter is rooted in Baldwin's prophecy that whites will ignore the truth and do violence to themselves unless blacks step in to open their eyes and tell them how to avoid chaos. In this sense Baldwin was a necromancer, since, as Marion Berghahn argues, he believed that African American writers should liberate white Americans from "ignorance" and "innocence" by testifying to the true world that Whites have ignored (177).

In an attempt to do therapy on the white psyche, Baldwin represents Gabriel as a preacher who uses religion in order to expiate historical sins. Yet Baldwin's hope can hardly be realized, since Gabriel reflects white people's denial of their historical sins. Gabriel is a paradoxical character who refuses to see the dark side of his self while he continues to point out the evil in other people: "Consistent with his inconsistencies, he [Gabriel] creates lies to confront and correct his truth. At heart, he is like Gatsby without stamina, wishing to be reborn after every transgression, seeking deliverance, in the sense of birth, from his own frail mind" (Rosenblatt 78). Gabriel, then, is a mirror image of the contradictions in the American culture that he seeks to purify. By representing Gabriel as an allegory for the ambiguity in American culture, Baldwin weakens the divide between blacks and whites, emphasizing the common tragedy of the two groups in the American experience.

Baldwin's theory of cross-racial relationships is visible in *Another Country* (1962) where he depicts black and white characters who live in a restless world. In this book, the character Rufus remembers the time when blacks and white pedestrians in Fifty-ninth Street of New York "came on board" and "rushed across the platform to be waiting [for the] local" (89). In Rufus's mind, these people lived in an unpredictable world where nothing but their ability to cross each other's lives could save them (89). Rufus, however, believes that cross-fertilization will be difficult to achieve, since he saw "many white people and many black people, chained together in time and space, and by history . . . all of them in a hurry. In a hurry to get away from each other" (89). In reaction to such isolation between blacks and whites, Rufus admitted that "we ain't never going to make it" and that "we been fucked for fair" (89). Rufus's perspective reflects Baldwin's theory of the permanent agitation in American society. This restlessness is, like slavery itself, deep-seated in American culture, since it explains the trauma of sexual oppression, violence, and economic exploitation that has produced fear of one another among blacks and whites, and impatience in the American city.

In *Go Tell It*, the restiveness in America is visible in the difficult lives of blacks, whose dreams of social and economic success are limited by discrimination. Richard comes to New York for success, only to be disillusioned by hostile white tenants and police. In New York, the police arrest Richard for having allegedly robbed a store. He is detained after a storeowner claims to have seen Richard in his store during a looting. The accusation makes

Richard realize that the white policemen are going to be prejudiced toward him, because he knows that "these white men would make no distinction between him and the three boys they were after: they were all colored" (171). Richard is released when the robbers turn themselves in. But he is indifferent about freedom, because prison nearly emasculated him. At the police station, Richard tells Elizabeth that "he had been beaten" and that "he could hardly walk. His body, she later discovered, bore almost no bruises, but was full of strange, painful swellings, and there was a welt above one eye" (170). Richard's predicament disheartens Elizabeth: "She had been trying to save money for a whole year; but she had only thirty dollars. She sat before him [Richard], going over in her mind all the things she might do to raise money, even going on the streets. Then, for very helplessness, she began to shake with sobbing" (172). Elizabeth's plight makes her realize that she is a victim of white exploitation, just as Rachel was during slavery. Elizabeth reiterates the sentiments that Rachel had about whites:

> She [Elizabeth] could not, that day, think of one decent white person in the whole world. She sat there, and she hoped that one day God, with tortures inconceivable, would grind them utterly into humility, and make them know that black boys and black girls, whom they treated with such condescension, such disdain, and such good humor, had hearts like human beings, too, more human hearts than theirs. (173)

Elizabeth's wish to see whites leave the "house of pride" and live in that of "humility" conveys Baldwin's condemnation of the social injustice that whites have perpetrated against blacks on grounds of racial hegemony.

During the civil rights era, old practices of white intimidation of blacks, such as mob violence and discrimination, flourished in the United States, seeking to stall the black struggle for equality and justice. As Jane Campbell argues in "Retreat into the Self: Ralph Ellison's *Invisible Man* and James Baldwin's *Go Tell It on the Mountain*" (1977), the 1950s and 1960s were times when there was an inconsistency "between symbolic and real legislation for blacks" (88). These were decades when, "as post-Reconstruction white Southerners strove to reinstate a more familiar system, white United States citizens of the mid-twentieth century seemed incapable of allowing unequivocal rights to Afro-Americans" (88).

Additionally, *Go Tell It* examines the ambiguity of racial oppression by establishing parallels between how John Grimes and Baldwin relate to American society. In the novel, Baldwin describes John as "a stranger" in a city where the lights "crashed on and off above him" (33). This total mockery and denial of John's existence is comparable to the contempt and rejection that alienated Baldwin in a secluding and illusive American society, from which he expatriated himself to live in France. In "James Baldwin: Expatriation, Homosexual Panic, and Man's Estate" (2000), Mae G. Henderson describes Baldwin's literal and real flight to Paris as an effort "to provide a space for the articulation of the homosexual dilemma within the context of postwar American culture" and an attempt "to open the space of black literary expression to subjects and experiences not deemed appropriate for black writers in the 1940s and 1950s" (313). In a comparable way, John's desire to hide from the delusional streetlights of New York is an attempt to escape the glimmer and fantasy that Baldwin viewed as signs of his estrangement in America. As Kathleen N. Drowne points out, Baldwin "was an honest witness to the painful realities of American culture. . . . Feeling alienated from his homeland and discouraged by the ambiguous but ubiquitous 'race problem,' he [Baldwin] fled to Paris, a city that could and did provide him necessary physical and psychological distance from his turbulent past" (72).

Yet, despite their sense of alienation in America, both John and Baldwin continue to regard the country as their home and remain proud of its heritage. With a determination that calls to mind Baldwin's attempts to understand his relations with America, John emphasizes his special place in the United States while being rooted in the African American experience and community.[6] John's hybrid perspective is visible in his vision of New York City from the top of a hill:

> He would be, of all, the mightiest, the most beloved, the Lord's anointed; and he would live in this shining city which his ancestors had seen with longing from far away. For it was his; the inhabitants of the city had told him it was his; he had but to run down, crying, and they would take him to their hearts and show him wonders his eyes had never seen. (33)

In this passage, John imagines the American city as a place where the celestial "shining city" that his ancestors dreamed about could exist. He reinvents New York as a place where God, community, and equality could prevail, opposing Gabriel's vision of the metropolis as a "*Broadway*," that is, "this city where, they said, his [John's] soul would find perdition" (33). By transforming Gabriel's *Broadway* into a city of the elected people, John conveys Baldwin's complex universal humanism, which James Hughes described in "Black City Lights": "With a passivity related to a cosmopolitan artistic grasp of universality, this just man [John Grimes] will await the arrival of the others necessary to constitute a city of the just. Their trust in its eventual existence is a very great secret indeed" (240). In this sense, Baldwin is part of the tradition of American intellectuals such as Vernon Louis Parrington and Perry Miller, who perceived American culture as diverse, unpredictable, and changing.[7]

Baldwin's theory of the unfinished and incomplete American culture is noticeable in the scene where John bumps into an old white man who was going up a hill:

> At the bottom of the hill, where the ground abruptly leveled off onto a gravel path, he nearly knocked down an old white man with a white beard, who was walking very slowly and leaning on his cane. They both stopped, astonished, and looked at one another. John struggled to catch his breath and apologize, but the old man smiled. John smiled back. It was as though he and the old man had between them a great secret; and the old man moved on. (34–35)

The passage describes the random way in which John and the old white man collide with each other unpredictably for reasons they cannot explain. The two characters share a connection about which they keep silent because of the complex unfolding of American history. As evident in the mutual and furtive look and smile that they exchange, the two characters are not ready to discuss the tragic history of oppression of black people. In this sense, the "great secret" Baldwin identifies in the relations between John and the white man is a metaphor for the hidden history of oppression of blacks that white America is still unwilling to tell, hear, or learn.

Like John, Baldwin strived persistently to understand the dilemma that America represented to him. His relationships with the country changed as he began to reinterpret this predicament. In *Nobody Knows My Name* (1961), Baldwin wrote that his shift of views about America occurred as a result of his European journey beginning in 1948, which made him realize that both white Americans and he were the products of historical displacement:

> In my necessity to find the terms on which my experience could be related to that of others, Negroes and whites, writers and non-writers, I proved, to my astonishment, to be as American as any Texas G.I. And I found my experience was shared by every American writer I knew in Paris. Like me, they had been divorced from their origins, and it turned out to make very little difference that the origins of white Americans were European and mine were African—they were no more at home in Europe than I was. (17–18)

By perceiving himself as a person who is as American as "any Texas G.I.," Baldwin was able to develop a universalism and a humanism that did not weaken his relationships with the black experience and community. As Irving Howe and David Levin have shown, Baldwin was a national writer who understood the contradictions in American history and culture.[8] However, as an African American writer, he was primarily engaged in the struggle against racism, injustice, and invisibility. As I will show in the following comparison of *Go Tell It* with *Beloved*, Baldwin was, above all, a critic of white America's image of black people.

Beloved

Set near Cincinnati, Ohio, in 1873, *Beloved* centers on Sethe, a formerly enslaved woman who had escaped from plantation slavery in Kentucky eighteen years earlier. Before her escape, she had sent her three children, two boys and one girl, to 124 Bluestone Road near Cincinnati, Ohio, where Baby Suggs, her free mother-in-law, lived. During her escape—on her way to Ohio—Sethe gave birth to a girl named Denver. Later, the slavemaster tracked her to Bluestone Road. She attempted to kill her children and succeeded in slaying her oldest daughter. She served a jail sentence and returned to 124, where the ghost of her murdered child dwelled for many years.

Recent reviews and critical essays on *Beloved* provide significant insights on Morrison's treatment of memory and history in the book. In "Toni Morrison's *Beloved*: Re-Membering the Body as Historical Text" (1999), Mae G. Henderson describes *Beloved* as "the imaginative and reconstructive recovery of the past" (84). In "The Disruption of Formulaic Discourse: Writing Resistance and Truth in *Beloved*" (1998), Lovalerie King depicts the novel as "a form of alternative discourse" that "takes its place in a continuing tradition of resistance" in African American literature (272). In *Forgetting Futures: On Memory, Trauma, and Identity* (2001), Petar Ramadanovic notes that *Beloved* raises questions about community and history "in the sense of the raising of the dead whose strange return is prompted by the dedication itself" (102). In a similar vein, in *Toni Morrison's Beloved and the Apotropaic Imagination* (2002), Kathleen Marks argues that *Beloved* is an example of "apotropaic imagination"and offers "a dangerous and yet fruitful way of confronting a painful past" (2). Nellie McKay describes *Beloved* as "the quest of history and the privilege of authenticating memory" (262). She continues: "Toni Morrison recreates a lost history. . . . Her history is particularly significant for it attempts to probe the psychological meaning of slavery through the experiences of the slave" (262). The above assessments also apply to *Go Tell It*, since Baldwin, like Morrison, rewrites history subversively while exploring the anxieties that slavery and racism have created in the African American psyche and in the relations between blacks and whites in American culture.

Like *Go Tell It, Beloved* examines the psychological and economic effects of slavery on African Americans. In *Beloved*, the effects are visible in the painful memories that Morrison's characters have of slavery. Talking with Beloved and Denver, Sethe tells them about her murdered mother, Nan, who, according to Baby Suggs, lived on a Southern plantation, where the whites raped her and forced her to give up her children (62). The enslaved black woman who cares for young Sethe explains to her that

> She [Nan] threw them all away but you. The one from the crew she threw away on the island. The others from more whites she also threw away. Without names, she threw them. You she gave the name of the black man. She put her arms around him. The others she did not put her arms around. Never. Never. Telling you. I am telling you, small girl Sethe. (62)

Nan's story is both individual and representative, evidencing repeated instances of her sexual and reproductive exploitation as well as that of enslaved black women in general.[9] Nan's experience recalls Rachel's, since both characters are black women whose physical, emotional, psychological, and economic suffering has never been paid for.

Like Nan, Sethe was a victim of white sexual abuse. Talking to Paul D, who is a long-time friend of Halle, the father of her children, Sethe remembers the day when white men violated her. Sethe describes to Paul D how schoolteacher had sent white men to rape her. Sethe says, "After I left you, those boys came in there and took my milk. That's what they came in there for. Held me down and took it. . . . Schoolteacher made one open up my back, and when it closed it made a tree. It grows there still" (16–17). The mark of the "tree" on Sethe's back symbolizes the brutal impact of the sexual violence that whites use to dehumanize, depersonalize, and control black people. The whites' selection of Sethe as the object of their sexual violence epitomizes their attempt to subordinate and humiliate not just Sethe, but also the ideals of subversive and resistant blackness and black womanhood that she represents.

After she described the sexual abuse of the whites, Sethe explains to Paul D the impact that such violence might have on Halle. She said,

> They took my milk and he saw it and didn't come down? Sunday came and he didn't. Monday came and no Halle. I thought he was dead, that's why; then I thought they caught him, that's why. Then I thought, No, he's not dead because if he was I'd know of it, and then you come here after all this time and you didn't say he was dead, because you didn't know either. (69)

Sethe did not know that Halle had been forced to watch her being raped, a scene that might have psychologically emasculated him. Paul D tells Sethe: "It broke him, Sethe. . . . You may as well know it all. Last time I saw him he was sitting by the churn. He had butter all over his face" (69). Paul D's confession helps Sethe understand the pain Halle went through before he disappeared. Sethe admits that Halle can never be the same person again after witnessing her abuse: "The milk they took is on his mind" (71). In this sense, she is conscious of the trauma created in the minds of the black men who witnessed the rape of black women.[10] Emasculation is a process in which whites seek to create a false sense of power by humiliating defenseless black men. As Gerda Lerner has shown, whites have historically used abusive methods such as rape in an attempt to maintain a false sense of superiority over black men (xxiii).

Sethe's attempt to understand Halle's plight suggests her awareness of the connections between the racial oppression of black women and men. As Lerner put it, "Black women have always been more conscious of and more handicapped by race oppression than by sex oppression. They have been subject to all restrictions against Blacks and to those against women. In no area of life have they ever been permitted to attain higher levels of status than white women" (xxii). Lerner's rationale is corroborated by the discrete social conditions of black and white women in *Beloved*. Neither Sethe nor Baby Suggs have the power of their white mistresses, Mrs. Garner and Mrs. Bodwin, who, in turn, have less power than their husbands do. Yet these white women were shielded from sexual abuse, hard work, and racism.[11]

Additionally, *Beloved* deals with the quandary that African Americans find themselves in when they seek to know which parts of history they should remember. This dilemma is visible when Sethe wants to know and forget about Halle at the same time. Sethe tells herself,

> If he [Halle] was that broken, then, then he is also and certainly dead now. And if Paul D saw him and could not save and comfort him because the iron bit was in his mouth, then there is still more that Paul D could tell me and my brain would go right ahead and take it and never say, No thank you. I don't want to know or have to remember that. (70)

Yet the narrator tells us that "her brain was not interested in the future. Loaded with the past and hungry for more, it left her no room to imagine, let alone plan for, the next day" (70). Sethe's double consciousness reveals the difficulty of selecting which parts of the past to remember when history is fragmented into discrete pieces. Transcending this dualism requires "a revisioning of the past as it is filtered through the present" (Rushdy 37).

Like Sethe, Elizabeth in *Go Tell It* has a dualistic attitude toward the past. She loves and supports her boyfriend, Richard. Yet when Richard commits suicide, Elizabeth—who seeks a quick way of accounting for this death and forgetting it—explains it as an "act of the living God" (174), indicating defeatism and a retreat into religious fatalism. Yet she is not strongly willing to forget Richard's death, since the church constantly reminds her of it and influences her to rationalize this loss in religious rather

than racial terms, which is a strategy of spiritual recourse against white violence. As Horace Porter argues, Elizabeth's religiosity is a desperate alternative in a situation in which her love alone cannot save Richard's life
(112). Yet, like Sethe, Elizabeth must survive and raise the child she had
with Richard before his death. Paradoxically, she cannot live without
remembering Richard's tragic end. Conscious of her challenge to raise his
child in a world that is continually oppressive, she finds succor in
Christianity:

> The consecrated cross I'll bear
> Till death shall set me free,
> And then go home, a crown to wear,
> For there's a crown for me. (152)

Moreover, Christianity allows Elizabeth to survive oppression, remember the
past, and atone for Richard's death, for which she feels partly responsible. As
Porter says, "Before Richard's suicide, Elizabeth discovers that she is pregnant
with his child. She lacks the courage to tell him as she had planned to do the
night before he killed himself—she didn't because she felt it might seem just
another burden. Ironically, Richard's sense of himself as a potential father
might have inspired a measure of optimism and saved his life" (112). Porter's
statement shows that Elizabeth truly loves Richard and that she partly shares
the responsibility for the tragic end of this man's life. In this sense, she is, like
Sethe, a brave and honest figure whose existence is overlaid with heartbreaking and brutal episodes that reveal the drastic emotional consequences of
racism on African American women's memories of their loved ones.

Like Go Tell It, Beloved examines the anxieties between blacks and
whites during slavery. The characters of Rachel in Go Tell It and Baby
Suggs in Beloved depict whiteness in racial and religious terms, revealing the
inimical relations between blacks and whites that Baldwin and Morrison
theorized in "The Price of the Ticket" (1985) and Playing in the Dark
(1992), respectively. The theory of whiteness that Stamp Paid articulates in
Beloved is comparable to Baldwin's concept of whiteness in "The Price of
the Ticket." In Beloved, the theorizing of whiteness is apparent when Baby
Suggs condemns whites for perpetuating injustices on blacks. Baby Suggs
tells Sethe: "Those white things have taken all I had or dreamed . . . and
broke my heartstrings too. There is no bad luck in the world but whitefolks" (89). Baby Suggs is saddened by her memories of her children who
were taken away from her during slavery.

> Thwarted yet wondering, she chopped away with the hoe. What could it
> be? This dark and coming thing. What was left to hurt her now? News of

Halle's death? No. She had been prepared for that better than she had for his life. The last of her children, whom she barely glanced at when he was born because it wasn't worth the trouble to try to learn features you would never see change into adulthood anyway. (139)

Baby Suggs's views on whiteness are also evident in her recollection of the experiences she and her son Halle had in Sweet Home. Baby Suggs served at Sweet Home for ten years as both a cook and a fieldworker until Halle bought her freedom by hiring out years of his Sundays. Mr. Garner, the owner of Sweet Home, made arrangements with Mr. and Mrs. Bodwin, two humanitarian abolitionists who offered to give Baby Suggs a home in exchange for menial work: "Baby Suggs agreed to the situation, sorry to see the money go but excited about a house with steps—never mind she couldn't climb them. Mr. Garner told the Bodwins that she was a right fine cook as well as a fine cobbler and showed his belly and the sample on his feet. Everybody laughed" (145). Baby Suggs then believed that the slaves of the Garners would soon be free. Her expectation was marred when, after the death of Mr. Garner, his brother-in-law—whom Sethe and the others nicknamed "schoolteacher"— imposed tough laws at Sweet Home. Morrison writes,

Voices remind schoolteacher about the spoiling these particular slaves have had at Garner's hands. There's laws against what he done: letting niggers hire out their own time to buy themselves. He even let em have guns! And you think he mated them niggers to get him some more? Hell no! He planned for them to marry! If that don't beat it all! Schoolteacher sighs, and says doesn't he know it? He had come to put the place aright. (226)

Halle had also made arrangements to purchase his own freedom for $123.70, the equivalent of one year of debt work, but schoolteacher put a stop to the practice of hiring out time. Halle tells Sethe, "Schoolteacher in there told me to quit it. Said the reason for doing it don't hold. I should do the extra but here at Sweet Home. . . . The question now is, Who's going buy you [Sethe] out? Or me? Or her [Beloved]?" (196). Schoolteacher's fear of black freedom led him to become racist, paranoid, and violent toward blacks. Accusing a slave called Sixo of stealing, "Schoolteacher beat him anyway to show him that definitions belonged to the definers—not the defined" (190). These incidents show that the white promise of freedom was unreal, and that the limited freedom of blacks was not given; it was paid for.

The illusive nature of the white promise of freedom is also noticeable in a dialogue in which Sethe and Baby Suggs express their differing views about whites. In this exchange of ideas, Baby Suggs develops a premise that counters each of the hypotheses that Sethe makes about whites. The dialogue reads as follows:

> "They got me out of jail," Sethe once told Baby Suggs.
> "They also put you in it," she answered.
> "They drove you 'cross the river."
> "On my son's back."
> "They gave you this house."
> "Nobody *gave* me nothing."
> "I got a job from them."
> "He got a cook from them, girl."
> "Oh, some of them do right by us."
> "And every time it's a surprise, ain't it?"
> "You didn't used to talk this way."
> "Don't box with me. There's more of us drowned than there
> is all of them ever lived from the start of time." (244)

This passage shows the discrepancies between Sethe's and Baby Suggs's opinions about freedom and white people. Unlike Sethe, Baby Suggs perceives freedom as a result of black struggles rather than of white benevolence. Unlike Sethe, who distinguishes between good and bad white people, Baby Suggs sees no variation among whites. Furthermore, unlike Sethe, who expresses gratitude to the white people who helped her get out of jail, Baby Suggs conveys no appreciation for any white person. Baby Suggs's opinions about whites diverge from those of Sethe mainly because Baby Suggs believes that the limited freedom she has was wrested from whites; it was not handed down to her. Being more mature and experienced than Sethe, Baby Suggs is able to see white people as part of a collective system of oppression from which freedom is to be taken, not granted.

Baby Suggs's conception of freedom as a state that blacks have achieved through their own sacrifices is worth comparing with Rachel's representation of liberty as a predestined status. In *Go Tell It,* Rachel represents freedom as the manifestation of divine predictions. In her lifetime, Rachel saw signs that foretold the end of slavery:

> All these signs, like the plagues with which the Lord has afflicted Egypt, only
> hardened the hearts of these people against the Lord. They [whites] thought
> the lash would save them, and they used the lash; or the knife, or the gallows, or the auction block; they thought that kindness would save them, and
> the master and mistress came down, smiling, to the cabins, making much of
> the pickaninnies and bearing gifts. These were great days, and they all, black
> and white, seemed happy together. But when the Word has gone forth from
> the mouth of God nothing can turn it back" (71)

Like Baby Suggs, Rachel does not perceive freedom as the outcome of white philanthropy. In her own terms, Rachel defines liberty as the result of divine intervention. There is a difference of views between Rachel and Baby Suggs, which can be understood only through a study of the two characters' versions of Christianity. Both Rachel and Baby Suggs are products of African American Evangelical Christianity, which, as Albert J. Raboteau shows in *Slave Religion: The "Invisible Institution" in the Antebellum South* (1978), developed in the South during the 1800s as a result of the Great Awakening. According to Raboteau, nineteenth-century black Christians, especially the Methodists and the Baptists, were drawn to the revivalism of the Evangelical clergy, who, unlike the Anglican clergy, emphasized "the experience of conviction, repentance, and regeneration" and "visualized the drama of sin and salvation, of damnation, and election" (132–133). Rachel and Baby Suggs preach vehemently about the sins of slavery, appropriating the traditional revivalists' emphasis on the centrality of personal experience in the narration of history. Yet Rachel's Christianity differs from that of Baby Suggs. Rachel's religious discourse, which focuses on the imminence of God's punishment of the planters, comes from the theology of chaos in fundamentalist Baptism, the tradition in which James Baldwin was reared. By contrast, Baby Suggs's rhetoric, which centers on the sacrifices black people have made in order to achieve freedom, could come from a variety of African American theologies. In her essay "Why Baby Suggs, Holy, Quit Preaching the Word: Redemption and Holiness in Toni Morrison's *Beloved*" (2001), Emily Griesinger argues that Baby Suggs's theology of holiness finds precedent in the Christian Holiness Movement that swept New England and the Midwest in the nineteenth century (693). While her brand of preaching finds antecedents in the sermons and testimonies of Black Evangelist women such as Jarena Lee, Zilpha Elaw, and Julia Foote, Baby Suggs' association with the Holiness Movement is visible when the narrator describes the black oracle as "an unchurched preacher, one who visited pulpits and opened her heart to those who could use it. In winter and fall she carried it to AME's and Baptists, Holinesses and Sanctifieds, the Church of the Redeemer and the Redeemed" (87). This statement shows that Baby Suggs's Christianity is a hybrid composite that is connected with many African American Christian doctrines.

Finally, *Beloved* is a critique of the white American ideology of racial supremacy. This critique is visible when schoolteacher develops racist attitudes toward blacks. Expressing the scientific racism that was popular in the second half of the nineteenth century, schoolteacher views black people as members of an inferior race who need to be saved from barbarity through exposure to white civilization. When he sees that Sethe has tried to kill her children, he thinks to himself, "All testimony to the results of a little so-called freedom imposed on people who needed every care and guidance in the world to keep them from the cannibal life they preferred" (151). In order to understand schoolteacher's racism, one must analyze the theory that Stamp Paid, the black man who helped Sethe escape to Ohio, develops about the white imagination of blackness. Stamp Paid's theory is as follows:

> Whitepeople believed that whatever the manners, under every dark skin was a jungle. Swift unnavigable waters, swinging screaming baboons, sleeping snakes, red gums ready for their sweet white blood. In a way, he thought, they were right. The more coloredpeople spent their strength trying to convince them how gentle they were, how clever and loving, how human, the more they used themselves up to persuade whites of something Negroes believed could not be questioned, the deeper and more tangled the jungle grew inside. But it wasn't the jungle blacks brought with them to this place from the other (livable) place. It was the jungle whitefolks planted in them. And it grew. It spread. In, through and after life, it spread, until it invaded the whites who had made it. Touched them every one. Changed and altered them. Made them bloody, silly, worse than even they wanted to be, so scared were they of the jungle they had made. The screaming baboon lived under their own white skin; the red gums were their own. (198–199)

Stamp Paid's theory of whiteness resonates with Baldwin's in "The Price of the Ticket." In this essay, Baldwin criticizes the invention of whiteness as an identity and a concept that legitimate the marginalization of and discrimination against blacks and other groups. According to him, in American culture, whiteness has been falsely constructed as a synonym for Americanness, when the unavoidable diversity in the country shows that "America is not, and never can be, white" (836). From his perspective, whiteness has been discriminately and fallaciously constructed because it is a social, political, and economic entitlement that white people receive effortlessly "with a painless change of name, and in the twinkling of an eye" (841). Baldwin is referring to the racist and prejudiced ways in which white Americans have prevented the upward mobility of black people by restricting class and educational progress, political power, and all other accomplishments that embody the American dream to whites alone.

The construction of whiteness in terms of privilege has created anxieties in the American psyche; it has also led to the continuous perception of blacks as less than human and blacks' attempts to prove whites wrong through imitation (835). Like Stamp Paid, Baldwin believes that it is unnecessary for blacks to prove a humanity they already have. Baldwin writes, "Not only was I not born to be a slave: I was not born to hope to become the equal of the slave-master" (831). Like Stamp Paid, Baldwin also knows that blacks cannot become white "partly because white people are not white: part of the price of the white ticket is to delude themselves into believing that they are" (835). In addition, like Stamp Paid, Baldwin understands the psychological reasons that prompt whites to insist on whiteness: "The price the white American paid for his ticket was to become white—: and, in the main, nothing more than that, or, as he was to insist, nothing less. This incredibly limited not to say dimwitted ambition has choked many a human being to death here: and this, I contend, is because the white American has never accepted the real reasons for his journey" (842).

Stamp Paid's and Baldwin's theories of the misrepresentation of blackness in American culture are consistent with Morrison's concept of "American Africanism" in *Playing in the Dark*. Morrison defines the term "American Africanism" as the study of the origins, literary uses, and constructions of the "Africanlike (or Africanist) presence or persona" in the United States and "the imaginative uses this fabricated presence served" (6). Like Baldwin, Morrison opposes the stereotyping of blackness in the white literary imagination. She writes: "I use [American Africanism] as a term for the denotative and connotative blackness that African peoples have come to signify, as well as the entire range of views, assumptions, readings, and misreadings that accompany Eurocentric learning about these people" (6–7).

Taking on Baldwin's tradition of necromancy, Morrison also examines the impact of the invention of whiteness in absolute terms on the American psyche. Her visionary ability is visible in *Playing in the Dark* where she interprets the imagination of whiteness and blackness in the ending of Edgar Allan Poe's *The Narrative of Arthur Gordon Pym*, which was written between 1837 and 1838. She finds passages in which the white protagonists, Pym and Peters, are described as floating "on a warm, milk-white sea under a 'white ashy shower.' The black man dies, and the boat rushes through the white curtain behind which a white giant rises up. After that, there is nothing. There is no more narrative. Instead there is a scholarly note, explanation, and an anxious, piled up 'conclusion.' The latter states that it was *whiteness* that terrified the natives and killed Nu-Nu" (32). According to Morrison, Poe's narrative represents whiteness as an image that expires and erases "the serviceable black figure, Nu-Nu" (32). Her argument echoes Baldwin's critique of the pathologizing of blackness in American culture.

Like Baldwin, Morrison depicts the theorizing of whiteness in American culture as a delusion. In *Playing in the Dark,* she writes: "Because they appear almost always in conjunction with representations of black or Africanist people who are dead, impotent, or under control, these images of blinding whiteness seem to function as both antidote for and meditation on the shadow that is companion to this whiteness—a dark and abiding presence that moves the hearts and texts of American literature with fear and longing" (33). The conception of *whiteness* as an identity that requires the death of the black body and subject is the psychic disorder that Morrison, like Baldwin, seeks to repair by examining "the impact of notions of racial hierarchy, racial exclusion, and racial vulnerability on nonblacks who held, resisted, explored, or altered those notions" (11). This American Africanist construct is what *Beloved* and *Go Tell It* have dismantled by exposing the scars of slavery and racism on the American psyche.

Conclusion

Go Tell It on the Mountain and *Beloved* explore the impact of slavery and racism on African Americans and European Americans since the time before the Emancipation Proclamation. The novels celebrate the resilience and humanity of African Americans, who overcame a myriad of social, political, and economic injustices through communal memory and resistance. Both works depict the discrimination and anxieties that slavery and racism have brought about in the relations between blacks and whites in America. In addition, they exhibit the dilemmas that the white morality of supremacy and oppression has created in the American psyche and culture. By tracing such anxieties to the violence of slavery and racism, Baldwin and Morrison have shown that the invention of whiteness as a hegemonic identity that is antithetical to Blackness is the major obstacle to successful cross-racial relationships in the United States.

NOTES

1. See Wright, *African Americans in the Colonial Era*, 57–58; and Stampp, *Peculiar Institution*.
2. See Franklin and Moss, *From Slavery to Freedom*, 58–59.
3. See Gutman, *Black Family*, 283–284.
4. See Bennett, *Before the Mayflower*, 87.
5. See Hine and Gaspar, *More Than Chattel*, 1.
6. See Fabre, *Unfinished Quest*, 226, 374; and Baldwin, *Nobody Knows My Name*, 17.
7. See Parrington, *Main Currents*, xvii; and Miller, *Errands*, 9.
8. See Howe, "Black Boys," 120; and Levin, "Baldwin's Autobiographical Essays," 239.
9. See Woloch, *American Experience*, 183.
10. See Lerner, *Black Women*, xxiii.
11. See Giddings, *When and Where*, 35.

WORKS CITED

Baldwin, James. *Go Tell It on the Mountain*. 1953. New York: Laurel, 1985.
————. *Another Country*. 1962. London: Michael Joseph, 1965.
————. *Nobody Knows My Name*. New York: Dell, 1961.
————. "The Price of the Ticket." 1985. In *James Baldwin: Collected Essays*. Ed. Toni Morrison. New York: Library of America, 1998. 830–842.
Balfour, Lawrie. *The Evidence of Things Not Said: James Baldwin and the Promise of American Democracy*. Ithaca, NY: Cornell University Press, 2001.
Bennett, Lerone, Jr. *Before The Mayflower: A History of Black America*. New York: Penguin, 1988.
Berghahn, Marion. *Images of Africa in Black American Literature*. Totowa, NJ: Rowman and Littlefield, 1977.
Campbell James. *Talking at the Gates: A Life of James Baldwin*. Berkeley, CA: University of California Press, 2002.
Campbell, Jane. "Retreat into the Self: Ralph Ellison's *Invisible Man* and James Baldwin's *Go Tell It on the Mountain*." In *Mythic Black Fiction: The Transformation of History*. Ed. Jane Campbell. Knoxville: University of Tennessee Press, 1977.
Drowne, Kathleen N. "'An Irrevocable Condition': Constructions of Home and the Writing of Place in *Giovanni's Room*." In *Re-Viewing James Baldwin: Things Not Seen*. Ed. D. Quentin Miller. Philadelphia: Temple University Press, 2000.
Fabre, Michel. *The Unfinished Quest of Richard Wright*. Urbana: University of Illinois Press, 1993.
Franklin, John Hope, and Alfred A. Moss, Jr. *From Slavery to Freedom: A History of African Americans*. 7th ed. New York: McGraw-Hill, 1994.
Giddings, Paula Giddings. *When and Where I Enter: The Impact of Black Women on Race and Sex in America*. New York: William Morrow, 1984.
Griesinger, Emily. "Why Baby Suggs, Holy, Quit Preaching the Word: Redemption and Holiness in Toni Morrison's *Beloved*." *Christianity and Literature* 50, no. 4 (2001): 689–702.
Gutman, Herbert G. *The Black Family in Slavery and Freedom, 1750–1925*. New York: Pantheon Books, 1976.
Hardy, Clarence E. *James Baldwin's God: Sex, Hope, and Crisis in Black Holiness Culture*. Knoxville: University of Tennessee Press, 2003.
Henderson, Mae G. "James Baldwin: Expatriation, Homosexual Panic, and Man's Estate." *Callaloo* 23, no. 1. (2000): 313–327.
————. "Toni Morrison's Beloved: Re-Membering the Body as Historical Text." In *Toni Morrison's Beloved: A Casebook*. Ed. Nellie Y. McKay and William L. Andrews. New York: Oxford University Press, 1999.
Hine, Darlene Clark and David Gaspar, eds. *More Than Chattel: Black Women and Slavery in the Americas*. Bloomington: Indiana University Press, 1996.
Holmes, Carolyn L. "Reassessing African American Literature through an Afrocentric Paradigm." In *Language and Literature in the African American Imagination*. Ed. Carol Aisha Blackshire-Belay. Westport, CT: Greenwood Press, 1992.

Howe, Irving. "Black Boys and Native Sons." In *A World More Attractive: A View of Modern Literature and Politics*. New York: Horizon Press, 1963.

Hughes, James M. "Black City Lights: Baldwin's City of the Just." *Journal of Black Studies* 18, no. 2. (1987): 230–241.

King, Lovalerie. "The Disruption of Formulaic Discourse: Writing Resistance and Truth in *Beloved*." In *Critical Essays on Toni Morrison's Beloved*. Ed. Barbara H. Solomon. New York: G.K. Hall, 1998. 272–283.

Leeming, David. *James Baldwin: A Biography*. New York: Knopf, 1994.

Lerner, Gerda, ed. *Black Women in White America: A Documentary History*. New York: Pantheon Books, 1972.

Levin, David. "Baldwin's Autobiographical Essays: The Problem of Negro Identity." *Massachusetts Review* 5 (Winter 1964), 239–247.

Macebuh, Stanley. *James Baldwin: A Critical Study*. New York: The Third Press, 1973.

McKay, Nellie. "The Journals of Charlotte L. Forten-Grimké: *Les Lieux de Mémoire* in African-American Women's Autobiography." In *History and Memory in African-American Culture*. Ed. Geneviève Fabre and Robert O'Meally New York: Oxford University Press, 1994.

Marks, Kathleen. *Toni Morrison's Beloved and the Apotropaic Imagination*. Columbia and London: University of Missouri Press, 2002.

Miller, Perry. *Errands Into The Wilderness*. New York: Harper & Row, 1964.

Morrison, Toni. *Beloved*. New York: Plume Books, 1998.

————. *Playing in the Dark: Whiteness and the Literary Imagination*. 1992. New York: Vintage Books, 1993.

Parrington, Vernon Louis. *Main Currents in American Thought: The Colonial Mind: 1620–1800*. Norman and London: University of Oklahoma Press, 1987.

Porter, Horace A. *Stealing the Fire: The Art and Protest of James Baldwin*. Middletown, CT: Wesleyan University Press, 1989.

Raboteau, Albert J. *Slave Religion: The "Invisible Institution" in the Antebellum South*. New York: Oxford University Press, 1980.

Ramadanovic, Petar. *Forgetting Futures: On Memory, Trauma, and Identity*. Lanham, MD: Lexington Books, 2001.

Rosenblatt, Roger. "Out of Control." *James Baldwin*. Ed. Harold Bloom. New York: Chelsea House, 1986.

Rushdy, Ashraf H. A. "Daughters Signifyin(g) History: The Example of Toni Morrison's *Beloved*." In *Toni Morrison's Beloved: A Casebook*. Ed. Nellie Y. McKay and William L. Andrews. New York: Oxford University Press, 1999.

Stampp, Kenneth M. *The Peculiar Institution: Slavery in the Ante-Bellum South*. New York: Vintage, 1956.

Stowe, Harriet Beecher. *Uncle Tom's Cabin; or Life among the Lowly*. 1852. Boston, MA: Houghton, Osgood and Company, 1879.

Sylvander, Carolyn W. *James Baldwin*. New York: Frederick Ungar, 1980.

Woloch, Nancy. *Women and the American Experience*. New York: McGraw-Hill, 1994.

Wright, Donald R. *African Americans in the Colonial Era: From African Origins Through the American Revolution*. Wheeling, IL: Harlan Davidson, 1990.

SECULAR WORD, SACRED FLESH:
PREACHERS IN THE FICTION OF BALDWIN
AND MORRISON

KEITH BYERMAN

Religion and spirituality have been among the most commented upon of themes in the works of James Baldwin and Toni Morrison.[1] While most evident in such works as *Go Tell It on the Mountain* (1953), *The Amen Corner* (1968), and *Beloved* (1987), these themes are manifest throughout their writings. For example, preachers—the focus of this study—appear frequently. Their roles may be minor, as in "Sonny's Blues" (1957), *Sula* (1974), and *Song of Solomon* (1977), but they are pervasive. What I wish to suggest in this analysis is the extent to which both writers use preachers to explore certain moral, social, and humanistic values, such as the equitable treatment of women, sensuality and physicality, sympathy, and love. In Baldwin, this embodiment is largely negational; that is, the preachers generally represent the opposite of these qualities. In Morrison, the range is broader, with such characters sometimes affirming and sometimes negating these qualities. It is not clear in either writer that preachers achieve anything positive for their communities. Either they bring disaster, as in the cases of Gabriel Grimes and Elihue Whitcomb (Soaphead Church), or they cannot prevent it, as in the cases of Baby Suggs and Richard Misner. Finally, I would suggest that preachers provide opportunities for both writers to comment on art as an alternative to religion as a means of articulating spiritual and humanistic values.

In Baldwin, the preacher's role is primarily one of providing leadership in defining a life of righteousness, which means, in effect, an anhedonic life. In his first appearance in *Go Tell It,* Father James, "a genial, well-fed man," publicly rebukes two of the young adults of the congregation for spending time together outside the church:

> For he knew them to be sincere young people, dedicated to the service of the Lord—it was only that, since they were young, they did not know the

pitfalls Satan laid for the unwary. He knew that sin was not in their minds—not yet; yet sin was in the flesh; and should they continue with their walking out alone together, their secrets and laughter, and touching of hands, they would surely sin a sin beyond forgiveness. (16)

It is the task of the minister to remind the congregation of the evils of the flesh, to compel them to turn away from desire, even when they do not yet recognize it as desire. Every preacher in Baldwin's writing, regardless of age or gender, performs this function. What interests Baldwin, as will be seen below, is the impact of this suppression and rejection of the body.

At the same time, Baldwin's ministers offer a substitute for physical experience through religious ecstasy. In *Go Tell It*, "The Outing" (1951), *Just Above My Head* (1979), and other texts, the author portrays bodies out of control under the influence of the Shout, an expression of religious ecstasy in traditional African American churches. In *Go Tell It*, the same Elisha condemned for his incipient desire is given sanction for a different kind of physical expression:

At one moment, head thrown back, eyes closed, sweat standing on his brow, he sat at the piano, singing and playing; and then, like a great, black cat in trouble in the jungle, he stiffened and trembled, and cried out. *Jesus, Jesus, oh Lord Jesus!* He struck on the piano one last, wild note, and threw up his hands, palms upward, stretched wide apart. The tambourines raced to fill the vacuum left by his silent piano, and his cry drew answering cries. Then he was on his feet turning, blind, his face congested, contorted with this rage, and the muscles leaping and swelling in his long, dark neck. It seemed that he could not breathe, that his body could not contain this passion, that he would be, before their eyes, dispersed into the waiting air. His hands, rigid to the very fingertips, moved outward and back against his hips, his sightless eyes looked upward, and he began to dance. Then his hands closed into fists, and his head snapped downward, his sweat loosening the grease that slicked down his hair; and the rhythm of all the others quickened to match Elisha's rhythm; his thighs moved terribly against the cloth of his suit, his heels beat on the floor, and his fists moved beside his body as though he were beating his own drum. And so, for a while, in the center of the dancers, head down, fists beating, on, on, unbearably, until it seemed the walls of the church would fall for very sound; and then, in a moment, with a cry, head up, arms high in the air, sweat pouring from his forehead, and all his body dancing as though it would never stop. Sometimes he did not stop until he fell—until he dropped like some animal felled by a hammer—moaning, on his face. And then a great moaning filled the church. (15; emphasis in original)

I have quoted this passage at length in order to suggest both the emphasis Baldwin places on the physical quality of the experience and the rhythmic nature of the language he uses to capture it. The church gives the body and its movements a freedom that is forbidden outside its boundaries. The young (and old) bodies kept under surveillance by the preacher and his minions are allowed full expression when within the gaze, and thus control, of church authorities. The violence of movement, the references to animals and the jungle, and the acceptance of dancing reveal a recognition of the power and needs of the body. Physicality, even to the point of something like orgasm, is not so much denied as directed toward the purposes of the church. Relatedly, the anger implicit in Elisha's performance (it should be noted that this is a repeated, almost ritualized activity) offers a release from the frustrations of living in a world in which black people, even those living in the North, suffer discrimination and deprivation. One role of the preacher in Baldwin's work is to shape and control these passions, in effect creating a theater of spiritual ecstasy within the set of the church.

The problem, as Baldwin sees it, with this performative function of religion, is that it has repercussions far beyond the "stage" of the storefront church. Because the ministers have the power to define acceptable (and thus "righteous") expressions of the body, they assume the authority to judge congregants and others on matters of sexuality, behavior, entertainment, work, style, and even luck and misfortune. Gabriel can forgive himself, but not his mistress or his second wife, for sex outside of marriage. Margaret, of *The Amen Corner,* tells a grieving mother to give up a happy marriage with a sinful husband or face the loss of a second child; she also insists that a member of her church give up his job as driver of a liquor truck. Julia, of *Just Above My Head,* refuses to allow her ailing mother to seek medical help because it would show a lack of faith in her own religious powers. It is in his analysis of these actions, rather than in attacks on the smugness, greed, and hypocrisy of ministers—which he also repeatedly shows in both his fiction and autobiographical writings—that Baldwin makes his deepest critique of preachers and of their churches. He sees them acting out the theology of "the mercilessly fanatical and self-righteous St. Paul."[2] Their work is dominated not by a gospel of love, but by a policing of the flesh. It may be more accurate to say that love is carefully kept within the boundaries of Pauline repression. Rigorous application of such regulations in Baldwin's fictional worlds seems to give the preacher-guardians permission to violate the rules themselves, as though their religious power granted them a dispensation.

The first, and in many ways most complex, of these figures is Gabriel of *Go Tell It.* Much of the commentary on him focuses on his authoritarian and judgmental personality in the present time of the novel.[3] But it is useful, I believe, to see him as a man of strong emotions torn between the demands of the flesh and those of the spirit. His tragedy (or pathos) is that he can neither reconcile those demands nor live without reconciling them. His dilemma produces, alternately, denial, rage, and projection onto others of his flaws. His appetite for alcohol and sex is legendary. His sickly mother both spoils him and prays for his salvation. As he tells the story later, he always had a sense of the sinfulness of his behavior. When his sister refuses to be the responsible child any longer and leaves for the North, his guilt becomes stronger even as his promiscuous behavior continues. The guilt seems to give an edge of intensity to his actions:

> And through all this his mother's eyes were on him; her hand, like fiery tongs, gripped the lukewarm ember of his heart; and caused him to feel, at the thought of death, another, colder terror. To go down into the grave, unwashed, unforgiven, was to go down into the pit forever, where terrors awaited him greater than any the earth, for all her age and groaning, had ever borne. He would be cut off from the living, forever; he would have no name forever . . . Thus, when he came to the harlot, he came to her in rage, and he left her in vain sorrow—feeling himself to have been, once more, most foully robbed, having spent his holy seed in a forbidden darkness where it could only die. (82)

What is noteworthy here is the grandiosity of his sin and the punishment it requires. He is not an ordinary sinner; he is a fallen angel deserving of a special damnation. And he does not merely engage in sex; he deposits "holy seed" in "forbidden darkness."

Gabriel is caught up in what might be called narcissistic righteousness even before his conversion. The world's (and God's) attention is focused on his evil; its extremity will make his salvation even more remarkable. Even before the change,

> He desired, with fear and trembling, all the glories that his mother prayed he should find. Yes, he wanted power—he wanted to know himself to be the Lord's anointed, His well-beloved, and worthy, nearly, of that snow-white dove which had been sent down from Heaven to testify that Jesus was the son of God. He wanted to be master, to speak with the authority which could only come from God. (81)

Thus, his path is determined not by the prayers of his mother or by the will of God, but by the overwhelming needs of his own ego. The great sinner must become the great saint and preacher.

Initially, he seems to be successful in this ambition. His local ministry attracts the attention of preachers elsewhere to such an extent that he is invited to participate in a large revival as the youngest of the ministers. What is significant for this analysis is not his sermon, which gains him attention, but what follows in his interactions with senior members of his profession. At a feast given in an "upper room" for all of them, Gabriel experiences his differences from them:

> He was not comfortable with these men—that was it—it was difficult for him to accept them as his elders and betters in the faith. They seemed to him so lax, so nearly worldly; they were not like those holy prophets of old, who grew thin and naked in the service of the Lord. These, God's ministers, had indeed grown fat, and their dress was rich and various. They had been in the field so long that they did not tremble before God any more. (92)

What causes Gabriel's loss of respect is the corruption of power and authority; these men have grown accustomed to a privileged status in the world. But such dishonesty, which has been the focus of a number of literary works and a large body of black folklore, is not Baldwin's principal concern. Rather, it is what comes out of the preachers' smugness and insensitivity.

One of them ridicules Deborah, who had been Gabriel's mother's friend and his chief admirer since his conversion. More important, she had been the victim of a gang rape by white men and thus something of a taboo figure in the black community. After defending her and being told that no harm was meant by the minister's comments, Gabriel further distances himself from the group. But the conflict leads him to consider the possibilities of a marriage to her. From the first thought, the intent is his own greater righteousness and moral authority. He will raise her from her pariah status by his act of generosity; such a special relationship will necessarily produce a line of faithful sons to carry on the work. Moreover, such a sacrificial gesture on his part will clearly make him more holy than the smug preachers around him.

Unfortunately for his dream of a "royal line," Deborah is sterile as a result of the attack on her. So while the work of the spirit goes forward, the work of the flesh must also be done. Gabriel finds life intolerable without the possibility of sons; Deborah moreover, is frigid. He turns to Esther for sexual satisfaction. Though the affair lasts only a few days, after which he turns in guilt away from her, the result is a pregnancy. Because he cannot accept desire as anything other than sin and because he will not acknowledge the fallibility of his converted self, he blames Esther and refuses to take any responsibility for her situation. He is only willing to steal some money from Deborah to give to Esther so that she will go away to have the child; this gesture is intended to protect *his* reputation, not hers. In Chicago, she gives birth to a boy she names Royal and then dies. The name is intended as an insult to Gabriel, who repeatedly talks of producing a religiously royal line of descendants. The child is returned to the community, where Gabriel has to watch him grow up to be a version of his own earlier self and eventually to be killed as a result. Not even his confession to Deborah of his paternity and her forgiveness can save him from bitterness. His ministry becomes a hollow performance because he senses the falseness of his preaching, based as it is on claims of purity. He lacks the strength to make the public confession that he demands of converts; he cannot trust either himself or the community of believers to forgive him. He hates Deborah for her generosity of spirit; he sees every person saved through his preaching as an accusation against him. Thus, he becomes a version of those smug preachers he had earlier disdained. But his is a deeper violation of faith: they had merely become comfortable with a desire for some of life's pleasures, whereas he loses the capacity for love and calls that loss "righteousness." It is appropriate then that when Deborah dies, he moves to the North but fails to find a congregation. He again marries a "fallen" woman in hopes of proving his moral superiority, but his frustration and self-hatred again rob him of any happiness.

By implication, then, Baldwin argues for an acceptance of and tolerance for human weakness over moral purity, in part because purity is not possible in a fallen world. The three women associated with Gabriel's sensual life—Deborah, Esther, and Elizabeth—all accept their bodies, no matter how imperfect. Deborah insists on continuing to live in the community and the church after her rape, while Esther and Elizabeth accept the responsibility for their behavior. Esther leaves not because she fears for her reputation, but because she is ashamed of Gabriel's cowardice. Elizabeth will repudiate neither her relationship with Richard nor the child, John, who was the illegitimate product of that relationship. None of these women lead happy lives, but all of them, unlike Gabriel, care for something beyond themselves. For Baldwin, Gabriel's self-absorption turned into self-hatred and self-righteousness is the greatest of sins.

Michael F. Lynch has argued that *The Amen Corner* is an extension of *Go Tell It*, in that the character of David in the play is one possible outcome of the story of John Grimes, who undergoes conversion at the end of the novel (47). But it can also be argued that Margaret Alexander is a Gabriel who had succeeded in getting a church of his own. She shows the same impulse toward self-righteousness, power, and control and the same disdain for the weaknesses of others. She also uses faith as a means of attack upon the body's needs for sustenance and pleasure. As minister of the church, she has imposed a rule of purity that cannot be sustained under the conditions of her congregants' lives. As mentioned above, she insists that one member give up driving a liquor truck, though she has no meaningful alternative employment for him. She tells Mrs. Jackson, who has just lost a baby, that the loss is God's warning to her about her life. What she refuses to do is acknowledge the woman's pain; instead, she sees this as another opportunity to win a convert. Mrs. Jackson leaves without joining Margaret in prayer, since she has been offered nothing that would make prayer worthwhile.

Ironically, it is this insistence on an unsympathetic righteousness that causes Margaret's loss of the church. Baldwin sets up a contrast between her present life and her past one, when she was married to Luke, a jazz musician. Luke's return when he is clearly dying becomes an opportunity for his and Margaret's son, David, to learn about his father and to give expression to his doubts about the church. This, in turn, allows members of the congregation, who have been chafing under Margaret's leadership, to attack her for *her* moral failings by pointing out that she cannot even bring salvation into her own home. They can reject her by claiming a greater righteousness for themselves.

But Baldwin seems to have in mind something other than what might be seen as Margaret's tragic flaw. Though she attempts, but fails, to regain control, what is more important is her understanding of what should have been important to her. She is the one who left Luke in order to pursue a religious life, though she had always lied to David that his father had abandoned them. Luke's pursuit of what she considered the "devil's work" meant that they had to separate. But what she comes to understand at the end of the play is that she in fact had always loved Luke and that her pursuit of the religious life had simply been a denial of that truth. She chose the Lord's work over the difficult work of love and, at the end, loses her husband to death, her son to life in the larger world, and her church to the smugly righteous.

Two points about this outcome are important for this analysis. The first is that Baldwin seems to be arguing at some level against the participation of women in church leadership. Brother Boxer, one of Margaret's critics, argues that she "started ruling other people's lives because she didn't have no man to control her" (84). While this might be read as a misogynistic comment from one of her enemies, she herself responds in the previous scene to her sister's statement that she had given her life to the Lord: "I'm thinking now—maybe Luke needed it more. Maybe David could have used it better" (82). Therefore, Baldwin's point here is probably not a theological one about the role of women in the church. Rather, since women—along with artists and homosexuals—are among the characters in his work often especially attuned to the difficulties and rewards of daily human existence, I would contend that Baldwin seems to be suggesting that Margaret should have known better than to pursue the false comfort of righteousness. In existential terms, hers was an act of "bad faith."

The second point concerns David's choice of art over the church. Baldwin's claim here would seem to be that the pursuit of the truth requires something other than the pursuit of righteousness, that it is art rather than religion that takes us to truth. The truth that interests David is a human, not a divine one. In his final confrontation with his mother, he says: "I know you think I don't know what's happening, but I'm beginning to see—something. Every time I play, every time I listen, I see Daddy's face and yours, and so many faces—who's going to speak for all that, Mama? I can't stay home. Maybe I can say something—one day—maybe I can say something in music that's never been said before" (79–80). What stands out here is the humility of his statement in contrast to the arrogance of the religious statements that are made. David understands that whatever he might accomplish will take a long time and may or may not actually be achieved. He also notes the importance of listening as well as performing. Moreover, he seeks to speak *for* and not *at* others, to give expression to real human experiences, not to rigidly control them. And finally, he believes that artistic originality is superior to the fixed forms of the church.

The final Baldwin text especially relevant to this analysis is *Just Above My Head*, with Julia Miller as the key figure. A child evangelist, she naturally invites comparisons to Baldwin's own experience in that role. But, I would argue, it is not so much this autobiographical element as it is the powerful and devastating effects of religion on human experience that Baldwin seeks to emphasize in what is arguably his most complex portrait of a preacher. Julia declares herself to be called to the pulpit at the age of seven, and her father, Joel, immediately takes advantage of her vocation by promoting her in the black churches of New York. However, because the story is told by Hall Montana, whose main concerns in the early part of the novel are not with the Miller family, the reader gets only sporadic views of Julia's ministry. These are further distanced by the fact that Hall and his parents do not particularly like her. Her inner life is only revealed to us after she has emerged from this role.

Significantly, Baldwin does not seem to question the authenticity of her calling nor the spiritual power of her preaching. At the age of seven, she declares herself an evangelist and begins speaking in various churches. Given that several characters criticize the ministers of these churches throughout the novel, in much the same language as had been used in the earlier works, it is noteworthy that the author appears to read the calling of Julia as an authentic spiritual experience. Unlike Gabriel, whose vocation seems to be the product of self-justification and glorification, hers is more on the order of a religious mystery: it simply happens. Her innocence only reinforces the claim. Moreover, her power as a speaker also seems very real:

> Whatever she was doing, she surely wasn't jiving: and that church seemed just about ready to take off and meet Jesus in the middle of the air . . . She moved as I have seen few people move, her hands, those eyes, those shoulders, that pulsing neck, and the voice which could not be issuing from a tiny, nine-year-old girl. For me, there was something terrifying about it, as terrifying as hearing the dumb stones speak, or being present at the raising of the dead. For, if the dead could be awakened, this small child's voice could do it—but who wants, really, to be present when the dead rise up? (68)

Though the narrator later questions her uniqueness as a preacher, at this moment he is overwhelmed by her power.

What concerns Baldwin, then, in this text, is not the authenticity of the vocation, but rather the effects of it. Julia's ministry does nothing less than destroy her family and nearly destroy herself. Her younger brother, Jimmy, is neglected by his parents in favor of his charismatic sister. He is punished whenever he tries to get any attention. Her parents, especially her father, become obsessed with her celebrity status, even though they are in many ways very secular people. When her mother, Amy, becomes ill, Julia forbids her to receive medical attention, claiming that to do so would be to doubt her spiritual power. Amy seems incapable of resisting her own child's arrogance, despite the concerns of other adults in the community; the father, too, willingly abdicates responsibility. Only on her deathbed does the mother understand and explain to Julia what they as a family have done to each other; in response to this insight, she admonishes her to take care of Jimmy.

To this point, *Just Above My Head* follows the pattern of Baldwin's earlier works: through self-righteousness, the religious leader brings misery to the family, to those who ought to be most loved and cared for. But in this work, Baldwin pushes the argument to an extreme. Not only is Julia chastened by her mother's death, to the extent that she refuses to preach anymore, but her father then begins sexually abusing her. Unlike Ralph Ellison in *Invisible Man* (1952) or Toni Morrison in *The Bluest Eye* (1970), Baldwin is not particularly interested in the motivations or psychology of the incestuous father. Joel simply claims that such behavior is not uncommon and then repeatedly rapes her and assaults her when she continues to refuse to return to the pulpit. He only stops when he beats her so badly that she is hospitalized and loses the baby (his baby) she is carrying. At this point, Joel disappears from the story in a drunken stupor.

One possible reading of this narrative is that Joel is not so much the abusive father as he is an avenging angel. Here the offending preacher is not only revealed to readers as a moral failure but is also punished for her flaws within the text. In contrast, Gabriel never becomes aware of his defects; *The Amen Corner* ends at the moment of Margaret's awareness. In *Just Above My Head,* Baldwin seems to have given full expression to his anger over the attitudes and actions of preachers. That Julia is a child when her trauma occurs suggests the depth of that anger; her presumed innocence because of her age is not a mitigating factor. To be a preacher at any age, it appears, is to be deserving of terrible punishment.[4]

Julia is saved by turning away from religion, though not necessarily from spirituality. Even before her father's attack, she has begun to take on a more secular appearance. After her recovery, she goes to New Orleans to reunite with Jimmy and carry out her mother's dying wish that she take care of him. She works various jobs, including prostitution, in order to bring them back to New York and into a different life. She remakes herself as a fashion model; the child's body that had been used within the church to denounce and suppress human need and desire has been remade into an adult one that expresses those things. In effect she becomes an artist of the body. By claiming the flesh, she reclaims herself. She is able to find spiritual peace not in any dogma, but in self-understanding and forgiveness, in acceptance of the situations and conditions of other lives, and in a quest for the truth about herself and others. The narrator says of religion, "It was all a lie, from top to bottom." He adds that the "energy called divine is really human need, translated" (343). If these words represent the author's view, then Julia can be said to be the character in his fiction who lives through that truth and emerges as a witness and survivor.

If for Baldwin the preacher is a key figure in the moral universe, one who, ironically, most often represents moral failure, for Toni Morrison, such characters are generally minor figures in her fictional world. Though they make an appearance in virtually every one of her novels, they are usually insignificant for both plot and theme. In most instances, their role is limited to offering advice or to performing rituals such as funeral sermons. They are seldom a target of moral or social commentary within the texts. This does not mean, however, that Morrison is unconcerned with spiritual matters; it means that unlike Baldwin, she does not so clearly divide the world between those devoted to the spirit and those committed to the flesh. While she has the same understanding that some people suppress desire and denigrate the body, she does not consistently link this perspective only to those in religious communities. The sources and motivations for denial are manifold in her work. At the same time, preachers in her work can speak not only for the spirit, but for the body and the world as well. The two most prominent of these—Baby Suggs and Richard Misner—are the focus of this discussion. What interests Morrison is not only the religious content of their preaching and advising, but also, like Baldwin, the effects of doing so. The argument here is that, although they are much more humanistic voices, they are also, at crucial points, ineffectual. Nothing they say or do can prevent the disasters that take place in] the novels. One possible interpretation of this fictional outcome is that Morrison is responding to Baldwin's call for a different kind of preacher by suggesting that such figures can do little in a fallen world.

In Baby Suggs of *Beloved*, Morrison creates a character that exemplifies Baldwin's insistence on suffering as the pathway to wisdom. The narrators of "Sonny's Blues" and *Just Above My Head*, for example, come to the understanding that although the world is a dangerous place, it is possible to gain some equanimity by paying attention to the stories of those who suffer. At the end of the latter work, the narrator uses a masculine pronoun but seems to be referring to Julia's experience: "The sermon does not belong to the preacher. He, too, is a kind of talking drum. The man who tells the story isn't *making up* a story. He's listening to us, and can only give back, to us, what he hears: from us" (590; emphasis in original). Baby Suggs, who has lost all of her children to slavery and whose body has been physically worn down by her own suffering, can nonetheless hear and respect the stories of others and offer them something back. She does so without reverting to the nostrums of dogma or to claims that the world is in fact a better or safer place than it is. In fact, she rejects the title of preacher, saying that she is "too ignorant" for such a role. She is guided by what is repeatedly referred to as her "great heart" to offer guidance to the community.

Though she is often invited to speak in the local churches, her primary pastoral activity takes place in the Clearing, a space that replicates the geography of black religious practice under slavery. In such locations, away from the white gaze, the enslaved could define for themselves their relationship to the divine and to the enslaver. Similarly, in the Clearing, Baby Suggs can conduct a healing ritual that is not about sin and righteousness so much as it is about catharsis and self-love. Every Saturday afternoon, members of the community join her in this hidden place. After calling out the children to laugh, the men to dance, and the women to cry, she encourages them to blend these expressions of emotion. She then offers her theology of the flesh: "This is flesh I'm talking about here. Flesh that needs to be loved. Feet that need to rest and to dance; backs that need support; shoulders that need arms, strong arms I'm telling you" (88). She provides a catalog of body parts that require such attention. This love is needed because "they" do not love black bodies; instead, "they" willingly abuse, exploit, and torture them. The only love possible in such a world is self-love, which is also the only means of healing. The weekly repetition of the ritual and the message suggests the depth of suffering and contempt that must be overcome. Through it, Baby Suggs has melded performative arts with a theology of love that seems to have healing effects on her community.[5]

However, two aspects of this ceremony have been overlooked. The first is the centrality of "they" to Baby Suggs' text. Her message of love is dependent on those who hate black flesh; it is not love for itself, but in resistance to the white other. It requires, in other words, the continuation of the white oppressor–black victim dynamic for its meaning. The black body has value primarily in the context of a condition of abjection. Baby Suggs' last words—"There is no bad luck in the world but whitefolks" (89)—may state a truth about her experience, but they also define the limits of her agency.

The second point is that her message is about *self*-love, not love for family or community. Each person must care for his or her own body, not those of others. While we may wish to read that larger feeling into her sermon (and references to her "great heart" encourage this), she always uses the singular when talking about the body and the parts of it that must be attended to. The appeal is to the individual and to the private self as the location of healing. As shall be seen, this narrow focus enables the disasters that soon follow.

The power of this message is tested upon the arrival of Sethe. Though Baby Suggs has been engaged in a process of forgetting a past linked to the loss of her children and husband during slavery, she immediately and joyously begins to take care of her daughter-in-law and her children. As part of the reunion, she organizes a feast of celebration. This event is presented as accidental in its origins: Stamp Paid goes to considerable trouble to find a large quantity of berries for the family, and this gift gradually becomes an extravagant meal for the community. But even as they enjoy her hospitality and generosity, her neighbors resent it, in part because they cannot match it. Their attitude causes them to remain silent when, a few days later, schoolteacher comes to find Sethe and her children and sell them back into slavery. And because she cannot escape, Sethe chooses infanticide over reenslavement.

Baby Suggs senses the error that she has made even before the terrible events take place. Part of this sense is her awareness of underlying antagonisms: her freedom was bought, not stolen; she came to the community in a wagon, not by running away; she seemed to have resources for extravagance that no one else could afford. Moreover, "She was accustomed to the knowledge that nobody prayed for her" (138). I want to argue that it is her message of self-love as a response to the hatred of the white other that fosters this resentment and disastrous silence. Her perspective blinds her to the problematic nature of her ministry and her celebration. Concerned only with her own joy and desire to express it, she cannot see its meaning through the eyes of the struggling community. To them, though she has suffered mightily, she seems inordinately lucky. Why should they pray for her when she seemed to have so much? Her message of self-love gives them permission to not be concerned with her spiritual or physical welfare. In addition, her focus on whites as the source of all trouble enables them to evade responsibility at the crucial moment.

After the killing, Baby Suggs gives up her ministry, believing both that she has nothing more to say and that what she did say was part of the problem: "Her authority in the pulpit, her dance in the Clearing, her powerful Call (she didn't deliver sermons or preach—insisting she was too ignorant for all that—she *called* and the hearing heard)—all that had been mocked and rebuked by the bloodspill in her backyard. God puzzled her and she was too ashamed of Him to say so" (177). This passage is similar to one in *Just Above My Head,* where the much more secular Hall says that we must learn patience with God. In both instances, the divine is seen as engaged in an act of deceit, resulting in harm to the innocent. Baby Suggs can no longer speak of love because love clearly leads to trouble. So she turns to the contemplation of color, which she tells Stamp Paid is something harmless. (Of course, we must note the irony of this since the fundamental problem *is* color, in the sense of race.) In effect, she turns her face to the wall, dying a few years later, indifferent to everything. Appropriately, her funeral only reinforces community hostility: Sethe refuses to eat the food brought by the neighbors, and they reject hers. "So Baby Suggs, holy, having devoted her freed life to harmony was buried amid a regular dance of pride, fear, condemnation and spite" (171).

Not only was her ministry ineffectual in preventing disasters from happening to her family and community, but her message itself exacerbated the problem. Even at the end, she could only see the world in racialized terms. Denver notes: "Grandma Baby said there was no defense [against whites]—they could prowl at will, change from one mind to another, and even when they thought they were behaving, it was a far cry from what real humans did" (244). Ultimately, she cannot grant to whites the condition of "real humans" and must thus grant to them the power of demons. The love she offers, then, must always fail because she has granted to evil control of the universe. If she cannot urge and trust her own people to love one another on the grounds that whites always take away the objects of that love, then the trauma and suffering will be unending. This, truly, is a story not to be passed on.

Paradise (1998) can be said to offer a modern version of this lesson. Here, however, the modern preacher is never taken seriously. Richard Misner has become the pastor of the Baptist Church in Ruby and thus head of the congregation of the most powerful men in town. But this fact does not gain him their respect. His decision to start a credit union and the reputation of his previous church for social activism are troubling to them if not yet threatening to their control of the community. "So the Morgans sorted Reverend Misner's opinions carefully to judge which were recommendations easily ignored and which were orders they ought to obey" (57). This is obviously a preacher very different from Baldwin's in his concern for matters of this world and different from Baby Suggs in that he is a fully trained member of the clergy. But unlike the others, he does not bring about suffering; he is merely incapable of preventing it.

The first crisis we see in his ministry suggests his limitations. K. D., the rather irresponsible heir to the Morgan fortune, has gotten Arnette pregnant, but more immediately important, has slapped her in public. His actions have provoked hostility in the small town. Since both families are members of his congregation, Misner makes an effort to resolve the problem. He assumes that negotiations are the key to a peaceful resolution. But he also believes that the families should be treated as equals, a view that is disturbing to the Morgans. In addition, he takes for granted that the women of the injured family have as much right as the men to participate. In all these things, he clearly misreads the reality, so while a resolution is achieved, it happens through an offer of money rather than through any sense of remorse or mutual understanding. The crisis ends not because of his values and skills, but because both families grasp something he cannot entirely see—the social and economic realities of the town.

The contrast to Misner is Reverend Pulliam, who is very much in the moralistic tradition portrayed by Baldwin. At the wedding of K. D. and Arnette, to which he has been invited to say a few words as a guest in Misner's church, Pulliam denounces both human love and God's interest in the individual as illusions. Love is a discipline, not a gift, and no one is worthy of it or capable of offering it on their own. Through his speech, aimed, as the text makes clear, primarily at Misner, Pulliam reinforces the patriarchal control seen as essential to the survival of the community.

In response to this attack, Misner, angered and concerned that his anger would manifest in his words and thus add only more inappropriateness to the ceremony, chooses instead a moment of theater. He silently takes the cross down from the wall and holds it before the wedding party. While the gesture, extended as it is over several minutes, is awkward, it in fact achieves his purpose. It offers a symbolic counterargument that love is freely given by the divine, a message that can be easily understood within this gathering of Christians. But more than this, it generates experiences of interiority as the participants consider the meaning of his action. Love is associated with self-awareness and self-expression rather than with discipline. And, to complete the Foucauldian metaphor, the punishment implicit in Pulliam's speech becomes forgiveness through Misner's performance. It is, in other words, art rather than sermon that suggests a way past Ruby's stifling environment.

But love, Morrison seems to be saying, is hard to come by in a community steeped in control, hatred, and the desire for purity. Misner can do little when the very identity of the town is a constantly reenacted history of exclusion and bitterness. He tries to understand that history through his conversations with Pat Best, the resident archivist, but his own impulses toward tolerance, diversity, and equality limit both his understanding and his effectiveness. His efforts to participate in civil rights activities and to listen to the children of the town are seen as merely contributing to the problems of Ruby. It is Pulliam who in fact has a better grasp of what the community believes is right and necessary.

Thus, Misner can do nothing to prevent or mitigate the massacre that opens and closes the novel. Hatred of outsiders and women outweighs love and acceptance. Because he is committed to love, Misner cannot even imagine the depths of antagonism within the Morgans and other men of the town. Unlike the author of the novel, he suffers from a failure of imagination when it comes to evil. His liberationist theology assumes a basic goodness in all people that will limit their behavior. What he can do is try to make sense of the story after the fact and as the town constructs self-justifying narratives and suppresses key details. Interestingly Pulliam has not been able to make the events "sermonizible" (297). Even when Deacon, one of the brothers, comes barefoot to the parsonage in what appears to be a gesture of medieval penance, Misner's ability to help him is limited. They never talk about the killing of the women, but rather about family history and its moral obligations. Deacon clearly seeks a path to forgiveness, but the sin to be forgiven remains unspeakable.

At the end, Misner is the one who is granted understanding of the town and its inner truth, but his knowledge cannot be spoken, in part because in contrast to Baby Suggs's sermons in the Clearing, "the hearing [cannot] hear." Unlike his predecessor, this preacher chooses to live and to live within the failed community. He understands that the people will need his help and his theology of love, now that their ideology of hate has brought them to the brink of destruction. Though he could not adequately imagine the present, he does have a sense of the future as something he can help them to shape. Whether he has real understanding and the power to make a difference is left open at the end of the book.

For Morrison, then, the preacher serves to articulate a humanistic vision in a fallen world. For her, the power of the spoken Word lies in its expression of a desire for transformation. What this means is that mere sermonizing is inadequate, since words alone cannot meet the needs of living beings.

Instead, their meaning must be performed so as to connect the body to the Word. Baldwin arrives at the same conclusion, I would argue, but from the opposite direction. Because his preachers insist on a moral dichotomy between the Word and the body, they eventually fail. They bring disaster to themselves and their families and communities because they reject the body's truth. In his works, their only hope is in finding wisdom after their fall, as in the case of Julia. The alternative presented in Baldwin's work is always the artist, usually a musician. Unlike Morrison, Baldwin has difficulty in bringing together these roles in one person. But like her, he knows that the true preacher is the one who understands that there is little salvation to be found in this fallen, suffering world.

NOTES

1. Recent comments on spirituality and religion include Allen, Bruck, Henderson, Newsome, Lynch, Olson, Scott, and Warren on Baldwin; and Alexander, Cullinan, Holland, Holloway, Holloway and Demetrakopolous, McCay, Mitchell, Morey, Ryan, and Taylor-Guthrie on Morrison.
2. *The Fire Next Time,* 58. See Michael F. Lynch, "*Just Above My Head:* James Baldwin's Quest for Belief" (1997), on some of the implications, especially in *The Amen Corner,* of a Pauline theology (49–50).
3. See Rosenblatt, Macebuh, Hubbard, and Margolies as examples of this critical approach.
4. While it is beyond the purview of this essay, it is, of course, possible to read Julia's punishment psychobiographically, as Baldwin's self-flagellation for once himself being a preacher. And making the father the agent of that punishment simultaneously implicates and exonerates David Baldwin for his role in young James's life.
5. See Hubbard, Krumholz, and Peach. Critics have repeatedly commented on the importance of this ceremony.

WORKS CITED

Alexander, Allen. "The Fourth Face: The Image of God in Toni Morrison's *The Bluest Eye.*" *African American Review* 32, no. 2 (1998): 293–303.
Allen, Shirley S. "Religious Symbolism and Psychic Reality in Baldwin's *Go Tell It on the Mountain.*" *CLA Journal* 19 (1975): 173–199.
Baldwin, James. *The Amen Corner.* New York: Dial Press, 1968.
———. *The Fire Next Time.* New York: Dial Press, 1963.
———. *Go Tell It on the Mountain.* New York: Dial Press, 1953.
———. *Just Above My Head.* New York: Dial Press, 1979.

————. "The Outing." *New Story* 2 (April 1951): 52–81.

Bruck, Peter. "Dungeon and Salvation: Biblical Rhetoric in James Baldwin's *Just Above My Head*." In *History and Tradition in Afro-American Culture*. Ed. Günter H. Lenz. Frankfurt: Campus, 1984. 130–146.

Cullinan, Colleen C. "A Maternal Discourse of Redemption: Speech and Suffering in Morrison's *Beloved*." *Religion and Literature* 34, no. 2 (2002): 77–104.

Ellison, Ralph. *Invisible Man*. New York: Random House, 1952.

Henderson, Carol. "Knee Bent, Body Bowed: Re-Memory's Prayer of Spiritual Re(new)al in Baldwin's *Go Tell It on the Mountain*." *Religion and Literature* 27, no. 1 (1995): 75–88.

Holland, Sharon P. "Marginality and Community in *Beloved*." In *Approaches to Teaching the Novels of Toni Morrison*. Ed. Nellie Y. McKay and Kathryn Earle. New York: Modern Language Association, 1997. 48–55.

Holloway, Karla F. C. "The Lyrical Dimensions of Spirituality: Music, Voice, and Language in the Novels of Toni Morrison." In *Embodied Voices: Representing Female Vocality in Western Culture*. Ed. Leslie C. Dunn and Nancy A. Jones. Cambridge: Cambridge University Press, 1994. 197–211.

Holloway, Karla F. C., and Stephanie A. Demetrakopolous. *New Dimensions of Spirituality: A Biracial and Bicultural Reading of the Novels of Toni Morrison*. New York: Greenwood, 1987.

Hubbard, Dolan. *The Sermon and the African American Literary Imagination*. Columbia: University of Missouri Press, 1994.

Krumholz, Linda. "The Ghosts of Slavery: Historical Recovery in Toni Morrison's *Beloved*." *African American Review* 26, no. 3 (1992): 395–408.

Lynch, Michael F. "*Just Above My Head*: James Baldwin's Quest for Belief." *Literature and Theology* 11, no. 3 (1997): 284–297.

Macebuh, Stanley. *James Baldwin: A Critical Study*. New York: Third Press, 1973.

Margolies, Edward. *Native Sons: A Critical Study of Twentieth-Century Black American Writers*. Philadelphia: J. B. Lippincott, 1968.

McCay, Mary A. "The River Narrative in Toni Morrison's *Sula*." In *Performance for a Lifetime: A Festschrift Honoring Dorothy Harrell Brown*. Ed. Mary A. McCay and Barbara C. Ewell. New Orleans, LA: Loyola University Press, 1997. 23–33.

Mitchell, Carolyn A. "'I Love to Tell the Story': Biblical Revisions in *Beloved*." *Religion and Literature* 23, no. 3 (1991): 27–42.

Morey, Ann-Janine. "Margaret Atwood and Toni Morrison: Reflections on Postmodernism and the Study of Religion and Literature." In *Toni Morrison's Fiction: Contemporary Criticism*. Ed. David L. Middleton. New York: Garland, 1997. 247–268.

Morrison, Toni. *Beloved*. New York: Alfred A. Knopf, 1987.

————. *Paradise*. New York: Alfred A. Knopf, 1998.

Newsome, Virginia. "Gabriel's Spaces in Baldwin's *Go Tell It on the Mountain*." *MAWA Review* 5, no. 2 (1990): 35–39.

Olson, Barbara K. "'Come-to-Jesus Stuff' in James Baldwin's *Go Tell It on the Mountain* and *The Amen Corner*." *African American Review* 31, no. 2 (1997): 295–301.

Peach, Linden. *Toni Morrison*. 2nd ed. New York: St. Martin's, 2000.

Rosenblatt, Roger. *Black Fiction*. Cambridge: Harvard University Press, 1974.

Ryan, Judylyn S. "Spirituality and/as Ideology in Black Women's Literature: The Preaching of Mary W. Stewart and Baby Suggs, Holy." In *Women Preachers and Prophets through Two Millenia*. Ed. Beverly Kienzle and Pamela J. Walker. Berkeley: University of California Press, 1998. 267–287.

Scott, Lynn O. *James Baldwin's Later Fiction: Witness to the Journey*. East Lansing: Michigan State University Press, 2002.

Taylor-Guthrie, Danielle. "Who Are the Beloved? Old and New Testaments, Old and New Communities of Faith." *Religion and Literature* 27, no. 1 (1995): 119–129.

Warren, Nagueyalti. "The Substance of Things Hoped For: Faith in *Go Tell It on the Mountain* and *Just Above My Head*." *Obsidian II* 7, nos. 1–2 (1992): 19–32.

UNSEEN OR UNSPEAKABLE?
RACIAL EVIDENCE IN BALDWIN'S AND
MORRISON'S NONFICTION

RICHARD SCHUR

L egal knowledge has always underwritten African American experiences and narratives. In *Whispered Consolations* (2000), Jon-Christian Suggs argues that African Americans between 1820 and 1954 utilized narrative to rewrite legal discourse because law had produced racial injustice. Only African American literary texts could do justice to black life, not law. After *Brown v. Board of Education* in 1954, Suggs argues, the patterns of African American narrative change once the law "sees" separate as unequal. For Suggs, African American fiction is liberated from discussing legal impediments to full citizenship when legal discourse itself, in *Brown*, adopts formal equality as the meaning of the Fourteenth Amendment to the Constitution. In other words, African American storytellers no longer have racial injustice rooted in legal doctrines as a major primary theme for their stories. *Brown*, in this formulation, announces new paradigms for educating the nation's youth and structuring social life and creates the need for developing new issues for African American storytellers.

In this chapter, my goal is to extend Suggs's analysis and consider the effect of post-*Brown* legal discourse on African American narrative. To accomplish that task, I create a dialogue between the nonfiction writings of James Baldwin (*The Evidence of Things Not Seen* [1985]) and Toni Morrison ("Friday on the Potomac" [1992] and "The Official Story: Dead Man Golfing"[1997]) and examine how these two influential African American writers have analyzed the continuing need for African American narratives to supplement and write over legal discourse. Their nonfiction essays describe how the legal and cultural terrain has been altered from the physical violence of Bull Connor to the representational violence of the Reagan era (welfare queens and Willie Horton). Along with critical race theorists,

Baldwin and Morrison helped articulate a legal strategy to confront the tactical shifts, both conscious and unconscious, made by civil rights opponents. The transition to the post–civil rights era transformed the grammar and syntax of racism, racialization, and white supremacy. The success of the 1963 March on Washington and the "I Have a Dream" speech altered how Americans, intent on maintaining de facto white supremacy, argued for a status quo. If political leaders previously relied on conscious racist language to keep African Americans "in their place," the 1970s and 1980s saw a resurgence of property rights and state's rights rhetoric that evaded overt references to race while tapping into racialized fears. Baldwin writes *"I'm not sure I want to be integrated into a burning house"* because legal doctrines had changed, but people's attitudes and behavior had not (italics in original, 23). For Baldwin, legal change without cultural transformation put African Americans at risk because racial barriers still existed, even if the signs announcing segregation had been removed.

If previous generations of African American storytellers emphasized the injustice of *substantive* law, such as property and criminal law, Baldwin and Morrison focus on the injustice of legal *processes* for eliciting testimony and recognizing the credibility of that testimony.[1] This shift speaks to a generational shift in emphasis or tone from civil-rights-era tactics for legal reform (changing the substance of law) to post–civil-rights-era concerns about the unconscious racism of legal discourse (the faulty process of law). The move from legal substance to legal process also involves shifting from the realms of thinking and argumentation to the problem of seeing, speaking, and hearing in a racialized world. In this chapter, I explore how Baldwin's and Morrison's nonfiction essays tend to recast legalized racism as a sensory problem, rather than one of rationality. The problem of race remains, but its meaning and operation have changed due to the growth of neoliberal rhetoric and policies during the post–civil rights era.

Baldwin's *Evidence* suggests that as a veteran of many civil rights struggles he saw the limitations of the NAACP (National Association for the Advancement of Colored People) efforts for legal reform and that he began articulating a new approach to law. Morrison carried on and developed further both Baldwin's critique of the civil rights legal legacy and the burgeoning critical race theory (CRT) movement that transformed the legal academy in the 1990s.[2] By connecting their criticisms of contemporary legal discourses, this chapter seeks to recenter discussions of Baldwin and Morrison, specifically, and African American literature, more generally, on questions of social justice. Their essays should not be confined or segregated to graduate-level seminars, but read alongside their more famous fiction to emphasize their profound dedication to the cause of social justice.

James Baldwin's *The Evidence of Things Not Seen*

In *Evidence*, Baldwin shifts the attention of civil rights activists from legal substance to legal process. During the civil rights movement, activists transformed the content of American legal doctrines because they trusted extant procedures to protect and promote the interests of historically marginalized groups (Peller 1993). *Evidence* was one of several moments during the 1980s when intellectuals, artists, and activists of color began to question the premises of the NAACP's legal strategy for attaining freedom and equality. Although courts had proved to be the most fertile ground for initiating social reform, over time they could not sustain that initial momentum (Spann 1993). For Baldwin, this failure to realize the goal of the civil rights movement followed from law's myopic vision of social life. Courts, judges, and juries could "see" only what their life experiences had conditioned them to see. The rules for discovering, presenting, and evaluating evidence had not been revised or rewritten during the civil rights movement because legal activists assumed that the eradication of racist legal doctrines would be sufficient to improve the lives of African Americans. There was little effort to change how legal discourse *viewed* African Americans, only how it thought about them.

In *Invisible Man* (1952), Ralph Ellison writes in the voice of his nameless narrator: "I am an invisible man . . . I am invisible, understand, simply because people refuse to see me" (3). Ellison's novel then proceeds to depict why society, in effect, forced the narrator to choose invisibility over a life doomed to misrecognition and false ideals. The NAACP sought to make courts and legislatures correct the irrationality of segregated schools and overt, intentional discrimination. They attempted to produce legal doctrines, such as the Voting Rights Act of 1965 and the Civil Rights Acts of 1964 and 1968, to respond to Ellison's narrator's crisis: legally created and enforced second-class citizenship. Legal discourse before *Brown* forced African Americans to live as "invisible men and women" because the law had illogically categorized African Americans and thus failed to appropriately interpret the Constitution. The law refused to apply legal doctrine rationally, so African Americans were functionally invisible.

In the late 1970s and early 1980s, twenty-eight black children were murdered in Atlanta. James Baldwin journeyed from France (then his home) to Atlanta to witness and write about the child-murder cases that resulted in Wayne Williams's conviction for two of the murders. Baldwin's *Evidence* depicts not so much the murders or Wayne Williams's trial, but how the post–civil rights era presented new challenges for civil rights activists. The title emphasizes the visual aspects of legal discourse to reflect law's racialized gaze where race shaped legal judgments and decisions even if conscious racist motives were no longer explicitly stated. If Ralph Ellison described the problem of invisibility, then Baldwin explores the crisis of racial misrecognition. Just as Percival Everett has rewritten Ellison's *Invisible Man* in his *Erasure* (2001), Baldwin recasts the civil-rights-era conundrum of doctrinal invisibility as the contemporary struggle against the erasure of black subjectivity from legal discourse.

While scholars have tended to ignore *Evidence* because of its eccentric and rambling prose, it nonetheless constitutes a significant—if not seminal—textual moment when civil-rights-era thinking about legal discourse modifies and gets transformed into post–civil-rights-era CRT. By putting this late-Baldwin nonfiction into dialogue with Morrison's nonfiction, I attempt to specify the moment when the civil rights era gives way to the post–civil rights era within African American cultural criticism and explore how the two underlying approaches differ, yet remain related. Baldwin's *Evidence* constitutes an exemplary articulation of the distinctions between civil rights and post-civil rights approaches to law: (1) Baldwin uses the Wayne Williams case to illustrate how the civil rights vision and trust in law failed to account for the manner in which a racialized culture limited the gains of the movement; (2) Baldwin turns to psychological causes for the persistence of racism, (3) Baldwin relies on optical or visual metaphors for the persistence of race, (4) Baldwin examines how language hides racialized meaning, and (5) Baldwin lays out the problems for a lay audience of the limits of rights discourse for African Americans. Baldwin's reliance on law's *vision* establishes a new line of inquiry for African American cultural criticisms of legal discourse—criticisms that will be developed further by Toni Morrison and CRT. The goal of *Evidence* is to represent how underlying cultural narratives and unconscious ways of seeing limit law's understanding of African American life and would likely further defer dreams of freedom and equality. Baldwin's descriptions of how justice operates thus illustrate the legal context and the African American cultural ethos for CRT's attempt to create both a theoretical and practical response to the limited gains produced by the legal activism of the civil rights movement.

Despite its rambling and overlapping style, most of Baldwin's text concerns itself with highlighting the gap between reality and legal constructions of that reality that ignore the plight of real African Americans. *Evidence* opens by comparing Wayne Williams's trial with a circus to undermine the illusion or assumption of impartial legal judgment. Rather, legal vision (and hence legal judgment) is pre-or overdetermined because it views an already structured spectacle whose very structure determines its meaning. Baldwin writes:

> For to suspend judgment demands that one dismisses one's perceptions at the very same moment one is most crucially—and cruelly—dependent on them. We perceive by means of the kaleidoscopic mirror of this life. This means

that our ability to perceive is at once tyrannized by our expectations, and at war with them. (1)

This passage signals a move away from the confrontation of clearly stated racist reasoning, the hallmark of civil-rights-era activism and jurisprudence. In its place, Baldwin announces a new terrain for the fight for freedom and equality: the realm of perception. As described by Baldwin, perception operates prior to rationality and impedes impartial judgment. Our preconceived notions "tyrannize" our logical faculties. On the one hand, such an analysis turns the supposed impartiality of law, symbolized by a blindfolded justice, into a cruel irony. Justice is blind not to diminish the possibility for bias, but because bias infects the perceptual faculties of any legal decision maker and renders null any attempts at impartiality. On the other hand, this description of legal vision transforms legal critique into a nearly hopeless task in which the culture and vision of legal actors must be altered before their reasoning can be.

A second key element in this opening passage is the "kaleidoscopic mirror." For Baldwin, perception itself functions as a kaleidoscope that shapes the location and time of our gaze, thus distorting the very objects we see. The courtroom and legal discourse operate as kaleidoscopic mirrors presenting us objects to view, but ones that get distorted precisely because they have been presented to us through the filter of law. Owing to the circularity of a kaleidoscope's lens, much of what we can "see" through law merely reflects, in Baldwin's words, "our expectations." Perhaps the apparent disorganization or circularity of *Evidence*'s structure constitutes Baldwin's effort to produce a literary kaleidoscope that constantly shifts order and placement of details from the Atlanta child-murder case to emphasize the circularity of Wayne Williams's trial despite its apparent unfolding in linear chronological time.

Throughout the extended essay, Baldwin returns to the distorting images legal discourse relies on and produces throughout the case:

What White men see when they look at Black men—insofar as they dare, or are able to perceive a Black as a man like themselves, like all men—I do not have the heart to conjecture. (21)

Blacks exist, in the imagination, and in relation to American institutions, in reference to the slave codes. (31)

Official language has no choice but to be that and is not to reveal so much as to distract and, as it were, console. (65)

The world's definitions are one thing and the life one actually lives quite another. One cannot allow oneself, nor can one's family, friends, or lovers—to say nothing of one's children—to live according to the world's definitions. (86)

Legality, according to an Atlanta lawyer I know, *is whatever you say is legal. Common law is what everyone agrees is legal.* (110; italics in original)

Although many of these quotations specifically deploy the language of vision, others do not. Nonetheless, I contend that these quotations and the many other potential aphorisms *Evidence* contains all focus on how perception tends to differ across racial lines and that these differences limit the possible effectiveness of civil-rights-era reforms in legal doctrine. The rules that ground legal decisions may be sound, but the determination of facts relies too much on white experiences and viewpoints and limits law's transformative potential.

In a move that might appear strange—given his literary, not legal, background—Baldwin reviews in minute detail evidentiary decisions. For example, he reviews the judge's decision to admit evidence of "prior acts" testimony. Baldwin tries to demonstrate that the judge is forced to draw an unconscious analogy between Wayne Williams's behavior as a black man and his own (or those of his friends) actions as a white man. This analogy, which is unspoken but essential to evidentiary determinations, requires judges to ignore or set aside race even when it may clearly differentiate between individuals' behaviors (15–18). Baldwin also explores the court's decision to admit evidence about the Williams's family carpet. The prosecution sought to admit scientific and photographic evidence as part of its effort to show a pattern of "prior acts" because the carpet fibers potentially showed Williams's pattern of curious and possibly criminal behavior. From Baldwin's perspective, this aspect of legal process, the rules of evidence, allows perception, not reason, to determine the fate of African Americans within the legal system. Determining what constitutes an appropriate or sufficient analogy of prior strange or odd behavior hinges on law's necessarily racialized vision, according to Baldwin. On the basis of his close observation of the Atlanta child-murder cases, Baldwin concludes that racialized vision and racist ideas infect legal outcomes primarily through decisions about the admissibility of evidence or the structure of the legal process rather than through racist legal doctrines (105–108). Baldwin's detailed evaluation of the court's decisions about evidence, nonetheless, might seem out of place within the text itself, despite their connection to his critique of law's vision. I would argue, however, that they form a necessary part of his kaleidoscopic critique of legal discourse that judicial assumptions and experience taint law's objectivity and infuse it with the subjective experience of white people.

The third element of Baldwin's exploration of how law's limited vision undermines its claims of objectivity and its ability to liberate African Americans is his focus on the discursive nature of blackness (a critique adopted almost in its entirety by Toni Morrison). Throughout *Evidence,* Baldwin examines how blackness is not simply an identity, but a description of reality.

Adopting and adapting the vocabulary and methodologies of a burgeoning postmodernism, Baldwin tries to show how blackness, the signifier, carries with it certain meanings that can be mapped onto places (Atlanta), people (Wayne Williams), and the government (Andrew Young, then the mayor of Atlanta). It also could be taken away from those very individuals or objects. Blackness is thus not a description of physical reality, but what Charles Mills has recently labeled *social ontology* or "a social structure of privilege and disadvantage . . . [that] uses biological markers" to distribute those privileges and disadvantages (7). Baldwin anticipates Mills's neologism and explores how decision makers relied on blackness to value or impart credibility to evidence and people. For Baldwin, the question the child murders presented was not only how do people translate Wayne Williams into a textual representation, but what do individuals *see* when they look at him or the evidence left behind in the Atlanta child murders. By focusing on how legal discourse *sees* controversies, Baldwin in effect unmasks the fiction that lady justice is blindfolded.

Toni Morrison's Nonfiction

After she published *Beloved* in 1987, Morrison "inherited" (along with a few others) Baldwin's role as a spokesperson for African American literary and cultural critics. Her first major foray into criticism, "Unspeakable Things Unspoken" (1989), explores the canon debates from the 1980s. In these debates, scholars, cultural critics, and educational experts sought to revise the rules for regulating or judging literature. Morrison intervened in this debate by demonstrating how race and the racial gaze have always structured literary judgment (11). For Morrison, the 1980s presented the question of whether scholars would or would not develop race-conscious methods and theories that could examine the role of race in literary discourse and create a more just national imagination (17). This essay "borrows" Baldwin's emphasis on the visual (through her use of *imagination, critical viewpoint,* and *narrative lenses* as key phrases) as fundamental to developing a more just *process* for arriving at literary judgments.[3] This essay also provides a fascinating discussion of Morrison's methods of creating "opening scenes" in her work. As a whole, however, it primarily adopts Baldwin's *view* about the evidence of things (i.e., race) not seen.

If Morrison continued to emphasize the visual, there would be little cause to explore the dialogue between Morrison and Baldwin. However, Morrison has increasingly focused on the role of narrative and what is "speakable" within literary, cultural, and legal discourse, thereby revising Baldwin's critique of legal discourse.[4] As legal discourse has become the primary setting for contemporary cultural controversies, Morrison's critique has shifted to how this discursive form shapes what can or cannot be spoken. For Morrison, the Thomas–Hill hearings (1991) and the O. J. Simpson case (1995) underlined the metaphorical nature of language, the relationship between narrative and justice, and the difference between justice and law. By examining how lawyers and legal decision makers deployed language in each high-profile case, Morrison confronts the myths, images, and tropes that structured these spectacles and informed public consumption of them.

The Clarence Thomas–Anita Hill Hearings

In 1991, George H. W. Bush nominated Clarence Thomas to fill Thurgood Marshall's vacant seat on the Supreme Court. This nomination caused considerable controversy because, although Thomas's appointment would mean that another African American justice would follow Marshall, Thomas had not worked in the civil rights movement, nor was he viewed as a strong proponent of civil rights law. Additionally, after Bush nominated Thomas, Anita Hill, a former employee of Thomas, came forward and alleged that he had sexually harassed her. Although the Senate ultimately confirmed Thomas, the Clarence Thomas–Anita Hill hearings presented an unusual moment in American history, but an emblematic one for the post–civil rights era: an African American woman testified against an African American male who sought one of the highest positions in the country. Thomas's appointment and the resultant sexual harassment hearings produced many newspaper editorials, many "water-cooler" conversations, and fuel for the fiery debate about the canon wars. In this context, Morrison invited many well-known academics to contribute to a volume of essays she planned to edit: *Race-Ing Justice, En-Gendering Power: Essays on Anita Hill, Clarence Thomas, and the Construction of the Social Reality* (1992).

In her introduction to the 1992 collection, Morrison explains how the Thomas–Hill hearings require some exploration of the nature of language and how activists for social justice in the post–civil rights era lack sufficient linguistic resources to describe adequately the condition of African Americans. Like Baldwin, she makes clear that legal discourse cannot "see" with the eyes or express the legal subjectivity of an African American. However, she goes further than Baldwin and connects the blindness of law's vision with its inability to develop legal processes through which truth, especially racial truth, can be spoken. The evidence of race can be neither seen nor spoken with American law because the civil rights movement focused on reforming legal doctrine, not legal process.

In her essay, Morrison writes: "The problem of internalizing the master's tongue is the problem of the rescued. Unlike the problems of survivors who may be lucky, fated, etc., the rescued have the problem of debt" (xxv). In her analysis, Clarence Thomas fascinated Americans because he appeared to be a contemporary version of *Robinson Crusoe's* Friday. If the civil rights generation protested their experiences of racial segregation and the continued meaning of race in contemporary life, Clarence Thomas seemed to indicate that race and racism constituted merely historical memories and that there was little need for more civil rights jurisprudence. Just as Friday proved to be a reliable servant for Crusoe, Thomas made it all too clear that he, like Friday, appreciated the efforts and accomplishments of European Americans and would make little effort to alter social relations. To Morrison, Thomas represented an individual who has so internalized the master's language that meaningful resistance becomes impossible. The story of Thomas matched dominant (i.e., white and male) stories about black upward mobility. Thus, audiences (both African American and white) eagerly consumed this story because Thomas did not offer a subjectivity that had been hidden by legal and cultural discourses. Baldwin would have described this as America's perceptions being "tyrannized by their expectations" about Thomas. For Morrison, law's language—not its vision—created this discursive impasse. In her essay, Morrison argues that American legal discourse produces a racialized subject, meaning that laws or events act upon African Americans instead of allowing African Americans to take meaningful action themselves. Morrison compares Clarence Thomas to Friday from *Robinson Crusoe* because his situation vis à vis American culture and American legal discourse is one in which his position was overdetermined and he followed perfectly the limited racial script offered to African Americans.

Part of the script included a claim of sexual harassment. Hill's allegations permitted Thomas to protest his "high-tech lynching" and remind America that it could help a black man overcome a charge of sexual harassment (as such charges were historically fabricated to legitimize extra-legal violence). Thomas's identity as an African American allowed him to argue, implicitly if not explicitly, that supporting him would enable a person to both demonstrate their "colorblindness" —a putative mark of racial sensitivity—and take a stand against the excesses of political correctness and sexual harassment law run amok. The complex vectors of race, sex, and gender make Baldwin's emphasis on vision too limited a lens to describe the cultural layers of power at work in this situation. In this essay, Morrison identifies this situation as a moment where legal discourse, both sexual harassment law and the constitutional procedure for confirming judges, lacks the vocabulary to attend to the multiple differences that operate.

For Morrison, Anita Hill pays the cost of this discursive failure because while Thomas can be understood or *viewed* as a caricature, she is completely incomprehensible. About Hill, she writes: "As in virtually all of this nation's great debates, nonwhites and women figure powerfully, although their presence may be disguised, denied, or obliterated" (xix). "Anita Hill's description of Thomas's behavior toward her did not ignite a careful search for the truth; her testimony simply produced *an exchange of racial tropes*" xvi italics mine). In these passages, Morrison argues that what "disguises, denies or obliterates" women and nonwhites in public discourse is "the exchange of racial tropes." She argues that the primary meaning that could be transferred successfully about Anita Hill was the white, male, heterosexual fantasy in which she would be a likely object for male desire. Legal language, because of the unconscious cultural assumptions embedded in it, proves insufficient to "tell a free story." In her account, language establishes the framework for vision, which in turn, produces fundamental injustice because linguistic structures limit what legal discourse sees and thus remedies through the appropriate legal doctrines.

For Morrison and CRT, the Thomas–Hill hearings underlined the metaphorical nature of language. Because language works through metaphor, language disrupts and detours any attempt at "pure" legal reasoning. The tropes that Hill could employ would prove ineffective in combating the words of Thomas and his supporters because her words relied too much on cultural narratives not shared by most whites or conservative African Americans, both male and female. Hill is incomprehensible under the dominant tropes that ground communication and enable the transfer of meaning, particularly within legal discourse. Her behavior seems irrational and ambivalent because her actions, especially her hesitancy to come forward, did not match dominant white, male standards for responding to an assault. As a result, she is "doomed" to the realm of insanity, magic, and fantasy. If the dominant culture views the experiences of an individual or group through the lenses of insanity, magic, and fantasy (because that person or group has no authorized language upon which to rely), then the harm endured will not be given equal protection of the law but will be disregarded as the stuff of fantasy or myth.

The O. J. Simpson Case

Five years after the publication of *Race-ing Justice, En-gender-ing Power,* Morrison authorized another collection of essays in her name. *Birth of a Nation'hood: Gaze, Script, and Spectacle in the O. J. Simpson Case* (1997) examined the cultural politics that surrounded the O. J. Simpson trial. Like the Thomas-Hill hearings, media attention transformed the Simpson case into a public spectacle in which American society explored questions about the role of race in culture and law. The state of California charged Simpson, a famous black ex–football star, with the murder of his white ex-wife and a male acquaintance after an infamous chase through Los Angeles in which local police officers followed Simpson at a slow speed. During this chase Simpson threatened that he would commit suicide. As with the Thomas confirmation hearings, gender and sexuality shaped the cultural politics of the case. Simpson had a relatively long history of physically abusing his ex-wife. This racially charged murder, which featured a black man who had allegedly engaged in a pattern of domestic violence against his white former spouse, allowed many historical stereotypes to be played out once again on the nation's television screen. As the case progressed, defense attorneys found evidence that the chief detective in the case had used racially derogatory terms to describe African Americans. Last but not least, the judge who presided over the case, Lance Ito, was Japanese American, suggesting that at least a certain amount of progress in race relations had been made between the 1960s and the 1990s.

In "The Official Story: Dead Man Golfing," Morrison explores how the case shed light on the ongoing national story about race. For Morrison, a "national narrative is born in and from chaos. Its purpose is to restore or imitate order and to minimize confusion about what is at stake and who will pay the price of dissension" (xv–xvi). Her essay does not simply follow the transfer of racial tropes within various accounts of the spectacle of the Simpson case, as she does with the Thomas–Hill hearings. Rather, she examines how racial tropes shape the narratives that can be told and circulated to create a supposedly national consensus. Locating and explicitly stating this national narrative is necessary work for Morrison, because the implicit national story about race is that conscious racism has been eradicated from public life and that therefore, the civil rights movement's goals have been realized. To critical race theorists and critics such as Baldwin and Morrison, the public's ongoing appetite for racial spectacles and the central role that legal discourse still plays in African American life suggests that more activism is needed to obtain true equality and freedom.

To explore how the national narrative influences a particular spectacle, Morrison tried to create a believable narrative of Simpson's guilt from the admissible evidence put forward during the trial without relying on the racial identification of the killer. She predicted that fiction readers would not accept such a story because "without the support of black irrationality . . . the fictional case not only could not be made, it was silly" (xii–xiii). In doing so, Morrison reveals the unconscious narratives about African

Americans and their behavior that still structure the dominant thinking even after the civil rights movement. She continues: "It was clear from the beginning that the real possibility of Mr. Simpson's innocence was a story that had no legs and would not walk, let alone sell" (xvii). These unconscious assumptions and narratives about race inclined or predisposed the American public to view Simpson as guilty regardless of the evidence that the district attorney's office presented.

Why is it that most whites, relying on legal discourse, "knew" that Simpson had to be guilty? The court of public opinion apparently relied on certain racialized narratives that the jury did not when it acquitted him. The Simpson case and the public reaction to it demonstrated the racialized narratives upon which legal discourse rests. As in the Wayne Williams case, few disagreed with the principle that murder should be prohibited. Rather, the divergent views produced by the case established that the "rational" and "neutral" application of principles, supposedly universally accepted, rely on unspoken racialized narratives. It was questions of evidence, especially how drops of blood were found on Simpson's clothes and car and whether some designer black gloves would fit, that proved crucial in the outcome of the case. Unlike Wayne Williams jury, this jury acquitted Simpson because his fame and the perception that a racist police officer may have planted evidence left "reasonable doubts" in the minds of jurors. Despite his legal acquittal, Simpson has been found guilty by media outlets and most (white) Americans.

In both essays, Morrison turns to Herman Melville's "Benito Cereno" to explain how racial tropes shape the national narrative and why Americans tended to view Thomas as innocent and Simpson as guilty. For Morrison, the story outlines the two roles available for African Americans in the national imagination: "naturally docile, made for servitude" or "savage cannibal" ("Friday" xv). According to Morrison, in Thomas and Simpson, America "had two black persons to nourish these fictions" ("Friday" xv). In reviewing the scene of Melville's tale, Morrison writes: "The American captain spends the day on board the *San Dominick*, happily observing, inquiring, chatting and arranging relief for the distressed ship's population. Any mild uneasiness he feels is quickly obliterated by his supreme confidence in his assessment of the order of things" ("Official" ix). Morrison's analysis of the story stresses that the captain misunderstands because he cannot comprehend the possibility of African revolt on a slave ship. "The long deferment of this realization is understandable partly because of his trusting nature but mostly because of his certainty that blacks were incapable of so planned, so intricate an undertaking" ("Official" x).

Captain Delano represents whites' views about Thomas and Simpson because most (white) Americans brought a "supreme confidence in [their] assessment of the order of things." Deferring the question of his guilt or innocence, Morrison uses the moment produced by the O. J. Simpson case to interrogate the national story about law and order and police corruption. For the guilt or innocence of Simpson requires an implicit assumption about how police authority is applied ("Official" xxi). The question—is he (i.e., Simpson) guilty?—was transformed, in the national imagination, to—are they (i.e., black people) guilty? ("Official" xxiv). As in her analysis of the Thomas hearings, Morrison has transcended Baldwin's emphasis on vision. Her argument takes a step back and attempts to connect how society and legal discourse see with the ubiquitous (but powerful) racial narratives because the truisms they contain "tyrannize" our perceptions, thus merely confirming our expectations.

Morrison explains that she began her essay with "Benito Cereno" "because the racist point of view of the narrator is hidden, the watcher is forced to discover racism as the paramount theme, the axis upon which all the action turns" ("Official" xxvii). By connecting the Simpson trial with interpretations and applications of Melville's short story (and the fugitive-slave cases) Morrison elevates the Simpson case, a public spectacle seemingly devoid of what traditionally passes for legal import, to the cultural, social, and *legal* importance of the fugitive-slave cases. In other words, a case with seemingly more public importance than precedential weight is a signal that racism and racialization continue to haunt law and legal discourse. Legal discourse still cannot adequately resolve the dilemma posed by racist and sexist national narratives that deny the rights of citizenship to African Americans. These "new" narratives, however, are more insidious because they enable a hierarchy of difference without speaking the language of difference. In the case of Thomas, his confirmation of white desire to believe that the civil rights movement had achieved its objectives appears to constitute a moment of genuine cross-racial understanding, but Morrison argues that this indicates the continued vitality of historical stereotypes. Similarly, the public insistence of Simpson's guilt, despite his acquittal, suggests that integration and the social transformations it produced have fostered a decline of values and contributed to an increase in criminal activity.

Morrison's criticism of the Thomas confirmation hearings and the Simpson trial attempts to make clear how unspoken racial narratives influence the way legal doctrines are applied, especially in the public imagination. In contrast to the strategy of civil-rights-era critics, Morrison attacks the limitations of the legal *process*. For Morrison, the language of the law and the cultural narratives that influence the law constitute a faulty structure of legal perception and vision, not a logical error that undermines the rationality of legal doctrine. This legal crisis, in which an ideology of whiteness structures and legitimates legal discourse, limits the litigation strategies developed by the civil rights movements. Morrison writes about what the civil rights movement failed to achieve through its intervention in legal discourse: an attack on a racialized national imaginary. Perhaps this explains why most of her novels take place before or during the civil rights era and include crimes but generally omit courtroom scenes, lawyers, and judges. It is not the substance of the law that necessarily furthers racial hierarchy, but the unconscious infection of race that limits what we see and what narratives we believe. For the ideal of equality to be realized, legal discourse must not only go beyond re-examining legal doctrine, but must also examine racialization's effect on the national legal imagination and how that shapes legal processes.

Conclusion

Contemporary efforts at cultural and legal reform have long speculated whether law and legal discourse can be effectively used for social change. Since the early 1980s, critical race theorists have explored whether legal discourse is the most efficacious discursive sphere for producing social, cultural, political, and economic change. These efforts constitute a critique of the NAACP's legal strategy that sought to use the law as the primary or leading tool for fostering racial equality during the civil rights era. While critical race theorists have offered a variety of answers to this question, nonlawyers have also developed a critique of law. Paralleling developments in CRT, Baldwin and Morrison have analyzed the relationship/impasse between legal discourse and black subjectivity in their nonfiction writings about highly publicized legal conflicts. In *The Evidence of Things Not Seen*, Baldwin examines how the veil of whiteness impedes the *vision* of legal actors and institutions as they proceed in developing a case against Wayne Williams, the so-called mass murderer of Atlanta. By contrast, Morrison explores the Clarence Thomas confirmation hearings and the O. J. Simpson case to demonstrate how racial tropes, national narratives, and the linguistic traces of racialization infect supposedly neutral and objective legal *language*.

In this essay, I have examined whether Baldwin's and Morrison's respective emphases on *vision* and *language* constituted complementary or contrasting criticisms of legal discourse. I ultimately conclude that their respective approaches exemplify the shift from faith to distrust regarding law within African American culture between 1970 and the late 1990s. Baldwin's analysis reflects a faith (not absolute, but faith nonetheless) that with proper vision legal discourse could arrive at properly equitable and just results. Morrison, by contrast, displays a more critical, less optimistic reading of legal discourse, one that is premised on the idea that equality and justice may be unrealizable ideals because language cannot accommodate enough subjectivities simultaneously.

In my reading of their nonfiction, Baldwin's restrained optimism about the possibility of legal visibility gets transformed into Morrison's pessimism (or perhaps realism) about the necessarily conflicted language of legal discourse. Comparative analyses of Baldwin's and Morrison's work are needed for both literary study and beyond. We need them to build a bridge between the civil rights and post–civil rights/hip hop generations. A number of writers on the hip hop generation—Bakari Kitwana, Todd Boyd, and Mark Anthony Neale in particular—have tried to show that the current generation's pessimism about law and social activism as articulated in hip hop and its materialism constitutes a break from the past. While neither Baldwin nor Morrison may have displayed other evidence of articulating a hip-hop-influenced critique, both share an ironic reading of contemporary race relations. While there is no evidence to infer their position about hip hop music and culture, it is clear that both Baldwin and Morrison share hip hop's instinct to question legal authority as it (over)regulates African American life.

By linking Baldwin and Morrison to hip hop culture, this chapter argues that we must extend Suggs's thesis from *Whispered Consolations*. Contemporary African American narratives continue to write over dominant American discourse, but in a new way. If previous generations relied on producing images of black respectability, texts of searing social realism, and arguments against the irrationality of legalized racism, CRT (as articulated by Baldwin and Morrison) and hip hop culture deploy irony (and, in the case of hip hop, parody) to deconstruct stereotypes of African American life in literary and legal discourse. As hip hop breaks down musical tradition and reconfigures it to follow an African-derived aesthetic, Baldwin's and Morrison's legal criticism attempts to rewrite legal discourse to allow African Americans to articulate legal claims and have legal decision makers view the evidence supporting those claims with color-conscious, not necessarily colorblind, eyes.

NOTES

1. This is, of course, a broad generalization rather than a description of all African American writing, past and present. Even if imperfect, the substance/process distinction is useful because it helps connect African American literature to specific moments of legal history.

2. The "Critical Race Theory" (or CRT) workshop began in 1989 as the idea of Kimberlé Crenshaw. Crenshaw convened the meeting to discuss how lawyers could continue the work of dismantling racial hierarchy in the context of a legal academy that had adopted an overly philosophical Critical Legal Studies, which had little to offer activists for racial justice (Crenshaw 2002, 1354–1365). The meeting brought together several scholars, including

Kendall Thomas, Neil Gotanda, Mari Matsuda, Richard Delgado, and Stephanie Phillips. The scholars shared two common interests. First, they shared an understanding that white supremacy inhered in dominant and formally equal institutions as endemic features rather than as deviations. They argued that lofty legal ideals, while in theory neutral and fair, have relied on unstated and unconscious racial assumptions. Thus, they expressed a certain amount of shared skepticism of legal principles such as the rule of law, objectivity, and equal protection as necessarily neutral legal principles. Second, they shared a commitment to altering the extant racial hierarchy in the United States (Crenshaw et al. 1995, xi). While not all attendees shared a common perspective on how to accomplish this change, all desired to use law to transform American culture. Critical race theory has gone on to transform how scholars explore the meaning of race in America. Just about every law school in the nation now has at least one or two faculty members whose work falls within the CRT paradigm. Lawyers and legal issues are increasingly finding their way into American Studies conferences and journals. Despite all of this cross-fertilization between law, literature, and cultural studies, James Baldwin's influence on CRT tends to be ignored.

3. Morrison's first novel, *The Bluest Eye* (1970), focused on how visual culture affects racial identity and shapes the national conversation about race.

4. To be fair to Baldwin, he clearly understood and made some reference to narrative in *Evidence* and his analysis of the Wayne Williams prosecution. In his earlier writing, he also pays considerable attention to the power of narrative. However, he does choose to emphasize visual metaphors within his critique so much so that Morrison's essays do, in fact, "re-focus" Baldwin's gaze.

WORKS CITED

Baldwin, James. *The Evidence of Things Not Seen*. New York: Henry Holt, 1985.

Boyd, Todd. *The New H.N.I.C.: The Death of Civil Rights and the Reign of Hip Hop*. New York: New York University Press, 2002.

Crenshaw, Kimberlé. "Critical Race Studies: The First Decade: Critical Reflections, or A Foot in the Closing Door." *U.C.L.A. Law Review* 49 (2002): 1343–1372.

Crenshaw, Kimberlé, Neil Gotanda, Gary Peller, and Kendall Thomas, eds. "Introduction." In *Critical Race Theory: The Key Writings That Formed the Movement*. New York: New Press, 1996. xii–xxxii.

Ellison, Ralph. *Invisible Man*. New York: Vintage, 1952.

Everett, Percival. *Erasure*. Hanover: University Press of New England, 2001.

Kitwana, Bakari. *The Hip Hop Generation: Young Blacks and the Crisis in African-American Culture*. New York: Perseus, 2002.

Mills, Charles. "White Being Black Being: Metaphysics of Race." In *Kerry James Marshall - One True Thing: Meditations on Black Aesthetics*. Chicago: Museum of Contemporary Art, 2004. 5–9.

Morrison, Toni. "Friday on the Potomac." In *Race-Ing Justice, En-Gendering Power: Essays on Anita Hill, Clarence Thomas, and the Construction of the Social Reality.* Ed. Toni Morrison. New York: Pantheon, 1992.

————. "The Official Story: Dead Man Golfing." In *Birth of a Nation'hood: Gaze, Script, and Spectacle in the O.J. Simpson Case.* Ed., Toni Morrison and Claudia Brodsky Lacour. New York: Pantheon, 1997.

————. "Unspeakable Things Unspoken: The Afro-American Presence in American Literature," *Michigan Quarterly Review* 28 (Winter 1989): 9–34.

Neale, Mark Anthony. *Soul Babies: Black Popular Culture and the Post-Soul Aesthetic.* New York: Routledge, 2002

Peller, Gary. "Criminal Law, Race and the Ideology of Bias: Transcending the Critical Tools of the Sixties." *Tulane Law Review* 67 (June 1993): 2231–2252.

Spann, Girardeau. *Race against the Court: The Supreme Court and Minorities in Contemporary America.* New York: New York University Press, 1993.

Suggs, Jon-Christian. *Whispered Consolations.* Ann Arbor: University of Michigan Press, 2000.

THE ART OF WHITENESS IN THE NONFICTION
OF JAMES BALDWIN AND TONI MORRISON

JONATHAN MIRIN

In the last chapter of E. Frances White's *Dark Continent of our Bodies: Black Feminism and the Politics of Respectability* (2001), White begins to compare James Baldwin's and Toni Morrison's points of view about the construction of white identity. She writes:

> For Baldwin, whiteness was about a false claim on innocence that depended on the demonization of blackness. My sense is that Morrison has been greatly influenced by her reading of Baldwin and has taken on a similar project. Both Baldwin and Morrison expose the fragility of whiteness and, in the process, disrupt any notion of pure whiteness, distinct from and in opposition to blackness. Morrison demonstrates that works from this country's master canon that seem to be about whiteness use blackness to construct white identity. (180)

White succinctly summarizes Baldwin and Morrison's relationship to each other in regard to their thinking about whiteness. Nevertheless, a range of questions are left open for the intrepid, racially minded thinker. How does Morrison's "project" complement or diverge from Baldwin's? How effective are their strategies in regard to exposing racial ideology, and to what extent are they implicated in the system they are trying to expose? As White notes, despite sharing the view that the unconscious is fundamental to "explain[ing] the roots of white racism . . . [as] White fear and guilt are projected onto black people," Baldwin's and Morrison's personal and cultural frameworks are distinct enough to create major differences in their approaches (181). Baldwin's perceptions of whiteness are rooted in a Christian/biblical worldview that weaves themes of innocence and redemption into his contemporary social analysis. His views of white people are inevitably linked to the amount of forgiveness he can grant them. Although he would not frame his quest in these terms, *Notes of a*

Native Son (1955) depicts his struggle to become Christlike enough to keep his own hatred from destroying him, in addition to relating his separation from the church. Over the course of his lengthy nonfiction career, this sense of the possibility of personal salvation is broadened to include everyone—all human beings are capable of elevating their consciousness out of the action/reaction cycle characteristic of conflict in general and ethnic strife in particular. Morrison's nonfiction, on the other hand, does not attempt Baldwin's style of personal vulnerability. In *Playing in the Dark: Whiteness and the Literary Imagination* (1992), Morrison writes both in response to and, to a lesser degree, for the literary establishment. In keeping with the more outward focus of what E. Frances White refers to as a "tradition whose roots are in slave narratives and whose mission has been to establish the humanity of black people," one senses that Morrison's essay-writing impulse is an effort to affect how the reader approaches whiteness in literature, the literary establishment itself, and the reader's perception of that establishment, rather than a tool for self-exploration (White 153). Baldwin's and Morrison's intertwined but separate trajectories, while providing the motivation and intellectual scope for their arguments, simultaneously provide the limitations for their thinking about whiteness.

The essays collected in *Notes of a Native Son* range from pop-culture analysis to autobiography to literary criticism, but all have some bearing on the ways white people construct their identity. In "Stranger in the Village," Baldwin's account of his stay in an all-white village in Switzerland, he is able to describe the European American character more vividly by comparing it with that of the European:

> If [Europe's colonies] posed any problem at all for the European conscience, it was a problem which remained comfortingly abstract: in effect, the black man, *as a man,* did not exist for Europe. But in America, even as a slave, he was an inescapable part of the general social fabric and no American could escape having an attitude toward him. Americans attempt until today to make an abstraction of the Negro, but the very nature of these abstractions reveals the tremendous effects the presence of the Negro has had on the American character. (170–171)

Perhaps Baldwin's clearest examples of these "abstractions" are the representations of blacks by whites in the arts, Uncle Tom, white actors in blackface, or the film *Carmen Jones* (a remake of *Carmen* with an all-black cast that Baldwin dissects in "*Carmen Jones:* The Dark is Light Enough"). However, his assessment includes the average person's internal manipulation of her or his own intellect and imagination to rationalize, interpret, or justify white America's history of its treatment of African Americans. For Baldwin, whites must choose the "abstract" as opposed to the "real" because the reality of the history of race relations is too horrific to be fully acknowledged without reassessing what being American means. He is at the beginning of his inquisition into this white state of "innocence" and the degree of its deliberate construction.

One can imagine Baldwin in the 1950s having a difficult time choosing which white-authored abstraction to analyze for the manner in which racial ideology supports the process of divorcing black characters from actual black lives. *Notes* settles on *Uncle Tom's Cabin* (1852) ("Everybody's Protest Novel") and *Carmen Jones*. Turning these lenses aimed at black America back on themselves, he performs the kind of critical act Morrison would call for some forty years later. He skewers both book and film by juxtaposing their makers' purported understandings of the black experience with the level of ignorance, willful or not, the works reveal. Harriet Beecher Stowe and 20th Century Fox assume that the inclusion of blacks in their products is evidence of a liberal aim. Baldwin sees them instead as indications of a "disturbance . . . which can [not] be eased by the doing of good works, but seems to have turned inward and shows every sign of becoming personal" (54). However, this situation was not yet a cause for lament without hope for him. In 1955, he was still able to see this book and film as smoke signals of a struggle toward conscience.

Yet *Carmen Jones* offends his sense of truth, among other things, deeply enough to prompt biting sarcasm. He writes: "It is important that the movie always be able to repudiate any suggestion that Negroes are amoral—which it can only do, considering the role of the Negro in the national psyche, by repudiating any suggestion that Negroes are not white" (*Notes*, 46). The "role of the negro" Baldwin describes is to be a repository for various unpleasant aspects of white America. The makers of *Carmen Jones*, in order not to disturb the smooth functioning of this scapegoat mechanism, "whitewash" the black actors' performances to the point where no elements of the black experience Baldwin might mistake as truthful remain. It appears that the intention behind the production was, at least at the conscious level, to depict blacks in a pleasant rather than unpleasant way. Ironically, this immerses the artists involved as deeply in racial ideology as if they had made a film the Klan would enjoy. By reacting so strongly to the unpleasant stereotype, they have created another fictitious code that whites can digest as code rather than as an attempt to portray reality.

Both Baldwin and Morrison are concerned with the possibility of representing the black experience in a manner that moves away from this reactive blindness toward their understandings of black experience. Indeed, this is a likely reason why they would spend the majority of their time writing novels. The accretion of the artful detail in the service of telling a human story is perhaps our most tantalizing way of imagining that we are out of ideology's grip. For Baldwin and Morrison, moving out of ideology into the realm of "truth" seems to be a longed-for possibility. Otherwise, why write? The creative impulse has a variety of motivations, however. Baldwin suggests that *Uncle Tom's Cabin* and *Carmen Jones* are evidence that the white man's inability to come to terms with slavery and its aftermath engendered a certain degree of creativity. European American writers, having strengthened their imaginations by practicing their craft, are instructive examples of this process. In *Playing in the Dark,* Morrison coins the term "Africanism" to describe the "ways in which a nonwhite, Africanlike (or Africanist) presence or persona was constructed in the United States, and the imaginative uses this fabricated presence served" (6). The descriptions of blackness she investigates offer more insight into the white describers than the black described. Quantum physics has been sure for some time that we cannot measure atoms without affecting the outcome. Nevertheless, the critical terrain Morrison stakes out seems relatively unexplored more than a decade after *Playing's* publication.

While her essay lacks Baldwin's autobiographical grit, she does manage some self-narrative in the first chapter. She describes her assumption of the African American's relative unimportance for white writers when she began reading American literature. However, when she began reading "as a writer," that assessment began to shift (3). Morrison states, "I began to see how the literature I revered, the literature I loathed, behaved in its encounter with racial ideology. American literature could not help being shaped by that encounter" (16). She goes on to describe the nature of this meeting between white writers and the black population of the United States: "What became transparent were the self-evident ways that Americans choose to talk about themselves through and within a sometimes allegorical, sometimes metaphorical, but always choked representation of an Africanist presence" (17). For Morrison, European American writers are neither able to avoid nor fully articulate the issue of race. It emerges, whether they are aware of it or not. Like Baldwin, Morrison grants these individuals a degree of blindness based on their immersion in a racist culture. The construction of the individual mind by the prevailing racial ideology is a given from which she begins her analysis. However "correct" this mode of understanding may be from the prevailing academic point of view, one senses that the underlying goal of the essay is to take the literary establishment to task for the erasure, conscious or not, of authentic black identities.

Nevertheless, Morrison seems less eager to forgive a writer like Hemingway, whose personal attitudes toward race appear less disguised. Her most telling example of the construction of white American male identity occurs in an analysis of *To Have and Have Not* (1937). She examines the construction of the lone, rugged, and free persona of Harry Morgan, whose qualities are amplified by the conveniently placed Wesley, a black man working as the first mate on Morgan's fishing boat. Morrison's argument about the importance of Wesley's lack of subjectivity for Harry's character is propelled by imagining the outcome if Hemingway had given Wesley agency:

> What would have been the cost, I wonder, of humanizing, genderizing this character at the opening of the novel? . . . Harry would lack the juxtaposition and association with a vague presence suggesting sexual excitement, a possible threat to his virility and competence, violence under wraps. He would finally, lack the complementarity of a figure that can be assumed to be in some way bound, fixed, unfree, and serviceable. (73)

Morrison suggests that the cipher of Wesley is a platform upon which Harry Morgan is built. The unthinking reader's respect and admiration for Harry is increased by what Baldwin might call the "abstraction" of the black first mate's personality.

However rich narratives like Hemingway's are for Morrison's analysis of Africanism, sometimes the real world spins stories, as the cliché goes, that would be hard to make up. The Clarence Thomas confirmation hearings inspired her to edit and write an introduction to a volume of essays titled *Race-ing Justice, En-gendering Power* (1992). It is not surprising that she would have an interest in this highly reactive story-telling spectacle, given the possibility of unearthing various truths beneath the public relations acrobatics. The analysis of racial ideology in mass media thus becomes another critical terrain that Baldwin mapped and Morrison takes up. However, during the lag time between their writings, the increased pervasiveness of television in American life allowed social reality itself to acquire a more performative quality. Her argument is that the truth of the two combatant's claims, let alone their distinct personalities, had no chance of emerging from beneath the avalanche of racial abstraction summoned up by the confirmation process:

> Without individuation, without nonracial perception, black people, as a group, are used to signify the polar opposites of love and repulsion. On the one hand, they signify benevolence, harmless and servile guardianship, and endless love. On the other hand, they have come to represent insanity, illicit sexuality, and chaos. In the confirmation hearings the two fictions were at war and on display . . . Thus the candidate was cloaked in the garments of loyalty, guardianship, and . . . limitless love . . . . The interrogator . . . was dressed in the oppositional costume of madness, anarchic sexuality, and explosive verbal violence. There seemed to be no other explanation for her testimony. (xv)

Morrison claims that for a citizenry beset with the host of moral, psychological and workplace issues surrounding race, the opportunity for a public exorcism of these suddenly and vividly "black" qualities was too tantalizing to resist. Her theatrical description suggests the burgeoning "news-as-entertainment" quality of the media's coverage. Essentially, the hearings afforded white America an opportunity to play out both of its most cherished black stereotypes, whereas *Carmen Jones* developed only the "benevolence, harmless and servile guardianship, and endless love" fiction embodied by Thomas. A large part of Morrison's and (for different reasons) white America's fascination with the hearings was that they featured these fictions simultaneously and in conflict. It would be difficult for a white screenwriter to conjure so compelling a scenario. Morrison persuades us that the news media and various Senate committee members, who were apparently in pursuit of the truth—or at least eager to appear so—were in fact hankering for the "reconfirmation" of comforting racial abstractions.

She deepens her analysis by comparing Thomas's ascent to power with Friday's indoctrination into his master's ways in Defoe's *Robinson Crusoe* (1719). Her strategy is to imagine the master/slave relationship from Friday's point of view, stating that

> Friday's real problem, however, was not to learn the language of repetition easily, like the parrot, but to learn to internalize it. For longer than necessary the first words he is taught, first "master," then "yes" or "no," remain all he is permitted to say. During the time in which he knows no other English, one has to assume he thinks in his own language . . . but Crusoe's account suggests . . . that before his rescue Friday had no language, and even if he did, there was nothing to say in it. (xxiv)

Morrison's contention is that Thomas, in order to receive the president's and then the Senate committee's blessing, had to exude a similar vacuum-like sensibility. He had to present himself as impervious to the weight of America's racial history in such a way that his only responses were forgiveness, acceptance, and an emphasis on the future. Like Friday, his speech had to conform strictly to the language of the powers he served if he hoped to pass their test.

Ironically, this portrayal of Thomas—not far from the innocence Baldwin sees whites as eager to confer on themselves—stands in opposition to Anita Hill's "anarchic sexuality and explosive verbal violence." By applying Sambo-like stereotypes such as the appeal of Thomas's laugh ("second in his list of 'the most fundamental points' about Clarence Thomas"), Senator Danforth opened the white gates to include a black man (xii). In other words, because Thomas possesses the ability to laugh loudly at "himself" he is no longer a threatening force against which whiteness can be defined. Rather, he can "come in from the field" because he has proven himself friendly, malice-free and innocent enough to join the innocent. His person has been reduced to a set of signifiers familiar enough for whites to think they know him when they are actually perceiving a walking, talking image of the collective white imagination. Morrison feels that Thomas participated in the blurring of his independent identity:

> [He] once quoted someone who said that dwelling on the horrors of racism invited one of two choices: vengeance or prosperity. He argued for a third choice: "to appeal to that which is good" . . . the footprint in the sand that so worried Crusoe's nights . . . disappears from his nightmares once Friday embraces, then internalizes, his master's voice and can follow the master's agenda with passion. (xxix)

Her argument is that Thomas's third option is designed to "appeal" to whites rather than to "that which is good."

It is one task to demonstrate, as Baldwin and Morrison do, that white identity is constructed through contrast with an artfully rendered blackness or "Africanism." It is another to identify the psychological mechanisms that underlie this process. In his book-length essay *The Devil Finds Work* (1976), Baldwin writes that "the root of the white man's hatred [of the black man] is terror, a bottomless and nameless terror, which focuses on the black, surfacing, and concentrating on this dread figure, an entity which lives only in his mind" (61). For Baldwin, the black person's literal and figurative distance in the white imagination is critical because white "terror" pre-exists and is dependent on the absence of an encounter with an actual human being. Fear and hatred require an object and it simplifies things if these emotions can be focused on a mysterious black "figure." Baldwin is prone to this type of group psychoanalysis, which may have been accepted more easily in 1976 than today. Now one can imagine any nervy undergraduate's first question being: "Which white person do you mean, Mr. Baldwin?" However, this is not simply a case of sloppy thinking on Baldwin's part. If he were to provoke cries of indignation from his white readers, that would be fine by him. In fact, provoking crises of conscience seems to be the number two job on his list—second only to working out a livable peace between himself and post-Vietnam America. Unlike Morrison, he does not feel obligated to develop an academically acceptable argument. If asked to prove his blanket statements, he might reply "wake up and look around." The description of "white man's hatred" seems most easily applied to whites who are overtly racist. However, by not specifying this subgroup, he provokes liberal whites—at least those reading closely—to consider the possibility of unconscious hatred and terror lingering beneath their good intentions.

Luckily, Baldwin's prodigious output allows for multiple takes on white identity. In *No Name in the Street* (1972), he has ample opportunity to depict the construction of white liberalism while narrating his experiences as a reporter and participant in the civil rights movement. Here Baldwin's own versions of whiteness acquire a complexity generally absent from his and Morrison's descriptions of identity construction by whites themselves. His most vivid description of the liberal-minded comes while discussing the "relatively wealthy and certainly very worldly" activist-citizens of the Hollywood hills (134). The general definition of a liberal from Baldwin's point of view at this moment in history seems to be a white person who is supportive of Martin Luther King and the movement, vocally or financially. He writes of mixed feelings about their fundraising activities: "In my own experience, genuine, disinterested compassion or conviction are very rare; yet, it is as well to remember that, rare as they are, they are real, they exist" (134). This "real" compassion is not another way to define the white self versus the black other. Instead, Baldwin raises the prospect of an impulse that is genuinely altruistic or "self-less."

A similar provocation toward inner work manifesting as social change occurs at the end of *The Fire Next Time* (1963). He claims that

> if we—and now I mean the relatively conscious whites and the relatively conscious blacks, who must, like lovers, insist on, or create, the consciousness of the others—do not falter in our duty now, we may be able, handful that we are, to end the racial nightmare, and achieve our country, and change the history of the world. If we do not now dare everything, the fulfillment of that prophecy, recreated from the Bible in song by a slave, is upon us: "God gave Noah the Rainbow sign, No more water, the fire next time!" (379)

Much has been made of the carry-over from Baldwin's teenage years as a young preacher in Harlem to the cadences of his prose. Here we see these rhythms employed to their full effect—exhortation of the flock. The reference to the Bible makes explicit the essentially Christian worldview that is a large part of the author's intellectual and emotional infrastructure. The "relatively conscious whites" are now cast in potential solidarity with their "relatively conscious" black brethren. Interestingly, the simile "like lovers" could refer to the relationship between blacks and whites or to conscious and unconscious citizenry. Again, he is less concerned with academic clarity than with the poetry of salvation.

Baldwin's infrequent descriptions of white people who fit into this "conscious" category point to his sense of their rarity. His sentence concerning "disinterested compassion" in *No Name* is the only moment in the essay where such a possibility is imagined. He describes the more typical liberal as someone

nagged by a sense that something is terribly wrong, and that they must
do what they can to put it right . . . . They do not, in any case, know what
to do . . . and so they give their money and their allegiance to whoever
appears to be doing what they feel should be done. Their fatal temptation, to
which, mostly, they appear to succumb, is to assume that they are, then, off
the hook. . . . [T]hey do not know how ruthless and powerful is the evil that
lives in the world. (134–135)

The general liberal response appears to lie somewhere between willful
innocence and guilt-driven ineffectuality. However accurate the above
description, there is the nagging suspicion that Baldwin has become entan-
gled in his own biblical framework of good and evil. He writes that whites
"do not know how ruthless and powerful is the evil in this world" while a
large part of his thinking around whiteness concerns the white construction of their own "not knowing" at the expense of a black population
burdened with all of the more-known, "evil" human qualities. Perhaps he
is giving his Hollywood friends a break, figuring they can't be blamed for
not sounding the depths of evil given the amount of sun in pre-smog Los
Angeles—but the degree of conscious effort required to maintain a state of
innocence remains unanswered.

White liberals come under particularly intense scrutiny when Baldwin
assesses their eroticization of blackness. It is not surprising that European
Americans would be eager to jettison their more promiscuous impulses,
given the amount and variety of guilts they have generated in response to
their Judeo-Christian spiritual tradition. Baldwin imagines the fate of
Malcolm X if Malcolm had actually been a "reverse racist" as he was portrayed in the media, stating that "he would have sounded familiar and even
comforting, his familiar rage confirming the reality of white power and sen-
suously inflaming a bizarre species of guilty eroticism without which, I am
beginning to believe, most white Americans of the more or less liberal per-
suasion cannot draw a single breath" (*No Name*, 97). Baldwin's claim is that
white liberals glean an erotic charge from their generic fantasy of black rage.
This conception of the black response to slavery reinforces the black/white
binary Baldwin is busy pulling apart. The refulfillment of the duality, despite
outward protestations, is eroticized by the white liberals who need it in order
to maintain and reinforce their identity as both white *and* liberal. Baldwin
suggests that the danger posed by Malcolm X, from any opposing political
perspective, was his ability to sidestep the desire for blind vengeance—much
to the chagrin of everyone who required this formulation of black reactivity
to know who they were. Consequently, it became necessary for the threatened parties to dumb-down his challenges to the status quo.

Morrison also explores this theme, but she does so through the literary
lens of the European American writer. Again, Hemingway's *To Have and*

Have Not provides her most vivid example, this time in the form of a metaphor that functions literally and figuratively: the hair lightening (whitening) of Marie, Harry Morgan's wife. Morrison writes that it is a "painful and difficult process that turns out to be well worth the pain in its sexual, protective, differentiating payout . . . . This enhanced sexuality comes on the heels of a sexual intrusion by a black man" (*Playing*, 78–79). The couple's desire is heightened by reinforcing the "black-white polarity" with the aid of chemicals. Morrison concludes that "here we see Africanism used as a fundamental fictional technique by which to establish character. . . . Harry and Marie . . . solicit our admiration by the comparison that is struck between their claims to fully embodied humanity and a discredited Africanism. The voice of the text is complicit in these formulations: Africanism becomes not only a means of displaying authority but, in fact, constitutes its source" (80). Her argument is that Hemingway's Cuban/African "milieu" is not an accident; indeed, Harry and Marie could not exist in all their "potency" anywhere else. They become who they are by virtue of the power they take away. Although Morrison toes the academic line in referring to Hemingway's words as the "voice of the text," she is clear about the way this story charges white sexuality at the expense of more "abstract," darker-skinned characters.

Morrison is not the only writer to take up where Baldwin leaves off. Perhaps the most widespread white fantasy of black sexuality is the myth of black male sexual prowess. Matthew P. Brown explores some of the more sinister ramifications of this cultural current in his essay "Basketball, Rodney King, Simi Valley" (1997). He describes the scene in the film *Grand Canyon* in which Kevin Kline's character sits in the stands at a Lakers game and the camera follows his guilt-ridden gaze from the black basketball players to the women in the stands. Brown writes: "In the social construction of desire, black masculinity is a zone of mythical sexuality that is the choice of women and the envy of the inadequate straight white male. This myth of potent sexuality—which in other contexts can threaten, panic, and justify terrible violence—is coded here as another erotic option, another form of beauty open to the privileged white male viewer" (108). In the same way that Baldwin describes white hatred thriving with an imagined rather than actual referent, Kline's distance from his objects of desire (in this case, the literal and psychological separateness of the spectator) creates room for fantasy. However, the subtext of desire is of secondary importance to the distance itself. Brown asserts that in other, weightier contexts than a Kevin Kline movie, distance allows for whatever type of projection is necessary to justify the viewer's desired conclusion. This metaphor becomes part of his analysis of the Rodney King verdict. He concludes that even though the videotape was definitive in its depiction of a vicious beating, jury members were able to justify exonerating the police by projecting onto King the intention of fighting back, running away, or whatever facets of racial ideology were required. The extent to which Baldwin laid the foundation for such analyses becomes more evident when we look at his comments concerning the white imaginative response to black sexuality in *No Name:*

> [And] it is absolutely certain that white men, who invented the nigger's big black prick, are still at the mercy of this nightmare, and are still, for the most part, doomed, in one way or another, to attempt to make this prick their own: so much for the progress which the Christian world has made from that jungle in which it is their clear intention to keep black men treed forever. (63)

If Baldwin had been alive to watch the Rodney King trial, he would likely have seen the proceedings as an example of the white jury's "mak[ing] King's] prick their own" by finding in favor of his assailants. This particular version of the phenomenon involved the denial of the legal power King had to enforce justice in addition to setting a tonal (if not legal) precedent for any other black man unwise enough to defend his right not to be beaten.

It could be argued that racism was largely a subconscious force working in the police officer's favor. However, the Baldwin who published *The Devil Finds Work* in 1976 would be less inclined toward forgiveness on these grounds than the one who wrote *Notes of a Native Son* in the first half of the 1950s. The interval featured twenty-plus eventful, difficult years during which Baldwin added to his role as writer those of activist and public witness to black suffering. These experiences were behind the emergence of a less conciliatory, more strident tone in his nonfiction. The Vietnam War was now officially over, but that event and its related atrocities in Southeast Asia seem to have been on his mind when he wrote that "the civilized have created the wretched, quite coldly and deliberately, and do not intend to change the *status quo;* are responsible for their slaughter and enslavement; rain down bombs on defenseless children whenever and wherever they decide that their "vital interests" are menaced, and think nothing of torturing a man to death" (*The Devil*, 16). The rage that Baldwin felt would kill him and that had prompted his original flight from America to Europe clearly had not disappeared. He had previously articulated an eloquent equation between whiteness and "the civilized" in "Stranger in the Village":

> The idea of white supremacy rests simply on the fact that white men are the creators of civilization . . . and are therefore civilizations' guardians and defenders. Thus it was impossible for Americans to accept the black man as one of themselves, for to do so was to jeopardize their status as white men.

> But not so to accept him was to deny his human reality . . . and the strain of denying the overwhelmingly undeniable forced Americans into rationalizations so fantastic that they approached the pathological. (*Notes*, 172)

Only by taking Baldwin's noun "creators" seriously in light of the authoring of seminal American documents such as the Constitution is it possible to imagine how the American populace was steeled for the simultaneous freedoms of individual liberty and slave-ownership. It is said that the best art comes from need, and in this case there was an economic and psychological imperative to create a social blueprint accommodating these contradictory "rights." Two hundred years later, Baldwin's ironic use of the term "civilized" had been sharpened by the United States' secret and less-secret attempts at bombing various darker-skinned cultures into extinction since the mid-1960s. Thus, "the wretched" suggests Vietnamese and Cambodians, and in 2005 it would also include the innocent people of Afghanistan, Iraq, and a growing list of other countries that have perished as a result of their proximity to the "vital interests" of the "civilized."

Yet Baldwin probably still felt that the only group suffering more than African Americans or the Vietnamese from this prolonged white identity construction project were whites themselves. This element of spiritual understanding, namely, the concept of the persecutors doing greater harm to themselves than to the persecuted, is notably more pronounced in his nonfiction than in Morrison's. In *No Name* he chooses to relate this paradox by describing it from another African American's perspective. Reverend Shuttlesworth visits Baldwin in his motel room in Birmingham and is continually checking the window to make sure no one plants a bomb in his car. Baldwin makes a comment on the Reverend's safety and

> a shade of sorrow crossed his face, deep, impatient, dark; then it was gone. It was the most impersonal anguish I had ever seen on a man's face. It was as though he were wrestling with the mighty fact that the danger in which he stood was as nothing compared to the spiritual horror which drove those who were trying to destroy him. They endangered him, but they doomed themselves. (67)

While the possibility of forgiveness is not stated here, it is implied. Baldwin sets himself up as the spiritually adept learning from an older, wiser teacher. He does not lay claim to Shuttlesworth's deep faith but rather infers it based on the careful observation of his face—creating a model for the comprehension of evil that allows at least for the possibility of the dissolution of the victim's rage. What revenge can be taken on the doomed?

The granting of forgiveness is not something Morrison works into her job description as an essayist. Nevertheless, an element of the empathy described above is present in her work. Morrison writes that her "project rises from delight, not disappointment" (*Playing*, 4). As a writer herself, she is able to engage in active sympathy with the ways writers "tell other stories, fight secret wars, limn out all sorts of debates blanketed in their text. . . . And . . . writers always know, at some level, that they do this" (*Playing*, 4). The phrase "at some level" suggests Morrison's willingness to grant the likes of Faulkner, Cather, Hemingway, and Melville the same kind of unconsciousness that Baldwin confers on white people as a whole. Indeed, a term like "forgiveness," which fits nicely with an author whose first debt is to the Christian tradition, feels awkward for Morrison. She is describing a situation in which the ways white writers offer a "choked representation of an Africanist presence" are substantially predetermined by culture. These authors are creating while immersed in a racialized society and consequently cannot be fully cognizant of all the ways their work reflects this fact. If there is sin without intention, then what does one forgive?

This assessment of the white canonical novelist's responsibility is distinct from that of the white canonical critic's responsibility. For Morrison, the critic is not as easily—if at all—given the benefit of the predetermined doubt. This is due in large part to the relatively greater consciousness she ascribes to their writing (or lack of it) on race. She states: "There seems to be a more or less tacit agreement among literary scholars that because American literature has been the preserve of white male views, genius and power, those views, genius and power are removed from the overwhelming presence of black people in the United States" (*Playing*, 5). Morrison still seems content to imply the volition to keep the canon in a racial vacuum rather than portray deliberate malice. Nevertheless, her disdain for the critical establishment on these matters is palpable when compared with the relative impunity she is willing to grant even Hemingway.

The types of measured empathy Baldwin's and Morrison's nonfiction suggest result in part from the historical breadth of their investigations. They are aware of the ways that individual human beings are shaped by the flow of cultural forces over time without negating the role of individual will. Morrison depicts the American writer's historical-cultural situation in regard to race by focusing on the conditions of creation from the creator's point of view: "Living in a nation of people who decided that their world view would combine agendas for individual freedom and mechanisms for devastating racial oppression presents a singular landscape for a writer" (*Playing*, xiii). She repackages the Founding Fathers' schizophrenia as an authorial opportunity. It is appropriate, given her text-driven agenda, that she trace the roots of European American identity back to the Constitution, stating that

> the ways in which artists—and the society that bred them—transferred internal conflicts to a "blank darkness," to conveniently bound and violently silenced black bodies, is a major theme of American literature. The rights of man, for example, an organizing principle upon which the nation was founded, was inevitably yoked to Africanism. Its history, its origin, is permanently allied with another seductive concept: the hierarchy of race. (*Playing*, 38)

The idea of racial hierarchy came to America on boats from Europe, but the early American writers Morrison examines could not have the same relation to blackness as their European counterparts because American-style slavery never existed on the Continent. If the concept had not already been accepted, the Constitution's authors would have had to reword the "Rights of Man" to specifically exclude the burgeoning black population. However, because this hierarchy was an intellectual underpinning of the culture, the Founding Fathers' declaration that "all men are created equal" could remain unqualified.

The fiction writers that Morrison examines follow their political predecessors' example by only allowing blackness to be seen through their principal (white) characters, undermining any possibility of black representations she or Baldwin might mistake as fully human. These white authors unknowingly set the stage for Baldwin and Morrison to pursue that neglected narrative task as their life work—work made more urgent, because "relatively [un]conscious" whites had set the mold for European American literature and scholarship, augmenting the ongoing spiritual debilitation of a populace collectively required to deny black humanity. Nevertheless, with most of them attempting the same illogical leap, European Americans were somehow able to take comfort in the lie's largesse. If the lie was not so directly personal for Morrison and Baldwin, it would not take as much magnanimity on their parts to realize the liar needs help.

Whether this "help" is wanted or can be received is another question. Baldwin's skeptical side, on display in an essay called "The Black Boy Looks at the White Boy" written for *Esquire* in 1961, thinks not:

> I had tried, in the States, to convey something of what it felt like to be a Negro and no one had been able to listen: they wanted their romance. And, anyway, the really ghastly thing about trying to convey to a white man the reality of the Negro experience has nothing whatever to do with the fact of color, but has to do with this man's relationship to his own life. He will face in your life only what he is willing to face in his . . . and I chickened out. (292)

Although couched in generalities until the last phrase, this statement emerges out of Baldwin's description of wanting to be honest with his new friend Norman Mailer in Paris, who, presumably, must be counted among the "relatively conscious" whites referred to at the end of *The Fire Next Time*. Baldwin's struggle is not abstract but immediate, as in: "Can I be vulnerable to this particular white man?" But the answer is contingent upon the degree of trust he places in Mailer and that trust depends on Baldwin's evaluation of what Mailer "is willing to face [in his own life]"—not his skin color. Baldwin transforms whiteness from an overarching racial question to a human one about the specific individuals involved and their particular bravery—or lack thereof.

The essay continues to chart their evolving friendship, but in the end the entire proposition of this particular white/black connection is again put into doubt when Baldwin asserts that "one can never really see into the heart, the mind, the soul of another" (303). If this is the case, then how could he make an accurate judgment about what Mailer was ready to hear? Of course, the piece itself is his way of communicating much of what he has not spoken aloud. His final sentence leaves the question of their continued friendship unresolved but returns to the kind of profound provocation toward work and conscience on the reader's—in this case Mailer's—part that characterizes so much of Baldwin's nonfiction:

> So that my concern with Norman, finally, has to do with how deeply he has understood these last sad and stormy events [of the civil rights movement]. If he has understood them, then he is richer and we are richer, too; if he has not understood them, we are all much poorer. For, though it clearly needs to be brought into focus, he has a real vision of ourselves as we are, and . . . where there is no vision, the people perish. (303)

In the end, it will not matter if Norman Mailer is white. The question is whether or not he has the ability to look at the white and black people of his country and present them with a truthful vision of themselves. The enduring value of this "love letter" as Baldwin calls it, is that any American artist—white or black—can read it and be provoked to search more deeply into the truth of their country's experience.

"The Black Boy Looks at the White Boy" concerns itself with the construction of an individual white man's identity. However, Baldwin's and Morrison's primary aim in regard to whiteness has been to unravel the ways white America has shaped itself in opposition to blackness. Early in *Playing*, Morrison writes that "Emerson's call for that new [white American] man in 'The American Scholar' indicates the deliberateness of the construction, the conscious necessity for establishing difference" (39). Baldwin and Morrison map distinct but analogous chains of ill effects resulting from the same historical cause: the birth of America's art of whiteness. Inevitably, the question arises: now what? Since *Playing's* publication 13 years ago, the questions about race in America have continued to evolve. Most visibly, intermarriage is creating a society that looks increasingly similar, at least in larger cities. However, even as we start looking more and more the same, Baldwin and Morrison would concur that if fear and hatred exist, so does the desire to establish difference in a way that allows them to be expressed. Will these emotions continue to play out between "shades" of people? Or perhaps as blackness becomes less distinct from whiteness, the importance of finding an enemy outside our borders will rise—however important it already appears. Baldwin encouraged his readers to use difference as a tool for looking deeper—toward similarity and the possibility of communal work toward shared goals of equality and harmony. Morrison focuses, at least in *Playing*, on the academy as one realm where further critical investigation of the white-dominated canon must occur before Baldwin's vision can be realized. Appropriately, her provocations are directed primarily toward an academic audience. However, anyone interested in the ways art and race intersect must look to Baldwin for a richer understanding of Morrison. Freud demurred, "Everywhere I go, I find a poet was there before me." In this case, a novelist, playwright, and essayist was there before her.

WORKS CITED

Baldwin, James. "The Black Boy Looks at the White Boy." 1961. In *The Price of the Ticket*. Ed. James Baldwin. New York: St. Martin's/Marek, 1985. 289–303.

———. *The Devil Finds Work: An Essay*. New York: Dial Press, 1976.

———. *The Fire Next Time*. 1963. *The Price of the Ticket*. New York: St. Martin's/Marek, 1985. 333–379.

———. *No Name in the Street*. New York: Dial Press, 1972.

———. *Notes of a Native Son*. Boston: Beacon Press, 1955.

Brown, Matthew. "Basketball, Rodney King, Simi Valley." In *Whiteness: A Critical Reader*. Ed. Mike Hill. New York: New York University Press, 1997.

Morrison, Toni. "Introduction: Friday on the Potomac." In *Race-ing Justice, Engendering Power*. Ed. Toni Morrison. New York: Pantheon Books, 1992. vii–xxx.

———. *Playing in the Dark: Whiteness and the Literary Imagination*. New York: Random House, 1992.

White, Francis E. *Dark Continent of our Bodies: Black Feminism and the Politics of Respectability*. Philadelphia: Temple University Press, 2001.

THE EVIDENCE OF THINGS NOT SEEN: THE ALCHEMY OF RACE AND SEXUALITY

E. FRANCES WHITE

What intellectual feats had to be performed by the author or his critic to erase me from a society seething with my presence, and what effect has that performance had on the work?

—Morrison, "Unspeakable Things Unspoken:
The Afro-American Presence in American Literature," 12

Toni Morrison asks of literary discourse, "What are the strategies of escape from knowledge? Of willful oblivion?" ("Unspeakable Things Unspoken" 11). She seeks to determine in what ways African American presence gets erased from discussions of American literature. The erasure takes place on several levels: African American literature is either ignored or undervalued; European American writers either fail to write black people into stories or, when they do, use their presence to define whiteness; and when blacks are present in Euro-American literature, literary critics fail to recognize that presence.

In the first part of this chapter, I take the tools that Morrison has developed for understanding race in literary discourse and use them to explore homosexuality in past and present discourses. Although I have no reason to believe that Morrison intended this use of her tools, I find them helpful in the exploration of certain complex questions that she has chosen not to pursue. In my view, this particular "escape from knowledge" has limited Morrison's own understanding of the ways that difference between European America and African America is constituted as well as of the multiple ways in which African Americans have created a rich culture of their own.

Originally published in a slightly different form as "The evidence of things not seen: the alchemy of race and sexuality" in *Dark Continent of Our Bodies: Black Feminism and the Politics of Respectability* (Philadelphia: Temple University Press, 2001), 151–183. Reprinted by permission of the author and the publisher.

James Baldwin was among the first writers to refuse this escape from knowledge about the connection between homosexuality and race. In the second part of this chapter, I look at the price that Baldwin had to pay for daring to break the silence on black homosexuality. Along the way, I also examine the limitations of Baldwin's insights. This investigation in no way indicates that I see Baldwin as having failed in some way; rather, it shows that the boundaries he set up were understandable attempts at self-protection.

When I first read Baldwin, I had no understanding of how difficult it must have been during his early career to imagine black male homosexuality. As I argue here, the enforced silence into which he wrote has roots as deep as slave times. Even Morrison, who imagines forced sexual acts on a chain gang in *Beloved* (1987), has the men of Sweet Home plantation turn to animals rather than to each other for sexual relief. Now, why could they not have comforted each other? If we cannot imagine black men giving black men comfort, we narrow our options for fighting racism.

Morrison's Views

I begin my exploration into race and heterosexuality by focusing on Morrison, the dean of black women writers, because of both the influence she has had on my thinking and the self-consciousness that she brings to her historical novels and literary criticism. As I suggest in *Dark Continent of Our Bodies: Black Feminism and the Politics of Respectability* (2001), the relationship between black women writers and black women historians is crucial for the development of black women's subjectivity. The two help each other to imagine the past. *Beloved* and *Jazz* (1992), two of Morrison's historical novels, bring a richness to the past that we historians could never achieve alone. Morrison herself is quite conscious of the role she plays in helping us gain access to that past. She has identified herself within a tradition whose roots are in slave narratives and whose mission has been to establish the humanity of black people. About the principal motivations that led to the writing of slave narratives, Morrison says:

> Whatever the style and circumstances of these [slave] narratives, they were written to say principally two things. One: "This is my historical life—my singular, special example that is personal, but that also represents the race." Two: "I write this text to persuade other people—you, the reader, who is probably not black—that we are human beings worthy of God's grace and the immediate abandonment of slavery." ("Marginalization and Contemporary Cultures" 299)

Morrison reminds us that even as these writers of slave narratives attempted to represent the race, they dropped a protective veil over their interior lives. "In shaping the experience to make it palatable to those who were in a position to alleviate it, they were silent about many things, and they 'forgot' many other things. There was a careful selection of the instances that they would record and a careful rendering of those that they chose to describe" (301). Although Morrison places herself in the tradition of these slave writers, she recognizes that the passage of time has created different conditions for the late-twentieth-century black (woman) writer. More than a century and a quarter after emancipation, we now have the freedom to peek behind the veil that literate African Americans drew over their lives. But to gain access to that veiled interior life of the enslaved, Morrison suggests, we have to make use of memories, recollections, and, most important, imagination. Thus Morrison engages in what she calls "literary archeology":

> On the basis of some information and a little bit of guesswork you journey to a site to see what remains were left behind and to reconstruct the world that these remains imply. What makes it fiction is the *nature* of the imaginative act: my reliance on the image—on the remains—in addition to recollection, to yield up a kind of truth. (302; my italics)

As Morrison implies, both the literary critic and the historian engage in acts of imagination. We nonfiction writers, too, must dig up the remains of the past and apply our imaginations. Otherwise, the oppressive limitations on representation in the past will continue to dominate.

Morrison is acutely aware of the narrative strategies that protected African Americans from scrutiny and yet managed to assert their presence. She has written movingly about the attempts to erase this presence from our literary traditions and history. Her review of Western canon formation carries with it an anger that reminds us of the power struggle behind the academic canon debates. In "Unspeakable Things Unspoken" (1989), Morrison exposes the hollowness of traditionalists' attempts to "maintain standards"—that is, to keep African American writers out of the canon. She shows very clearly the way that the ever-contested value "quality" "is itself the subject of much rage and is seldom universally agreed upon by everyone at all times" (2).

Morrison, however, does not simply want African American writers to be included in the master canon; she also wants a rereading of that canon to recognize the presence of Africanisms. By "Africanisms" she means "the denotative and connotative blackness that African peoples have come to signify, as well as the entire range of views, assumptions, readings and misreadings that accompany Eurocentric learning about these people" (*Playing in the Dark* 5–7).

Africanisms are figures of speech that help Americans imagine the negative, the abnormal, evil, or, by contrast, their opposites—the positive, the normal, and the good. They are useful tropes because they communicate so much without explicitly signaling the author's meaning and without diffusing the power of that meaning in the process. Thomas McLaughlin has provided a useful explanation of the way such tropes or figures of speech work:

> Figures [of speech] convince, though, not by a strictly logical presentation but by an appeal to the irrational, the part of the mind that delights in their multiple meanings and deep reassurances. Figures reassure our belief in dominant systems of thought in that they rely on accepted categories and analogies. In this sense figures appeal to our desire to possess an untroubled, self-evident truth. (88)

Similarly, Africanisms appeal to, for example, often unconscious fears about African Americans deeply embedded in this society. Alternatively, they can be used to conjure up desire, freedom, individualism, and much more (Morrison, *Playing*). They can play such wide-ranging roles because of African Americans' centrality in the formation of American identity. From the beginning, we have symbolized the opposite of whiteness. To recognize the boundaries of freedom, for example, European Americans used the changing meaning of black slavery. As Morrison suggests,

> Through the simple expedient of demonizing and reifying the range of color on a palette, American Africanism makes it possible to say and not say, to inscribe and erase, to escape and engage, to act out and act on, to historicize and render timeless. It provides a way of contemplating chaos and civilization, desire and fear, and a mechanism for testing the problems and blessings of freedom. (*Playing* 7)

In *Playing in the Dark* (1992), Morrison exposes Africanisms in Euro-American literature and the collective white unconscious at the same time that she highlights the willful failure of literary critics to acknowledge their presence. Critics, she points out, have developed a discourse around the master canon that denies the centrality of race in this literature. Traditional literary criticism has constructed American literature as if it were universal and race neutral by failing to bring critical scrutiny to the obvious existence of the Africanism trope.

In the next two sections of this chapter, I explore two historical periods that have been the subjects of Morrison's novels: (1) the slave era, during which many of the issues that remain central to American culture—such as the relationship between freedom and gender—first emerged, and (2) the 1920s, during which urban life began to dominate black culture. In examining the treatment of these two periods in her novels, I extend Morrison's notions of erasure and the power of Africanisms to the topic of homosexuality.

Morrison's Blues

We can agree, I think, that invisible things are not necessarily "not-there"; that a void may be empty, but not a vacuum.

—Morrison, "Unspeakable things Unspoken:
The Afro-American Presence in American Literature," 11

Morrison's work has helped those interested in race turn their attention away from an exclusive and isolated focus on blackness toward the simultaneous construction of whiteness and the interaction between the two. Morrison acknowledges the importance of reading African American writers, but (as I have suggested) she also wants us to reread the "master" works in the canon with a new sensitivity. Additionally, she acknowledges the way that feminist literary criticism has transformed our readings of works in the master canon to include a focus on the construction of the "Whiteman."

I suspect that it is not incidental that Morrison seems unaware of a similar project that has been carried on in gay studies by such literary critics as Eve Sedgwick. In *Between Men* (1985), Sedgwick helps us understand the importance of studying sexuality by reminding us that sexuality is an "especially charged leverage-point, or point for the exchange of meanings *between* gender and class (and in many societies, race), the sets of categories by which we ordinarily try to describe the divisions of human labor" (11). Sexuality helps to establish difference among races and between genders.

Clearly, many black writers, critics, and historians have recognized the way that American literature has used sexuality to establish difference between African Americans and European Americans. Morrison herself makes a point of this. In *Beloved*, for example, the owners of the Sweet Home plantation use the control of black women's sexuality to subjugate their enslaved black men. The violent assault against Sethe carries as much meaning as it does because her sexuality is violated:

> "After I left you, those boys came in there and took my milk. That's what they came in there for. Held me down and took it. . . . Them boys found out I told on em. Schoolteacher made one open up my back, and when it closed it made a tree. It grows there still."
> "They used cowhide on you?"
> "And they took my milk."
> "They beat you and you was pregnant?"
> "And they took my milk!" (16–17)[1]

Sethe is much more concerned about the sexual violation she has experi-enced than about the horror of having her back lashed beyond recognition. Sexuality here functions as a trope for lack of freedom; through their sexual domination, whites exercise ultimate control over what the most basic freedom would render private and personal. Indeed, this violation is as important to Sethe's husband, Halle, as it is to her. Hiding out in the hayloft, Halle watches as the young white men suck his wife's breasts. Paul D, another ex-slave from the Sweet Home plantation, informs Sethe of Halle's response:

> The day I came in here you said they stole your milk. I never knew what it was that messed [Halle] up. That was it, I guess. All I knew was that some-thing broke him. Not a one of them years of Saturdays, Sundays, and night-time extra never touched him. But whatever he saw go on in that barn that day broke him like a twig. (69)

Morrison does not limit her use of the trope of sexuality to heterosexual relations. In a significant scene that is so subtly written that some readers may miss its import, the trope of homosexuality defines difference between the races. Morrison describes in detail the daily rituals of a chain gang in which Paul D finds himself. Each morning, the men chain them-selves together and then kneel, awaiting "the whim of a guard, or two, or three":

> Chain-up completed, they knelt down. The dew, more likely than not, was mist by then. Heavy sometimes and if the dogs were quiet and just breath-ing you could hear doves. Kneeling in the mist they waited for the whim of a guard, or two, or three. Or maybe all of them wanted it. Wanted it from one prisoner in particular or none—or all.
>   "Breakfast? Want some breakfast, nigger?"
>   "Yes, sir."
>   "Hungry, nigger?"
>   "Yes, sir."
>   "Here you go."
> Occasionally a kneeling man chose gunshot in his head as the price, maybe, of taking a bit of foreskin with him to Jesus. Paul D did not know that then. (108–109)

Here Morrison uses homosexuality as a literary trope, just as many white writers have used Africanisms. The ritual of homosexual oral sex between master and slave clearly marks the black male captive as enslaved and subjugated. To paraphrase her account of the use of Africanisms, homo-sexuality here has a simplistic, though menacing purpose to establish hier-archic difference (*Playing* 63).

This is certainly a rare example of a black writer imagining a slave past that includes homosexual rape as a possibility. Indeed, without citing evidence, bell hooks expresses what seems to be the belief of many: "The sexism of colonial white male patriarchs spared black male slaves the humiliation of homosexual rape and other forms of sexual assault. While institutionalized sexism was a social system that protected black male sexuality, it (socially) legitimized sexual exploitation of black females" (24). The implications of homosexual rape and its relationship to heterosexual rape are significant. Why have African American intellectuals not explored this issue?

With Morrison-like curiosity, we should ask why historians have presented the African American past as if the only sexual concerns that black men had during slavery were castration and whether they could protect (and, for some, control) black women's bodies.[2]

I must admit that I, too, feel ambivalent about lifting the veil from the possibility of homosexual rape. After all, homosexuality has already had such bad press—why add to that by pointing to instances in which it would be seen as sordid and despicable? Admittedly, acknowledging the existence of heterosexual rape during slavery does not make most people think that the entire institution and various practices of heterosexuality need to be condemned, so perhaps people would not jump to such conclusions about homosexuality either. But, of course, homosexuality and heterosexuality are not parallel and equal constructions: the latter depends on the former for its claim to normalcy.

In *Beloved*, Morrison partially lifts the veil from what must have been a terrifying experience—black men's loss of control over their *own* sexuality. As I have suggested, even to acknowledge the existence of homosexuality—especially of homosexual rape—speaks into a context heavily laden with heterosexist assumptions. (Morrison's heterosexist assumption is that *watching* Sethe's violation could drive Halle crazy, whereas the actual violation of Paul D seems less traumatic.)

Are there clues—or remains—that we could use to unveil more completely a homosexual past? We know that homosexual behavior was not foreign to the slave South. Martin Duberman's published correspondence between two Southern white slave holders—Jeff Withers, who helped draw up the government for the Confederacy, and large-plantation owner James H. Hammond, well known in local and national politics—suggests that the two men were in a homosexual relationship during their youth.

Duberman uses the clues from this correspondence and from Hammond's life to speculate that "sexual contact between males (of a certain class, region, time, and place), if not commonplace, was not wholly proscribed either" (161). With irony, Duberman reminds us that "to date we have accumulated only a tiny collection of historical materials that record the existence of *heterosexual* behavior in the past. Yet no one claims that that minuscule amount of evidence is an accurate measure of the actual amount of heterosexual activity which took place" (161). Even Duberman, who has often written on African American history, is strangely silent about cross-race homosexual activity. Perhaps he did not want to taint homosexuality by acknowledging that homosexual relationships, like heterosexual ones, can take place between unequals.

In contrast, Robert K. Martin has turned to popular literature of the mid-nineteenth century to show the ways that white male writers used Africanisms to create an element of sexual danger in a text. In examining how men of color functioned in the homosocial worlds of these writers, Martin suggests that nineteenth-century fictional male couples who were the models for Mandrake and Lothar and the Lone Ranger and Tonto serve

> as a physical confirmation of what can only be suggested in the text, as the realization of male sexuality in a union with the dark and forbidden. To be a male homosexual is thus to couple with the devil, to embrace the primitive, for it was these figures that the African represented metonymically in the popular culture of the mid-nineteenth century. (177)

In Theodore Winthrop's popular novel *Cecil Dreeme,* the main character, Byng, thinks to himself about his slave, Densdeth, "I saw on the steamer that you were worth buying, worth perverting" (quoted in Martin 177). Martin points out that Byng has managed to turn things around, to make it seem as if Densdeth has control over him. Martin argues:

> For Byng finds himself here feminized, that is, read as the woman to be purchased and corrupted; but the presence of the concept of "perverting" makes it clear that this feminization is precisely what is feared in homosexual panic: the loss of male autonomy and power. To accept the embrace of Densdeth is to succumb to Densdeth"s other self, the dark African, to accept, symbolically at least, anal penetration (entry into the darkness within) and thus to make oneself over as female, a commodity to be exchanged. (177–178)

Martin brings together an understanding of Africanisms, homophobia, and sexism in a complex way. He takes these structures of dominance as literary tropes that depend on fears that were deeply embedded in the psyches of many nineteenth-century white men. Byng's relationship with Densdeth represents the possibility of homosexual desire between master and slave. In this perverse projection, the actual power relationship has been inverted; the master imagines himself as a woman dominated by his black slave. From the evidence of narratives like this, it would seem that black men certainly entered the homoerotic imagination of at least some white men. With such clues, it is not hard to imagine that some masters did in fact rape their enslaved black men.

Of course, I am not implying that homosexual rape was as widespread as heterosexual rape. I certainly do not want to be misread as suggesting that slave plantations and farms were gay dens of iniquity. What is important is the *potential* for homosexual rape rather than its actual prevalence. We need to ask why we persist in seeing the sexual emasculation of black men as stemming from their actual castration or their inability to protect black women from rape rather than also from their inability to protect *themselves* from rape.

And what of homosexual desire *between* black men? Is it unreasonable to ask that Morrison, Duberman, and other intellectuals imagine *that?* Male slave narratives are understandably silent on questions of sexuality. As Morrison explains, they were often silent about or "forgot" things that their intended audience would find intolerable to confront. Moreover, the struggle to transform oneself from a slave into a literary subject—to narrate one's story—was ultimately a bid for the power to assert one's humanity. For black men, the struggle to write and publish was symbolic of the act of establishing manhood. As Henry Louis Gates Jr. succinctly puts it, "The purported connection between the act of writing and the 'rights of man' did not escape the notice of the slave" (xxvii). With the stakes so obviously high, we need not be surprised, then, that slave narratives reveal nothing about homosexual behavior. Since homosexual activity was seen as sinful, male slaves had reason to draw a veil over their lives.

Given that Morrison has set herself the task of drawing back the veil from that life, I wish she had gone a step further. It strikes me as a failure of imagination that, in describing the relationships among the Sweet Home plantation men, she sees no possibility that they might sexually comfort each other. We know enough about bisexuality among African American men today to see that heterosexual desire does not preclude homosexual desire.

Morrison's narrative serves to undermine the old sexist belief that black men who watched their women get raped suffered more than these women did. To my mind, she could have taken this effort further if she had been able to imagine more powerfully the sexual humiliation suffered by the men in her novel. Given the unequal power relationship between the Sweet Home masters and their enslaved men, she would have been able to explore more deeply the relationship between power and desire. Finally, if she had imagined African American men comforting each other, she might have helped us think our history differently.

Representing the Renaissance

In moving from *Beloved* to *Jazz,* Morrison follows the great African American migration from the former slave South to the urban North during the early twentieth century. Set during what many have called the Harlem Renaissance, *Jazz* places sexuality and gender at the center of the struggles African Americans faced to build new communities in the North. In a book that points to both the fragility and the necessity of community, characters flee antiblack pogroms in the South and dodge antiblack riots in the North, all the while searching for fulfilling relationships with one another. There is a freedom in *Jazz* that we do not see in *Beloved*—a freedom that includes the opportunity to look for love and sex without the direct interference of the masters. At one point in the novel, Morrison describes a party: "It's good they don't need much space to dance in because there isn't any. The room is packed. Men groan their satisfaction; women hum anticipation. The music bends, falls to its knees to embrace them all, encourage them all to live a little, why don't you? since this is the it you've been looking for" (188). Jazz is a music of improvisation—which is precisely the skill African Americans used to adapt in the urban North. Through the jazz idiom, Morrison helps us imagine the emerging desires of the new urban working class. She has her unnamed narrator tell us of the hopes that led African Americans to Harlem:

A city like this one makes me dream tall and feel in on things. Hep. . . . When I look over strips of green grass lining the river, at church steeples and into the cream-and-copper halls of apartment buildings, I'm strong. Alone, yes, but top-notch and indestructible—like the City in 1926 when all the wars are over and there will never be another one. The people down there in the shadow are happy about that. At last, at last, everything's ahead. The smart ones say so and people listening to them and reading what they write down agree: Here comes the new. Look out. There goes the sad stuff. The bad stuff. The things-nobody-could-help stuff. . . . History is over, you all, and everything's ahead at last. (7)

In *Jazz,* Morrison provides a wealth of vivid images of the past; but, again, her heterosexist bias limits her imagination. To paraphrase her words in another context ("Unspeakable" 12), I wonder what intellectual feats she had to perform to erase the homosexual presence from the Harlem of the 1920s. It seems to me infinitely more difficult to escape from the knowledge of homosexuality when imagining the 1920s than when imagining the 1820s.

What clues has Morrison willfully overlooked? By the 1920s, gay communities were becoming increasingly visible in large cities.[3] As I argue later, evidence suggests that African Americans participated in the sprouting of these communities and that Harlem blacks played a particularly prominent role in their development. Judging from the number of notable people who engaged in homosexual activity, I speculate that the great migration that brought so many African Americans north coughed up a number of "sexual deviants."

Work on blues singers of that era is instructive here. A number of recent writings (including work by Faderman and McCorkle) have drawn attention to the homosexual behavior of many famous blues singers, such as Alberta Hunter, Bessie Smith, and Ethel Waters. Hazel Carby sees such artists as folk heroes who helped African Americans make the transition from the rural South to the urban North. Carby notes that they spoke easily of sexual matters. Indeed, a number of their lyrics, such as Ma Rainey's "Prove It on Me Blues" and Lucy Bogan's "B. D. Women Blues," represented lesbian behavior and beliefs.

It would be a mistake to conclude, as many have, that the openness of some blues singers about homosexuality suggests that black communities were necessarily tolerant of homosexual behavior. After all, many conservative Christians saw blues singers as agents of the devil, and efforts to divert attention from open discussions of sexuality—heterosexual or homosexual—were surely not limited to the middle class. Nonetheless, the lyrics and the behavior of some blues singers clearly indicated the presence of homosexuality during the 1920s. Although blues singers did not represent the views of all African Americans, they were able to express some of the desires and discontent of an important minority of women precisely because, as "sexual perverts," these singers stood in an uneasy relationship to the community. This outsider status allowed them to comment openly on their society.

Indeed, so many of the prominent blues singers engaged in homosexuality that perhaps we should hypothesize on the connection between "deviant" sexuality and cultural production. When we turn to the writers, artists, and other intellectuals of the 1920s, we find that a similarly large number engaged in homosexual activity. In *Color, Sex, and Poetry* (1987), Gloria T. Hull identifies the cross-racial male homosocial network that dominated the Harlem Renaissance. Indeed, the fact that Alain Locke was a misogynist homosexual was key to the functioning of the Renaissance; he preferred men as writers and as lovers, and his contacts with the white homosexual literary world were invaluable. Similarly, in the diaries and letters of women writers such as Alice Dunbar-Nelson and Georgia Douglas Johnson, Hull finds evidence of a female homosocial network that included women connected by homosexual desire.

Eric Garber also finds evidence of strong homosexual networks in the Harlem artistic scene. He details the importance of those networks for the white voyeurs who traveled to Harlem for sex and danger. Ironically, Garber, like earlier whites who associated blacks with sexual freedom, both fetishizes and objectifies the black homosexuals he describes.[4] Nonetheless, he helps us see the important role both of African American culture in the formation of homosexual communities and of homosexuality in the formation of black communities. In Morrison's language, the Africanisms of blackness represented sexual freedom. Not surprisingly, then, whites felt freer to explore homosexuality in the communities where they could be sexually expressive with relatively few consequences. Black homosexuals became important models of how white homosexuals should act.

Thus, although it is true that conservative elements in the African American community of the 1920s condemned most open expressions of sexuality, it is also true that homosexual and bisexual desires were clearly fighting for space and representation. Significantly, that space emerged among artists, both bourgeois and popular.

Morrison has chosen to ignore this struggle. *Jazz* sensitively explores the challenges African Americans faced in forming heterosexual bonds in the urban North of the 1920s. But these were not the only bonds available to them. By failing to explore the possibility of homosexual bonds, Morrison leaves unveiled both the complexities of the black community's internal relationships and the relationships between blacks and whites. With our view thus obstructed, we can neither explore the problematic relationship between the emerging black and white gay and lesbian communities nor fully understand the ways that race influenced these relationships. Moreover, we cannot appreciate the full range of ways in which African Americans adapted to urban life. As they struggled to escape the legacy of slavery and the realities of Southern segregation, they asserted control over their sexual lives. And for some, this control included the exercise of homosexual desire.

Clearly, Morrison has made an impressive contribution to American letters. Her criticism and fiction speak to long-standing debates about the nature of American society that have traditionally been dominated by white male authors. And she has managed to add a black feminist voice to these debates. In the process, among her many other achievements, she exposes racism in the collective white unconscious and shows the ways that sexuality can be used to construct hierarchical differences between genders and races.

Yet by failing to explore homosexuality more fully, Morrison has limited our understanding of the complex ways sexuality is used. The history of blackness and the history of sexuality are intertwined, and both heterosexuality and homosexuality can act as leverage points for expressing the unequal difference between whites and blacks. Given the close relationship between race and sexuality, it seems inevitable that the rise of homosexuality as an important category and of homophobia as a central preoccupation is also bound to the history of blackness. Her many other contributions notwithstanding, Morrison's heterosexist project leaves a heavy veil in place over this history.

Baldwin: Unspeakable Things Finally Spoken

It was James Baldwin, more than anyone else, who created a space for a kind of male homosexual presence that had previously been unimaginable. As I will argue, this space was not uncomplicated, but it was fertile. To understand Baldwin's work on homosexuality, let us first turn briefly to his related views on race.

Baldwin was the first writer I encountered who gave brutally honest, nonfictional testimony to the impact of racism on aspiring, young black intellectuals. Several of his essays in *Notes of a Native Son* (1955) address his concern with escaping from being merely a "Negro" or even merely a Negro writer. When he wrote this book, I think he was only beginning to understand the many ways that *he* had accepted the word "Negro" as a term of diminishment.

Baldwin's response to racism's tendency to limit the complexities of his thinking and the complexities of what could be thought about him was to attack the racial categories that oppressed him. In a famous article on Richard Wright, Baldwin argues that the concept of race, so central to understanding American culture, also blinds us to certain conditions; our racial categories conceal what he considered to be truth. Baldwin's insights are striking for their early breaks with race as an essential category. He often emphasized the barriers to insight created by racial categories. These categories allowed whites to project from their collective unconscious the fear and guilt they felt toward blacks.

I suspect that Baldwin's discomfort with being categorized as gay was partially fueled by this insight about race. Like a number of gay men of his generation, Baldwin struggled against such labels in an effort to persuade heterosexuals to focus on the similarities the two shared. For him, heterosexual men, like homosexuals, had to learn to accept their desires in all their instability and fluidity; the task for both was to escape what Baldwin called the prison of masculinity. Thus, he sought to disrupt the category "man" by demonstrating that the binary straight/homosexual binary is a false one.

This concern about the similar problems faced by all men emerges in Baldwin's novels. The copy on the book jacket of the 1962 Dial Press edition of *Giovanni's Room* (first published in 1956), Baldwin's most talked-about book in the gay literary canon, is revealing. It reads: "*Giovanni's*

Room is both a novel of extraordinary literary quality and a completely honest treatment—perhaps the most outspoken yet—of an extremely controversial theme: 'David's dilemma,' writes Mr. Baldwin, 'is the dilemma of many men of his generation; by which I do not so much mean sexual ambivalence as a crucial lack of sexual authority.' To Baldwin, this book is not, as one might think, about homosexuality; rather, it is about the quest of all men to come to terms with their own desires.

Baldwin's attempts to explain and stress the similarities between homosexuals and heterosexuals occupied him throughout his writing career. In *Just above My Head* (1979), he takes up this theme early in the book. Tony, the son of the narrator, Hall Montana, asks his father about the sexual orientation of his uncle, Arthur.

> [Tony:] "A lot of the kids in school—they talk about him."
> "They say—he was a faggot." . . .
> [Hall:] "I know—before Jimmy—Arthur slept with a lot of people—mostly men, but not always. He was young, Tony. Before your mother, I slept with a lot of women . . . mostly women, but—in the army—I was young, too—not always. You want to know the truth, your uncle, and I'll be proud of him until the day I die. . . . Whatever the fuck your uncle was, and he was a whole lot of things, he was nobody's faggot."
> "Tony—didn't me and your mother raise you right? Didn't I—tell you a long time ago, not to believe in labels?" (36–37)

That Arthur slept with men does not distinguish him from straight men. Indeed, Baldwin's ideal homosexual man was one who lived in a heterosexual world despite his sexual attraction to other men.[5] For Baldwin, homosexuals were not marked by any significant difference, partly because he felt that we are all bisexual or androgynous in the sense that we all contain both male and female elements. Toward the end of his life, in "Here Be Dragons" (1985), he returns to the topic of similarities among men. He concludes, "But we are all androgynous, not only because we are all born of a woman impregnated by the seed of a man but because each of us, helplessly and forever, contains the other—male in female, female in male, white in black and black in white" (690).

Baldwin wanted to explain to the world and to himself that his attraction to men did not make him abnormal and that it certainly should not exile him from the race. This concern may have intensified as Baldwin's desire to be viewed as a race person grew and as he became increasingly immersed in the black liberation struggles of the 1950s and 1960s. In *No Name in the Street* (1972), Baldwin talks about the effect of the civil rights movement on his thinking. He began to understand the necessity for acknowledging, and even, at times, moving and writing from, rage. Although he continued to call on love as the ultimate means to avoid a racial holocaust, he no longer expected black writers to distance themselves from their feelings about racism. As I read his work, he seemed to be writing increasingly for black audiences rather than for white liberals.

Baldwin acknowledged that many of his new insights and attitudes came from younger men in the movement. Unfortunately, his bonds with these young black men were challenged by homophobia. Nowhere was this challenge more clear than in the famous confrontation between Baldwin and Eldridge Cleaver. In his celebrated essay entitled "Notes on a Native Son" (1968), Cleaver acknowledges that he initially found Baldwin's writings on race insightful but later began to think that Baldwin hated black masculinity. Cleaver uses Baldwin's brave revelations about racism's impact on his psyche—revelations that were meant to exorcise him of this affliction—to make Baldwin pay for his honesty and vulnerability. For Cleaver, Baldwin's homosexual desires were signs of his racial pathology. He argues that Baldwin's racial self-hatred led to a racial death wish—a bizarre desire that, in Cleaver's mind, also motivates black nationalists. "The attempt to suppress or deny such [homosexual] drives," writes Cleaver, "leads many American Negroes to become ostentatious separationists, Black Muslims, and back-to-Africa advocates" (101).

For Cleaver, black homosexuality becomes the expression par excellence of a racial death wish:

> The case of James Baldwin aside for the moment, it seems that many Negro homosexuals, acquiescing in his racial death-wish, are outraged and frustrated because in their sickness they are unable to have a baby by a white man. The cross they have to bear is that, already bending over and touching their toes for the white man, the fruit of their miscegenation is not the little half-white offspring of their dreams but an increase in the unwinding of their nerves— though they redouble their efforts and intake of the white man's sperm. (102)

Cleaver here makes his point through a gendered analogy: homosexuals are failed men who must hate themselves.[6] Somehow, the betrayal of the black (male) homosexual is made to seem reminiscent of the mythical betrayal of black women who slept with white masters and then gave birth to mulatto children. For Cleaver, this kind of racial self-hatred led Baldwin to criticize Richard Wright because he "despised—not Wright, but his masculinity. He cannot confront the stud in others—except that he must either submit to it or destroy it. And he was not about to bow to a *black* man" (160). I suspect that Cleaver felt that faggots were men who

were penetrated—that is, they were like women—whereas men who penetrated men and/or women were real men. Moreover, as William J.
Spurlin speculates, Cleaver's anxieties about black gay men and his feminization of Baldwin "raise for speculation whether it was he or Baldwin
who was the more eager for the 'fanatical, fawning, sycophantic love [and
acceptance] of whites'" (114).

Baldwin's response to Cleaver was surprisingly restrained. In *No Name in
the Street* (1972), he suggests that Cleaver is like a zealous watchman who
fears that Baldwin has allowed the Establishment to use him. But in
essence, Baldwin maintains, they agree: what threatens black masculinity is
white power. Baldwin hypothesizes that Cleaver has him "confused in his
mind with the unutterable debasement of the male—with all those faggots,
punks, and sissies, the sight and sound of whom, in prison, must have made
him vomit more than once" (171–72).

Of course, like his fictional character Arthur in *Just Above My Head*,
Baldwin was no faggot. Clearly, he wanted to distance himself from the
"debased" homosexuals of the prisons. Although understandable, this strategy was double-edged. To protect himself from vicious attack, Baldwin
turned to a politics of respectability. *He* was a respectable man, even if
homosexual. Baldwin wanted to separate himself from those homosexuals
whose behavior proved them to be debased. This strategy, however, leaves
too many homosexuals exposed to homophobic disciplining. Moreover, it
does not sufficiently undermine the homosexual/heterosexual, binary
because the category "man" depends on too many exclusions—including
the exclusion of woman. These points have become increasingly clear in
more recent years from gay studies and gay politics, both of which have
been influenced by Baldwin's insights (see, for example, Harper).

Ironically, it was Baldwin's own narrow vision of masculinity that left him
exposed to attacks like Cleaver's. Baldwin could not defend himself as a man
against the assertion that he was like a woman. Although, as he suggested in
"Here Be Dragons," he believed that all males contain elements of the female,
he devalued womanhood. And he made the mistake of allowing Cleaver to
set the terms—terms that assumed that "woman" is an inherently diminished
position. Baldwin never recognized heterosexuality's investment in the rigid
and gendered boundaries for desire. By allowing the terms of masculinity to
remain intact and gender to remain fixed, he had no recourse in the face of
Cleaver's denigrating assaults. As long as gay men could be disparaged as failed
men—as essentially women—Baldwin would have no comeback.

It is sadly ironic that in desiring members of his own sex, Baldwin risked
losing the protection provided by the very men he so dearly loved. As he
suggests in *Just Above My Head*, loving black men can be a revolutionary
act in this racist society. Indeed, I have rarely read anyone else who writes

so lovingly about black men; Baldwin wrote from a devotion to his brothers born of living in their lives *and* holding them in his arms. Yet his love
placed him outside the norms of both the dominant society and the black
community. In *No Name in the Street,* as he speaks affectionately of black
militants such as Cleaver, Baldwin can barely conceal the pain he must have
felt at Cleaver's harsh indictment.

I had the chance to see Baldwin interact with younger black men from
the black power movement. From 1982 until the end of his life, Baldwin
was a Five College faculty member in western Massachusetts. In the first
year of his appointment, he was based at Hampshire College, where I was
on the faculty; he then moved to Hampshire's nearby consortial school, the
University of Massachusetts at Amherst. Many of his associates were former
members of the Student Nonviolent Coordinating Committee (SNCC)
and other black power organizations. Baldwin was famous for his traveling
retinue; I figured I would fit right in. Much to my surprise, however, there
did not seem to be much space for a black lesbian feminist.

Hints about why, beyond my own shy personality, I might have found
Baldwin's space uncomfortable can be found in a dialogue between Audre
Lorde and Baldwin that took place at Hampshire College in the fall of
1984. The transcript was excerpted in *Essence* magazine. Baldwin and Lorde
disagreed early and often. I cannot help feeling that some of Lorde's anger
was directed toward the way Baldwin tried to suppress his sexual difference
even though Lorde spoke mostly of gender difference, Baldwin seemed—
at first, anyway—to be looking for common ground, but Lorde, who had
staked her reputation on exposing difference and hidden power, would
have none of this:

> *Lorde:* Truly dealing with how we live, recognizing each other's differences
> is something that hasn't happened . . .
> *Baldwin:* Differences and samenesses.
> *Lorde:* Differences and samenesses. But in a crunch, when all our asses are in
> the sling, it looks like it is easier to deal with the samenesses. When we deal
> with samenesses only, we develop weapons that we use against each other
> when the differences become apparent. And we can wipe each other out—
> Black men and women can wipe each other out—far more effectively than
> outsiders do. (Lorde and Baldwin 74)

Lorde clearly understands the ways that differences can be used against people
even as these differences are being denied. Baldwin countered Lorde's arguments about difference by misrepresenting her: he maintained that she was
trying to blame black men for the condition of black women and children.
Finally, exasperated by Lorde's relentless and aggressive efforts to get through
to him about difference and sexism, he cut her off with an angry retort: "But

don't you realize that in this republic the only real crime is to be a Black man?
. . . How can you be so sentimental as to blame the Black man for a situation
which has nothing to do with him?" (Lorde and Baldwin 133). For Baldwin,
black sexism flows from white racism. Obviously, in making the point that
black women endure racism not simply as blacks but also as black women,
Lorde has spoken past him. Baldwin showed no willingness to recognize the
complex ways in which categories such as race and gender intertwine.

The dynamic of the Baldwin-Lorde debate reveals Baldwin's resistance to
the theoretical contribution of feminism and his commitment to male-dominated models for understanding race. Lorde was irrelevant to him; his interest
was limited to relations among black men and between black and white men.
He played out these interests in the largely male following that surrounded
him in Amherst. In this context, I found myself uncomfortably suppressing my
own concerns about sexism and homophobia. My concerns seemed to threat-
en the very fragile male bonds that kept his following together.

When I was around "Jimmy," I sensed the reconstruction of an elaborate closet. We all knew that there were so many ways in which Baldwin
was out: he was regularly surrounded by men who were interested in him,
and his fiction clearly spoke for him. But this kind of open homosexuality
threatened the terms of masculinity and the politics of respectability in
which many in his following were invested; somehow he needed to find a
way for homosexuality to be recognized but ignored. What an enormous
task! Manhood had to be constructed as if it were undifferentiated by sexuality and as if it stood for the race as a whole. Unfortunately, this homosexual panic created—and continues to create—real barriers to the prospect
of black men comforting each other. As long as the African American community colludes in an escape from knowledge about black homosexuality,
this kind of caring must remain in the closet.

My comments about Baldwin should in no way be read as a rejection of
him or his work. He was a man of his times, and he took us an impressively long way toward understanding the alchemy of race and sexuality.
His writing gave us many tools for exploring the sexualities of African
Americans—a topic that had long been suppressed for reasons of self-protection. I have chosen to investigate his limitations here because a clearer
sense of them can help us to unpack the complexity of his insights. Baldwin
remained trapped by some of his struggles against homophobia, and he
never overcame his deeply ingrained sexism. These limitations—as well as
his openness—cost him, because racism and homophobia can injure the
spirit and break down the body. By breaking the silence on black homosexuality through his writings, Baldwin both opened possibilities for
younger generations of black intellectuals like me and risked losing the love
of the very black men whom he so clearly loved.

Conclusion

> The object of one's hatred is never, alas, conveniently outside but is seated
> in one's lap, stirring in one's bowels and dictating the beat of one's heart.
> And if one does not know this, one risks becoming an imitation—and,
> therefore, a continuation— of principles one imagines oneself to despise.
>
> —Baldwin, "Here Be Dragons," 686

During the few short years that James Baldwin taught in western Massachusetts, I often heard him say, "White is a metaphor for safety." It took me a long time to realize that he repeated that line so often because he knew that it was a hard concept to grasp; after all, people were just beginning to talk about whiteness as a constructed identity. The meaning of his phrase lay at the heart of much of what he was about. He wanted us to know that blacks and whites do not have separate histories and that there could be no white people without black people. For Baldwin, whiteness was about a false claim on innocence that depended on the demonization of blackness.

My sense is that Morrison has been greatly influenced by her reading of Baldwin and has taken on a similar project. Both Baldwin and Morrison expose the fragility of whiteness and, in the process, disrupt any notion of pure whiteness distinct from and in opposition to blackness. Morrison demonstrates that works from this country's master canon that seem to be about whiteness use blackness to construct white identity. Baldwin attacks not only the false white/black binary, but also male/female and heterosexual/homosexual ones. As we saw previously, according to Baldwin, we all contain "the other—male in female, female in male, white in black and black in white" ("Here Be Dragons" 690).

Both Morrison and Baldwin critique the ways that black people have been erased from a history that seethes with their presence. And they are concerned about the myths and metaphors of race. Morrison writes about the ways that race establishes difference within our national literature, whereas Baldwin sees whiteness as a metaphor for safety. Although Morrison's work is more developed in her understanding of the way our culture has developed blackness as a figure of speech for the abnormal and evil, Baldwin's work is striking for its early break with the notion of race as an essential category. Baldwin often stressed both the destructiveness of and the barriers to insight created by racial categories.

Although both Morrison and Baldwin are impressively attuned to the nuances of black culture, they display a sense of irony that underneath it all blacks are not so different from whites. Both authors rely on the unconscious to explain the roots of white racism: white fear and guilt are projected onto black people. The entire nation suffers from the white escape from knowledge. Since the unconscious is so closely bound up with sexuality, racial and sexual identity become intimately linked.

The ways that Baldwin and Morrison see the impact of this intertwined relationship differs. Morrison tends to use sexuality as a leverage point of power between unequals. In particular, homosexual behavior becomes a powerful trope for unequal relationships. The chain gang scene in *Beloved* represents this use of homosexuality. The power of the scene derives from the fact that Morrison almost buries it by focusing on seemingly minor peripheral details. Yet once the reader visualizes the scene, the horror unfolds. Black men are chained together, and every one of them is at the mercy of the guards. Every punishment is a collective punishment. Since death deprives the guards of the use of another black male body, their ultimate punishment of the men in the chain gang becomes not execution but a psychological attack—the invasion of their sexuality and the sense of themselves as men. That the men in the chain gang experience this invasion collectively forces them to bury this secret deep in their (our) cultural psyche. Darieck Scott has come to similar conclusions: "The repressed memory [of African American men] might also be of the horror of homoerotic domination and desire enacted by and engendered in sexual exploitation" (229). If Morrison's scene were situated in the context of an African American literary culture that recognized a range of male-to-male relationships, from forced to loving, it would not contribute to the erasure of black homosexuality. But *Beloved* speaks into a homophobic silence. From Morrison's insights on race, I have been led to ask what intellectual and political feats she has had to perform to erase black queers from her consciousness.

Like Morrison, Baldwin knew that the histories of race and sexuality are inextricably intertwined. Perhaps because Baldwin was more intent on finding space for male homosexual relationships in a hostile environment, he placed greater emphasis on the similarities between the homosexual and the heterosexual. More than Morrison, he was concerned with exposing false binaries: black/white, male/female, gay/straight.

Baldwin and Morrison have greatly enriched our understanding of race and sexuality. The boundaries of their understanding provide fertile ground for exploring the way that race and sexuality operate together.

NOTES

1. This passage was first brought to my attention in a student paper written by Neeshan Mehretu (1992). I have been influenced by Mehretu's reading of this quoted passage and the one that follows from Morrison's *Beloved*.

2. For an exception, see William S. McFeely's *Frederick Douglass* (1991). McFeely speculates that Edward Covey, a notorious "slave breaker" in Eastern Shore, Maryland, engaged in frequent homosexual rape of slaves who fell under his power, including Frederick Douglass himself.

3. See Chauncey, *Gay New York* (1994) and Faderman, *Odd Girls and Twilight Lovers* (1991).

4. For a critique of Garber's work, see Reid-Pharr's "The Spectacle of Blackness" (1993) For a more sensitive view, see Faderman's *Odd Girls and Twilight Lovers.*

5. For a similar conclusion, see James Campbell, *Talking at the Gates* (1991).

6. I thank Margaret Cerullo and Marla Erlien for helping me see this.

WORKS CITED

Baldwin, James. *Giovanni's Room.* 1956. New York: Dial, 1962.

————. "Here Be Dragons." In *The Price of the Ticket: Collected Nonfiction 1948–1985.* New York: St. Martin's Press, 1985. 677–690.

————. *Just Above My Head.* New York: Dell, 1979.

————. *No Name in the Street.* New York: Dial, 1972.

————. *Notes of a Native Son.* Boston: Beacon, 1955.

Campbell, James. *Talking at the Gates: A Life of James Baldwin.* New York: Viking, 1991.

Carby, Hazel V. "It Be's Dat Way Sometime: The Sexual Politics of Women's Blues." *Radical America* 20 (Fall 1986): 239–49.

Chauncey, George. *Gay New York: Gender, Urban Culture, and the Making of the Gay Male World, 1890–1940.* New York: Basic Books, 1994.

Cleaver, Eldridge. *Soul on Ice.* New York: Dell, 1968.

Duberman, Martin. "'Writhing Bedfellows' in Antebellum South Carolina." In *Hidden from History: Reclaiming the Gay and Lesbian Past.* Ed. Martin Duberman et al. New York: New American Library, 1989.

Faderman, Lillian. "Harlem Nights: Savvy Women of the '20s Knew Where to Find New York's Lesbian Life." *Advocate,* 1991, 573.

————. *Odd Girls and Twilight Lovers: A History of Lesbian Life in Twentieth Century America.* New York: Penguin, 1991.

Garber, Eric. "A Spectacle of Color: The Lesbian and Gay Subculture of Jazz Age Harlem." In *Hidden from History: Reclaiming the Gay and Lesbian Past.* Ed. Martin Duberman et al. New York: New American Library, 1990.

Gates, Henry Louis, Jr. "Introduction: The Language of Slavery." In *The Slave's Narrative.* Ed. Charles T. Davis and Henry Louis Gates, Jr. Oxford: Oxford University Press, 1985.

Harper, Phillip Brian. *Private Affairs: Critical Ventures in the Culture of Social Relations.* New York: New York University Press, 1999.

hooks, bell. *Ain't I a Woman: Black Women and Feminism.* Boston: South End Press, 1981.

Hull, Gloria T. *Color, Sex, and Poetry: Three Women Writers of the Harlem Renaissance.* Bloomington: Indiana University Press, 1987.

Lorde, Audre, and James Baldwin. "Revolutionary Hope: A Conversation between James Baldwin and Audre Lorde." *Essence* 15, no. 8 (1984): 72–74, 129–30, 133.

Martin, Robert K. "Knights-Errant and Gothic Seducers: The Representation of Male Friendship in Mid-Nineteenth-Century America." In *Hidden from History: Reclaiming the Gay and Lesbian Past.* Ed. Martin Duberman et al. New York: New American Library, 1989.

McCorkle, Susannah. "Back to Bessie." *American Heritage* 48, no. 7 (November 1997): 54–64.

McFeely, William S. *Frederick Douglass.* New York: W.W. Norton, 1991.

McLaughlin, Thomas. "Figurative Language." In *Critical Terms for Literary Study.* Ed. Frank Lentricchia and Thomas McLaughlin. Chicago: University of Chicago Press, 1990. 80–90.

Mehretu, Neeshan. "The Representation of Black Women's Sexuality and the Connection of History with Slavery and Lynching." Paper presented for Race, Sexuality and Representation in U.S. History at Hampshire College, 1992.

Morrison, Toni. *Beloved.* New York: Knopf, 1987.

———. *Jazz.* New York: Knopf, 1992.

———. "Marginalization and Contemporary Cultures." In *Discourses: Conversations in Postmodern Art and Culture.* Ed. Russell Ferguson et al. Cambridge, MA: MIT Press, 1990.

———. *Playing in the Dark: Whiteness and the Literary Imagination.* Cambridge, MA: Harvard University Press, 1992.

———. "Unspeakable Things Unspoken: The Afro-American Presence in American Literature." *Michigan Quarterly Review* 28, no. 1 (1989): 1–34.

Reid-Pharr, Robert F. "The Spectacle of Blackness." *Radical America.* 24, no. 4 (1993): 57–65.

Scott, Darieck. "More Man Than You'll Ever Be: Antonio Fargas, Eldridge Cleaver, and Toni Morrison's *Beloved.*" In *Dangerous Liaisons: Blacks and Gays and the Struggle for Equality.* Ed. Eric Brandt. New York: New Press, 1999.

Sedgwick, Eve Kosofsky. *Between Men: English Literature and Male Homosocial Desire.* New York: Columbia University Press, 1985.

Spurlin, William. "Culture, Rhetoric, and Queer Identity: James Baldwin and the Identity Politics of Race and Sexuality." In *Baldwin Now.* Ed. Dwight A. McBride. New York: New York University Press, 1999.

White, E. Frances. *Dark Continent of Our Bodies: Black Feminism and the Politics of Responsibility.* Philadelphia: Temple University Press, 2001.

Winthrop, Theodore. *Cecil Dreeme.* Boston: Ticknor and Fields, 1862.

FEMININITY, ABJECTION, AND (BLACK) MASCULINITY IN JAMES BALDWIN'S *GIOVANNI'S ROOM* AND TONI MORRISON'S *BELOVED*

KEITH MITCHELL

Women are like water. They are tempting like that, and they can be that treacherous, and they can seem to be that bottomless, you know?

——James Baldwin, *Giovanni's Room*

A fully dressed woman walked out of the water.

——Toni Morrison, *Beloved*

Julia Kristeva describes the abject as that which "draws me towards the place where meaning collapses" (*Powers of Horror* 2). In African American letters, one of the ontological and epistemological places where many African American writers and thinkers, such as Frederick Douglass, W. E. B. DuBois, Leroi Jones, Amiri Baraka, and Henry Louis Gates, Jr., have theoretically tried to define meaning and failed is the notion of black masculinity. In many regards, too, they have failed to understand the oppressive nature of compulsory heterosexuality in the black community. Fortunately, the advent and aftermath of the black feminist movement in the early 1970s and recent interests in African American queer theory has made it abundantly clear that heterosexist ideas about black masculinities and sexualities need to be challenged.

The recent changes in thinking about black masculinity and sexuality are mainly due to groundbreaking work in African American queer theory posited by such scholars as Roderick A. Ferguson, E. Patrick Johnson, Devon W. Carbado, Jennifer DeVere Brody, Charles I. Nero, Patricia Collins, Dwight A. McBride, and bell hooks, among others, as a remedy for the exclusionary practices of African American literary and social theory. Moreover, a number of these scholars have begun to challenge how revered black writers, such as the two I examine in this chapter, Toni Morrison and James Baldwin, represent black masculinities and sexualities in their work. It is ironic, for instance, that in *Beloved* (1987) Paul D states that "to get to a place to love anything you could choose—to not need permission for desire—now *that* was freedom" (162). Unfortunately, because of deep-rooted prejudices within the black community, African American gays and lesbians often do not have that freedom to love openly whom they choose. Moreover, Baldwin's philosophy of love and sexual desire, which he espouses in his fiction and essays, often relies on bisexuality or androgyny, as a means of garnering a precarious acceptance by keeping one foot in the realm of heterosexuality.

Given the heteronormative discourses regulated by most straight African American male intellectuals and writers, and perhaps to a lesser extent by their female counterparts, one would think that a redefinition of black masculinity would come from the more marginalized members of the African American intellectual and literary community; for example, black queer writers and black women writers, such as Baldwin and Morrison. However, as I will demonstrate in a close reading of Baldwin's *Giovanni's Room* (1956) and Morrison's *Beloved*, even in the novels of two of the world's most highly regarded African American writer-critics, we encounter the reification of ideas about (black) masculinity and (black) patriarchal heteronormativity predicated by the dominant society. More specifically, I will demonstrate how Baldwin's and Morrison's reification of (black) masculinity is predicated upon the disdain for and the suppression of "femininity" in (black) males, the destruction of what Barbara Creed calls the "monstrous-feminine," and the disavowal of the maternal body as abject.

As the late African American literary and cultural critic Claudia Tate has expressed, most African American scholars distrust psychoanalytic theory as a critical tool for better understanding racism and oppression against African Americans. Yet Tate appropriates and subverts Freudian and Lacanian psychoanalytic theory to expose their inherent racism and to use psychoanalytic theory to write about desire, sexual difference, and black literary and cultural production.[1] Thus, French psychoanalyst and cultural critic Julia Kristeva's important work concerning the nature of abjection is the starting point of my argument in this chapter.[2]

As Kristeva points out, "What we designate as 'feminine,' far from being a primeval essence, will be seen as an 'other' without a name, which subjective experience confronts when it does not stop at the appearance of its identity" (*Powers*, 58). Kristeva makes clear that in order for a baby to become a "subject," it must reject the maternal body; before this process, the baby does not differentiate itself from its mother's body. As a subject in process, initially, "the enfant is still in an imaginary union with its mother

. . . well before it begins to learn language and enters into Jacques Lacan's symbolic realm" (47). Before entering into the symbolic realm, the realm of language, culture, and civilization, "[the subject] is not quite yet on the borderline of subjectivity. Abjection will help it get there. And the first 'thing' to be abjected is the mother's body, the child's own origin" (48).

As the infant, at least initially, cannot see itself as a separate entity from its mother, its sense of itself is that it is a part of its mother, inside of her. As it moves toward subjectivity, it sees itself as wholly separate from its mother, which it has only been able to do upon its disavowal of the maternal body. However, this does not mean that the semiotic/imaginary realm, with which the maternal body is associated, completely disappears once the child becomes a subject in the symbolic realm. Kristeva makes it clear that the abject, associated with the maternal body, borders the symbolic realm and enables the subject in process to remain a subject. It is only through the continual process of disavowing the abject that the subject can maintain its integrity.

That which disrupts subjectivity is abject, and Kristeva associates the abject, in contiguity with (the symbolic) order represented by society and patriarchal law, not only with the feminine (maternal body) but also with the unclean: vomit, filth, dirt, spit, urine, blood, feces, tears, milk, sperm, and even fingernail parings. The ultimate symbol of abjection for Kristeva, however, is the cadaver or corpse, which in both *Giovanni's Room* and *Beloved* is represented by the maternal/feminine abject. The cadaver, like other abject material, lies outside of, but nevertheless borders, the symbolic order and subjectivity.[3] I argue that *Giovanni's Room* and *Beloved* not only negate other possible ways of constructing (black) masculinity by abjecting the maternal/feminine body, but also use the abject maternal/feminine body as a way of reifying (black) masculinity and heteronormativity.[4]

Commenting on the psychological, erotic, and physical prison house that American men, both black and white, find themselves in, Baldwin states in his important essay on American (black) masculinity, "Here Be Dragons" (1985):

> The American ideal . . . of sexuality appears rooted in the American ideal of masculinity. This ideal has created cowboys and Indians, good guys and bad guys, punks and studs, tough guys and softies, butch and faggot, black and white. It is an ideal so paralytically infantile that it is virtually forbidden—as an unpatriotic act—that the American boy evolve into the complexity of manhood. (678)

In many ways, Baldwin's ideas about sexuality are precursors of current trends in feminist and queer theory. For example, Judith Butler claims that gender is performative and that sexuality is inherently fluid. Baldwin's aim, like Butler's, is to deconstruct binary oppositions based on societal laws that seek to pigeonhole people in terms of gender and sexuality. Significantly, however, Baldwin includes race in his attack on heteronormativity as another important component of black and white patriarchal oppression. In order to break down patriarchal dichotomies, Baldwin speaks of the notion of androgyny, which, I believe, is key in understanding why he chose to write about homosexuality through white characters rather than black characters in his novel *Giovanni's Room,* and also to set the novel in another country, France, where, given America's conservative political landscape and the publication history of black novelists in America during the 1950s, the subject matter would certainly be more palatable for (black) American readers.[5]

In seeking to understand Baldwin's racialized sleight of hand in writing *Giovanni's Room,* I would agree with Siobhan B. Somerville that in analyzing literature one must "listen for the inexplicable presence of the thing not named" (*Queering the Color Line* 6).[6] "The thing not named" in *Giovanni's Room* is the Africanist presence in the text, and not homosexuality. Baldwin makes metaphorical references to race and racialization in order to show that such categories as race, gender, and sexuality are socially constructed. In this sense, by making all of the characters in the novel white, he "queers" racial categorization. About the power of naming and categorization, he says, "Once you have discerned the meaning of a label, it may seem to define you for others, but it does not have the power to define you to yourself" ("Dragons" 681).

Perhaps the most important question is whether or not Baldwin's polemic is actualized in *Giovanni's Room.* I would suggest that perhaps in later novels such as *Another Country* (1962) and *Tell Me How Long the Train's Been Gone* (1968), Baldwin's art and polemic complement each other better than in *Giovanni's Room.* In fact, I would say that even as Baldwin attempts to destabilize the heteronormativity surrounding (black) masculinity in positing "femininity," effeminate homosexuals, and women as abject in *Giovanni's Room,* he actually reinscribes heteronormativity. One of the primary psychological dilemmas that the protagonist of *Giovanni's Room,* David, wrestles with is how to reconcile his masculinity with his homosexuality.

At the beginning of the novel, the reader gets a fairly accurate picture of David. He is a near-thirty-year-old white male who is living in Paris as an expatriate. Ostensibly, he has come to Europe to find himself and to ask his girlfriend, Hella, also an American expatriate, to marry him. When he arrives in Paris, she is traveling in Spain and is slated to meet him in Paris later in the month to give him her answer to his proposal. Baldwin immediately establishes the idea of feminine abjection and monstrosity by naming

Giovanni's girlfriend Hella. In Norse mythology, Hella is the goddess of the dead. She has complete sovereignty over those who die, and she decides their fate. In her kingdom of Niflheim, the dead suffer unimaginable tortures—all except those who die heroically in battle; fallen heroes end up in Valhalla, the Hall of Heroes. Additionally, Hella is described, in Norse mythology, as half-white and half-black or half-living and half-dead. Thus, in naming David's girlfriend, Baldwin, metaphorically, deconstructs yet reinscribes black and white racial binaries; at the same time, he establishes Hella, a woman associated with death, as an abject figure.[7]

Even though there are no clearly identifiable nonwhite characters in *Giovanni's Room*, I believe that Baldwin makes a connection between the oppression and persecution of African American and that of (black) American men who do not limit themselves to the constrictive paradigms associated with compulsory heterosexuality. As an African American male who is also not heterosexual, it seems perfectly reasonable for Baldwin to be unable or unwilling to separate the discrimination and oppression against him due to his race from the discrimination and oppression against him due to his sexual orientation. In "Here Be Dragons," he deals with heteronormative oppression by addressing issues that also apply to racial oppression in America and refuses to label himself as a black gay man or a gay black man. As such, his polemic has radically important implications for the notion of (black) male subjectivity.

Even today, most black Americans refuse to accept the connection that Baldwin makes between (homo)sexual oppression and racial oppression. It is the general consensus, as Charles I. Nero and E. Frances White point out, that among black folks and African American intellectuals alike, homosexuality is a perverse symptom of the white race's innate depravity and that homosexuality connected to "femininity" is pathological: "the white man's disease." And "femininity" is linked to abjection. If we extend abjection as a metaphor to include the black race, as many of history's most influential Western thinkers have done, then Baldwin's elaborate schema of linking sexual oppression with racial oppression is not lost in *Giovanni's Room*, even if race and sexuality are painted in whiteface. Because women and homosexuals are at the margins of black and white patriarchal heteronormative society, these two marginalized groups are seen as an ever-potential threat to the cohesiveness of the social body. In accordance with Mary Douglas's remarks, I would argue that for Baldwin, "the body is a model that can stand for any bounded system. Its boundaries can represent any boundaries that are threatened or precarious" (*Purity and Danger* 115). Moreover, as Judith Butler, elaborating on Douglas's work, says, society considers homosexual acts as transgressing bodily boundaries, which, metaphorically, include the social body.

If we examine David's character at the beginning of *Giovanni's Room*, he represents the oppressive, masculine, American social body that Baldwin justly criticizes in "Here Be Dragons" and other essays. As David reflects upon his past and present relationship with his "girl Hella," we begin to see the cracks in his heterosexual performance as he reminisces about his first sexual experience with his childhood friend, Joey.[8] What begins as late-night rough-housing between two seemingly straight best friends soon develops into a mutually satisfying sexual encounter. The next morning, at least initially, David is in a state of bliss as he peers over at Joey, who remains asleep next to him: "Joey's body was brown, was sweaty, the most beautiful creation I had ever seen till then" (8). However, shame, guilt, and homosexual panic soon upend his blissful state of mind as consequences of his lovemaking with Joey, a boy, begin to disturb and distort his bodily perceptions. David's previously integrated (heterosexual) sense of himself begins to unravel as in the next instance he sees his body as "gross and crushing" and his "desire [as] monstrous" (9). He describes Joey's body as "the black opening of a cavern in which he would be tortured till madness came [and where] [he] would lose [his] manhood" (9). Metaphorically, he links Joey's body or "black hole" with a scene reminiscent of hell in Dante's *Inferno*, as well as his own fall from grace.[9] As a result, he begins to fight desperately against what he sees as a "feminizing" assault on his masculinity. Indeed, he leaves before Joey awakens and abruptly ends their friendship.

Even prior to his sexual escapade with Joey, as the novel points out, David has always been afraid of the feminine, which he vividly connects with death and abjection. For example, he has nightmares about his dead mother, in which he envisions her as having eyes "blind with worms, her hair as dry as metal and brittle as a twig, straining to press me against her body; the body so putrescent, so sickening soft, that it opened, as I clawed and cried, into a breach so enormous as to swallow me alive" (GR 11–12). To Kristeva, the corpse or cadaver represents the epitome of the abject; she clearly distinguishes between accepting that death happens to all living creatures and being confronted by death through the materiality of the dead body:

> As in true theater, without makeup or masks, refuse and corpses *show me* what I permanently thrust aside in order to live. These body fluids, this defilement, this shit are what life withstands, hardly and with difficulty, on the part of death. There, I am at the border of my condition as a living being. (*Powers* 3)

David's confrontation with the materiality of his mother's death causes him to have terrible nightmares and to fear that all of the life will be drained from his body as it was from hers.[10] His fear of being consumed by his mother's abject, monstrous-feminine desire is a fear of the loss of his masculine subjectivity. This fear of feminine libidinal consumption, in turn, manifests in his rejection of his homosexual relationship with Joey.

Because of his guilt over his relationship with Joey, David comes to despise both his father and his Aunt Ellen, who comes to live with David and his father after the death of David's mother.[11] David also begins to despise his own body. In fact, his body and his same-sex desires become a prison, rather than a release, for him. He begins acting out, coming home drunk and belligerent. He even attempts suicide. His father dismisses his reckless behavior as a phase; but in the back of his mind, David knows that his behavior is based on his relationship with Joey and guilt about not ever being able to live up to his father's expectations of what it means to be a "real man." David laments: "The incident with Joey had shaken me profoundly and its effect was to make me secretive and cruel. I could not discuss what had happened to me with anyone . . . And it changed, it thickened, it soured the atmosphere of my mind" (15–16).[12] David's thoughts after having sex with Joey and his equating it with death, hinges on the abjectness he feels about homosexuality.[13]

Throughout *Giovanni's Room*, David's encounters with women, maternal figures, and effeminate nonheteronormative characters illustrate his sexual ambivalence and his desire to rid himself of what he sees as the castrating and feminizing implications of same-sex desire. He is especially repulsed by transvestites, whom he sees as an unholy hybrid of masculinity and femininity. Indeed, he describes a transvestite that he meets at Guillaume's bar as "a mummy or a zombie, of something walking after it had been put to death" (38). Again, the abject feminine threatens his masculine subjectivity.

The binary opposition between heteronormative gender identification breaks down as David tries unsuccessfully to categorize the transvestite in prescriptive gender terms of male or female. Unable to do so, he refers to the transvestite as "it," which places the transvestite in the category of the unknown. What David is most afraid of is the stereotypical, effeminate spectacle of homosexuality that the transvestite embodies for society. On the other hand, David's homosexuality is masked by his masculine performance. In other words, his same-sex desire is not visibly marked; he can pass, performatively, as straight any time he desires, except perhaps when around those who can sense his masquerade. For example, when a sailor catches him cruising him at the American Express Office and guesses his sexual orientation, David panics and picks up a girl to prove to himself that he is still heterosexual. In effect, an effeminate gay man who cannot conceal his sexuality is arguably more of a man than David because he has to face head-on the slings and arrows of heteronormative society. David's het-erosexual performance is always in danger of being discovered by those who are able to see through it. Thus, he is always hyperconcerned about keeping up heterosexual appearances. His sexuality is, invariably, "[regulat-ed] within the obligatory frame of heterosexuality" (Butler 136).

Butler's theory is useful in understanding David's heterosexual perform-ance and homosexual panic in *Giovanni's Room*. In other words, just as the transvestite's or drag queen's degree of agency or transgression against het-eronormativity is limited, so is David's so-called straight drag, because he is afraid to openly love Giovanni, or anyone else for that matter. Even when David and Giovanni attempt to live together as a couple, while David's girlfriend Hella is away, David wants to maintain a heterosexual perform-ance even within the confines of safe, queer spaces, such as Giovanni's room and Guillaume's bar.

As David's anxieties about his relationship with Giovanni increase expo-nentially, he decides to tell Giovanni that he is going to leave him. In a heated argument, Giovanni tells David, "You want to go out and be the big laborer and bring home the money, and you want me to stay here and wash the dishes and cook the food and clean this miserable *closet of a room* and kiss you when you come home through that door and lie with you at night and be your little *girl* (142; emphasis mine). In a state of rage, Giovanni accurately accesses David's psychological confusion as David refuses to believe that sexual preference and nonheteronormative behavior do not define one's manhood.

Through David's feelings about masculinity and femininity in gay male culture, Baldwin makes clear that a bifurcation exists between effeminate homosexuals and masculine homosexuals, a bifurcation that does not accu-rately reflect what actually occurs in black and white gay male culture.[14] As such, Baldwin erects a seemingly unbreachable boundary between effeminate homosexuals, such as Guillaume and Jacques, and masculine homosexuals, such as David and Giovanni, who, though they engage in homosexual behavior, are much more respectable and less threatening to societal norms because they do not fit gay stereotypes. David and Giovanni's heterosexual courting rituals mock Guillaume and Jacques's "impersonal homoerotic sex" (Nero 406).[15] But this is only because David and Giovanni have the luxury of *passing* as straight men. Unlike the transvestite whose drag and effeminacy marks him or her, neither David's nor Giovanni's homosexuality is visibly marked.[16] Both men do not wish to acknowledge that whatever "feminini-ty" they see in the transvestite, effeminate gay men or women is also a part of them.

David and Giovanni display internalized homophobia and misogyny throughout the novel. They despise Jacques and Guillaume, two older, effeminate homosexuals who befriend them in Paris, and they falsely believe that their relationship is morally superior to the one-night stands that Jacques and Guillaume engage in, when, in fact, their relationship is merely a fabrication of a heterosexual relationship. The courtship rituals that David and Giovanni engage in are framed within a heteronormative, patriarchal matrix. They deem any other sexual relationship between gay men as dirty, predatory sexual behavior.[17] David and Giovanni's relationship in *Giovanni's Room* subverts as well as codifies heteronormative relationships because these two nonheteronormative men "queer" cultural stereotypes pertaining to gay men; but at the same time, their relationship is, in the main, based on heterosexual modes of thinking and behaving.

Men without Women

As David and Giovanni's relationship eventually begins to deteriorate, David becomes more and more anxious to leave Giovanni, who has truly fallen in love with David. Because of the oppressive nature and demands of masculinity and its trappings, David cannot emotionally give himself to Giovanni or anyone else of either gender because he does not love himself. Their relationship ends when Giovanni loses his job at Guillaume's bar, the one steady source of income that he and David had to live on. When David returns to the apartment, he finds Giovanni in a state of "hysteria and despair" (104).[18] David recalls that

> Giovanni suddenly sat down on the edge of the bed . . . in a state of rage . . . He looked up at me. His eyes were full of tears. "They're just dirty, all of them, low and cheap and dirty . . . All except you" . . . He held my face between his hands and I suppose such tenderness scarcely produced such terror as I felt then. *"Ne me laisse pas tomber, je t'en prie,"* he said and kissed me, with a strange insistent gentleness, on the mouth. His touch never failed to make me feel desire; yet, his hot sweet breath made me want to vomit. (105)

In this scene, Giovanni is vulnerable, which terrifies David; for the first time, he sees Giovanni as weak. Giovanni occupies the "feminine" position in the relationship, where once, because of his economic power, he was at least on equal (masculine) terms with David. In French, Giovanni begs David to not let him fall. He needs David's emotional support, but David is unable to give it to him. We may situate this scene in a larger context: that of femininity and abjection.[19] Giovanni's words not only foreshadow his death but also metaphorically link him to the abject. Moreover, in this scene, Giovanni's "feminization," as exhibited by his vulnerability, tenderness toward David, and his tears, also metaphorically links him to the feminine abject and the monstrous-feminine.[20] David becomes so disgust-ed by Giovanni's "feminine" behavior that he almost vomits. David's retching is the physical manifestation of his wish to expel his same-sex desire for Giovanni. However, in the same instant that David attempts to maintain his masculine subject integrity by abjecting Giovanni, he abjects himself, as his "body extricates itself, as being alive" from the maternal body/Giovanni's body and the border between life and death.

Ironically, Giovanni has similar feeling about Guillaume's "feminini-ty" before Guillaume fires him because Giovanni refuses his sexual advances. Giovanni tells David, "I found Guillaume in his dressing gown, covered with perfume. I do not know why, but the moment I saw him like that, I began to be angry. He looked at me as though he were some fabulous coquette—and he is ugly, ugly, he has a body just like sour milk" (107). By positioning "femininity" as abject, Baldwin upholds heteronormative societal values because he implies that "femi-ninity," as a trait in (gay) men, as well as women, has no real value or purpose in society, despite his argument in "Here Be Dragons" and other essays in which he writes about sexuality and gender. Baldwin does appear to have issues concerning homosexual behavior and black male propriety. About certain issues concerning homosexual behavior, Baldwin's stance is rooted in an African American bourgeois sensibility. I would even argue that the intolerant Baptist teachings that Baldwin tried to rid himself of return to haunt the moral trajectory of the narra-tive. Although certainly a groundbreaking novel, *Giovanni's Room,* in its own subtle way, is, in fact, nearly as disturbing as Eldridge Cleaver's homophobic diatribes in *Soul on Ice* (1968).

One of the most telling scenes illustrating Baldwin's rather conservative and bourgeois attitudes toward homosexual relationships is when Giovanni, in a fit of manic hysteria, attempts to re-create the room where he and David live as a love nest that mimics heteronormative domesticity. In his attempt to revamp the cramped, filthy room, Giovanni peels off large pieces of wall paper.[21] However, the opposite wall, which "was destined never to be uncovered . . . [depicts] a lady in a hoop skirt and a man in knee breeches [who] perpetually walked together, hemmed in by roses" (86). I read this scene in two ways: on the one hand, that the wallpaper remains untouched speaks of the power, permanency, and oppression of compulsory heterosexuality, while on the other hand, this scene also speaks of Giovanni's longing for heteronormative domesticity *within* a matrix of same-sex desire—a scenario that David wants nothing to do with because he still believes that he has a chance for a normal life with Hella.

Thus, instead of showing the possibilities of desire outside of the trap of compulsory heterosexuality, the novel delineates nonheteronormative people and women as not only lack but also as pathological.[22] Moreover, "femininity," as I have attempted to show, is repeatedly positioned in *Giovanni's Room* as monstrous and abject in order to promote heteronormative notions of (black) masculinity. As such, Baldwin falls into the very trap of masculine, patriarchal oppression from which he tries to extricate himself and the rest of American society.

"Playing with the Possibilities That Are Also There"[23]

Much like James Baldwin, Toni Morrison has been lauded for her work, especially her novels, in which through oppositional discourse she addresses, transgresses, and subverts white patriarchal ideology and its oppressive nature concerning people of color. Although her work centers primarily on issues concerning black women, it also addresses complex relationships between black men and black women as well as equally important issues about the construction of black masculinity in American society. Her work is a literary and historical (re-)membering of specific African American social and historical moments, which seek to excavate heretofore untold narratives omitted, erased, or distorted by the official historical record.

Nonetheless, as Morrison astutely critiques discursive practices of Western writers and thinkers and their inability to adequately deal with people of African descent, she too must be criticized for her failure to adequately explore certain aspects of African American life, such as nonheteronormative relationships in African history and culture—relationships that have been vital to African American cultural and historical production. Charles I. Nero's essay "Toward a Black Gay Aesthetic" (1991) does just this. In his critique of Morrison's sustained homophobia in her literary work, Nero charges that "Toni Morrison has woven into her novels [the] idea of homosexuality as alien to African cultures, as forced upon black men by racist European civilizations, and as the inability to acquire and sustain manhood" (401–402).[24] Similarly, in her essay "The Evidence of Things Not Seen," E. Frances White also takes Morrison to task for not addressing issues of same-sex desire among black men in the communities she portrays in her novels. Using Morrison's own theoretical and critical assertions about "the fact of blackness" in her collection of essays *Playing in the Dark: Whiteness and the Literary Imagination* (1992), White asserts that Morrison's work is limited in its scope because Morrison fails to address "the fact of queerness" in the African American community and that Morrison reifies heteronormative patriarchal paradigms that are as damaging to same-sex-desiring black men (and women) as white, patriarchal discourses have been to heterosexual black men and women. Just as white discursive practices have tried to render invisible or erase black men and women from official historical, political, social, and literary records, so too has Morrison managed to do in not writing about the complexities of same-sex-desiring African Americans.

White's essay critiques Baldwin and Morrison by contextualizing their depictions of black masculinity in relationship to African American social and historical truths. For example, she critiques Baldwin for his lack of sensitivity to issues concerning black women, while critiquing Morrison for her lack of sensitivity to issues concerning nonheteronormative relationships between black men. White writes that in his lifetime "Baldwin showed no willingness to recognize the complex ways that categories such as race and gender intertwine" ("The Evidence" 178). About Morrison, she writes, "From Morrison's insights on race, I have been led to ask what intellectual and political feats she has had to perform to erase black queers from her consciousness" (182).

Confining my argument to *Beloved* and *Giovanni's Room,* I would suggest that one of the intellectual feats that Morrison (and Baldwin) has had to perform in order to render black gays and lesbians invisible and to promote heteronormative behavior within the black community is, ironically, the rendering of aspects of black, female subjectivity as abject. By doing so, I would argue, Morrison, like Baldwin, reifies compulsory heterosexuality and buys into the notion of homosexuality as pathological, "the white man's disease," and that heterosexual relationships are the only types of relationships that are legitimate under the larger umbrella of African American historical and social truths. In short, any behavior by black men or women that is deemed out of the gendered norm in Morrison's black literary imagination is rendered invisible or readily expunged. I would argue that like Baldwin, Morrison, in her own way, does not put into practice what she preaches when it comes to challenging patriarchal standards of behavior; at the ends of all of her novels, heteronormative social behavior is invariably maintained: case in point, *Beloved.*

At the beginning of *Beloved,* the reader encounters a haunted house, Morrison's feminine space that is not only abject but is also abject-ed by the rest of the black community made up of "a town full of disgust" (5): "124 was spiteful. Full of a baby's venom. The women in the house knew and so did the children" (3). By creating this female, ex-centric space of evil—a house haunted by a vindictive, female ghost-baby—Morrison makes it clear that this all-female space is not normal, especially since the ghost-baby is able to drive away all of the male members of the besieged family: Buglar, Howard, and the dog, Hereboy.[25]

Left alone on the outskirts of the rest of the black community that surrounds it, the women of 124 are left to fend for themselves. Sethe and her daughter, Denver, "understood the source of the outrage as well as they knew the source of light" (4). As Sethe recalls, the source of the outrage is the

> soul of her baby girl. Who would have thought that a little old baby could harbor so much rage? Rutting among stones under the eyes of the engraver's son was not enough. Not only did she have to live out her years in a house palsied by the baby's fury at having its throat cut, but those ten minutes she spent pressed up against dawn-colored stone studded with star chips, her knees wide open as the grave, were longer than life, more alive, more pulsating than the baby blood that soaked her fingers like oil. (5)

Morrison is lauded, and rightfully so, for her magnificent poetic prose. However, as in the above quotation, sometimes the prose is so dazzling that readers and critics gloss over the full import of the words on the page. Central to my argument is to show how Morrison uses feminine abjection and the monstrous-feminine to reify, in general, the black community's insistence on heteronormative behavior, underscored by black masculinity and the maintenance of the patriarchal black family unit. The language in the above passage is gothic; the setting is gothic. First we have Beloved's rage, which symbolizes the mad (in both senses of the word) black female.[26] That this madness manifests itself in the form of a female ghost-baby sets up the depiction of other black femaleness in the novel as abnormal, unnatural, abject. Moreover, the image of Sethe copulating in a cemetery, "her knees wide open as the grave [and] the baby blood that soaked her fingers like oil," in exchange for a headstone for her murdered child, poignantly shows Sethe's desperation but also decidedly links her to death and the abject.

   While I acknowledge, as many other critics do, that Morrison uses the ghost-baby and the degradation of black women (and men) to show the devastating, inhumane treatment of slaves, which in turn caused many slaves to internalize this degradation, it seems that Morrison's trope of the abject black female ultimately supports the idea that the black community, in order to survive, must uphold heteronormative behavior and practices; this includes the idea that black men and black masculinity can *only* be viewed in terms heterosexuality: any signs of frailty, passivity, or weakness in black males is unacceptable. For example, it is only when Sethe and Denver are at their wits' end concerning the ghost-baby's raging against them and 124 that eighteen years after her escape from the Sweet Home plantation, Paul D, "the last of the Sweet Home men," comes to the rescue, as if Sethe magically conjures him up from the recesses of her (re-)membering (6).

As soon as Paul D enters the house, his battle against the ghost-child begins:

> Paul D tied his shoes together, hung them over his shoulders and followed [Sethe] through the door straight into a pool of red and undulating light that locked him where he stood.
> "You got company?" he whispered, frowning.
> "Off and on," said Sethe.
> "Good God." He backed out of the door onto the porch. "What kind of evil you got in here?" (8)

As this female-centered household and the women in it symbolize the abject, Paul D, for a time, becomes the *pharmakos*, or cure, as he attempts to reestablish normativity and boundaries between the living and the dead, between mother and daughter, between instinct and reason, and between Sethe and himself. He beats back the ghost-child by literally smashing up the room where she manifests herself, bringing to bear the sheer force of his black masculine will against the crawling-already? baby girl's spirit of Sethe's murdered child: "With a table and a loud male voice he had rid 124 of its local claim to fame" (37).

Paul D's arrival at 124 marks a brief return to a semblance of normalcy, which causes Denver and Sethe to begin to re-vision the reality of their situation: the lack of maleness in their home, their loneliness, and their isolation from the rest of the black community. Before,

> there was no other room [in 124] for any other thing or body until Paul D arrived and broke up the place, making room, shifting it, moving it over to someplace else, then standing in the place he had made.
> After Paul D came, [Sethe] was distracted by two orange squares [on Baby Suggs' quilt] that signaled how barren 124 really was.
> [Paul D] became responsible for that. Things became what they were: drabness looked drab; heat was hot. Windows suddenly had a view. And wouldn't you know he would be a singing man. (39)

Just as women are generally associated with passivity, men are associated with action. Sethe puts up with the ghost-baby's shenanigans. Out of guilt and loneliness for her dead daughter, she makes no effort to remove its presence. Paul D, however, takes immediate action, flexing his muscles and his manhood to rid 124 of the thing that denies him a space in Sethe's life. He not only has to fight for a place in which he can find comfort and pride in being a black man with a family, but he must also deal with Denver's fears that he will take the place of her father, Halle, who has been missing for eighteen years and presumed dead. Yet, Denver holds on to the hope that Halle, her "Angel man," will miraculously return to take her away from her near-unbearable, lonely existence on Bluestone Road, away from the house that she regarded as "a person rather than a structure" (29).

If we look at 124 as a space of dislocation, "time out of joint," we can make a tangential analogy between 124 as a metaphor for what Julia Kristeva calls the semiotic state and the rest of the black community and the town as a metaphor for the symbolic realm. For Kristeva, "the semiotic represents nature/[maternal]body/the unconsciousness," and the semiotic is [also] associated with the prelinguistic (McAfee 17). The symbolic, on the other hand, is associated with "culture/mind/-consciousness," and it is associated with patriarchy (McAfee 17). Yet, the semiotic always makes itself felt, despite the "dominance" of the symbolic realm. In fact, the symbolic is dependent on the semiotic for its existence, and vice versa. Therefore, I would suggest that when the ghost-child, Beloved, returns to 124 as "a fully dressed woman [who walks] out of the water," her existence (the semiotic) is the lynchpin that enables Paul D (the symbolic) to regain his manhood, for Denver to leave 124 and interact with the surrounding black community, and for heteronormative relations, specifically between Sethe and Paul D, to be reestablished. In short, Beloved, the abject ghost-woman, must be put back in her place to establish (symbolic) order/black patriarchy at 124, where previously there was none.[27]

In *Gone Primitive* (1990), Marianna Torgovnick seeks to establish the importance of the concept of the primitive, no matter how odious the word and its terminology might be, to "conceptions . . . that drive the modern and the postmodern across a wide range of fields and levels of culture, [and] as a part of the ambiance and aura of our culture" (21). Throughout *Beloved's* narrative, Morrison makes clear the disjunction between the maternal body and matriarchy (normally associated with the primitive) and the paternal body and patriarchy (normally associated with civilization). Once Beloved has ensconced herself in Sethe's home, Paul D is especially interested in knowing where Beloved came from, for he sees the blossoming ties between Sethe, Denver, and Beloved as having the potential to close permanently the physical, emotional, and psychical space he has worked so hard to establish:

"I asked you who brought you here?"
"I walked here," [Beloved] said. A long, long, long, long, long way. Nobody bring me. Nobody help me."
"You had new shoes. If you walked so long why don't your shoes show it?"

"I want to know," [Paul D] said, holding the knife handle in his fist like a pole."

"I take the shoes! I take the dress! The shoe strings don't fix!" she shouted and gave him a look so malevolent Denver touched her arm.

Paul D had the feeling a large, silver fish had slipped from his hands the minute he grabbed hold of its tail.[28] That it was streaming back into the dark water now, gone but for the glistening marking its route. (65)

As Paul D attempts to make clear to both Beloved and Denver his place in Sethe's heart and home, he also uses his interrogation of Beloved to re-member his manhood. The image of the knife is a phallic image, which is both psychological and mythological. The knife, which resembles a (fishing) pole symbolizes Paul D's manhood. The knife image then transforms to symbolize Paul D's efforts to pluck answers from the murky waters of Beloved's unconscious. However, Beloved's memories are so fragmented that she cannot convey to him much information about her arrival at 124, even if she wanted to. Her inability to clearly express her thoughts and desires in a coherent fashion also places her in the semiotic realm. In addition, her dead-on arrival out from the stream behind 124, as a fully dressed woman, associates her not only with the feminine abject body but also with the unconscious. Water is one of the primary images that one associates Beloved with in the novel.[29] As Togorvnick explains,

The "oceanic" must be ousted from a place in the foreground because it would displace the individualistic paternal line to which Freud wishes to trace civilization, its benefits and its discontents. The "oceanic," with its absence of boundaries and divisions, is something we need to be protected from if we are to take our places in the "mature" culture of the West. (207)

Beloved's return to Sethe and her greed for this plentitude of mother-love and nurturance is displayed through her jealousy of Sethe and Paul D's relationship and Sethe's "willingness to pay attention to other things. Him mostly. Him who kept [Sethe] hidden at night behind doors" (101).[30] Beloved's plan is to move Paul D from the environs of 124, away from her dearly beloved mother, Sethe. And at first she is successful, as for some inexplicable reason Paul D becomes restless living under Sethe's roof. Through sexual seduction, slowly but surely, Beloved moves Paul D, which brings back memories of his humiliation after he failed to escape from the Sweet Home plantation and his subsequent hellish trials in a chain gang in Alfred, Georgia: the cause of his humiliation "was being moved, placed where [Beloved] wanted him, and there was nothing he was able to do about it" (126) although Paul D realizes that Beloved "is doing it to [him]. Fixing [him]" (127). Beloved fixes Paul D literally and figuratively.

She (magically) causes Paul D to move away from 124, into town and away from Sethe. And because he, a grown man, is psychologically defeated by a supposedly harmless, young girl, Beloved has fixed him as one would geld a stallion. Worse, he cannot confide in Sethe, the woman he wants to love and protect, at the risk of drawing her attention to his feelings of his lost manhood.[31] And so he leaves an unholy trinity—Sethe, Beloved, and Denver—to their own devices. Without a man around the house to protect her and without the protection of the rest of the black community, Beloved, the insatiable ghost-child, is free to wreak havoc against Sethe. She thinks that she has destroyed the possibility of Sethe and Paul D building a home and a life together. Thus, Paul D's black, patriarchal heteronormative existence is also "fixed."

As a "Ulysses" character, movement is a very important trope in the novel, as associated with Paul D and his sense of manhood. In fact, four major scenes deal with Paul D's ability to control his movements, his own body. The first scene is when he looks back on his life as a Sweet Home man and questions whether or not working as a slave for Mr. Garner, the plantation owner and his master, meant that he was freer, and thus, more of a man than other slaves on the surrounding plantations. It is Halle, after having gotten a taste of freedom by hiring himself out to surrounding plantations, who first understands that the Sweet Home men are only men because their master, Mr. Garner, says that they are, and not because they *know* that they are. On the Sweet Home plantation, Halle, Paul D, and the other male slaves are men only conditionally, as Paul D soon learns. Shortly after his failed escape from Sweet Home and schoolteacher's depravity, Paul D is shackled and a bit is put in his mouth to prevent him from screaming. He cannot move. But it is his encounter with the rooster, Mister, that capitalizes his psychological trauma. He tells Sethe:

> It wasn't the bit . . . [It was] Mister, he looked so . . . free. Stronger, tougher. Son a bitch couldn't even get out the shell by hisself, but he was still king and I was . . . Mister was allowed to be and stay what he was. Even if you cooked him you'd be cooking a rooster named Mister. But wasn't no way I'd ever be Paul D again, living or dead. Schoolteacher changed me. I was something else and that something else was less than a chicken sitting in the sun on a tub. (72–73)

For his part in the failed escape from Sweet Home, Paul D winds up in a prison chain gang. In this situation, his manhood is literally measured by his connection to the other black men on the gang. His movement, as an individual, is dependent on the movement of the other black men chained to him. If the prison guards allow one member of the chain gang to move, they all must move in turn. Again, control over his own body, his man-hood, is taken away from him. Next, Beloved's conjurations, which remove Paul D from 124, aid in his emasculation. Upon hearing from Sethe that she had wanted to murder her children but only managed to kill Beloved, Paul D leaves her and Denver.

When Stamp Paid, a respected member of the surrounding black community, walks to 124 Bluestone Road for a visit,

> He heard a loud conflagration of hasty voices—loud, urgent all speaking at once so he could not make out what they were talking about or to whom. The speech wasn't nonsensical, exactly, nor was it tongues. But something was wrong with the order of the words and he couldn't describe or cipher it to save his life. All he could make out was the word mine. (172)

For Paul D to reclaim his manhood and his position in a black heteropatriarchal society, Beloved, like all abjections that threaten to overrun the symbolic order, must be expelled so that Sethe and the rest of the surrounding black community can remain safe and intact. Nevertheless, we must remember Beloved's importance to the sustenance of said community. As "a source of evil mingled with sin, abjection becomes a requisite for reconciliation in the mind, between flesh and the law" (Kristeva, *Powers* 127–128). When Stamp Paid goes to see Ella, another respected member of the black community, about the strange happenings in 124 since Paul D's departure, Ella knowingly replies, "Well, Paul D must know who she is. Or *what* she is . . . You know as well as I do that people who die bad don't stay in the ground" (188).[32] Ella's immediate connection of Beloved with something that has invaded and transgressed boundaries, 'took flesh and came in her world,' is what ignites her and the other black women in the community to come to Sethe's rescue (257). "What constitutes the strongest association between monstrosity and female corporeality," as Carmen Bujdei asserts, "is the notion of a fluid transgression of the boundaries between inside and outside, self and other" (1). In fact, Ella sees Beloved's presence in the community as an outrage: "She didn't mind a little communication between the two worlds, but this was an invasion" (257).

As thirty of the community's black women gather near 124 Bluestone Road to confront what they believe to be an incarnation of the devil himself, the very atmosphere of the surrounding area, as if nature or the natural order has been defiled, is filled with a stench "[that] had traveled to the country: from the canal, from hanging meat and things rotting in jars; from small animals dead in the fields, town sewers and factories. The stench, the heat, the moisture—trust the devil to make his presence known" (256). On their knees in front of 124, the community of black women, in an expression of love, compassion, and fear, begin to pray. Then, they cease to pray and begin to hum, and they "took a step back to the beginning. In the beginning there were no words. In the beginning there was the sound, and they all knew what the sound sounded like" (259). Because the women instinctively know to vanquish Beloved, who appears pregnant, and what she represents, they "employ a maternal regulation or law which prefigures . . . paternal law," even more ancient than the words evoked in prayer to exorcize the ghost-woman and to reestablish order (McAfee 17).[33] The women instinctively understand Beloved's (the semiotic's) importance and her/its relationship to the community's existence (the symbolic realm): one cannot function without the other.

The scene in which Beloved, pregnant, stands on the porch with her hand tightly clasped in Sethe's, who, next to her, looks more like the child than the mother, signifies a grotesque switch in the mother–daughter knot. At this point in the narrative, Sethe and Beloved are one. As such, standing to face the women in the community, Beloved, "the maternal body," is the very embodiment of "the subject in process/on trial [en process]" (Kristeva, *Revolution in Poetic Language* 22). If Beloved succeeds in destroying Sethe, the fear is that her presence (the semiotic) will usurp communal integrity (the symbolic). As mysteriously as she appears, under the onslaught of the women's choral assault, Beloved explodes before their very eyes.

Nonetheless, as in the semiotic realm's relationship to the symbolic realm, and the abject's to the community, Beloved, or at least her memory, does not entirely disappear, and it is clear that she will continue, at least marginally, to have an effect on the community's collective consciousness: "Later one little boy put it out how he had been looking for bait back of 124, down by the stream, and saw, cutting through the woods, a naked woman with fish for hair" (267). Beloved's abject absence/presence in the community, materially and psychically, is necessary, like the semiotic, in order for the community (the symbolic) to function. In addition, Paul D's return to Sethe after Beloved disappears marks the expulsion of the abject feminine from the community.[34] Now, he is free "to put his story next to hers" (*Beloved* 273), for without Beloved's presence, her intervention, all of the unspeakable things that Sethe and Paul D had wanted to say to one another could not have been fully expressed. Once Beloved is gone, Sethe can now "cry and tell him things [women] only told each other" (272). Paul D's masculine presence at the end of the narrative allows for the potential revitalization of communal bonds between Sethe and the rest of the black community; but also, his story, laid next to hers, offers a picture of the revitalization of black masculinity and black patriarchal heteronormativity in light of a perverse system of human subjugation and depravity.

In writing *Giovanni's Room* and *Beloved*, respectively, James Baldwin and Toni Morrison seek to expose systems of oppression that threaten (black) masculinity and, by extension, (black) heteronormative relationships. For Baldwin, the threat comes from America's obsession with the weighty questions of race and sexuality, which leaves very little room for nonheteronormative sexual variations. By cleverly displacing America's racial and (homo)sexual panic onto white, nonheteronormative men, Baldwin attempts to force us to revise our ideas of what constitutes (black) masculinity. However, in doing so, he actually reifies heteronormativity by discursively marking "femininity," effeminate gay men, and women as abject. These types of characters, in order for patriarchal heteronormativity to survive, must be suppressed, which is why, outside of his murder of Guillaume, Giovanni must die at the end of the novel.

In another context, but with similar results, Morrison's project of re-membering African American history in *Beloved* and her other novels makes it perfectly clear that re-visioning the past does not include African American men (and women) who do not prescribe to patriarchal, heteronormative standards of behavior. In this regard, like Baldwin, Morrison, who is known for her cogent, oppositional discourse to the warped realities formulated by a larger, more dominant Western culture, erases important aspects of the African American experience that would, to an even greater extent, flesh out the rich history and contributions of all African Americans, and not just those who conform to the very same patterns of behavior and notions of normalcy prescribed by white society that Baldwin and Morrison are supposedly fighting against.

NOTES

1. See Claudia Tate's pioneering works Domestic *Allegories of Political Desire* (1992) and *Psychoanalysis and Black Novels* (1998).
2. See Barbara Creed, *Monstrous-Feminine*.
3. According to Kristeva, abject entities remove themselves, but not totally, from the symbolic order. That is, they escape "social rationality," "logical order," "classification system[s]" or "structure" ("Powers" 256). Along this line of thinking, I include water, because of its ubiquity, as representing both the feminine and the abject in *Giovanni's Room*.
4. In order to speak about Morrison's *Beloved* and Baldwin's *Giovanni's Room*, I place the word "black" in parentheses to address the observation that there are no phenotypically black characters in *Giovanni's Room*. However, as I will demonstrate, Baldwin deconstructs the binarism of the color line in *Giovanni's Room* in order to show that compulsory heterosexuality and notions of masculinity transcend color; and in fact, there are "black" characters in the novel.

5. Although a number of African American gay and lesbian writers have been published in the United States since the 1950s, their work is even more marginalized in the white publishing mainstream than that of heterosexual, African American writers. In fact, even within current African American literary, theoretical, and cultural circles, with few exceptions, black queer authors continue to be marginalized.

6. This quotation is originally from Willa Cather's essay "The Novel Déméuble," in *Not under Forty* (New York: Knopf, 1922), 50.

7. As the goddess of the dead, Hella dwells beneath one of the three roots of the sacred ash tree Yggdrasil and resides in her hall, Elvidnir (misery), in the underworld (Helheim). Hers is the World of Darkness. Moreover, she is the daughter of Loki, the spirit of mischief and evil, and the giantess Angerbotha. Odin, the All-Father, hurled Hella into Niflheim, the realm of cold and darkness, itself also known as Hel. Hella is responsible for terrible calamities, sickness, and catastrophes.

8. I want to make a distinction between two important concepts in queer theory and gender studies: performance and performativity. According to queer and gender theorists such as Judith Butler, Nikki Sullivan, and Phillip Brian Harper, performance can be seen as related to the theatrical and performativity "can be seen as a mode of discursive production" (Sullivan 89). Performance implies subject agency, and is thus perhaps more political, while performativity is a deliberate reification of heterosexual norms.

9. David's description of Joey's body as a black hole, of course, is a metaphor for anal sex. But Joey's body, I would argue, is also metaphorically associated with the (black) homosexual male body. I believe that it is no coincidence that Joey's color is brown. This is not to claim, however, as a few critics have done, to unequivocally stake that Joey is African American, but his color, in keeping with Baldwin's aesthetics of ambiguity, certainly makes this a possibility.

10. One of the important theories concerning the relationship between the semiotic and the symbolic is that the semiotic and the symbolic are often concepts at odds with one another. For Kristeva, the semiotic and the symbolic form a fluctuating dialectic in which the semiotic and the symbolic depend on one another for existence: "As the discharge of drives, the semiotic is associated with the maternal body, the first source of rhythm, tone and movement for every human being . . . The symbolic element of signification is associated with the grammar and structure of signification . . . Without the symbolic all signification would be babble or delirium. But, without the semiotic, all signification would be empty and have no importance to our lives " ("Kristeva and Feminism") Thus, the constant shift between the semiotic drive and the symbolic is crucial to the formation of the speaking subject. This is an especially important idea if we examine David's fear of the semiotic as embodied by the feminine and, in terms of nationalism, Europe. For David, we might say that women (his dead mother, his Aunt Ellen, his girlfriend Hella, Guillaume, Jacques, and later Giovanni, and his lover Sue) represent the semiotic, while America, David's father, and, as David believes, he himself represent the symbolic, higher order.

11. Aunt Ellen is another metaphorically "black" character in the novel. David describes her as "a little older than his father, a little darker, always over-dressed, overmade-up, with a face and a figure that was beginning to harden . . . . [S]he was dressed, as they say, *to kill*, with her mouth redder than any blood, dressed in something which was either the wrong color, or too tight, or too young . . . . When I was a little boy and I watched her in company, she frightened me (11–12; emphasis mine). Again, women and femininity are associated with death, the grotesque, and the abject. Indeed, David's descrip-tion of Ellen is similar to his description of the transvestite he later meets in Paris in his friend Guillaume's bar.

12. Baldwin deftly shows the coming-out process and the agony for many gay, bisexual, lesbian, and transgender (GBLT) people that this process entails. David not only comes to hate his father for his ineffectiveness and for his own inability to live up to his father's expectations about what a real man is, but he also despises his overbearing Aunt Ellen, who tries, to some degree, to take the place of his deceased mother. David's depression becomes so profound that he tries to commit suicide by smashing his car into a tree. He also joins the army, ostensibly to prove to himself that he is a real man; but even in the military he finds himself engaged in illicit one-night stands with homosexual men, whom he describes as fairies, and with women whom he uses to prove to himself that despite his same-sex desire he is still a (straight) man.

13. Because homosexual sex does not lead to procreation, theorists such as Martin Duberman, Judith Butler, bell hooks, Julia Kristeva, and Douglas Crimp show in their work how social institutions, such as the church, erroneously connect homosexuality to other abjections: bestiality, corpses, dirt, and deadly illness-es, which break down the boundary between inside and outside.

14. David stereotypically equates feelings with femininity and stoicism with mas-culinity.

15. The irony is that David engages in anonymous sexual encounters with both men and women while he is in Paris. His heterosexual liaison with the American expatriate, Sue, is one such encounter. However, his thoughts about her reveal his androgynous (bisexual) nature. When he returns with Sue to her apartment, he "realized that [his] *performance* with Sue was suc-ceeding, even too well . . . . [He] traveled through a network of Sue's cries, of Sue's tom-tom fists on [his] back . . ." (100). As we examine how the narrator constructs Sue, we see that he not only constructs her genderwise as an androgynous character, but he also constructs her as racially ambigu-ous. For example, the sound of the tom-toms in the above passage metaphorically marks Sue as a "black" woman. In addition, when David first meets Sue, she is described as "[wearing] her curly blond hair cut very short, she had small breasts and a big behind, and in order to show the world how little she cared for appearance or sensuality, she almost always wore tight blue jeans." (95) In short, Sue is masculinized and racialized. Later, after they have had sex at Sue's apartment, David is pleasantly sur-prised that "when she came back [from freshening up] she was wearing a

dress and some real shoes, and she had sort of fluffed up her hair. I had to admit she looked better that way, really more like a girl, like a school girl." (101) Thus, David is pleased that Sue looks more feminine, and he feels better about himself as a real man.

16. Nonetheless, Giovanni is "feminized" early in the novel when David first meets him in Guillaume's bar and teasingly says, "But the French say . . . that the Italians are too fluid, too volatile, have no sense of measure." (36) The idea of fluidity, of course, is associated with water, which has the capacity to cross boundaries. In addition, Freud associates water (the oceanic) with femininity, a dangerous female sexuality, and "the dark continent," as another metaphor for dangerous female sexuality.

17. Here, I am not making moral judgments that support either form of behavior as the "correct" way for nonheteronormative people to behave in society. Mine is simply a reading of how Baldwin sets up a bifurcation, in terms of homosexual behavior, in the novel, which appears to favor a mimicking of heteronormative social behavior for homosexuals.

18. Historically, the psychiatric community has associated women with hysteria, because they believe that women are not in control of their emotions.

19. Julia Kristeva explains that the word "corpse" or cadaver comes from the Latin word *cadere*, "to fall" (*Power* 3).

20. Despite its theoretical flaws, one should understand that for a long time, well into the feminist movement of the 1960s, in psychoanalytical and social discourses, Freud's arguments concerning masculine and feminine behavior stood unchallenged: woman is passive, man active. Active is gendered "masculine," "passive" feminine. (Davis 3)

21. The room itself is a metaphor for how David comes to view his relationship with Giovanni: dirty and threatening.

22. Fueled by frustration, desperation, and humiliation, Giovanni, after David abandons him, murders Guillaume, who wrongly accuses him of being a thief. When Guillaume is murdered, he is wearing a lounging gown and heavy perfume. In killing Guillaume, Giovanni not only exacts revenge against his tormentor but also symbolically kills his own "feminine" side. Subsequently, Giovanni is executed (guillotined) for the murder. This is an obvious symbol of castration, which completes Giovanni's feminization as well as his abjection.

23. This quotation comes from Albert Murray's *The Omni-Americans: Black Experience and American Culture* (New York, 1970), 58.

24. Nero makes reference to Morrison's novels *The Bluest Eye* (1969), *Tar Baby* (1981), and *Beloved*. He just as easily could have included *Sula* (1973) and *Song of Solomon* (1977).

25. I refer to the house at 124 Bluestone Road as "ex-centric" not only because of the paranormal happenings that take place in it but also because the house, and the women in it, lies isolated on the edge of town and away from the rest of the black community; where once 124 was the center of activity, when Baby Suggs was alive, for black people in the community it is no longer so.

26. That the narrator describes the house as full of a baby's venom evokes the age-old mythic trope, in both Western and non-Western cultures, of women as evil and associated with the Devil. In addition, snakes, according to Kristeva, are abject because they are seen as neither.

27. In the novel, Paul D is initially reluctant to establish a place with Sethe at 124 Bluestone Road. In this regard, as Torgovnick suggests, "Westerners who journeyed to remote societies (Henry Stanley, Lawrence Blair and Lorne Blair, [and] Tobias Schneebaum) called their journeys 'odysseys' and model themselves, often self-consciously, on the intrepid Odysseus" (24). Paul D's itinerancy, as he eventually makes his way to 124, also establishes his character as an Odysseus/Ulysses figure. Part of Paul D's role in *Beloved* is to impose a normalizing societal and civil code to 124 Bluestone Road. In other words, Paul D (and later Denver) reestablishes ties between 124 Bluestone Road/nature and civilization/the black community.

28. According to Eric Ackroyd, in many cultures "silver has associations with the moon and may therefore symbolize the feminine, intuition, or the unconscious" (3)

29. In mythology and psychoanalysis, water is associated with the feminine and the maternal body. Moreover, because of its ubiquity, water is also associated with a dangerous female sexuality, the unconscious, and the primitive. In short, the oceanic represents the id.

30. Beloved is especially upset that she literally cannot see Sethe when Sethe is in the bedroom making love with Paul D. Beloved's greed, physical and psychological, is a metaphor for uncontrollable female desire.

31. When Paul D begins to realize what Beloved is doing to him, his countermeasure to "document his manhood and break out of the girl's spell—all in one," is to ask Sethe to have his children, which she politely refuses because she feels she is "too old to start that all over again." (128) Paul D believes that having children and being a father would give him the opportunity to fully regain what was lost to him—his manhood.

32. This statement also applies to the scene at the end of *Giovanni's Room* in which David tears up the note that Giovanni sends to him through Jacques before he even reads it. He tosses it in the wind. However, "as [he] turn[s] and begin[s] walking towards the waiting people, the wind blows some of them back on [him]." (169)

33. In this scene, the narrator describes that "the singing women recognized Sethe at once and surprised themselves by their absence of fear when they saw what stood next to her. The devil-child was clever, they thought. And beautiful. It had taken the shape of a pregnant woman, naked and smiling in the heat of the afternoon sun. Thunderblack and glistening, she stood on long straight legs, her belly big and tight. Vines of hair twisted all over her head. . . . Her smile was dazzling" (261). Beloved's demise is also a communal rejection of the presence of the abject maternal body.

34. Importantly, when Paul D meets Denver on his way to see Sethe, she calls him Mr. D, which is not only a sign of respect but also marks the reassertion that Paul D is part of the community, a man, and a human being.

WORKS CITED

Ackroyd, Eric. "Colors." *Myths, Dreams, Symbols.* http://www.mythsdreamssymbols.com/ddcolors.html (accessed on February 26, 2005).

Baldwin, James. *Another Country.* New York: Dial Press, 1962.

———. *Giovanni's Room.* 1956. Delta Publishing: New York, 2000.

———. "Here Be Dragons." *The Price of the Ticket: Collected Nonfiction 1948–1985.* New York: St. Martin's Press, 1985. 677–690.

———. *Tell Me How Long the Train's Been Gone.* New York: Dell, 1968.

Bujdei, Carmen. "The Body Monstrous (Fragments) Towards Unsettling Notions of the 'Monstrous Feminine.'" *Clouds Magazine* Summer 2004. http://www.cloudsmagazine.com/18/Carmen_Bujdei_The_Body_Monstrous.htm (accessed on March 10, 2005).

Butler, Judith. *Gender Trouble: Feminism and the Subversion of Identity.* New York and London: Routledge, 1990.

Cleaver, Eldridge. *Soul on Ice.* New York: Dell, 1968.

Creed, Barbara. *Monstrous-Feminine: Film, Feminism, Psychoanalysis.* New York and London: Routledge, 1993.

Davis, Doug. "Notes on Freud's Theory of Femininity." http://www.haverford.edu/psych/ddavis/p109g/freudfem.html (accessed on January 25, 2005).

Douglas, Mary. *Purity and Danger: An Analysis of the Concepts of Pollution and Taboo.* New York and London: Routledge, 1995.

Ferguson, Roderick A. *Aberrations in Black: Toward a Queer of Color Critique.* Minneapolis and London: University of Minnesota Press, 2004.

Freud, Sigmund. *Civilizations and Its Discontents.* Ed. A. Dickson. Trans. James Strachey. *Pelican Freud Library 12.* Harmondsworth: Penguin, 1984.

Johnson, E. Patrick. *Appropriating Blackness: Performance and the Politics of Authenticity.* Durham and London: Duke University Press, 2003.

Kristeva, Julia. *Powers of Horror: An Essay on Abjection.* Trans. Leon S. Roudiez. New York: Columbia University Press, 1982.

———. "The Powers of Horror." In *The Portable Kristeva.* Ed. Kelly Oliver. New York: Columbia University Press, 2002. 229–63.

———. *Revolution in Poetic Language.* New York: Columbia University Press, 1984.

McAfee, Noelle. "Abjection." In *Julia Kristeva.* New York and London: Routledge, 2004. 45–57.

Morrison, Toni. *Beloved.* 1987. New York: Plume, 1988.

———. "Unspeakable Things Unspoken." *Michigan Quarterly Review* 28, no. 1 1989): 1–34.

———. *Playing in the Dark: Whiteness and the Literary Imagination.* Cambridge and London: Harvard University Press, 1992.

Nero, Charles I. "Toward a Black Gay Aesthetic: Signifying in Contemporary Black Gay Literature." In *African American Literary Theory: A Reader.* Ed. Winston Napier. New York and London: New York University Press, 2000. 399–420.

Oliver, Kelly. "Kristeva and Feminism." 1998. http://www.cddc.vt.edu/feminism/Kristeva.html (accessed on March 7, 2005).

———. *Portable Kristeva*. Ed. Kelly Oliver. New York: Columbia University Press, 2002.

Somerville, Siobhan, B. *Queering the Color Line: Race and the Invention of Homosexuality in American Culture*. Duke University Press, 2000.

Sullivan, Nikki. *A Critical Introduction to Queer Theory*. Washington Square: New York University Press, 2003.

Tate, Claudia. *Domestic Allegories of Political Desire: The Black Heroine's Text at the Turn of the Century*. New York: Oxford University Press, 1992.

———. *Psychoanalysis and Black Novels: Desire and the Protocols of Race*. New York: Oxford University Press, 1998.

Torgovnick. Marianna. *Gone Primitive: Savage Intellects, Modern Lives*. Chicago: University of Chicago Press, 1990.

White, E. Frances. "The Evidence of Things Not Seen." In *Dark Continent of Our Bodies: Black Feminism and the Politics of Respectability (Mapping Racisms)*. Philadelphia: Temple University Press, 2001. 151–183.

NOTES ON CONTRIBUTORS

Carol Henderson Belton is Associate Professor of African American and American Literature at the University of Delaware, Newark campus. Her publications under her writing name "Carol E. Henderson" include a book published by the University of Missouri Press, *Scarring the Black Body: Race and Representation in African American Literature* (2002) and numerous essays and reviews on African American literature in reference volumes, edited collections, and journals. She was special editor for a collection of essays on James Baldwin's *Go Tell It on the Mountain* (*MAWA Review*, 2005), and has an edited collection on Baldwin entitled *James Baldwin's Go Tell It on the Mountain: Historical and Critical Essays* forthcoming from Peter Lang Publisher, fall 2006. She has three essays forthcoming: "Refiguring the Flesh: The Word, The Body, and the Process of Being in *Beloved* and *Go Tell It On The Mountain*" in *James Baldwin and Toni Morrison: Comparative Critical and Theoretical Essays*, Ed. Lovalerie King and Lynn O. Scott (Palgrave 2006); "Allegories of the Undead: Rites and Rituals in *Tales from the Hood*" in *Folklore and Popular Film*, Ed. Mikel Koven and Sharon Sherman (Utah State University Press 2006); and "Notes of a Native Daughter: The Nature of Black Womanhood in Wright's *Native Son*" in an edited collection of critical essays to be published in Spain. She is currently at work on two manuscripts: *Footprints: One Sistah's journey from AFDC to Ph.D.* and *Shadow-Boxing: The African American Male Image from Print to Film*.

Keith Byerman is Professor of English and Women's Studies at Indiana State University and associate editor of *African American Review*. He is the author of books on W. E. B. Du Bois, Alice Walker, and John Edgar Wideman, and on folklore in recent African American narrative. His *Remembering the Past in Contemporary African American Fiction* was published in 2005 and *Critical Essays on John Edgar Wideman* (coedited with Bonnie TuSmith) in 2006. In 2004, he received the Theodore Dreiser Research/Creativity Award.

Trudier Harris is J. Carlyle Sitterson Professor of English at the University of North Carolina at Chapel Hill, where she teaches courses in African American literature and folklore at undergraduate and graduate levels. Author and editor of more than twenty volumes, she is currently at work on "The Scary Mason-Dixon Line: African American Writers and the South." Her memoir, *Summer Snow, Reflections from a Black Daughter of the South* (Beacon, 2003), was selected to inaugurate the One-Book, One-Community Reading Program in Orange County, North Carolina in 2003–2004. In 2005, she won the UNC System Board of Governors' Award for Excellence in Teaching. Also in 2005, she received the John Hurt Fisher Award from SAMLA "For Career Achievement in Letters."

Anna Kérchy holds an MA in English and French from the University of Szeged, Hungary, and a DEA in Semiology from Université Paris 7, France. She is about to defend her dissertation on textual grotesqueries and corporeal freakings in contemporary women's writing in English. Her major fields of interest include gender-, body-, and performance studies, contemporary women writers' fiction, and feminist and poststructuralist literary theory. She has taught courses at the Institute of English and American Studies of the University of Szeged, and published numerous articles, essays, and reviews in English, French, and Hungarian on these themes.

Lovalerie King is Assistant Professor of English at Penn State University-University Park. She is the author of *A Students' Guide to African American Literature* (2003) and numerous articles, essays, and reviews in *The Oxford Companion to African American Literature, The Dictionary of Literary Biography, The Cambridge Companion to the African American Novel, African American Review, MELUS, Callaloo,* and other publications. Forthcoming projects include a book-length study of the topos of property, race, and ethics in African American literature and an introduction to Zora Neale Hurston.

Babacar M'Baye is Assistant Professor of African and African American Literature and Culture at Kent State University. His publications include "Colonization and African Modernity in Cheikh Hamidou Kane's *Ambiguous Adventure*" (*Journal of African Literature and Culture*, 2006), "Africa, Race, and Culture in the Narratives of W. E. B. Du Bois" *Philosophia Africana: Analysis of Philosophy and Issues in Africa and the Black Diaspora*, August 2004), "The Image of Africa in the Travel Narratives of W. E. B. Du Bois, Richard Wright, James Baldwin, and Henry Louis Gates, Jr." (*The Sonia Sanchez Literary Review*, Fall 2003) and "Dualistic Imagination of Africa in the Black

Atlantic Narratives of Phillis Wheatley, Olaudah Equiano, and Martin R. Delany" (*The New England Journal of History*, Spring 2002).

D. Quentin Miller is Associate Professor of English at Suffolk University. He has published or edited three books: *Re-Viewing James Baldwin: Things Not Seen* (2000), *John Updike and the Cold War: Drawing the Iron Curtain* (2001), and *Prose and Cons: New Essays on U.S. Prison Literature* (2005). He is also the editor of the composition textbook *The Generation of Ideas* (2005) and one of the co-editors of the *Heath Anthology of American Literature*. His essays have appeared in such journals as *American Literature*, *Legacy: A Journal of American Women Writers*, *English Language Notes*, and *American Literary Realism*. He is developing a book-length study of James Baldwin.

Jonathan Mirin is a playwright, actor, and co-artistic director of the Piti Theatre Company based in Shelburne, Massachussetts, and Les Ponts-de-Martel, Switzerland. His solo performance piece *Riding the Wave.com* premiered at the 2004 New York International Fringe Festival. Other plays have been performed at the Edinburgh Fringe Festival, Florida Studio Theatre, and off-off Broadway. He is currently writing a musical based on *Alice's Adventures in Wonderland* called *Alice in America* as well as a novel based on *Riding the Wave.com*.

Keith Mitchell is Assistant Professor of English and Ethnic Literatures at the University of Massachusetts at Lowell. He has published a number of essays and encyclopedia entries on African American, West Indian, and Southern American writers such as Gayl Jones, Paul Marshall, Wilson Harris, Joseph Zobel, and George Moses Horton. He is currently doing archival work on the Harlem Renaissance poet Gwendolyn Bennett and working on an essay on the one-act plays of African American poet Jay Wright.

Keren Omry was awarded her PhD in English Literature at the University of London, where she explored the relationship between jazz and African American literature of the twentieth century. She is currently developing her investigation of racialized discourses in contemporary Jewish American and African American texts, writing on a jazz aesthetic of ethnic identity. Furthermore, she is researching and due to publish her work on Octavia Butler and science fiction, investigating how the dialogue between aesthetics and technology is articulated in terms of gender and genre.

Michelle H. Phillips taught high school English for the past five years while pursuing her Master's degree at the University of Massachusetts-Boston. She is currently enrolled in the English PhD program at Rutgers University, where she plans to specialize in Gender and Sexuality Studies.

Richard Schur is an Assistant Professor of Interdisciplinary Studies at Drury University. His articles on African American literature and critical race theory have appeared in journals such as *Contemporary Literature, American Studies, Biography,* and *Law & Inequality.* His current project explores the legal ramifications of post-soul aesthetics in contemporary African American art and literature.

Lynn Orilla Scott is a Visiting Assistant Professor in James Madison College at Michigan State University. She is the author of *James Baldwin's Later Fiction: Witness to the Journey* (2002) and several articles, essays, and reviews on American and African American literature.

E. Frances White is Vice Provost for Faculty Affairs at New York University. She is the author of *Dark Continent of Our Bodies: Black Feminism and the Politics of Respectabiity* (2001), *Sierra Leone's Settler Women Traders* (1987), and other volumes on black women.

INDEX

Printed in the United States
92642LV00001B/38/A

9 781403 970732